A PIRATE'S EMBRACE

"Enjoying the view?"

Rosalind whirled to confront Blackbeard in person. "They won't be fooled," she cried. "They'll sink you anyway; you won't get away with your foul plot."

His eyebrows raised. "You have an annoying habit of talking too much."

Annoying? She'd show him!

"I don't care if you shoot me as you did Reginald," she said haughtily. "I intend to warn the men on the *Michigan*. You can't stop me from screaming."

"Oh, no?" he asked softly.

She spread her arms, her back to the rail. "Shoot me, then," she cried hysterically. "Kill me!"

Instead, he tipped back her bonnet and pulled her against him. Before she could struggle, his lips were on hers. He held her so closely she couldn't breathe; and though she tried to pull away, it was impossible.

His beard was soft against her face instead of harsh as she had expected, and the pressure of his mouth forced her lips apart. She gasped in surprise, shivering when she felt his tongue caress the inside of her mouth.

Fire burned upward from deep inside her, spreading hotly through her, slowing her struggles, urging her to answer his kiss. No, she thought, I won't. Never.

But she had no more control over what was happening inside her than she had control over him. Despite her vow, she felt herself begin to melt into his embrace.

Love's Desire
Jane Toombs

ZEBRA BOOKS
KENSINGTON PUBLISHING CORP.

ZEBRA BOOKS are published by

Kensington Publishing Corp.
850 Third Avenue
New York, NY 10022

Zebra and the Z logo Reg. U.S. Pat. & TM Off. The Lovegram
logo is a trademark of Kensington Publishing Corp.

First Printing: February, 1995

Printed in the United States of America

And the blood doth seethe with fever
For Love's savage sister, Lust . . .
                    —Anonymous

One

Rosalind Collins pulled the black veil over her face before she climbed from the carriage. She could almost hear Aunt Rhoda's voice in her ears.

A lady is always proper.

Other than her dove-gray Talma cloak, she was entirely dressed in black—a glace linen day dress with a modified hoop for traveling, black boots, black gloves, and black spoon bonnet. Aunt Rhoda wouldn't have approved of the cloak, but Rosalind had no black shawls and there hadn't been enough money to buy one.

Poor Aunt Rhoda. Tears gathered in Rosalind's eyes, but she blinked them away. No amount of tears would bring back her aunt, who had died so miserably in the unending April rains. Yellow Jack, the doctor had called it.

"I've treated a good many cases this spring," he had told Rosalind. "And quite a few smallpox cases as well. Must be the war; all these people traveling around stir up infection. I hope Boston's not in for an epidemic like New York's." He had shaken his head. "Your vaccination will protect you from smallpox, but I have nothing to prescribe against the miasma responsible for yellow fever, nothing at all. It might be best to leave Boston for the time being."

Rosalind rearranged her veil and clutched her carpetbag in a gloved hand. It hadn't been fear of yellow fever but dire necessity that had brought her here to this Sandusky, Ohio, dock. But no good would result from brooding about the past, she must concentrate on the present for she still had a long way to go.

The May sun was warm on her shoulders as she joined the passengers filing up the gangway to the deck of the *Phoenix.* The boat's name, she told herself, was a good omen—the phoenix symbolized renewal, a new life. As hers was to be. Once aboard, she stood at the rail watching the deckhands load the last of the mail and freight. When the deck under her feet began to throb and water churned white as the sidewheeler pulled away from the pier, she felt a thrill despite her misgivings. This was her first real adventure!

She took a deep breath of the creosote-tainted air, detecting a faint odor of rotting fish that made her wrinkle her nose. Still, the smell was preferable to the smokiness and grime of the railroad stations where she'd changed trains on the way to Ohio. While Aunt Rhoda's house hadn't been near the water, Boston was a seaport and Rosalind had always liked the sight and smell of the ocean. Looking out over Lake Erie, she almost felt at home.

"That's Johnson Island," a woman's voice said.

Rosalind turned her head and saw a stout middle-aged woman in black bombazine standing next to her. "That's where they keep the Confederate prisoners," she told Rosalind, "right there on Johnson Island." She smiled. "I'm Mrs. Donal. What's your name, my dear?"

"Miss Rosalind Collins." Rosalind stifled a sigh. She had nothing against Mrs. Donal, but the woman was typical of others she'd met during her journey. Though her aunt had often warned her about the dangers of being accosted by strange men, so far not a single one of them had so much as said a word to Rosalind. However dangerous, mightn't talking to a young man prove to be more interesting than the staid conversation of middle-aged women?

"In mourning, dear, aren't you?" Mrs. Donal asked.

"For my aunt," Rosalind said. "I lived with her."

Mrs. Donal peered at her as though trying to see her face through the veil. "Are you all alone in the world, a young girl like you?"

"I'm eighteen," Rosalind said, "and I'm going to my father."

"Where might that be, dear—Detroit?"

"No. He lives by Lake Superior in the Upper Peninsula of Michigan."

Mrs. Donal tut-tutted. "So far away. You really shouldn't be traveling by yourself. Especially to a remote spot like that. I understand the entire Upper Peninsula is nothing but wilderness."

"I believe my father lives in a village." A touch of tartness crept into Rosalind's voice, covering her uncertainty. Mrs. Donal seemed to be trying to frighten her. Heaven knows she was nervous enough about the trip already.

"I'm sure it can be no more than the most primitive of settlements. I've been told on good authority that the entire area is at least fifty years behind the times. I expect you'll be the only woman wearing a hoop in your father's village."

Though she disliked being thought rude, Rosalind turned her head away from the older woman and, shielding her eyes against the sun, stared at the green water of Lake Erie.

Tomorrow, she told herself, I'll be on the steamer *Illinois,* outbound from Detroit, sailing up Lake Huron. In a matter of days I'll be with my father and everything will be all right. I won't pay any attention to this woman's crepe-hanging.

Apparently unoffended, Mrs. Donal nudged her, saying, "There's the *USS Michigan*."

Looking where she pointed, Rosalind saw a sidewheeler with sails anchored off Johnson Island. "Are those cannon on the ship?" she asked.

"She's a gunboat, not a ship," Mrs. Donal corrected. "Ships sail on the ocean; boats sail on the lakes. Last year the *Michigan*'s cannons stopped those sneaky Rebel-sympathizers—Copperheads, we call them—from trying to set free the Johnson Island prisoners. No Copperhead is going to get past a Union gunboat; you can be sure of that."

Rosalind knew nothing of any attempt to free Confederate prisoners; in fact, she'd never even heard of Johnson Island, much less the prison there. Aunt Rhoda had done her best to ignore the war, chiding Rosalind when she had made any mention of it.

"All these abolitionists rushing about shouting slogans are as vulgar a lot as I've ever encountered," Aunt Rhoda had complained. "I find myself as unsympathetic toward them as I am toward the slave-owners. Although, to give credit where credit's due, the Southerners I've met have always been ladies and gentlemen. The entire situation is ill-advised and no good will come of it. Enough said."

Rosalind sighed inaudibly. No good *had* come of it. Newly commissioned Lt. Reginald Morley had kissed her goodbye before he left Boston with his unit for the front. The kiss had been a chaste promise that he'd return; but in less than a month he was dead, felled by a Confederate bullet.

"Does your father have an interest in copper mining?" Mrs. Donal asked. "There's not much else in the Upper Peninsula except wild Indians and wolves."

"I believe he does," Rosalind said, wishing the woman

would find someone else to talk to. Older woman, she'd discovered on this trip, were inclined to be overly curious about her circumstances.

While still in Boston, she'd learned they could be secretive, too. The letter she'd found in Aunt Rhoda's Bible after her aunt's death had said Rosalind's father owned part of a copper mine. It was dated March 4, 1864, and had been from William Wadstrom, Aunt Rhoda's Boston attorney.

"I am advised," the letter read, "that Jephthah Collins has invested in the Nonpareil Mine, said mine at present producing a considerable copper tonnage. Since he has not remarried, I would think he should be held responsible for supporting his daughter . . ."

Rosalind hadn't immediately taken in the sense of the letter because the name, Jephthah Collins, had seemed to leap off the paper at her. Her father was alive! Why had Aunt Rhoda always insisted he was dead? Her aunt must have known this was a lie. Furthermore, she must have had some notion of where he was since she'd obviously asked her lawyer to investigate him with a view to approaching Jephthah for money. For, as Rosalind had discovered quite soon after the funeral, Aunt Rhoda had been practically penniless.

"Sell the house," Mr. Wadstrom had advised. "You can't afford to keep it."

Only when Rosalind had shown him the letter she'd found in the Bible did the lawyer admit that her aunt had asked him to trace the whereabouts of Jephthah Collins.

"Does he—does my father know about me?" Rosalind had demanded. "Aunt Rhoda let me believe he was dead. Did she also tell him I was dead?"

The lawyer had offered no answers beyond the fact that her father was alive and apparently financially secure. Mr.

Wadstrom had protested when Rosalind had announced her intention of joining her father as soon as possible.

"Allow me to write and make further inquiries first," he had cautioned.

"There's no time. You've already said there's almost no money for me to live on and the sale of the house may take forever. I prefer to spend what money I do have on the fare to the Upper Peninsula of Michigan. To Ojibway, where my father lives."

Mr. Wadstrom's attempts to change her mind had been to no avail, though she had been shocked to discover that not only were there no railroads to the Upper Peninsula but no proper roads either. One traveled by water.

"But the Great Lakes are fresh water. Don't they freeze in the winter?" she had asked.

"One doesn't travel in the winter," the lawyer had said.

"Then I'd best leave well before then," she'd told him. "I have nothing to keep me here—my only relative is my father." She wasn't as confident as she'd pretended to be. What if Jephthah Collins refused to acknowledge her?

"Your poor mother died in the wilderness," Aunt Rhoda had often said. "I never saw your father again after he brought you here and left you with me. He perished in that awful country, just as your mother did."

But he *hadn't* perished. Her father was very much alive. Why had he left her with Aunt Rhoda and never returned?

Rosalind realized with a start that Mrs. Donal was speaking to her. "I—I'm sorry. I didn't hear what you said."

"We'll soon be stopping at Middle Bass Island to refuel," Mrs. Donal told her. "Then it's on to Detroit." She shook her head. "I don't envy you that long trip up the lakes. You'll be at least a week getting where you're going. And you'll arrive in a wilderness neither fit nor safe for a young girl on her own."

Rosalind reflected that if the rest of the trip were as it had been so far, she'd be in no danger. Despite Aunt Rhoda's warning about the peril of being approached by strange men, that danger had so far failed to materialize. Not a single man had so much as spoken to her, much less made advances.

It was obvious she was in mourning and she had been careful to keep her veil down. Was that the reason? Janet Morley had always deplored her own overly curly brown locks, insisting blue-eyed blondes like Rosalind were what men preferred. Janet's brother Reginald had certainly praised Rosalind's hair and eyes, claiming he loved her and asking her to wait for him until the war ended. And now he was dead. While she grieved for him, at the same time she wondered if any other man would ever admire her. Or want to marry her.

"There." Mrs. Donal pointed. "If you look, you can just make out Middle Bass Island."

Seagulls swooped past the boat, evoking memories of Boston harbor. Somehow she hadn't expected gulls to be as prevalent on the Great Lakes as on the ocean. She dismissed the gulls from her mind when a two-master, sails billowing in the wind, suddenly cut across in front of the steamboat. A bearded man aboard the sloop shouted and waved.

After a moment, the deck shuddered under Rosalind's feet as the *Phoenix* slowed. She glanced at Mrs. Donal. "Is something wrong?"

"I think the sloop's in trouble," the older woman said. "She's riding far too low in the water. Could be we're going to take her crew aboard."

The sloop disappeared around the other side of the *Phoenix* and, by the time Rosalind and Mrs. Donal had walked over to see what was happening, there were so many other passengers along the rail watching they couldn't find a vantage spot.

"Rough-looking customers," a man in front of Rosalind said. "Wouldn't be surprised if they're a bunch of them skedaddlers. I'm surprised the captain stopped for them."

"Even if they're cowards, you can't stand by and let them drown," another man pointed out.

"What's a skedaddler?" Rosalind asked Mrs. Donal.

"A man who skips off to Canada to avoid being drafted into the Union Army. When they think the war might be coming to an end, they sometimes slip back home again. I've got no use for them, and neither does any other right-minded person."

"Is that who we're saving from the sloop?"

"I don't know," Mrs. Donal said. "I can't see any more than you can."

"The captain's taking a chance of getting our side stove in with that sloop nudging us the way she is," a man observed.

"Here they come," another man said. "Stand back. Let them get up the ladder."

By standing on tiptoe and craning her neck, Rosalind was able to see a man with a black beard climb over the boat's rail. He leaped to the deck, but she could still see his head for he towered over the passengers. He seemed to be helping other men climb aboard.

Blackbeard, she thought. He really did look like a pirate. But she'd always heard there were no pirates on the Great Lakes.

"You overloaded," a man told Blackbeard as the crew

from the sloop kept climbing over the rail. "Too many men aboard such a dinky boat—no wonder you had to call for help."

"What the hell! They're even bringing their belongings," someone complained. "Sea chests and all."

A sharp crack startled Rosalind into grasping Mrs. Donal's arm.

"They're shooting!" the older woman cried, huddling closer to Rosalind. "They've got guns."

"All right, we don't want to hurt anyone." The deep voice belonged to Blackbeard. "Do what we ask, and you'll be safe enough."

Rosalind caught a glimpse of him as he raised a pistol into the air and fired another shot. Then the thrust of the crowd backing away from the guns separated her from Mrs. Donal. She stumbled, nearly losing her footing. Her bonnet was knocked from her head and hung down her back, still held by the ribbons around her neck.

"Pirates!" someone exclaimed.

"Pirates on the Great Lakes?"

"All passengers into the lounge cabin." The order rang out loud and clear.

Again Rosalind moved helplessly with the others. People pressed close to her on all sides, and she lost sight of Mrs. Donal in the crowd. Rosalind was only two inches over five feet and, feeling crushed in the mob, began to panic. Reaching out, she touched a metal rail and clutched it, holding on first with one hand, then with both.

Flattened against the outside wall of the cabin, her cheek pressed against the wood, frightened into near mindlessness, she sobbed without tears as the other passengers swirled past her.

She was becoming aware that the pressure against her

had eased when a hand grasped her arm roughly. She screamed as she was whirled about and stared with terror into a grinning red face.

"Well, well," the man said. "I caught me a pretty one, sure enough."

Rosalind screamed again, thrashing wildly in an effort to break free from his grip. He thrust his face close to hers, and she smelled whiskey fumes.

"Now, lookee here, gal," he muttered. "I . . ."

"What's going on here?" she heard another man's voice, strong with command.

Her captor released her and Rosalind slumped against the cabin wall, staring at the second man, tall and dark. Blackbeard.

"She ain't in the cabin with them others, sir," Redface said placatingly. "I was aiming to make her get inside."

"No need to scare her to death by manhandling her," Blackbeard told him. "Go forward and help with the crew. I'll manage the little lady."

"Yessir," Redface said, sketching a salute before hurrying to obey the order.

The trembling Rosalind took a deep breath as she tried to collect her wits. How right Aunt Rhoda had been!

"Can you walk?" Blackbeard asked her, not unkindly.

"I—I don't know," she quavered.

Before she realized what he intended, he stepped forward and scooped her up into his arms, carrying her easily. She gazed into walnut-brown eyes.

"Can't really blame Amos," he murmured. "You *are* a pretty little thing." When he smiled, his teeth white against the dark beard, the left side of his mouth turned up more than the right.

He opened the cabin door, set her on her feet and exited,

leaving her with the other passengers. Rosalind was immediately surrounded by solicitousness.

"That scoundrel didn't harm ye, did he?" A middle-aged man asked, his face choleric above mutton-chop whiskers.

"The nerve of the man!" A woman exclaimed, her voice high and shrill. "Are you all right? I've some smelling salts."

Rosalind tried to smile, fighting off her sense of suffocation. "I'm not hurt," she managed to say.

"Dirty Rebs, that's what they are," the woman said. "After those prisoners on Johnson Island again, I've no doubt."

"How could the captain have been so easily gulled?" Muttonchops asked.

Rebels? Rosalind wondered, her mind beginning to work coherently again. Disguised Confederate soldiers? The man saluting Blackbeard had called him "sir." The deference due an officer?

"What will happen to us?" she asked.

"They said we'd be safe," the woman said, "but who can trust a Reb? As likely as not they'll murder every last one of us so we can't talk."

The cabin bristled with uneasiness and fear by the time the pirates opened the door again. A dozen plans had been put forward and discarded by the male passengers, who could find no way to get around the fact that the doors were guarded by armed men and none of the passengers carried so much as a derringer.

Blackbeard stood framed in the doorway, gun in hand. Rosalind shrank back when he motioned to her with his pistol. "Outside," he snapped.

"Look here," Muttonchops protested. "You can't . . ."

Blackbeard cut him off. Raising his voice, he announced, "I'm taking six of the women. I'll personally guarantee no harm will come to them if the rest of you make no attempt to escape from the cabin. The women will be hostages for your good conduct."

"How can we trust the word of a—a pirate?" Mutton-chops demanded.

Blackbeard drew himself even more erect. Rosalind thought dazedly that he was the tallest man she'd ever seen. And, if he hadn't been an enemy, quite possibly the most handsome.

"You can trust the word of a gentleman," he said. Then he smiled and added, "Also, you have no alternative."

He selected the nearest six women quickly—Rosalind, the shrill-voiced lady, two middle-aged women, an elderly lady and her scarcely younger female companion.

As he ushered them out, he said, "I repeat—we intend these ladies no harm. Provided—" He allowed the closing door to punctuate his threat.

Rosalind found herself on the deck with the other five women and Blackbeard. His brown eyes met hers and he flashed his uneven smile, bowing slightly. She flushed and looked away, fumbling with the ties of her bonnet, suddenly wanting to set the black veil between herself and this frightening man.

"Now, ladies," he said, "if you'll be so kind as to stand by the rail—three of you to starboard and the other three on the port side. Stand far enough apart so there's a space between each of you, and when we approach—" He hesitated, then went on. "When we approach another ship, I expect no outcry. Be sensible, and you'll all be perfectly safe."

He waved the elderly lady, her companion, and one of the middle-aged women to the rail nearest them. The

roughly dressed man lounging against the cabin wall, gun
in hand, nodded, saying, "I'll watch 'em, sir."

Rosalind's eyes narrowed. "Sir," again.

"Around to the other side," Blackbeard told the three
remaining women, herding Rosalind and the other two
ahead of him. She settled her bonnet onto her head and
pulled the veil over her face only to have him reach out,
lift the veil, and fold it back onto the bonnet's brim. She
glared at him, fear swallowed by indignation.

"Can't you see I'm in mourning?" she demanded.

"Mourning or not, I like to look at you," he said. "Keep
your face uncovered."

Again she noticed his lopsided smile, one she might have
found charming if he weren't so arrogant as well as an
enemy.

"You're a Confederate officer, aren't you?" she asked.

His eyes, gone hard and cold, raked her. She swallowed
nervously but refused to flinch when he caught her arm
and hurried her along with the other two women until they
were at the opposite rail.

"Watch them," he ordered the armed man on this side
of the deck.

Rosalind tingled with apprehension mixed with a dollop
of pride at her own temerity. How had she dared ask him
such a question? He'd been so furious he might have shot
her and thrown her overboard then and there.

Still, she'd hit the mark, she told herself. Reaching up
to pull down her veil, she discovered a hole torn in the
mesh from his rough handling and scowled. What inso-
lence—having the nerve to say he wanted to look at her.

Reginald's face came into her mind and she recalled his
gentle kiss before he'd left to die on the battlefield. Killed
by the Rebs, by men like these on the boat. Like Black-

beard. She straightened her shoulders and lifted her chin. I'll avenge Reginald, she vowed. Somehow I will.

The two other women were not close enough to ask if they had any idea where the boat might be bound. Rosalind's gaze searched the water. Where was the island Mrs. Donal had pointed out to her before the sloop had appeared? She saw land ahead; but in the dimming light of early evening, she found it impossible to decide whether it was an island she looked at or part of the mainland.

The lights of other boats twinkled in the dusk, the nearest quite large. What were those protrusions she saw? Could it be cannon jutting from the decks? Was that the *USS Michigan?*

Of course it was. The Rebs had turned the *Phoenix* about and were headed for Johnson Island, planning to free the prisoners. But what about the gunboat? With her cannons she could shoot the *Phoenix* and all aboard her to kingdom come.

Rosalind's skin prickled, and the hair rose on the nape of her neck as understanding came to her. That's why Blackbeard has women standing along the rail, she realized. He knows the *Michigan* won't fire on a steamer carrying women passengers, no matter how close the boat comes to them. She clung to the rail, briefly closing her eyes.

What can I do? she asked herself. How can I foil Blackbeard's plan?

"Enjoying the view?"

Rosalind whirled to confront Blackbeard in person. "They won't be fooled," she cried. "They'll sink you anyway; you won't get away with your foul plot."

His eyebrows raised. "You have an annoying habit of talking too much."

Annoying? She'd show him!

"I don't care if you shoot me as you did Reginald," she said haughtily. "I intend to warn the men on the *Michigan*. You can't stop me from screaming."

"Oh, no?" he asked softly.

She spread her arms, her back to the rail. "Shoot me, then," she cried hysterically. "Kill me!"

Instead, he tipped back her bonnet and pulled her against him. Before she could struggle, his lips were on hers. He held her so closely she couldn't breathe; and though she tried to pull away, it was impossible.

His beard was soft against her face instead of harsh as she had expected, and the pressure of his mouth forced her lips apart. She gasped in surprise, shivering when she felt his tongue caress the inside of her mouth.

Fire burned upward from deep inside her, spreading hotly through her, slowing her struggles, urging her to answer his kiss. No, she thought, I won't. Never.

But she had no more control over what was happening inside her than she had control over him. Despite her vow, she felt herself begin to melt into his embrace.

Two

Rosalind felt she was drowning within Blackbeard's embrace, and she hadn't the will to save herself. His kiss and the hard length of his body against hers created a fiery yearning that demanded to be satisfied.

"Major Eaton?" The voice seemed to come from far off, a mere thread of a voice.

Suddenly Blackbeard thrust her away and she found herself standing alone on her trembling legs.

"Damn it, no names!" Blackbeard—Major Eaton?—snapped at the man who'd come up to them unobserved. "Do you want us to wind up with stretched necks?"

"Sorry, sir."

Rosalind, ashamed and embarrassed, put her hands to her burning face. Before she had a chance to move Blackbeard's arm snaked around her waist pulling her close again, this time with her back against him. His hand clamped over her mouth, preventing her from uttering a sound.

"There's no answering signal, sir," the man said. "We've flashed ours three times, waited, then three times again. Something most have gone wrong over there."

"You're sure there's been no return signal?"

"Certain, sir. What should we do now?"

"We risk discovery if we stay. Chances are some boat

has already spotted the *Phoenix* headed the wrong way."
There was a silence while Blackbeard considered their next
best course of action.

"We'll turn back for Detroit," he said at last. "We can
refuel on one of the islands."

"Yessir."

"Get the ship turned about. I'll deposit the little lady
where she'll do the least harm and then come to the wheel-
house."

Rosalind found herself thrust unceremoniously into the
cabin once more.

"They failed," she told the other passengers. "Something
went wrong on Johnson Island and they didn't get the signal they needed, so they're turning tail and running."

"Where are we headed now?" a man asked.

"He said they'd refuel at an island, then go on to Detroit."

"Likely they'll jump ship at Sandwich," another man
said. "They'll be safe enough in Canada, worse luck."

"Sandwich?" Rosalind asked.

"On the Detroit River. It's a Canadian town. Canada's
full of Rebel spies, and our government can't touch 'em."

The door opened, and Rosalind gasped; but it was only
one of the Rebs bringing back the other women who'd been
outside.

Huddled in the cabin with the rest of the passengers
throughout the long night hours, she fought to stay awake
for, despite the discomfort of the crowded quarters, her
eyes persisted in drooping shut.

I want to see Blackbeard once more, she told herself.
Or should she be thinking of him as Major Eaton? Whoever
he was, she meant to tell him how rude he'd been. Aunt
Rhoda had believed Southerners were gentlemen—but this

Confederate major wasn't! He'd had no right to kiss her against her will . . .

As she swayed groggily against the wall, a door opened and a shout went up. She shook her head to clear it. The captain of the *Phoenix* stood in the doorway.

"We're safe, all of us," he said. "The Rebs are gone."

Many of the passengers surged onto the deck, but Rosalind remained in the cabin. Though relieved, to her dismay she found she was also disappointed because she'd never see Major Eaton again. Only because she'd lost her chance to tell him exactly what she thought of his behavior, she decided. Yes, that was why.

When she began to relive the soft brush of his beard against her face, the fire of his kiss, the exciting feel of his body against hers, she thrust the images from her mind. She would *not* remember.

Through the open door she saw dawn streaking the sky, and alarm shot through her. Would she arrive in Detroit in time to catch the steamer *Illinois?*

She'd already paid for her ticket and had exactly three dollars and seventy cents left in her reticule. What if she missed the *Illinois?* Where would the money come from for the fare on another boat? What if she had to stay in a hotel overnight? Or maybe more than one night, since she doubted that boats sailed to the Upper Peninsula every day. What would she do?

She walked slowly onto the deck and found the rail lined with people speaking in loud, excited voices.

". . . hope they all hang . . ."

"Damn spies. My boy's with the Ohio 130th . . ."

"You can't trust anyone these days," a woman in brown merino said. "The Confederates have spies everywhere."

"Now, Martha, don't get worked up," the man next to her cautioned.

"The war just goes on and on," she said. "Why can't we end it? I won't have my Billy a soldier."

"He's but fourteen, Martha. There's no cause to—"

"He talks of nothing but joining up." Martha's voice rose. "He follows the reports of every battle. I can't bear the thought of—"

"Please, Martha, pull yourself together." The man put his arm around the woman and led her away from the rail.

Rosalind took their place, pulling her cloak closely about herself as the chill morning wind blew over the water. Land loomed to either side telling her the *Phoenix* must be in the Detroit River. To her right she saw fortifications and caught a glimpse of a red-coated sentinel. How close Canada was!

But when would they arrive in Detroit? Would she be in time? She stepped away from the rail to search for a crew member she could ask. When she found the captain, he listened to her with sympathy but shook his head.

"There's no chance of catching the *Illinois* if she left on time," he said. "I believe the *Pewabic*'s leaving tomorrow, though. You might try for a passage on her after you talk to the steamship company and get your money refunded. I'll see you settled in a hotel myself and have your trunk stored somewhere on the wharf; don't you worry about that."

The sun was well risen before the *Phoenix* docked. Rosalind found the hotel recommended by the captain to be both clean and inexpensive. In her room, she washed and repaired her toilet before going to the steamship office and telling her story to a clerk.

"It's a shame you missed the *Illinois*," he said when she

finished. "And I quite understand it was not your fault. We've all heard about the Reb's takeover of the *Phoenix*— what a terrible experience it must have been for you. There's no question that the company will refund your fare in full."

Rosalind breathed a sigh of relief—prematurely as it turned out.

"Unfortunately, I'm not authorized to refund money," the clerk added. "If you'll complete these forms, I'll see that they reach the main office as soon as possible. The refund shouldn't take more than a week at most."

"But I can't stay in Detroit that long," she protested.

"No need to, Miss Collins. The *Pewabic* sails tomorrow morning and the refund can be sent to your address in Michigan."

"I don't have enough money to purchase another fare," she admitted. "Isn't there some way my refund could cover the cost?"

He shook his head regretfully. "I'm sorry but I don't have the authority to arrange such a thing."

"Who does?"

The clerk apologized again, telling her the manager was in Chicago for three days.

"But I can't miss another boat," she said plaintively. "I haven't the money to stay here in Detroit and wait for either the manager to return or the refund to be paid."

The clerk spread his hands. "I'm so dreadfully sorry, Miss Collins."

Rosalind gave up and retreated to her hotel room where she lay on the bed fully dressed, staring up at the cracked plaster of the ceiling. What was she to do? Her money would cover tonight's lodging only. Despite her anxiety, her lack of sleep made her eyes heavy and she dozed off, waking with a start now and again, only to slip under once more.

It was all Major Eaton's fault, she thought groggily. What a detestable man. Had they caught him yet? She'd like to see him hanged.

Then she was asleep again and dreaming of his black beard soft against her cheek and his warm lips possessing hers . . .

She came to full alertness with her body throbbing and perspiration covering her face and neck. She stared about the unfamiliar room in bewilderment. Where was she? Only a moment ago she'd been aboard the *Phoenix* in Major Eaton's arms. When she realized she'd been dreaming, she flung herself from the bed and poured cold water from the pitcher into the basin to bathe her face.

How could she possibly have allowed herself to dream about such an insolent man, a man who was her enemy as well? The major was nothing like gentle and kind Reginald. Reginald had never taken liberties; he'd never even attempted to kiss her until the morning he'd left Boston with his unit. Even then, his kiss had been respectful.

But Reginald was dead. Killed by Confederate soldiers. Soldiers like Major Eaton. She would never dream about that wretched Reb again.

After tidying herself, she went downstairs for supper and ate hungrily, aware she'd paid all but her last few cents for the meal. Afterwards, there was nothing to do but return to her room and go to bed.

Rosalind woke at dawn, having made no decision about what she'd do. Deciding there was the off chance the captain of the *Pewabic* might be cajoled into taking her aboard on promise of payment once she received the refund, she dressed quickly, packed her carpetbag and left the hotel.

She hurried along Jefferson Avenue and, once she arrived dockside, asked a wagoner where she might find the *Pewabic*.

When she reached the boat, wooden crates were still being hustled aboard, men swarmed over the deck, and the urgency of imminent departure filled the air. Her notion of speaking to a busy captain seemed foolish—he'd only send her back to the steamship office and that hapless clerk. And, while she'd heard of people stowing away on boats, she wouldn't have the slightest idea how to go about it.

But what else was there to do? Tentatively, she approached the gangplank. As she stood at the foot, looking up the sloping ramp to the deck, a well-dressed man in a brown suit and wearing a top hat, started down. He was speaking to someone behind him and so didn't immediately notice her. Because his face was turned away from her she didn't see it until he was almost upon her. As he moved aside, thinking she wanted to get by, she glanced at him, then stared. Surely she knew him.

Clean-shaven, the skin of his jaw somewhat lighter than the rest of his face, dark hair, a thin white scar running along his left cheek, a scar that lifted the corner of his mouth ever so slightly—who was he?

"Pardon me," he said making to pass her, lifting his hat but not really looking at her.

The voice, she'd know that voice anywhere.

"Major Eaton!" she exclaimed.

He halted, frowning as he gazed intently at her. "I beg your pardon," he said. "I believe you've made a mistake."

She was dressed differently than she had been on the *Phoenix*, with a bonnet that shaded her face and wearing a shawl over a dark-gray walking dress, shortened so her boots showed. Perhaps he didn't recognize her.

The second time he spoke, his voice sounded slightly different than she remembered. But, despite that and, though he was beardless now, she was all but positive he was Blackbeard.

"I believe Major Eaton was your name on the *Phoenix*," she said. "How dare you show yourself in Detroit?"

"Miss, I have no idea who you think I might be," he said coolly. "We've never met before."

Rosalind took a deep breath. Could she be wrong? "I don't think I'm mistaken," she insisted.

He bowed slightly. "Are you boarding the *Pewabic?*" he asked.

"I wish I could," she said, wondering if he meant to drop his claim that she'd mistaken him for some other man. "Unfortunately, due to unforeseen circumstances on the *Phoenix,* I missed my boat yesterday. Now I'm stranded here in Detroit with no money to pay for passage on another boat."

She noticed that the muscles in his jaw tightened.

"I had my fare paid on the *Illinois,*" she went on, hoping she was discomfiting him, "but due to the delay, she sailed before the *Phoenix* docked."

A man and woman approached along the dock. He glanced at them, then back at her.

"Although you've confused me with someone else," he said, speaking quickly in a low voice, "I can't turn aside from a lady in distress. Please accept my paid passage aboard the *Pewabic*. I'll notify the captain and collect my belongings from the cabin."

She blinked in surprise and, before she had time to recover, he hurried back up the gangplank and disappeared. Clutching her carpetbag tightly, Rosalind followed slowly. Could she have made a mistake? After all, this man had no beard. And his voice—had it been quite the same? It would be inexcusable if she'd confronted a stranger.

Yet she was almost positive he was Major Eaton, minus his beard. If he'd smiled at her, wouldn't the scar have pulled the left side of his mouth higher, making the smile lopsided? Of course the beard would have hidden the scar . . .

When she found the captain of the *Pewabic,* he confirmed her good fortune. "Mr. Rackham told me a young lady would be sailing with us in his place."

"Who?" she asked, startled.

"Mr. Daniel Rackham," the captain repeated.

Mr. Rackham. She nodded. Why not? If he were a fugitive, he would hardly use his real name or his army rank. She glanced all around, but he was nowhere to be seen among the men on deck.

"Do you have a trunk, Miss Er—" the captain asked.

"Miss Collins," she told him. "And, yes, I do."

"I should advise you, Miss Collins, that we'll be sailing within the hour and so you haven't much time to put baggage aboard."

Rosalind rushed to the dock in search of a man to collect her trunk from the storage warehouse. She waited nervously for his return and paid him with her last few coins. No sooner was her trunk aboard than the gangplank was raised and the ropes cast off. Though she scanned the pier carefully, she saw no sign of "Daniel Rackham."

I ought to tell the captain who he really is, she thought. After all, he is an enemy. On the other hand, it's probably too late.

No wonder Major Eaton had been so eager to give up his cabin to her—it insured her immediate departure from Detroit, giving him time to escape by other means. She frowned, wondering why he'd booked passage on the *Pewabic* to begin with. The boat was sailing north and he'd want to travel in exactly the opposite direction, wouldn't he? Wouldn't a Confederate officer be eager to go south as rapidly as possible? Wouldn't he be anxious to remove himself from enemy territory where he might be captured and imprisoned? And quite possibly hanged?

Rosalind pictured those bright brown eyes glazed in death and bit her lip. She might hate and despise him, but somehow she'd changed her mind about wanting to see him hanged. Then she shook her head. For all she knew, Major Eaton had no intention of fleeing from the North. He might well be still involved in a plot to free the Reb prisoners on Johnson Island. She had absolutely no sympathy for him, none at all. He deserved to be hanged.

As she undressed that night in her tiny cabin, she wondered what would have happened if she'd received an immediate refund and thus been able to book passage aboard the *Pewabic*. What would have happened once the boat had left dock and she had met Major Eaton face to face? Would he have insisted he was Daniel Rackham and tried to brazen it out? Would she have denounced him?

She went to sleep still thinking about him, and once again he invaded her dreams.

In the next few days, Rosalind discovered she was the only unmarried woman aboard the Pewabic, if you didn't count the fifteen-year-old daughter of a copper mine superintendent who was traveling with her mother, Mrs. Stanley, to Houghton.

The girl, Emma, sought out Rosalind, quite possibly to get away from her over-protective mother. Emma was plump, childish-looking, and a chatterbox. Nevertheless, it was pleasant to talk to someone near her own age.

When Rosalind recounted her adventures aboard the *Phoenix,* Emma promptly told everyone she met so that Rosalind found herself a heroine in the eyes of the other passengers. Their eager interest made her feel guilty about withholding information concerning Major Eaton. Wasn't she loyal to the Union? Why was she protecting an enemy? But, guilty or not, she kept quiet about his escape.

"Nothing ever happens to me," Emma pouted. "I just know I'll hate Houghton. There's nothing but a lot of trees and rocks and Papa says the snow piles up every winter so high that one has to tunnel out." She shivered. "I'll have no girl friends. And the men! They're all miners and as crude as they can be. Foreigners from Europe."

"There must be other men like your father," Rosalind pointed out. "Men with families. And surely Houghton has teachers and doctors. Some of them ought to have sons and daughters for you to meet."

Emma was not easily consoled. "Mama read in a newspaper that Michigan's Upper Peninsula is a wild Siberia. Cold and sterile, it said. Why did we ever have to leave Detroit?"

From what Rosalind had seen of Detroit, it couldn't hold a candle to Boston; but she was careful not to mention this to Emma. She struggled not be become infected with the young girl's gloom but couldn't help wondering exactly what she was letting herself in for. Had Mrs. Donal been right about conditions in the Upper Peninsula?

I'm going to my father, she told herself firmly, and that's what matters. Surely he'll be as thrilled and happy to see me as I will be to see him.

It wouldn't be wise to dwell on any doubts she might have, because she simply had no choice.

"What does your father do?" Emma asked.

"He has an interest in a copper mine near Ojibway."

"Oh? Which one?" Emma, for all her complaints about living in the wilds of Houghton, knew far more about the Upper Peninsula and copper mining than Rosalind did.

"The Nonpareil," she told Emma.

Emma frowned. "That's between Ojibway and Houghton. I've heard Papa speak of the Nonpareil as a spotty producer."

Rosalind smiled vaguely, uncertain what that might mean. Since the lawyer's letter to her aunt had indicated the mine was doing well, she decided to pay no attention to Emma's words.

Rosalind didn't spend all her time with Emma. Two of the men aboard the boat paid her a great deal of attention. Their company made the ten-day trip with all its layovers and refueling stops pass quite pleasantly. Especially since the scenery quickly grew monotonous—water, gulls, pine forests along the shore and, occasionally, other boats.

As they traveled steadily northward, the weather grew cooler; and after they passed through the Soo Locks at Sault Ste. Marie and into Lake Superior, the wind turned chill and rain swept across the gray water.

Rosalind didn't mind. Not with two admiring young men to amuse her. Fair-haired Kenton Ames was twenty but so immature that Rosalind felt she was the elder instead of two years younger.

"I'm 'on leave' from Harvard," he told her. "Father needed me to fill in temporarily as timekeeper at one of his mines at Red Jacket. So difficult to find intelligent help, you know. Naturally, I was happy to oblige."

Listening to him ramble on, she surmised that he was actually in disgrace for some escapade he was ashamed to discuss with her and that his wealthy father had chosen this method of punishment. She refrained from asking Kenton why he wasn't in the army—Reginald had been twenty when he had ridden away from her for the last time. She didn't wish to see Kenton share his fate.

She found Jacob Thompson far more interesting. He was older, over thirty, a lawyer from Philadelphia on his way to Houghton. She thought him a handsome man with his curling chestnut hair, luxuriant mustache to match, and observant hazel eyes. He wore no uniform, either; but maybe, as a lawyer, he'd paid another man to take his place in the army. Rosalind wasn't quite sure she approved of that, but it was difficult to dislike Jacob.

At first she'd thought he might be a bit too curious about why she was in a cabin originally booked by Daniel Rackham. Why would he know the man's name? But later she dismissed her suspicions when Jacob explained that Phillip Rackham had been his best friend back in Philadelphia and he'd intended to discover if Daniel were any relation.

"Your presence aboard the *Pewabic,*" Jacob assured her, "is worth any number of my friend's possible relatives. I can't thank the man enough for relinquishing his cabin to such a charming young woman."

Not everyone liked Jacob as much as she did. "A young woman like you, traveling alone, must be careful what company she keeps," Emma's mother warned Rosalind. "I wouldn't trust that Mr. Thompson with his easy tongue."

Rosalind ignored her advice, enjoying the extravagant compliments Jacob paid her.

"You're that rarity," he told her, "a truly beautiful blond. We men always expect golden-haired women to be beautiful, and we're constantly being disappointed. You, though, are true perfection."

She went as far as to allow him to hold her hand; but when he tried to kiss her one evening, she turned her face so his mouth barely brushed her cheek. She might have found the kiss more exciting if she'd never met Major Eaton.

Finally, all her shipboard friends disembarked at Houghton. The few remaining passengers didn't interest her, and she couldn't wait to dock at Ojibway. But when at last the *Pewabic* entered the Ojibway harbor, Rosalind wondered if she'd come to the end of the earth. There was nothing to see except a wooden pier and a scattering of unpainted frame and log buildings. She watched smoke blow briskly from dozens of chimneys and wondered if the wind always came so coldly from the north. May might be well established, but she could swear she felt a hint of snow in the air. Well, she would just have to make the best of it.

Rosalind disembarked and arranged for her trunk to be delivered to the Bigelow House—"the only place you'd want to stay at, miss"—then trudged up a plank walk leading from the harbor to the town proper, soon coming to the main street. This road, muddy ruts in a nearly solid blanket of horse manure, ran between low frame-buildings boasting false fronts. Cedar lampposts marked the street intersections.

She had to lift her skirts to pick her way across the street to reach the Bigelow House. She couldn't, of course, stay there with no money; but surely someone at the hotel could tell her how to reach her father.

"Jephthah Collins?" the desk clerk repeated. "Why, yes,

everyone knows Mr. Collins. He has a fine new home up on the hill by the river."

"I'm his daughter," she said.

"His daughter? You're his—daughter?" The clerk's thin eyebrows raised nearly to his hairline.

"Could you tell me how to get there, please?" As she went on to tell him about the trunk, Rosalind did her best to imitate both Aunt Rhoda's no-nonsense voice and her imperious manner, but inwardly she trembled, her stomach in a knot.

The clerk's surprise had reminded her of what she hadn't cared to face—her father would be astounded to see her. He'd very likely be angry she'd come to Ojibway without letting him know in advance. What if he didn't like her? Or didn't want her?

"It's a ways to walk, miss," the clerk said. "Over a mile. I could get you a hired rig if—"

"Thank you, I prefer to walk," she said haughtily, not caring to arrive in a hired carriage and immediately have to ask her father for money to pay the driver.

"You must have come off the *Pewabic,*" the clerk said. "Any news of the war?"

Rosalind shook her head, Major Eaton's sardonic smile invading her mind as it so often did her dreams. "If you could tell me the way to my father's house—" she repeated.

The house was not in the town proper and, after half a mile of muddy walking, Rosalind decided her boots were ruined forever. She could see the house long before she reached it, standing tall and white and lonely on a bluff above the river. There were no trees in front, but a grove of pines snuggled close behind the house. She counted three stories and noticed the porch was columned.

Actually the house wouldn't look out of place in Detroit,

she thought—or even Boston. Somewhat cheered, she inhaled the cool damp air and relaxed a little. Her father had taste as well as money. He'd find she'd been well trained in the proper way to run a household by Aunt Rhoda. Everything would be all right. He'd accept her—of course he would.

If only she could have managed to arrive in style. The bottom of her skirt had become so soiled she doubted if the material would ever come clean again.

Toiling up the hill, with the river below to her right, she saw farm buildings and fields under cultivation on the lower, opposite side. When at last she faced Jephthah Collins's front door, she paused to catch her breath.

She'd had a long and unexpectedly difficult trip, taken against the lawyer's advice, but here she was. Pirates, a Rebel plot, a dangerous man, no money—nothing had kept her from her father. A sense of exhilaration filled her as she climbed the steps to the porch.

The front door was varnished and set with a copper knocker in the shape of a bear's head. Rosalind picked up the copper head in her gloved hand and rapped it smartly against the striker plate. Once. Twice. Three times, for luck.

After a few moments, she tried again. No one came to the door. A great weight settled in her chest. It had never occurred to her that she might come all this way from Boston to Ojibway and not find anyone at home.

What was she to do now?

Three

"It's an ungodly name," Father Paquet said. "None of the saints—"

"Damn it, man, she has to be baptized," Jephthah Collins insisted. "Do you think I want to be responsible for dooming her soul to everlasting purgatory? I gave her the name eighteen years ago, when she was born, and she's been Coesius Collins ever since. Baptize her, for the love of God."

Cosy listened to her father argue with the priest, her face showing no trace of her interest.

"The name is Roman—Latin. Isn't that good enough for you, Father?"

"Latin?"

"Look at her eyes—as green as a cat's. They've been the same since she was born. The name means cat's eyes. Like her mother's." Jephthah Collins bowed his head. "God rest her soul."

Cosy's expression didn't change even though she was well aware her father was putting on an act for the priest. She wondered why this baptism was suddenly so important to her father after all these years. She didn't care one way or another. Hungry Moon had taught her enough of the ways of the Great Spirit so that she felt no fear. Kitchi

Manitou meant her no harm no matter what Father Paquet decided to do.

"I shall baptize her as Coesius Mary Collins," the priest announced finally.

Jephthah shrugged. "I have no objection."

Louella Genette had taught Cosy about the Virgin Mary and the Baby Jesus. She was secretly pleased that Father Paquet should think she merited such a name, but her pleasure did nothing to dislodge Hungry Moon's teachings.

With Hungry Moon to guide her, she'd learned how the Great Spirit looked after the earth and everything on it—including the People. She'd also learned Anishinabe ways, including those of a medicine woman—how to gather wild plants for food, for healing, and for death. She'd learned how to dry and preserve them as well as the rites for placating the spirit of the plants.

Cosy had come to the Anishinabe camp when she was nine; and Hungry Moon had welcomed her into her lodge, happy to have a girl she could raise as her daughter since she had no child of her own. Since Hungry Moon belonged to the Loon totem, Cosy had wanted to belong, too.

"Koko, my little owlet," Hungry Moon had told her, "you have a father who is not of the People; and though your mother was, she came from a different totem. Some of your spirit will always belong with us; but you must not wish to become like me, for your father will not leave you in my village for long."

"But I *want* to be a medicine woman like you," Cosy had protested. "My father is gone; you said you didn't know where. You don't even know if he'll ever be back."

"I've had a dream," Hungry Moon had said and Cosy had ceased her protests, knowing dreams were a thing of the spirit and often showed what would be.

"In my dream, Mukwah, the black bear, came into my lodge," Hungry Moon had said, her voice low with sadness. "When Mukwah left, a white owl was perched on his shoulder. For six winters you've been my owlet, my little white bird, but what the dream told me was that your father would come for you."

How quickly the years had passed in Hungry Moon's village. The six years she'd lived with the medicine woman had been the happiest of her life. But Hungry Moon's dream had been a true one. When Cosy reached fifteen, her father appeared again, his blue eyes smiling, and told her she must go to another place to live, a place where she'd learn the ways of his people.

Though she'd wept inside, she'd shed no tears leaving Hungry Moon. The People didn't cry in front of strangers—which her father had become to her—and she had tried to behave as though she were one of the People.

She hadn't protested. As a dutiful daughter she'd obeyed her father even though at first she'd hated living in the house her father had brought her to. She had preferred the round lodges of the People to the wooden boxes of her father's people. And, though she had respected her, she'd not taken to the woman with hair the color of pale fire who had lived with her in the house and taught her to read and write and do sums.

Remembering the advice of Hungry Moon—only fools don't partake of a feast offered in good will—Cosy had done her best to absorb everything she could, discovering in the process that learning *was* a feast. And in time, she'd become fond of her teacher, Louella Genette, who'd been unfailingly patient and kind, while at the same time insisting that Cosy learn white ways.

Just before she had turned eighteen, her father had uprooted her once again. Only when she had known she must leave her had Cosy realized how much she'd come to depend on Miss Genette. She had known her teacher was in love with Jephthah Collins and she had felt sorry for her because he never stayed long with any woman. Cosy had been distressed but not surprised when he had dismissed Louella Genette abruptly, showing little sympathy when she had cried and clung to him.

Cosy had felt her father had demonstrated the truth of Hungry Moon's warning that a woman had to take great care when choosing a man to love.

"A woman must be wise enough to control the force within her that urges mating," she'd cautioned.

I won't ever let any man hurt me like that, Cosy had vowed as, tears streaming down her face, she had waved goodbye from the dock when the boat pulled away with the weeping Miss Genette aboard.

"Don't mind about Lolly Genette leaving," Jephthah had said to Cosy, not understanding that she minded *for* Miss Genette as well as because she was losing her friend and teacher.

Shortly afterward, they'd moved into the new house her father had built and less than a moon later her father had brought her to this priest to be baptized.

Cosy bowed her head before Father Paquet and allowed him to anoint her and name her Coesius Mary Collins. As Father Paquet droned on, calling her a daughter of the church, Cosy was reminded of what she'd once overheard a woman ask Miss Genette.

"Why does Mr. Collins take so much trouble to educate a half-breed daughter? It isn't as though she'll amount to anything—no decent man will ever marry her."

Louella Genette had realized that Cosy had heard and

later she'd tried to explain. "Those with small minds label others," she's said. "Pay no attention. Besides, the word half-breed is inaccurate. You're only one-quarter Indian."

Cosy still wondered why Miss Genette hadn't said it the other way—that she was three-quarters white. The white part of her was what she wished to exchange, not the small portion that bound her to the People.

"Do you understand what I'm telling you, my child?"

Bringing her attention back to the priest, Cosy said, "Yes, Father Paquet. I am to cross myself only in the name of the Father, the Son, and the Holy Ghost."

"And to worship no other gods," he added.

Should she lie? She had no intention of giving up Kitchi Manitou, and Hungry Moon had warned that a lie pricked the teller with the irritating persistence of a porcupine quill.

"She understands, Father," Jephthah said impatiently, saving her from making a decision. "I'll take the place of the godparents I wasn't able to provide and see she attends to her devotions. You've been kind to both of us, Father, very kind."

Cosy watched him take money from his pocket and slip it into the priest's hand, murmuring, "For your mission."

"Thank you," the priest said. "God grant you a safe journey home."

Moments later they'd left the small log church and were climbing into the buckboard once again. The driver clucked to the team, calling the horses by name, and the wagon lurched ahead.

"Most goddamned uncomfortable vehicle built by man," Jephthah said. "I hope to hell we get the railroad soon." He turned to her. "Are you all right, Cosy?"

"Yes, Father," she answered.

The May breeze carried the chill of snow from the deep

woods but also the sweet scent of trailing arbutus, the earliest of spring flowers.

At the bottom of the small storage chest her father had bought for her, Cosy had placed her hide pouches containing the ground roots and dried leaves of the medicine plants she'd gathered for Hungry Moon. Though her father had insisted she'd have no further need for Indian clothes, her deerskin moccasins decorated with porcupine quills and stained with dyes were in the trunk, too, along with her doeskin skirt, tunic, and leggings.

Cosy clung to her seat as the buckboard jounced over the rutted road, puzzled as to why her father had brought her to this log church on the Nonpareil Mine road instead of having her baptized in St. Patrick's in Ojibway. He was friendly with Father Dunne from St. Patrick's. Why have his handyman Jim take them all this way on a cold May day? Why bypass a priest he knew and liked for a stranger who traveled between the mines, a priest he'd never met before today?

Was he ashamed to have left her baptism so late? Or was there some other reason?

She dredged up what she remembered of her early years when she'd traveled with her father from one mining settlement to another—to Houghton, to Rockland, to LaPointe, then back to Ojibway, month after month, year after year, before he'd finally left her at the Anishinabe village. In the white settlements he'd always found a woman to take care of her—and of him as well, she'd realized when she'd grown older—but none of them had lasted long. Hungry Moon was as much of a mother as she'd ever had, and she still missed her Anishinabe foster mother.

"What do you think, Jim?" Jephthah asked the buckboard driver. "We in for some rain?"

"Might make the mine location first," Jim answered. "Hope it ain't one of the gully-washers so we get holed up there two, three days."

Cosy glanced upward, evaluating the clouds, aware the air was heavy with dampness. Yes, it would rain, she decided; but there wasn't the look or the feel of a real storm, more likely a fine, misty rain, a cold rain that wouldn't prevent them from returning to her father's two-story new house in Ojibway in the morning.

She shifted on the hard planking, still bothered about the way her father had gone about the baptism. On the surface Jephthah was a friendly, smiling man, but he didn't really give of himself. The man underneath, what Hungry Moon called the heartwood of a person, he kept concealed from everyone. He'd been kind and generous to Cosy since she'd moved into the new house with him, but she'd learned by observation that her father never did anything without a reason. True, there was the blood tie between them, but she doubted if that were enough to account for all the attention he'd lavished on her lately.

Coesius Mary Collins was going to be of some use to him in a way she didn't yet understand. He'd been preparing her for this unknown purpose for three years—making her learn white ways from Miss Genette while providing her with new clothes to go with her new ways.

"I expect we'll be able to leave for home tomorrow," Jephthah said.

"I reckon," Jim replied, turning his head to shoot a stream of tobacco juice into the bushes. "You been calling the shots right lately."

Jephthah laughed, his blue eyes bright and confident. Now that she was older, Cosy understood why women were attracted to her father. He stood over six feet and had not

run to fat, nor had he grayed overmuch—just a touch at
the temples, setting off his dark, wavy hair. He also took
the trouble to be clean-shaven, which was unusual for a
white man.

She smiled, responding to his good humor. If she re-
served her trust, it was only because she'd been taught to.

"Rule yourself," Hungry Moon had emphasized. "Young
girls must learn ways to win other than by force or they'll
suffer as women. Don't strive against fate. See how the
young birch bends and sways with the wind and yet grows
straight."

"Ah, Cosy, you've a lovely smile," her father said. "A
pity you bestow it so seldom."

She took his words and held them close, treasuring the
rare compliment. Daylight was fading, and the lowering
clouds hastened the twilight. A thin rain began, and her
father wrapped them both in a blanket.

As it grew darker, Jim stopped the team and fastened a
lantern to the front of the wagon box before they went on.
And then night settled over them. Huddled next to her
father, Cosy heard the first long cry of a wolf running in
the woods and she raised her head to listen. After a moment, another wolf, farther away, responded.

"Shouldn't bother us none," Jim said. "Plenty for 'em
to eat this time of year."

She hadn't been worried about the wolves attacking.
What their cries had reminded her of was Black Water.
Though he lived in Hungry Moon's village, his people, who
lived to the west under the crouching mountain, belonged
to the Wolf totem. She pictured him in her mind—as tall
as her father but slim, the fastest runner in the village, a
better marksman than any other, and a superb swimmer.

When she'd lived in the People's village, she'd known by

Black Water's glances that he had preferred her to the other girls; but he had known she was taboo and he hadn't chanced angering Hungry Moon, the tribe's medicine woman. She had power equal to old Fire-in-the-Sky, the chief.

As soon as Cosy had begun to change from a girl to a woman, Hungry Moon had warned the young men away from her. And had warned her, too. "You are not to tempt them," Hungry Moon had told her. "They all want you, lovely as you are, but you must keep to yourself and leave the men alone. Your father expects it and so do I."

Hungry Moon hadn't hidden the reason for the youths' attraction to Cosy—the urge to mate that men carry like a burden through most of their lives. A woman's burden was different. "Never forget, little owlet," she'd cautioned, "that mating leads to children and it is women, not men, who bear the babies. Choosing the wrong man can leave a woman alone with a child with no hunter to bring food to the lodge."

Was Black Water the wrong man? Cosy sighed. She'd never know because she doubted she'd ever see him again.

Certainly not if her father could prevent it. "You can speak to the squaws you know, Cosy," he'd told her over a year ago when, as she was walking with Miss Genette in Ojibway, she'd recognized Black Water among a group of the People and called to him.

"But," her father had added sternly, "I don't ever want to hear of you talking to or being with any of the braves. Do you understand me?"

She had had no need to ask why. He had been telling her what Hungry Moon had taught her long ago—Cosy Collins was not to mate with a man of the People. Because she had had no choice she'd obeyed him.

It didn't stop her from dreaming about Black Water, though. Compared to him, the white men she'd met seemed too loud and too fat. Not that she'd met many. Miss Genette had been as diligent as Hungry Moon at keeping her away from men.

Cosy saw the first glint of light in the darkness ahead just as Jim announced, "Here we are. Even with the rain and all, we made it in time so you won't miss that dinner."

What dinner? Cosy wondered. Her father didn't enlighten her. When the wagon stopped in front of a large frame house, her father jumped off, then lifted her down and escorted her to the front door.

A plump middle-aged woman answered his knock, immediately inviting them inside.

"This is my daughter Cosy, Mrs. Appleton," Jephthah said.

The woman put her arm over Cosy's shoulders. "You poor, dear girl, you must be exhausted," she exclaimed. "What a shame you had to travel in this miserable weather!"

She swept Cosy up a flight of stairs and into a bedroom with green wallpaper above the maple wainscoting. After two years, Cosy had grown accustomed to houses and she quickly realized this one was furnished even more grandly than the new home her father had built.

"What pretty eyes you have, my dear," Mrs. Appleton said as she urged Cosy out of her wet cloak. "Exactly the color of the finest Chinese jade. I'm sorry you won't have a chance to rest before dinner, but I'm afraid there isn't time."

Cosy touched the green dress she wore—damp, but not unduly so. She noticed in the pier glass that the rain had encouraged the faint curl in her dark hair.

"My dear, you look perfectly charming," Mrs. Appleton assured her. "No need to worry; young girls are always lovely."

Uncertain what was to come—a dinner, yes, but who would be at the table?—Cosy followed her hostess down the stairs and into a parlor where three men stood talking. Next to her father was a gray-haired man she took to be Mrs. Appleton's husband and a younger man, who stared at her when she came into the room.

She conquered her first impulse to lower her eyes in the fashion of the women of the People—both Miss Genette and her father had discouraged that habit—and, raising her chin, looked into the man's otter-brown eyes.

His dark hair curled along his collar and a thin white scar ran along his left cheek, making that side of his mouth turn up a trifle so that he seemed to be amused. He was the tallest man in the room. And very handsome.

In a sudden flash of inspiration, it came to her that this man was the reason why her father had brought her to the log church on the mine road to be baptized. She'd thought the baptism itself was of the utmost importance to her father but now she knew better. Careful not to reveal any hint of what she was thinking, she glanced at her father, then back at the tall, dark stranger.

What was Jephthah Collins's purpose in bringing her to meet this man?

"My daughter, Coesius," Jephthah said.

The man bowed slightly, saying, "Daniel Rackham, very willingly at your service, Miss Collins."

Four

Rosalind awoke to the gloomy gray light of a cloudy day. For a moment she thought she was still aboard the *Pewabic,* but then she saw the unfamiliar room and heard the clatter of a horse and wagon passing on the street below and she remembered where she was and what had happened after she'd disembarked from the boat at Ojibway.

Sitting up in bed, she hugged herself as she stared at the Worthington stove that stood on a zinc square. The chill in the room told her last night's comforting fire had burned itself out.

The desk clerk at the Bigelow House had been most accommodating after she'd returned in the rain yesterday, tired and dispirited. As he'd conducted her to this more-than-adequate room, he'd said, "If'n your father's not home, I'll wager he's out at the Nonpareil Mine. Yessir, that'll be it, right enough. Likely he gave the help a day off; otherwise, they'd've let you in. I reckon he'll be back by tomorrow."

The clerk mentioned not a word about the room charge. Because she had no money Rosalind knew her father would have to be responsible and it made her uneasy to be running up bills for him to pay before he even knew she'd arrived in town. But it couldn't be helped and so there was no

point in worrying about how he might feel or even wondering what the hotel charged.

Because of Ojibway's isolated location, she hadn't expected much of the Bigelow House and was pleasantly
surprised to find it the most deluxe hotel she'd stayed in
on her journey from Boston. Outside, it was no more than
a five-story frame box, but the interior accoutrements were
luxurious. Gilt. Velvets. Brocade. Rich carpets. She had a
suite—a sitting room and a bedroom.

Shivering in the penetrating cold, she eased from the
brass bed and made her way to the curly maple commode
whose top held a large white china bowl and a water pitcher
decorated with blue lilies. Glancing at her image in the
mirror above the commode, Rosalind sighed and fluffed
her hair. Travel did not add to a lady's attractiveness.

Last night she'd set aside the dark-blue skirt of her riding
habit to be worn with a plain, white bodice-shirt. A match-
ing dark-blue jacket, Wellington boots, and her pork-pie
hat without, thank goodness, a veil, would complete her
outfit. The ensemble would hold up well for the ride on
the buckboard that would deliver her trunk to her father's
house sometime today. She had no intention of ruining
another dress and pair of shoes by walking along the
muddy roads.

When she entered the lobby after eating in the well-ap-
pointed dining room—white table linen and silver in the
wilderness of the Upper Peninsula!—the clerk hastened to
her side.

"I heard tell your father's back in town," he said. "Came
in late this morning, he did." Glancing at the grandfather
clock next to the stairs, he added, "Close on to noon. If'n
you want, I'll fetch a wagon driver to take your trunk up
the hill."

Thanking the clerk, she hurried to her room to finish packing her carpetbag. Setting it in the hall next to her door to be carried down by a porter, she descended the steps once again and left the hotel.

Outside, the rain had stopped but the air hung heavy, as though another downfall might begin at any moment. A cold, damp wind blew off Lake Superior, making Rosalind wish she'd worn a shawl. Like ladies' fashions, spring in the Upper Peninsula obviously lagged far behind Boston.

When the wagon pulled to a stop in front of the Bigelow House, she climbed up onto the wooden seat while the bearded driver went inside to collect her trunk and carpetbag. Once he'd loaded her belongings into the back of the wagon, he clambered up beside her and clucked to the horses causing the buckboard to jolt along the main street of the town, mud splattering to either side.

"Hear tell you're Collins's daughter," the driver said. "Kind of a surprise. None of us knew old Jephthah had—" Pausing, he eyed her sideways. "I got to say *your* ma couldn't've been no Injun squaw."

Of course not! Rosalind thought indignantly. What an odd thing for him to say. Was he trying to insult her? Making no reply, she turned away.

"Where ye from?" he asked, not at all abashed by her attempt to ignore him.

"Boston," she said coolly.

"Came in on the *Pewabic* yesterday, didn't ye? Heard they had a Reb spy scare down to Detroit. The mate said folks downstate was all worked up over some Reb pirates what took over a boat. Ye know about that?"

Deciding he'd keep asking if she didn't answer, she made up her mind to reveal as little as possible. "I don't know anything more than you've already heard," she told him.

"Some folks up here think the Rebs have been working on the Canucks, trying to start some kind of invasion from over the border so's we'd be fighting Canucks in the north and Rebs in the south. Mind you, I don't believe half of what I hear round and about but there ain't no love lost between them Canucks and us, that's for sure."

Rosalind pondered the driver's words. Could Major Eaton or Daniel Rackham or whatever his name was be involved in inciting the Canadians to join the Rebs as well as trying to free the Johnson Island prisoners-of-war? An image of his crooked smile flashed in her mind. To think he'd had the nerve to kiss her! She pressed her gloved hand to her lips as though to wipe away even the memory of that kiss. Why did his image keep lingering in her mind?

Firmly ejecting the Rebel major from her thoughts, Rosalind turned her attention to the storefronts along the road. Men in slouch hats ambled along the wooden plank walks set above the mud of the street, and she noticed that some of the men wore Indian moccasins even though they didn't seem to be Indians. How peculiar! Children clattered by, running past on the wooden boards, and an occasional woman walked by. None of the women wore a hoop, exactly as Mrs. Donal from the *Phoenix* had predicted.

Everyone gazed at her with such frank curiosity that Rosalind, unnerved, finally looked straight ahead. She was relieved when the wagon left the main street and turned into a narrow lane that led to the bluff where Jephthah Collins had built his imposing house. She caught a glimpse of it, white against the dark green of the pines behind. Smoke curled from the four chimneys.

As the horses toiled up the hill's narrow, rutted road, Rosalind clutched the seat to avoid falling off. Behind them a buggy came up, drawn by a brown horse that snorted impatiently when he had to slow for the slow moving wagon ahead.

Because she didn't want to seem to be staring at the driver of the rig, Rosalind gave him no more than a glance. Could it possibly be her father? To tell the truth, even if she'd had a better look, she wouldn't have been certain because she'd never seen a picture of her father. Aunt Rhoda's only description of Jephthah Collins had been, "a dark man, inside and out."

Rosalind's heart beat faster in anticipation. He'd be surprised. Amazed. But happy to see her—surely. After all, she was his daughter. No doubt he was as curious about her as she was about him. Would he be pleased at the way she looked? Oh, why couldn't the driver hurry the horses a bit?

Finally the buckboard reached the crest of the hill and the wagon lurched into the circular drive leading to the portico. Rosalind bit her lip nervously, suddenly unsure of her welcome. When at last the driver stopped the horses, she jumped off before he could offer to help her. The buggy pulled up immediately behind the wagon and she hesitated, uncertain whether to go immediately to the front door or wait to discover the identity of the man in the buggy.

She eyed the tall man as he climbed out and drew in her breath, shocked. He glanced at her as he started toward the house and stopped short.

"What the hell are you doing here?" he demanded.

Rosalind recovered her wits. "Why Major—uh, Mr. Rackham!" she exclaimed.

"What are you doing here?" he repeated.

"I've come to see my father," she said tartly. "I might well ask what you're—?"

"Your father is Jephthah Collins?"

"Yes."

"Allow me to pay your driver," Daniel Rackham said, "since I assume you still have no money." He eased past her and strode to the buckboard.

Rosalind clutched her gloved fingers together as though that could repress the humiliation she felt as she watched the driver take the money Daniel Rackham offered him. How she loathed having to allow this arrogant man to pay the fee. And how she loathed Daniel Rackham, for that matter.

The driver unloaded her trunk and carpetbag onto the porch, tipped his hat, and swung up onto the seat. Not until the wagon was headed down the hill did Daniel hold out his arm in a mute offer to escort her to the door. As she braced herself to refuse, he said, "I'm pleased you remembered my correct name."

She noticed again how the scar made the corner of his mouth lift as though with secret amusement. "If you insist your name is Daniel Rackham," she said coolly, "I shan't argue."

"Good. You might have told me *your* name somewhat earlier, Miss Collins."

"You didn't ask."

He did smile then and, though this man was not bearded, she remembered Major Eaton smiling at her on the *Phoenix,* his teeth white against his black beard, and was almost positive that, beard or not, this was the same smile. And the same man, no matter what he chose to call himself.

"It might be best if we allowed ourselves to be formally introduced to one another," he suggested, nodding toward the house.

Rosalind blinked, belatedly understanding his suggestion that they pretend to having never met before. Perhaps he was right. Her father would hardly approve of their highly unorthodox meeting. She didn't herself, even though she certainly wasn't to blame for anything that had happened. On the other hand, if she pretended that Daniel Rackham was a stranger, it might prove difficult to reveal her suspicions about him to her father. Coming to a decision, she smiled at Daniel, but said nothing. Nor did she take his arm as she walked to her father's door. He kept pace beside her. When she glanced sideways, he nodded briefly, as though accepting her challenge. At the door, he raised the copper bear's head knocker and rapped twice.

Almost immediately the door swung open and she saw a sallow-skinned middle-aged woman in a dark dress. Rosalind's heart sank. A stepmother?

"I'm Mr. Rackham," Daniel said to the woman. "Mr. Collins is expecting me."

"Yes, sir," the woman replied.

The housekeeper, Rosalind thought, relieved. Licking suddenly dry lips, she said, "I'm here to see Mr. Collins, too."

Daniel raised an eyebrow in her direction.

The housekeeper glanced at her appraisingly, then nodded. "If you'll follow me."

They passed through the large entry hall into a room with walnut paneling that gleamed richly in the light from hanging brass and crystal lamps. A deep-red Oriental rug covered most of the parquet flooring.

A man with dark hair lightly touched with gray rose from an overstuffed chair and approached them. Despite her growing trepidation, Rosalind noticed he was almost as tall as Daniel. "Glad to see you found my place, Dan," he said, starting to hold out his hand. His blue eyes shifted to Rosalind and he halted, his hand partly out-thrust.

"My God!" he exclaimed.

"Fa—father?" Rosalind quavered.

"Little Rosie—it can't be!"

"I—yes, I've come from Boston to live with you."

"I'm surprised Rhoda would permit—" Jephthah paused and shook his head. "She wouldn't. Rhoda's dead, isn't she?"

"Aunt Rhoda died in April," Rosalind confirmed. "Until then I didn't know you were alive."

Jephthah came closer and caught her hands in his. "Rosalind. My little Rosie. You do favor your mother—your hair, your eyes and, yes, your beauty. When I married her, I thought Cecily was the prettiest thing I'd ever seen."

"Miss Collins and I met outside your door quite by accident, sir," Daniel Rackham put in. "I had no idea this was to be a reunion. If you'd like me to come back later . . ."

"No, no." Jephthah raised a hand. "Let's all sit down. I think we could do with a bit of brandy." His hand went out to ring a bell but, before he could, a dark-haired young woman glided into the room.

A maid? Rosalind wondered but only for an instant. She was too well dressed to be a servant. Her cerise-velvet gown was expensive, and the dressmaker had taken care with the fitting so the gown revealed the wearer's well-developed bosom before the skirt flared, held out by hoops. Whoever the woman was, she wore the latest fashion.

Rosalind tried to swallow her dismay as it came to her that her father might have taken a young bride. Would she find herself sharing the house with a stepmother no older than herself?

"Good afternoon, Miss Collins," Daniel Rackham said to the young woman, bowing slightly. "A pleasure to see you again."

Miss Collins? Rosalind stared at her coiled dark hair, the same color as Jephthah's.

Daniel turned to her, smiling slightly. Or perhaps it was only the scar. "Miss Rosalind Collins," he said, "allow me to present Miss Coesius Collins."

The girl's green eyes gazed at Rosalind with surprise that was quickly masked. She inclined her head and spoke in a husky voice that held a trace of foreignness, a slight accent. "I am happy to meet you."

Rosalind nodded, unable to speak. As if of one accord, both she and Coesius turned to look at Jephthah.

He spread his hands and smiled, his blue eyes shining. "Both my girls together," he said. "I never dreamed I'd have the two of you under one roof." As he spoke he rang the bell, and a moment later the housekeeper entered.

"Mrs. Howard," he said, "a bottle of my French brandy, if you please. Also, we'll be having another guest for dinner tonight. And not only tonight—my daughter Rosalind has come to stay."

Mrs. Howard glanced at Rosalind, her hazel eyes hooded. She looked at Jephthah again and said, "How very nice for you, sir. I'll have Hilda bring the brandy."

I don't think Mrs. Howard likes having me here, Rosalind thought as she seated herself on an elaborately carved rosewood sofa upholstered in a burgundy brocade. After Coesius sat on a chair near her, the two men also took seats.

Rosalind smiled at Jephthah and said, "I didn't know you had remarried, Father. You see, Aunt Rhoda scarcely ever mentioned your name."

"The old bitch didn't—" Jephthah paused. "That is, your aunt was none too fond of me. Blamed me for taking your mother away from her family. And when poor Cecily died, Rhoda came to hate me."

Cecily. Rosalind savored the sound of her father saying her mother's name. She wanted to ask a thousand questions about her mother, but this was not the time. Not with Daniel Rackham here. And not in front of Coesius, either, even if the girl was her half-sister.

She hadn't pictured this kind of reunion with her father. They should have been alone. If they had been, she might have had the nerve to kiss him and he might then have clasped her in his arms. Perhaps they both would have shed a few tears . . .

Instead, here was a strange half-sister. And Daniel Rackham. How had he gotten to Ojibway so quickly? In the shock of seeing him and of meeting her father, she hadn't thought about where she'd last seen him—on the wharf in Detroit after he'd given her his cabin aboard the *Pewabic*. She'd obviously sailed before he had and yet here he was. Not only here, but already acquainted with both her father and Coesius.

"How odd that we're sisters and have never known of one another," Coesius said. "I used to dream of having a sister."

Rosalind forced a smile, not at all certain she'd ever wished for a sister. A father, yes.

"My mother, like yours, no longer lives," Coesius said. "She's been dead for many years."

An unhappy thought struck Rosalind, if her father had raised one daughter he could have raised two. But he hadn't. She'd been forced to stay in Boston while he kept Coesius with him. Why? Because her father preferred her half-sister to her?

"How old are you?" she asked Coesius abruptly.

"Eighteen this month. And you?"

"I—I was eighteen in April," Rosalind managed to say,

her mind roiling in confusion. How could she possibly be only one month older than her half-sister.

Coesius, equally taken aback, stared at her in consternation.

Jephthah cleared his throat. "Well, Rosie, my dear, I'm glad you've come to me. We'll have a long talk after dinner." He rose from his chair. "Dan and I have some business to discuss now, so if you girls will excuse us—"

He paused as a stocky olive-skinned maid came in with a tray of stemmed glasses and a bottle of brandy which she set on a high table before hurrying from the room. Jephthah poured a small amount of the amber liquid into two glasses, handing one to Rosalind and one to Coesius. Then he picked up the tray with the remaining glasses and the bottle and left the room, trailed by Daniel, who nodded to them as he went out.

Rosalind took a sip of her drink before asking, "Have you known Mr. Rackham long, Coesius?"

"I met Mr. Rackham only last night at the Appletons' on the mine location."

"The Nonpareil Mine?" Rosalind asked.

"Yes."

So Daniel had been in the area since yesterday at least. How had he gotten here before her? It was true the *Pewabic* had seemed to dawdle her way up the lakes. Perhaps he'd found a faster boat.

"How was your journey from Boston?" Coesius asked. "I've never been out of the Upper Peninsula of Michigan, not even to Detroit. Is Detroit a very large city?"

Rosalind nodded. "Boston is a bigger city than Detroit; but, compared to Ojibway, Detroit is huge. How large is this town, do you know?" She ignored the question about her trip since she had yet to decide how much she wished to tell and to whom.

"About 2,500 people live in and around Ojibway, my father says." Coesius smiled shyly. "I haven't grown accustomed to the idea that he's your father, too."

Rosalind's effort to return the smile was stiff. "Your name—Coesius—is most unusual."

"Father calls me Cosy. I hope you will, too. I find your name beautiful. Rosalind, like in Shakespeare's play."

Rosalind couldn't help being pleased even as she wondered how her half-sister had managed, in this backwoods, to receive an education that included Shakespeare. Cosy was not exactly pretty, but she was undeniably attractive with her cerise gown setting off her black hair, ivory skin, and green eyes.

"A woman on the boat told me no one wore hoops in the Upper Peninsula," Rosalind said. "I see she was wrong."

"I dress this way to please Father," Cosy said. "Actually hoops are a terrible nuisance, don't you think?"

"They can be on occasion," Rosalind admitted. "But I do like to be in fashion."

Cosy set her stemmed glass on a marble-topped table—she'd scarcely touched the brandy, Rosalind noticed—and rose from her chair. "Would you like to choose a room? We have four empty bedrooms for you to select from."

Rosalind agreed, chiding herself for her feeling that Cosy had no more right to be mistress of this house than she. Her half-sister was only trying to be courteous.

The front staircase led up from the entry and, as they walked toward the stairs, Rosalind noticed how generously proportioned the foyer was, with a hanging copper chandelier unlike any she'd ever seen. The leaded diamond panes to either side of the front door cast ever-changing rainbows of light despite the gloom of the day.

They climbed the carpeted staircase, which curved to a landing where a large model of a sailing ship stood on a pedestal. Rosalind paused to glance at the intricately crafted and minutely detailed model. Obviously her father prized it or he wouldn't have displayed the boat so prominently. She repeated the name on the bow. *"Kaug.* What a strange word."

Cosy, ahead of her, turned back. "Father calls the *Kaug* his treasure ship though I don't know why. Kaug means porcupine in the Anishinabe—that is, the Chippewa—tongue. Like the name of the mountains to the west."

"Mountains?"

"The Porcupine Mountains. You may have noticed them when your boat sailed into the bay. The mountains lie to the west of Ojibway. They're the highest land in the Upper Peninsula."

"You're well informed. But I find myself curious as to why you said 'Anishinabe' when you meant Chippewa. Are they a local Indian tribe?"

"Yes. The word they use is Anishinabe, not Chippewa. It means *the People."*

When they reached the top of the stairs, Rosalind paused again, glancing along the central corridor and noting the many closed doors to either side. "Where do the servants sleep?" she asked. "In the attic?"

"No, the attic is too cold in the winter and too hot in the summer. They don't live in. Father prefers it that way."

Rosalind chose the first room she looked into, her fancy taken by the blue rose-patterned wallpaper above the walnut wainscoting. Gazing at the heavily scrolled headboard and footboard of the large walnut bed that dominated the room, she nodded in approval. Though the furnishings weren't particularly feminine, she felt at home, reminded of what Aunt Rhoda had always called her "good pieces" of furniture. She placed her reticule on the marble-topped dresser with an air of proprietorship.

"I'll have Jim—he's our handyman—bring up your trunk," Cosy said. "Hilda can help you unpack if you wish."

"Thank you," Rosalind said. After her half-sister left the room, she closed the door and leaned against it.

She was in her father's house. She'd journeyed far and overcome unexpected obstacles only to find he already had a daughter. One her own age. Which was impossible. Since her father couldn't have been married to two women at the same time, that made one of his daughters illegitimate. Disturbed at where her thoughts had led her, Rosalind frowned and crossed to the window to gaze down at the town below the bluff. The scattered buildings lay at the juncture of the river and the lake.

Ojibway. Her new home. The end of the world, according to Mrs. Donal. Did she truly belong here?

Aunt Rhoda had spoken several times of her sister's wedding to Jephthah Collins, mentioning how some of the best families in Boston had attended and how wealthy relatives of Jephthah's had traveled all the way from the islands in the Caribbean. A society wedding, according to Aunt Rhoda. Certainly there could be no question that a marriage had taken place between Cecily Hansen and Jephthah Collins. Then Cecily had gone to the wilds of upper Michigan with her husband, and Rosalind had been born less than a year later.

Aunt's Rhoda's words echoed in Rosalind's mind. "He brought you to me and handed you over with never a word of remorse or regret over poor Cecily's death. All he said was I must raise you in the Roman Catholic faith, though he never mentioned being a Catholic when he married your mother in the Episcopalian church."

Had Jephthah settled a sum of money on Aunt Rhoda for her upbringing? Rosalind wondered. They hadn't lived extravagantly, but they'd been comfortable, she and her aunt. She'd gone to a good school and had had fashionable clothes.

What had her father left behind when had he made his journey to Boston, that fateful journey when he had met Cecily Hansen? Had he already known the woman who was to be Cosy's mother? Was it possible he was already married to that woman at the time he came to Boston? Was her father a bigamist?

Rosalind shook her head. If he'd been married to Cosy's mother first, then she, Rosalind, would be the—the bastard. She took a deep breath and turned away from the window. Impossible! She refused to believe it.

The wagon driver's odd remark came back to her ". . . *your* ma couldn't't've been no Injun squaw . . ."

Rosalind's eyes narrowed. Had he been implying Cosy's mother was? Her half-sister did have dark hair, but her skin, while not as fair as Rosalind's, wasn't copper-colored. And her eyes were green. On the other hand, Cosy had a slight accent. And she knew Chippewa words; she'd called them *the People*. Her people? Was Cosy part Indian? Had her mother been Jephthah's mistress?

It seemed probable. How shocked Aunt Rhoda would be! She was shocked herself. How could her father possibly expect her to share the same house with his illegitimate, half-breed daughter?

Five

Rosalind's musings were interrupted by a knock on her bedroom door. She opened it and found the handyman with her trunk. Hilda followed him in.

"Come to help you unpack, miss," Hilda muttered.

The maid, sallow-skinned with lank dark hair and oddly shaped, Oriental-looking eyes, had an unfortunate manner, Rosalind thought. Though poor Hilda was far from attractive, if she stood up straight and spoke clearly, she'd make a much better impression.

After the handyman was gone, Rosalind opened the trunk. "I'll set aside the soiled clothes," she told Hilda, "and you can take them away to be cleaned. I'll manage the rest of the unpacking myself."

Hilda said nothing, standing by stolidly and accepting the garments handed to her.

"I believe that's all," Rosalind said at last.

Hilda's dark eyes met hers for a moment before the girl ducked her head, but it was long enough for Rosalind to see the enmity in the maid's gaze. Why in heaven's name should this lump of a servant dislike her? she wondered. The girl hardly knew her, and she certainly hadn't been unpleasant to Hilda.

"Yes, miss," Hilda mumbled and turned away with the clothes.

Rosalind, accustomed to sharing a pleasant, accommodating maid with Aunt Rhoda, shook her head as she watched Hilda leave the room. She didn't want this sullen girl helping her dress or doing her hair.

Though she'd managed to dress herself while traveling alone, Rosalind saw no reason she should have to keep doing so. She truly needed a personal maid. Hooking one's own gown up the back required the ability of a contortionist. If her father didn't object to hiring one more servant, she'd choose the girl herself.

Reaching into the trunk, she removed her favorite delft-blue evening dress and frowned. It was sadly wrinkled and it would have to be pressed before she wore the gown to dinner tonight. Since she was almost positive the enigmatic Mr. Rackham would be their dinner guest, she was determined to look her best.

The blue gown, made to be worn with a hoop, not only favored her coloring but had a low enough neckline so she could wear the sapphire. Aunt Rhoda's pendant, a pear-shaped sapphire surrounded by tiny diamonds, had been left to Rosalind. She'd tried on the pendant in the privacy of her Boston bedroom and marveled at the brilliancy of the jewel, but this would be the first time she'd worn it for anyone else to see.

Wait until he sees me, Rosalind told herself, smiling at her image in the looking glass above the marble-topped dresser. There'll be nothing to remind him of the frightened girl he took advantage of on the *Phoenix*. Whatever he calls himself, Major Eaton or Mr. Rackham, he'll see he'd best tread carefully with me. I know secrets he wouldn't care to have revealed.

What was his business with her father? Rosalind put her thumb to her lips, biting worriedly on the nail. Her father

must be a staunch Union supporter; she couldn't imagine
him being a Rebel-sympathizer. No doubt he'd be horrified
to discover he was dealing with a Confederate officer in
disguise. Or worse—perhaps even a spy.

Wasn't it her duty to tell him what she knew about
Daniel?

On the other hand, what harm would it do to watch and
wait for a few days? Who knew, given time she might be
able to trap Daniel into revealing, in front of her father,
just exactly what he was. Rosalind nodded as she pictured
Daniel's humiliation as her father denounced the Confed-
eracy in general and Daniel in particular. There was nothing
she'd rather see than Daniel Rackham brought to his knees.

The matter temporarily disposed of to her satisfaction,
Rosalind hummed "Home Sweet Home" as she puttered
about in her room, fitting her belongings into the wardrobe
and the dresser. She was where she belonged at last—with
her father. If things were not exactly as she'd imagined
they'd be—who could have expected an illegitimate half-
sister?—still, she was home.

That evening, as, without any help, she struggled into
the freshly ironed blue gown, someone tapped at her door.
"Who is it?" she asked.

"Cosy. May I come in?"

"Please do." Rosalind's invitation was heartfelt. She was
never going to be able to manage the gown on her own,
and she much preferred Cosy's assistance to Hilda's.

Her half-sister paused in the doorway. "Oh, how lovely
you look!" she exclaimed.

Rosalind smiled in thanks. "Would you be an angel and
do up my buttons?" she pleaded.

Glancing sideways into the mirror as Cosy worked on
the fastenings, Rosalind noticed that her half-sister, still

wearing the cerise-velvet, had added a copper ornament to the bodice of the gown. The design was unusual—some sort of strange creature that appeared to be half-man, half-bird.

"I've never seen anything quite like your brooch," she said.

"Hungry Moon gave me this amulet," Cosy told her, "and Father had it made into a pin so I could wear it. He says no Chippewa fashioned the amulet, that the workmanship comes from an earlier time, perhaps from the copper-seekers who came to Kitchigami—that is, Lake Superior—before the People did."

Rosalind stared at her in the mirror. What was Cosy talking about? "Hungry Moon?" she asked. "Is that a person?"

Cosy finished fastening her up and stepped back. "She's a medicine woman I lived with for six years at a time when Father was too busy to look after me."

Rosalind was aghast. "Hungry Moon's an Indian? Did you actually live in an Indian camp with her? In a wigwam?"

"Yes. Her Chippewa village is near the Ojibway River, several miles upstream from here."

Rosalind wondered if Cosy's mother had come from that same village. If not, why had Jephthah sent his daughter there? Had he handed Cosy over like a puppy, the way Aunt Rhoda claimed he'd done with Rosalind? She felt a prick of empathy for her half-sister.

"It must have been dreadful living with the Indians," she said, shuddering.

Cozy shook her head, her mouth drooping sadly. But all she said was, "I came to tell you we'll be having sherry in the parlor before dinner. Will you come down with me now?"

They found Jephthah and Daniel waiting in the parlor. Seeing the two men side by side, Rosalind was struck by a certain similarity. It was more subtle than mere appearance. There was an aura of masculinity, a male quality she couldn't define.

"You're a fortunate man, sir," Daniel said. "Not one, but two beautiful daughters. The sun and the moon. Day and night."

Jephthah smiled. "I haven't adjusted to their both being with me yet, but you're absolutely correct—they're a pair of lovelies." He beamed at Rosalind, then Cosy. "Sherry?" he asked.

Cosy murmured a polite refusal, but Rosalind accepted a glass of sherry. Though it was true that wine had a tendency to go to her head, she'd barely taken two sips of the brandy her father had offered her earlier.

"I was admiring Cosy's copper ornament," she said. "How surprised I was when Cosy told me it was a gift from a Chippewa medicine woman whom she'd lived with for some years."

Jephthah's smile faded. "Yes. It seemed like the best arrangement at the time."

"You lived with the Indians?" Daniel asked, focusing his attention on Cosy. "Interesting. How did you like it?"

"I got along quite well." Cosy was deliberately being evasive, Rosalind thought.

"This medicine woman is unusually intelligent," Jephthah put in. "I daresay Hungry Moon has more cures to her credit than many of our doctors."

"Did the medicine woman teach you to heal?" Daniel wanted to know.

"I learned a little," Cosy said, and Rosalind heard the reluctance in her voice. For some reason Cosy didn't want to talk about her time with the Indians. Quite likely it was because she was embarrassed. Rosalind could hardly blame her.

Watching Daniel's eyes shift from Cosy to Jephthah and back, Rosalind tensed. Was she missing something? Was Daniel's interest in Cosy because he found her attractive or for some covert reason that had to do with Jephthah? Not that she cared a whit if Daniel preferred Cosy to her. He was nothing to her, nothing at all.

"I suppose that expensive gew-gaw you're wearing came from your aunt," Jephthah said to Rosalind. "You do the jewel far more justice that Rhoda ever could."

Daniel's gaze swung to Rosalind. "I can't decide which is the deeper blue or sparkles the most," he said, "your eyes or the sapphire."

For a moment Rosalind basked in his obvious admiration, then took herself firmly in hand. He was deliberately trying to charm her. Why? No doubt because he meant to do everything in his power to keep her from exposing him. She raised her chin and donned her haughtiest expression.

"Ah, but I see the difference," Daniel said, his lips quirking in that lopsided smile. "The sapphire is undoubtedly expensive but you, Miss Collins, are a jewel beyond price."

Jephthah cleared his throat. "I believe it's time to go into the dining room," he said gruffly, holding out his arm to Rosalind.

She could see he was annoyed. Why? Because Daniel had complimented her? What harm was there in what Daniel had said to her? Puzzling over this, she allowed her father to escort her into the dining room where she noticed, hanging over the mahogany sideboard, a large oil painting of a ship in an ornate gold frame. She thought she recognized the *Kaug*.

"Is that your treasure ship?" she asked her father.

He was seating her as she spoke, and there was a slight pause before he pushed her chair closer to the table. "Where did you hear that?" he demanded.

"Cosy mentioned it when I admired the model on the landing."

"Yes, I suppose I do think of the *Kaug* as my treasure ship," he said but made no further explanation.

Rosalind saw Daniel Rackham scan the picture with raised eyebrows as he seated Cosy at a table long enough to easily accommodate twelve. Her father apparently did nothing on a small scale.

The food was plain but good. After a delicious leek and potato soup, Hilda brought in fish on a wooden plank, surprising Rosalind because she'd never seen fish served in that way before. Perhaps it was an Upper Peninsula peculiarity. The fish itself was white, with a flavor more delicate than the ocean fish she was used to. She found it succulent.

"Planked whitefish," Jephthah explained. "One of our Great Lakes specialties."

Though Rosalind sipped sparingly of the wine served with dinner, she felt her head begin to buzz and wished she'd had the sense to abstain, like Cosy. Sensing Daniel watching her, she found herself glancing at him with a challenge in her eyes.

"Do you miss Boston?" he asked.

His tone was polite enough. But inside, where it doesn't show, he's laughing at me, she told herself. He thinks his charm has overwhelmed me to the point where I won't speak out. Or else he believes I'm afraid to.

"I don't miss Boston," she said carefully. "At least not

yet. So far Ojibway seems most interesting. As was my journey here."

"There's an Irish blessing—or is it a curse?—that goes, 'May you live in interesting times.' "

Staring at that infuriating lopsided smile, she fumed.

"Perhaps it *is* a curse," she said. "Not as much the events of the times as the people who cause those fateful, *interesting* events. Specifically—"

Aware of her father's puzzled expression, Rosalind paused and didn't go on. She wasn't quite ready to expose Daniel. But she would. Soon. Without being fully aware of what she was doing, she took another sip of wine.

Cosy's face, as usual, showed nothing of what she thought. Cosy was an enigma. A puzzle.

Puzzles are made to be solved, Rosalind told herself fuzzily. Cosy needn't believe I can be fooled by her silence for long.

By the time dessert was served, Rosalind had eaten so much that she thought at first she couldn't make room for the apple pie, but one bite convinced her to try.

"This is heavenly," she murmured.

"Ojibway apples," Jephthah said. "Some enterprising chap across the river has established an orchard. Mrs. Howard dries them in the fall so we can enjoy apples in one form or another the year round."

Eventually Rosalind found herself on her feet, this time with Daniel's arm supporting her as her father and Cosy went on ahead. When she started to follow them, Daniel held her back, pulling her aside so the two of them were not within view of the others.

"I notice wine makes you talkative," he said. "A bit *too* talkative."

"I plan to tell my father the entire story of my journey here," she said defiantly.

"He won't believe you. Especially since I reached Ojibway before you did."

"I still don't understand how you did that," she admitted. To her dismay she heard herself slur some of her words.

Daniel's grin told her he'd heard it, too. "Best limit your wine. Drinking can prove dangerous."

"You can't frighten me!"

"Ah, but how I enjoy trying." Then he pulled her into his arms, his lips claiming hers in a challenging kiss that sizzled through her, heating her blood, making her melt against him as she answered his kiss with a passion she had no idea she possessed.

For a timeless moment she floated in a blissful dream. He was like no other man she'd ever known and she lost herself in his warm embrace, held tightly against him in a kiss she hoped never would end.

Belatedly regaining her wits, she pulled away and would have slapped him if he hadn't captured both her hands in his. "Let me go," she snapped. "You have no right to touch me!"

"You enjoyed that as much as I did." His voice was soft and caressing.

"I did not!"

"Shall we try it again to see which of us is right?"

She sputtered, too furious to speak coherently.

"You're quite correct," he said, as though she'd answered. "Regrettably, this isn't the time or the place. Shall we rejoin your sister and father?"

Cosy had noticed how Daniel had lingered with Rosalind, but she knew her father hadn't paid attention. When they reached the parlor, she said to Jephthah, "My sister is very pretty."

"She looks like her mother," he said. "Cecily was frail; I hope Rosie doesn't take after her that way. You know a thing or two about illness—keep an eye on Rosie and don't let her sicken."

"I'll do all I can, Father," Cosy said, thinking to herself that Rosalind looked to be in perfect health.

Why had her father never told her about her half-sister? Could it be because he hadn't married Rosalind's mother? He certainly *had* married Cosy's mother. Hungry Moon, who never lied, had said she'd watched while a blackcoat, a Catholic priest, had married Jephthah to Antoinette DuBois.

"Your mother was carrying you inside her at the time," Hungry Moon had told Cosy, "so you were there, too, even though you didn't know it."

Cosy had heard it was against the white man's law to be married to two wives at the same time and so what was she to believe—that her father had broken the law or that he had never wed Rosalind's mother?

"What the hell's keeping those two?" Jephthah growled.

Cosy, who'd noted how Rosalind's gaze had rarely left Daniel during the dinner, had no intention of sharing her growing suspicion that her sister and Daniel Rackham were not strangers to one another. "I hear them coming now," she said.

"You don't look Indian now that I've got you dressed in proper clothes," Jephthah said, "but you've got Indian hearing, damned if you don't."

Cosy smiled, taking his words as a compliment.

When Rosalind and Daniel walked into the parlor, she understood immediately that something had happened be-

tween them because her sister's face was flushed and
Daniel's eyes glinted with triumph.

Daniel puzzled Cosy. At the mine location, having dinner
with the Appletons, he'd behaved as though he admired her.
But once Rosalind had appeared, he'd switched his attention
to her. It made little difference to Cosy, but she had the
feeling that her father would be displeased once he realized
the extent of Daniel's interest in her sister. For some reason
she didn't yet understand, she was convinced her father
intended that Daniel be interested in her, not Rosalind.

"Ah, Dan," Jephthah said, "a bit of brandy to settle the
food?"

"Thank you, sir."

To Cosy's relief, Jephthah didn't offer brandy to his
daughters. It was awkward to keep refusing. She didn't care
for alcohol of any kind. It was like some of the plants she'd
gathered with Hungry Moon, useful when used to numb
pain but a poison to be treated with great care and never
to be taken to excess. For many of the People, alcohol had
proved to be more dangerous than the white man's diseases.

"Is Mr. Rackham associated with you in the Nonpareil
Mine?" Rosalind asked Jephthah.

Cosy stared at her sister. Father discouraged any questions from her about his business. What would he say to
Rosalind?

He frowned. "Don't worry your pretty little head over
what doesn't concern you."

"I thought he might be," Rosalind said, "since Cosy told
me she'd met Mr. Rackham at the mine."

Jephthah's frown deepened. "It was a social visit."

Cosy marveled at her sister's persistence as Rosalind,
undiscouraged, turned to Daniel. "What *do* you do, Mr.

Rackham? Are you interested in boats?" Malice lurked beneath the sugar of Rosalind's tone.

Cosy's glance evaluated all three of them. Her father was annoyed, and her sister was playing some game only she and Daniel understood. Daniel's expression gave no clue to his feelings.

"As a matter of fact, yes," he said. "I'm a diver."

"Women don't understand business, Dan," Jephthah warned. "There's no point in discussing it in front of them."

Rosalind's attention remained on Daniel. "Do you mean a deep-sea diver?" she asked, her eyes wide and astonished.

"Rosalind!" Jephthah's voice was sharp. "I most particularly do not want it bruited about that Dan is a diver. Do you hear?"

Rosalind blinked, then nodded.

"There will be," Jephthah went on, "no more discussion of the subject. Do you understand, Rosie?"

Rosalind bit her lip and looked down at the floor. "I'm sorry if I've displeased you, Father. I didn't realize there was any secret."

Jephthah scowled. "I didn't say there was a secret! I simply don't want you talking about it."

"Perhaps we should call it a secret," Dan said. "If we do, your daughters will certainly not breathe a word to anyone."

"The more people who know something," Jephthah muttered, "the less likely any secret is to be kept."

Daniel's face darkened. "Amen," he said.

To Cosy's amazement, Rosalind smiled.

"I'll admit you have a point, Dan," Jephthah said after a moment's silence. "The girls will see us coming and going, and they're bound to be curious—women always are." He paused, strode to the door of the parlor, and closed it. "I don't want the servants to hear."

"Can't you trust them?" Daniel asked.

Jephthah shrugged. "More or less. None of them live with us, so that helps. Jim's rarely in the house and, in any case, he's closemouthed. Mrs. Howard is a pussy-footer; you never know when you're going to look up and find her standing there. Walks real quiet, like an Indian. But she doesn't listen at doors and she wouldn't let Hilda eavesdrop, either. Still, it never hurts to be careful."

Cosy knew Mina Howard walked softly because she'd grown up in a Potawatomi village to the south before she married Jed Howard, a sailor who'd gone down with his boat. Mina was called a half-breed, an ugly word because it was meant to be ugly. Hilda Maki, for all her dark coloring, was not of the People but had come from Finland.

"You've heard me talk about the treasure ship, Cosy," Jephthah said. "And, Rosie, you've seen the model and the picture of the *Kaug*. Well, the old *Kaug* is just that—a treasure ship. Sunken treasure. The *Kaug* went down in '55, and she's lying on the bottom of Superior just waiting for Dan to bring up her gold."

"Gold?" Rosalind echoed.

"When she sank, the *Kaug* had over $50,000 in gold in her safe according to records I had one hell of time locating. I have reason to believe there was more gold than was officially listed. And I happen to be the only man alive who can locate the exact spot in the lake where her bones rest. I've looted her once and I hope to again. A storm shifted her, you see, and she lies in deeper water now, too deep to reach without the aid of a diving suit. That's where Dan comes into the picture."

"Does the *Kaug* belong to you?" Rosalind asked.

Jephthah grinned. "Rosie, my dear, here on the lakes, once she sinks, it doesn't matter whom a boat once belonged to. Whoever arrives first gets what's left of her. That's why we have to keep this a secret."

"I understand," Rosalind said. "I shan't breathe a word to anyone."

Cosy nodded in agreement.

"If you girls will excuse us, Dan and I have a few matters to discuss in my study," Jephthah said. "It won't take long. In the meantime, Cosy, ask Mrs. Howard to serve coffee in here."

Though there was a call bell in the parlor, Cosy never used it. Leaving Rosalind in the parlor, she hurried from the room, intending to go to the kitchen. But she found Mina Howard standing in the entry, near the front door.

Before Cosy could speak, Mina asked, "Have you heard the owl?"

Cosy shook her head.

"He has called many times tonight," Mina said, gazing intently at Cosy. "We have never had an owl so near us before. I wonder why we do now?"

Was there another meaning in Mina's words? If so, Cosy failed to understand what it might be. "I'll listen," she promised. "Father would like to have coffee in the parlor, please."

"Hilda will bring the coffee." Mina slanted one last look at Cosy before walking quickly toward the kitchen.

Cosy watched her go and paused in thought. It was true no owl had frequented the woods near the house before, but was it important? Why had Mina stressed that she'd heard an owl calling tonight?

The People believed that some owls were ill-omened birds. Is that what Mina had meant? Cosy stepped to the front door, opened it and listened. Very faintly she heard a few early frogs singing in the marsh down along the river. Far away someone's dog barked. No owl hooted. Shrugging, she closed the door and was about to rejoin her sister in the parlor when she remembered something from long ago. When she'd lived in Hungry Moon's village, there'd been someone who'd teased her with the owl's call, knowing that Hungry Moon called her *Owlet*.

Her heart leaped in her breast and her breath caught when she realized that the owl's call might be for her. Was it possible? So many moons had passed that she'd given up hope of ever seeing him again . . .

Six

Cosy, tempted to slip into the night to see if the owl calls really were meant for her, hesitated. What if her father finished his business discussion with Daniel and came looking for her? She didn't dare take the chance.

Reluctantly, she turned away from the front door and retraced her steps. Before she reached the parlor, Daniel and her father emerged from the study and the three of them joined Rosalind.

Rosalind immediately singled out Daniel. "I think diving for gold sounds terribly exciting," she said. "But mightn't it be dangerous?"

Cosy thrust from her mind any speculation about who might be waiting outside the house and made herself concentrate on Daniel's answer.

"I wear a diving suit and helmet," he explained. "I'll show you the equipment when it arrives."

"A helmet?" Cosy echoed. "A diving suit?" Though the men of the People were excellent swimmers and divers, they wore as few clothes as possible in the water.

Daniel nodded. "An Englishman named Augustus Siebe invented the diving suit some fifty years ago. The helmet is fastened to the suit and air lines are connected to the helmet so the diver can breathe underwater. Anyone can learn to use the suit."

Rosalind widened her eyes. "Not me!"

Jephthah laughed. "Diving's certainly no job for a woman."

"I once saw a diving suit in the Boston Museum," Rosalind said. "The helmet was grotesque—like a Cyclops—and it looked very heavy. After you don the helmet and suit, Mr. Rackham, how do you get into the water? Do you wade in from shore? Do you jump off a boat?"

"He climbs down a ladder along the side of a specially equipped boat," Jephthah told her. "There's a man on the boat whose sole job it is to pump air down to Dan. And that ends the conversation on this particular subject. Do you understand?" After a pause, he added, "I want to remind you girls again that this is not to be spoken of to anyone. If word gets out, we'll be plagued by treasure-seekers from all over the country, following us, trying to steal what's rightfully mine."

Cosy puzzled over his words. The *Kaug* was a wrecked boat lying on the bottom of Kitchigami and, according to her father, belonged to whoever found her. He considered the boat his because he'd already located her once. But if someone else discovered the new location before Daniel had a chance to dive down into the depths, who would the gold rightfully belong to? She shook her head. It didn't matter. She was on her father's side; she wanted him to succeed.

"I'll tell no one, Father," she assured him.

"I've already promised," Rosalind chimed in. "Not that I know anyone here to talk to, in any case."

"I'm sure you made acquaintances on the *Pewabic*," Daniel said. "I believe you'll find the Upper Peninsula is a small world compared to Boston."

"Why, yes, I did meet a few people on the boat,"

Rosalind said, "but they all got off in Houghton. Though now that I think about it, one of the men *did* say he'd be calling on me."

Jephthah frowned. "A young lady traveling alone should have enough sense not to speak to strange men."

"Have I uncovered a shipboard romance?" Daniel asked, his gaze on Rosalind.

She flushed, turning her face away from him. "No, certainly not! A most respectable lady introduced me to this gentleman from Philadelphia. Mr. Thompson is an attorney, as I recall."

Cosy, watching Daniel and Rosalind, became more certain than ever they knew each other from somewhere else. When they'd arrived, Daniel had claimed they'd happened to meet outside the house. Eyeing him thoughtfully, she wondered if he was like Sun Dog, one of the older men at the Anishinabe village. While not an out-and-out liar, Sun Dog always bent the truth to his own advantage.

Was Daniel inclined to do the same? Had he and Rosalind met each other before they arrived in Ojibway? But if Daniel weren't telling the truth, that meant Rosalind wasn't either.

"Rosie," Jephthah said, "as I recall, Rhoda had a piano. I assume she saw to it you learned to play the thing."

Rosalind nodded.

"Your mother was an accomplished singer," he went on. "Have you inherited her beautiful voice?"

Rosalind blinked. "I don't know. I do sing."

"After I built this house, I bought a piano—a rosewood spinet—for the music room," Jephthah said. "It's been untouched since the day it arrived. Would you play and sing for us?"

"If you like," Rosalind said.

As she followed her sister into the music room, Cosy didn't mention how she'd sat on the piano stool and admired the spinet—the first piano she'd ever seen. She'd secretly touched its white and black keys with careful fingers, marveling at the melodic sound each key made.

She stood back while Rosalind seated herself on the stool, raised the lid of the piano, and poised her hands above the keys for a moment, then began playing. Cosy stared, astonished and impressed by her sister's ability to coax such sweet sounds from the spinet.

" 'Black is the color of my true love's hair . . .' " Rosalind sang.

Cosy listened to the plaintive melody and her sister's high, thin voice lamenting a lost lover. She took a deep, quavering breath, touched by the emotion Rosalind put into the song. Noting how entranced her father was, Cosy felt a prick of jealousy mixed with a pinch of alarm.

Daniel, too, seemed caught in the web of Rosalind's music, but that didn't matter to Cosy. What bothered her was Jephthah's obvious admiration of his long-lost daughter. Would he come to prefer her sister to her—or did he already?

Hungry Moon's words echoed in her head. "We each have at least one talent given to us by the Great Spirit. Never envy that of another; instead, learn to use the talent you do have."

Her foster mother had spoken the truth, but Cosy didn't envy Rosalind's ability to play the piano as much as she minded her father's appreciation of that ability. He'd never admired Cosy in such a way.

Rosalind was as pretty as the pink summer roses that grew in Mrs. Wentworth's garden at the foot of the hill. Cosy stifled a sigh. She might as well not be present for all the attention either man was paying her. Just two days ago, she'd been the center of attention at Mrs. Appleton's dinner table. Daniel had paid her compliments, and her father had seemed pleased and proud of her.

Yet Father kept me near him, Cosy reminded herself, while leaving my sister in far-off Boston with an aunt. The knowledge brought her small comfort—there'd been no convenient aunt to leave her with.

"Your grandfather was a French fur-trapper who married a woman of the People," Hungry Moon had said. "She died when Antoinette was quite small. Your grandfather didn't know how to raise a girl-child in either our way or the way of his people, so Antoinette never learned how a woman should behave. She became foolish, not wise, through no fault of her own. Pretty and foolish breeds danger and grief."

Cosy knew from Hungry Moon that her grandfather had died soon after she was born, leaving no one but her father. If only he'd given her to Hungry Moon to raise from the beginning, if only he'd left her in the People's village, surely she'd have been happier. She would never have learned white ways; the ways of the People would be hers. And perhaps one day she and Black Water would have . . .

"Do you sing, Cosy?"

Startled from her reverie by Daniel's voice, she shook her head. "Not songs like Rosalind sings."

He smiled, the scar near his mouth making the smile crooked. "Do you believe love is as hopeless and sad as this song tells us? Do you think all lovers are faithless?"

Avoiding the first question, she answered the second. "Some lovers surely are, for that's the way of men."

He raised one eyebrow. "Not women?"

"Not often, because women are meant to be healers, not those who wound," she said, quoting Hungry Moon.

"Wise words from one so young."

Not wishing to speak further of love, Cosy changed the subject. "My sister plays the song well. I've never heard it before. I only know children's songs and those from the village."

"By village, do you mean the town of Ojibway?"

"No, the Chippewa village, upriver. There, the music is not the same as here."

"Maybe sometime you'll sing a Chippewa song for me so I can hear the difference."

Cosy didn't answer immediately, uncertain what to say. She had no desire to sing for Daniel, but she couldn't tell him that.

The piano fell silent, but almost immediately Rosalind began another tune. As she sang, "Do you remember Sweet Alice, Ben Bolt?" she flashed a glance over her shoulder at Daniel and, as if summoned, he stepped closer to the piano.

Cosy drifted in the opposite direction, toward the windows. Before reaching them, she held, listening. Did she hear, threading through Rosalind's playing and singing, the insistent hooting of an owl?

Looking back at her father and Daniel, she found their attention focused on Rosalind. Cosy took a deep breath. Did she dare? If her father asked her where she was going, she had an excuse—to see why it was taking so long for the coffee to arrive.

Making up her mind, she glided quietly behind and past them through the door of the music room. No one said a word, making her wonder if any of them had even noticed her departure. She entered the dining room, eased through the side door leading to the flagstone terrace where, though hampered by her hoop, she lifted her skirts and ran through the moonlit night as swiftly as she could toward the sound of the hooting.

She'd almost reached the trees when a dark figure stepped from among them. "Koko," he said softly in the People's tongue. "I wondered if you'd forgotten how I used to call to you."

Cosy halted, staring, unable to believe her eyes. "Black Water," she whispered after giving an involuntary glance back at the lighted windows of the house. "What are you doing here?"

"Hungry Moon sent me." He reached for her hand, grasped it, and drew her into the darkness under the trees.

When he stopped and turned to her, he released her hand. She could no longer see his face, but the moon had already shown her the gleam in his eyes as he gazed at her and her heart thundered in her chest.

"Hungry Moon has dreamed," he said.

Cosy tensed. The dream must have been important or her foster mother wouldn't have sent Black Water, the fastest runner in the village, as her messenger.

"She has dreamed of the white owlet," Black Water went on. "Is all well with you?"

"Well enough. Tell me of the dream."

"Mukwah walks manlike through the forest with the white owl on his shoulder."

"Hungry Moon had that dream before I left the village," Cosy said. "She had it before my father came to take me away. The black bear is my father and I am Koko, the owlet."

"It is true. But Hungry Moon dreamed more. Another bird flies toward the bear and the owlet—the osprey, the fish hawk. Instead of alighting on Mukwah's other shoulder, the osprey flies at Koko with menacing talons, forcing her off Mukwah's shoulder and away. Then the osprey perches where Koko was."

Cosy thought of Rosalind playing the piano and singing so sweetly of love betrayed.

"Do you know the meaning of this?" Black Water asked.

Cosy swallowed twice before she could answer. "My sister has come from beside the Great Salt Water to live in my father's house."

"Ah," he said. "The meaning of the dream is clear. Beware, for this sister means to displace you. Hungry Moon dreams true."

"I heed the warning," Cosy said, thinking to herself that Mukwah still had one empty shoulder. Did that mean she might find a place for herself despite Rosalind's becoming her father's favorite?

"Have you chosen a husband?" Black Water asked.

She caught her breath at his unexpected question. "No."

Black Water put his hands on her shoulders, pulling her close before she realized what he meant to do. "I would choose you for my wife," he whispered.

"My father—" she began, confused by her breathlessness and the pounding of her heart. She'd never been held like this by any man and the heat of his body both warmed and frightened her.

"Leave your father." Black Water's hand caressed her cheek. "We will marry."

She pulled away from him. "I can't marry without his approval. Maybe if I talk to him—"

"There was more to the dream," Black Water said. "Koko, dispossessed, flies to a pine tree and, thinking herself safe, prepares to rest. But below, a fox watches and waits; and on the branch above crouches a lynx, his eyes on the white bird."

"I don't understand the fox or the lynx," she admitted.

"They are men. Men who mean you no good. Who are they?"

"Two men? How can that be when not even one man menaces me?"

"Like the owl, unaware of the fox waiting below and the lynx crouching above her, you don't understand that these men are close by. You must know who they are."

Cosy bit her lip. "But I don't."

"There's a man in your father's house."

Daniel Rackham? Surely he was no danger to her. "That man works for my father," she told Black Water. "If he's watching anyone, it's my sister. He's interested in her, not me."

"You can't be sure. Come with me now. We'll be happy together."

She *would* be happy with Black Water, Cosy told herself. Hadn't she always admired him? But she needed time to think about marriage. Besides, she disliked going against her father's wishes. Perhaps now that he had another daughter, he might agree to let her marry Black Water.

"I must speak to my father first," she said.

"My pretty Koko, he's like all whites. He doesn't think a man of the People is good enough for his daughter. He'll never agree to let you come with me. I've always wanted you, even when you were a little girl learning to talk to the plants. I've waited long—but I can't wait forever."

"Were you in Hungry Moon's dream?" Cosy asked hesitantly.

Black Water sighed. "No. Hungry Moon has never had a dream for me."

"Then we must be patient," Cosy told him. "My father

may agree, after all. Since Rosalind has come, he's already changed. I don't think he values me in the same way he does his other daughter."

Black Water's finger touched her cheek again. A moment later, in the way of the People, he was gone with no farewell.

Her head awhirl, Cosy hurried back to the house and let herself in through the side door. She could hear voices coming from the music room, her father and Daniel singing with Rosalind.

" 'Listen to the mocking bird . . .' " the words ran, " 'for the mocking bird is singing o'er her grave . . .' "

Cosy shivered and told herself it was from being out in the chill of the night, not from the words of the song or from Hungry Moon's dream, true though it might be.

She reached the parlor, stopped and stared unseeingly at the coffee Hilda had left for them, a song of the People thrumming through her head.

> "The day passes and the year
> The wind and the moon
> Travel and are gone
> So the flesh, the house of the spirit
> Passes away
> To the quiet place . . ."

In her mind she pictured the villagers around the fire, one singing, others chorusing "Hee Yah" in counterpoint to the singer's words. She could almost smell the pungent odor of burning wood blending with the ever-present clean scent of the pines, could almost hear the rush of the nearby river. Tears stung her eyes.

"Did you manage to scare the owl away?"

Daniel's words jarred her. Blinking back her tears, she turned to face him. Was he the dream fox? The lynx? As she tried to collect her wits, Rosalind and Jephthah followed Daniel into the parlor.

Cosy, bewildered by her own feelings and upset by both Hungry Moon's dream and Daniel's question about the owl, could only pretend to drink the coffee. She sat quietly as the others talked.

She was relieved when Jephthah said, "I think it's about time you took your sister up to bed, Cosy. She's had a long journey here and I know she must be tired."

"But, Father," Rosalind protested, "I thought we'd have a chance to talk, just you and I."

He reached across and patted her hand. "Tomorrow's soon enough, my dear."

Rosalind frowned but rose obediently. She bent and kissed him on the cheek, murmuring, "I'm so glad to be here. Goodnight, Father."

Cosy felt her heart wrench at her father's pleasure in Rosalind's kiss. She'd never kissed her father in her life— nor had he kissed her.

"Good night," Daniel said, glancing from her to Rosalind, where his gaze lingered.

Upstairs, Cosy would have left Rosalind at her door, but her sister caught her hand. "Please come in for a minute," she said. "I need help with this gown."

Once Cosy had undone the back fastenings, Rosalind shrugged out of the gown, removed her hoop and slippers, then flung herself onto the bed in her underclothes, propping her head up with pillows. "Do sit down," she ordered, so Cosy sat in the carved rocker.

"What do you think of him?" Rosalind asked.

"Mr. Rackham?" Cosy asked to gain time since she was somewhat surprised by the question.

Rosalind laughed. "That does seem to be his name."

"He's handsome," Cosy said cautiously.

"Do you think he's mysterious?"

Cosy blinked, taken aback.

"Oh, you know what I mean," Rosalind said. "As if he's hiding something."

Cosy had been speculating that Rosalind and Daniel were hiding a previous acquaintanceship, but she hadn't felt Daniel himself was particularly mysterious.

"We all hide things, don't we?" she said, unable to come up with a better answer.

"I don't mean some tiny, little, unimportant secret," Rosalind countered, gazing knowingly at Cosy. "I mean a dangerous secret. I wouldn't trust Daniel if I were you. *I* certainly don't. That is, I don't intend to trust him."

"Father does."

Rosalind's brows drew together. "Maybe I ought to warn him."

Unable to keep back the question that had been plaguing her all evening, Cosy asked, "Were you acquainted with Daniel Rackham before?"

Rosalind sat up straight. "Me? Surely you heard him say we met at the front door."

"For the first time?" Cosy persisted.

"I don't know why you're harrying me," Rosalind cried plaintively, running a hand through her hair. "You must be aware I'm completely exhausted."

Cosy rose. "I'm sorry," she said.

"I'm sure you didn't mean to be unkind. We must try to be friends."

Though she saw no particular friendliness in Rosalind's blue eyes, Cosy nodded.

"After all, we *are* half-sisters," Rosalind went on, "and sisters should like each other."

"Yes, they should," Cosy agreed. And with a small nod, she left Rosalind's room.

Later, in her room," standing by the French door leading to her balcony, moonlight streaming over her, Cosy went over the evening's events. Even though Rosalind seemed to be their father's favorite, she told herself, she would try very hard to banish envy from her heart. She wasn't certain whether or not she could truly like her new sister, but at least she could make an attempt not to envy her.

Pushing open the door, she breathed deeply of the damp night air faintly scented with pine and sighed, remembering how, under the pines, Black Water had held her in his arms. He hadn't tried to kiss her. Would she have let him? No man had yet kissed her, and she was curious to know what it would be like.

She heard the front door open and close. Soon after, the clip-clop of hooves told her Daniel was riding back to Ojibway for the night. She wondered how Rosalind really felt about Daniel. Did he make her sister's heart beat faster the way her own did when Black Water touched her cheek? She didn't mind Rosalind's interest in Daniel or Daniel's in Rosalind. Why should she? He was not the man she wanted.

Cosy couldn't convince herself Daniel was the fox or the lynx in Hungry Moon's dream. In what way could he be a threat to her? As for the rest of the dream, surely there was room in her father's house for two daughters. If he hadn't wanted her to live with him, he wouldn't have taken her away from Hungry Moon, had her learn white ways, and—just two days ago—even arranged for her baptism.

She hadn't known about Rosalind until her arrival, but all along her father had been aware of his Boston daughter. Cosy wondered if he would have sent for Rosalind some day or gone East to see her. Father rarely spoke of his plans, and she'd learned early not to ask.

How brave her sister had been, traveling alone by train and steamer all the way from the Atlantic Ocean. Rosalind couldn't have known Cosy existed any more than Cosy had known about Rosalind. She must have been shocked to find a half-sister in her father's house, a half-sister her own age.

Only father knew the truth. Though she wasn't sure he'd tell her, Cosy made up her mind to try to find out. But what if the truth were unpleasant? She shook her head. Whatever she learned from him would be better than not knowing.

A high-pitched bark, quite unlike a dog's, came faintly to her ears, making her hunch her shoulders. What she heard was a fox, hunting in the night, searching for its prey.

A fox was clever and quick, seeking the right time and place to strike. Though not as powerful as a lynx, it was a killer. Hearing the fox was a sign, she told herself, that Dan was the fox in Hungry Moon's dream.

If Dan were the fox, who could the lynx be? Not Black Water, because her foster mother had never dreamed of him. Yet Hungry Moon always dreamed true. Sooner or later, the man who was the lynx would appear. And a lynx was far more dangerous than any fox.

Dangerous to her? She shivered. Hugging herself, she refused to believe she was afraid. How could she fear a man she hadn't yet met? Her chill, she decided, came from nothing more than the cold night wind.

Seven

The next morning, Mina Howard intercepted Cosy in the entry on her way to her father's study. "You answered the owl's call last night," she said.

After looking around to be certain they weren't overheard, Cosy said, "There was a dream message for me from Hungry Moon."

Mina's eyes widened. "A warning?" She glanced toward the staircase. "About *her?*"

Aware that Mina meant Rosalind, who hadn't yet come down for breakfast, Cosy nodded. Mina was her friend, but she didn't wish to share any more of the dream with her.

"Is she going to stay, your sister?" Mina asked.

"Yes. She has no other home."

"Men like pretty girls with yellow hair," Mina said. "No doubt she'll soon marry." She touched Cosy's shoulder, offering comfort, and turned away.

Cosy found her father at his desk. "What would you say," he asked her, "if I told you I've asked Dan to live with us for awhile?"

"Has he agreed?" Cosy parried, uncertain as to what answer her father expected from her.

"Not yet, but I'm sure, with your help, I'll be able to persuade him. The Bigelow House can get mighty tiresome after a while. I know, I've had to put up at many a hotel in my time."

"How long will Mr. Rackham be staying here?"

Jephthah tipped his chair back. "I hope to entice him into staying until every ounce of gold is off the bottom of Lake Superior. That may take all summer." He gazed intently at Cosy. "I need Dan, need him badly. It's taken me a long time to find a diver and I want to keep him."

Taking advantage of the fact her father seemed to be in a mood to answer questions, Cosy asked, "How *did* you find Mr. Rackham?"

At first she thought he wasn't going to reply but finally he said, "I heard about Dan from Charles Appleton some time ago, but I wasn't able to contact him. The man never stays in one place for any length of time. When Appleton told me Dan was in Houghton and planned to visit him, I couldn't have been more delighted." Jephthah frowned. "But, as I said, Dan's a nomad and I want to make sure he doesn't wander off before the job's done."

"If you want Mr. Rackham to stay here," Cosy said carefully, "I have no cause to object."

Jephthah's frown deepened. "Come now, Cosy, you needn't be so standoffish to the man. I want you to urge him to stay with us. Call him Dan; be a bit friendly; make him feel welcome. He's a far better bet than those Indian braves you yearn after. Don't think I haven't seen you stare at them in town when you think I'm not watching. They aren't for you, Cosy. You're no Indian. You're a Collins; you're my daughter, and you'll do as I say."

Cosy's heart sank. How could she possibly mention Black Water to her father? Her disappointment gave her the courage to ask, "Am I really your daughter? Rosalind and I are the same age and that's not possible unless you married two women at the same time."

He brought his chair down with a thump. She steeled herself for an angry outburst, but all he did was shake his head.

"I hoped I'd never have to confess to you that my marriage to your mother was a sham," he said slowly. "I tried to make the best of it; when she died, I took you to raise. Would I do that if you weren't my daughter?"

Cosy shook her head, too stunned to speak. She, after all, was the bastard. Rosalind's mother had been his legal wife, not Antoinette DuBois, the half-breed.

"I may be your daughter," she said at last, "but I'm also part Anishinabe, like my mother."

He scowled. "Are you defying me? If I say you're not Indian, you're damned well not! I wish to hell I'd never left you with that squaw, but I had no choice. She—"

"Hungry Moon was good to me," Cosy protested.

"She did her best to turn you into an Indian," Jephthah grumbled. "Although she did keep the young bucks away— I'll grant her that." He stood up and took Cosy's hand, holding it between both of his. "I need your help with Dan, Cosy. You like him all right, don't you?"

She nodded warily.

"I'm not asking too much of you when I say be nice to him, am I?" Jephthah asked.

"I'll do as you say, Father. But Mr. Rackham—"

"Dan. Call him Dan, for God's sake."

"I think Mr.—Dan—is more interested in Rosalind than he is me. Perhaps she—"

"No!" Jephthah roared, dropping her hand. "He's *not* interested in Rosie."

Cosy held her tongue, aware her father was really saying

he refused to permit Dan and Rosalind to be interested in one another. Why? He thought Dan was good enough for Cosy, but not for Rosalind—was that the reason? She strove to hide her growing dread that, since her half-sister's arrival, one thing after another in her world was changing for the worse.

Jephthah took a deep breath and let it out slowly. "You're wrong about Dan's interest, Cosy. Smile at him once or twice and you'll see. Remember, though, that I do expect you not to lose your head. Your mother had an unfortunate tendency to—"

"Am I interrupting?" Rosalind asked as she walked into the study. "I'm sorry I missed having breakfast with you, Father, but I don't know when I've slept so long and so well. Maybe it's because I've found a home." She smiled at him.

Jephthah put his arm around Rosalind's shoulders and gave her a brief hug. "Have you had your breakfast?"

"No," she said, "I wanted to talk to you first."

"That will never do." He turned to Cosy. "Have Mrs. Howard fix a tray for Rosie and bring it in here."

I *won't* be envious, Cosy admonished herself as she hurried to the kitchen. Father needs me, too. Didn't he ask for my help in keeping Mr. Rack—no, Dan—here?

Once she'd told Mina about a tray for Rosalind, Cosy ran up the back stairs to make certain the unused bedrooms were presentable and decide which one to offer to the diver. She'd have to remember to call him Dan to his face or her father would be annoyed. And she'd try to be friendly, though she suspected it would be of little use in distracting Dan's attention from her sister.

Once she'd chosen a bedroom, Cosy came down the front stairs just in time to answer the knock at the front door.

Daniel Rackham stood on the porch. Behind him, rain slanted down.

"Hello, Cosy," he said with his crooked smile.

Wordlessly, she stepped aside to let him in.

"What, no greeting?" he asked.

"Good morning, Mr.—Dan," she said.

His eyebrows rose. "I'm pleased to hear you call me Dan. I was beginning to think you didn't like me."

"I like most people," she told him.

"Is that your way of making me aware I'm nobody special as far as you're concerned?" As he spoke he took off his damp hat and coat and hung them on the entry rack.

"Father has asked me to invite you to stay with us," Cosy said hurriedly, hoping her smile didn't look forced. "I hope you'll agree."

"I've always found it difficult to refuse a pretty girl. Therefore, I accept. I look forward to becoming a temporary member of the Collins household. Are you pleased with my answer, Cosy?"

Though she recognized the teasing light in his eyes, she wasn't accustomed to having a man tease her. Flustered, she blurted out the first thing that came into her head. "I hope we can be friends. My father would like that."

His eyebrows rose high again. "Your father? How about you?"

"Oh, yes, I want to be friends."

Dan shook his head. "You don't sound properly enthusiastic. You're an enigma, Cosy, and puzzles have always fascinated me. Your sister, on the other hand, is as crystal clear as a pane of glass. But she does enjoy playing games and that, too, can be intriguing. All in all, I expect to enjoy my stay here with Snow White and Rose Red."

Cosy vaguely recalled Louella Genette reading a fable

to her about two sisters named Snow White and Rose Red, but she'd forgotten the details of the story and remembered only that it had something to do with a bear.

"What do you really think of me?" Dan asked.

Because she hadn't made up her mind about him, Cosy didn't know how to reply. Instead she said, "My sister thinks you're mysterious."

Dan laughed. "And so I am. Sweet Rosalind is quite right. But what's *your* opinion?"

"You're the fox." Even as she spoke, Cosy regretted her words.

"A fox, am I?" Dan laughed. "You *are* perceptive."

In the study, Rosalind sipped the tea Hilda had brought. "I wish I'd known you earlier," she said to Jephthah.

He sighed. "You came at the right time. I could offer you no kind of life before now."

"Were you intending to write Aunt Rhoda and send for me?" she asked.

He shook his head. "To be frank, no. Of course I had no idea the woman had allowed you to think me dead. But Boston is a civilized city and I knew you'd be far more likely to make a good match there than you would here. Ojibway is fine for me and even for Cosy. We're used to rough ways. You've been raised differently."

"This house is as grand as most in Boston," Rosalind protested.

"I'm glad you like it. And glad you're here. Here to stay, now that Rhoda's dead. We do have a few refinements; we're not completely without culture—the music society for one. And there are a few decent unmarried men about, men with manners and ability. Some of them will go far and take a wife with them as their fortunes improve. Your prospects aren't entirely dismal, Rosie."

Deciding there was no need to tell her father about being practically engaged to poor Reginald Morely—after all, he was dead—she said, "I don't know that I care to marry right away. I'd like to see a little more of life first. Aunt Rhoda kept me practically under lock and key. She seemed to be afraid of men."

Jephthah smiled sourly. "A bitter woman. Still, I knew I could count on her to do her best for you. When your mother died, I didn't know where else to take you."

Rosalind set her cup down and leaned forward. "You really couldn't have been married to my mother and to Cosy's mother, too. You weren't, were you?"

Jephthah cleared his throat. "You're free with your words, young lady."

"Well—were you?" Rosalind persisted, determined to find out the truth.

For a long moment she thought he wasn't going to answer. "Yes and no," Jephthah said at last. "I did go through a ceremony with Cosy's mother."

Rosalind stared at him.

"I had no choice," he protested. "Antoinette DuBois's father was a tough old French trapper. When he found us together, he held a rifle to my head until I agreed to marry her. I didn't dare tell him I was already married; he'd have blasted my brains out. How was I to know he'd find a priest within the hour and hold me to my promise? What could I do but go through with it? The old trapper was satisfied—he had no idea his daughter wasn't legally married to me. I did the best I could; I took care of Cosy when her mother died, just as though she'd been born of a legitimate union."

Rosalind, aware that she and Cosy were the same age,

understood that her father must have been with Antoinette DuBois barely a month after his marriage to her mother. How could he!

"Did you love my mother?" she demanded.

"Cecily was a lovely woman," he said evasively. "Rosie, didn't your aunt ever tell you that men and women differ as to what 'love' means to them?"

"She told me men were to be avoided if at all possible."

"And did you believe her?"

Rosalind couldn't help smiling. "What would you think if I said yes?"

Jephthah grunted. "I'd call you a liar. I'm not blind, you know. Last night I noticed you making eyes at Dan." He leaned forward, lowering his voice. "Dan's not the man for you, Rosie. I expect you to take heed of what I say."

She bristled, forgetting for a moment her vow that she wouldn't have Daniel Rackham if he were the last man on earth. "Why isn't he for me?"

Jephthah frowned. "Dan's not the marrying kind. Here today, gone tomorrow. With your looks, you can have any man you choose, girl. Forget Daniel Rackham."

Rosalind tossed her head. "I'm not interested in him anyway."

"Good, then we won't discuss it further. What we will do is have a party here soon to christen the house properly. Everyone will want to meet you—women as well as men. Though the truth is, there isn't a girl in Ojibway that can hold a candle to you, Rosie."

"My sister is very attractive."

"Oh, Cosy. Yes, she's more than passable."

"Perhaps you intend Mr. Rackham for her?"

"Damn it, girl, you have a tendency to let your tongue

run away with you. Cosy will do what I say and so will you!"

"Yes, Father." Rosalind lowered her head. She'd meant to tell her father about her misadventures on the journey and the mysterious Major Eaton who was masquerading as Daniel Rackham. But her father's insistence that she must obey him irked her. She might not be interested in Dan; but no one, not even Jephthah Collins, was going to tell her whom she could smile at and whom she couldn't.

She'd keep Dan's secret for a while longer. It would be more fun anyway to drop hints to her father about the pirated boat with Dan present. How she'd enjoy watching Dan's face as he wondered how much she intended to reveal.

"Whatever Rhoda's faults," Jephthah said, "she did help you become an accomplished young lady. I'm proud of you."

Rosalind gave him her most dazzling smile.

"However," he added, "you do have the tendency to be too forward in your ways. Men sometimes misunderstand. You must curb this wayward impulse."

Rosalind's smile vanished. "I never expected you to sound like Aunt Rhoda, Father! Heavens, I'm not a child. I traveled the entire way from Boston to Ojibway by myself without any difficulties whatsoever."

"With nary a mishap?" Dan said from behind her. "A remarkable feat, indeed."

As he advanced into the room, she shot him a speaking look. Ignoring her, he said to Jephthah, "Excuse me, sir, I hadn't realized you were occupied with your daughter."

"Rosie and I were just finishing our little chat," Jephthah said.

Realizing she was being dismissed, Rosalind got up from her chair. "Good morning, Mr. Rackham," she said coolly.

"Please, won't you call me Dan?" he asked. "Your sister does."

Rosalind glanced at her father before saying, "Of course, Dan. And you must call me Rosalind, as if we were friends."

He bowed slightly to her, but his words were addressed to Jephthah. "I've been informed a room in your home has been set aside for my use while I'm in Ojibway. Thank you for your kind and generous hospitality. It would be churlish of me to refuse."

"Then you accept?" Jephthah asked.

"For a time, at least."

A thrill ran through Rosalind as she realized Dan was going to be staying in the house.

"I believe Cosy said I was to have the gray bedroom," Dan said.

Rosalind did her best to hide her smile. Gray—the Rebel color. How appropriate.

"You should certainly plan to stay until the weather is decent enough to get at the *Kaug*," Jephthah said to Dan.

"I hope I can, sir. Do you have any idea how soon we can start?"

"I wish I did. This damn Superior is as moody and unpredictable as a woman."

"With your daughter so newly arrived herself," Dan said, "she may not wish to put up with a semi-permanent guest so soon."

"Rosie will have no complaints," Jephthah said, eyeing her sternly. "As for Cosy, I'm sure she'll be happy to see more of you."

Rosalind frowned. Why on earth was her father all but dumping Cosy into Dan's lap? With a start, she noticed Cosy standing in the doorway and wondered how long she'd been there. Certainly long enough to have heard the last part of the conversation. Rosalind intended to find out how her sister felt about their father's ploy.

"I'll come upstairs with you, Cosy," she said, "to be sure we don't overlook anything that will provide for our guest's comfort. We certainly wouldn't want Mr. Rackham—that is, Dan—to complain that our hospitality was lacking in any way."

Without waiting for Cosy to agree, Rosalind swept her from the study. As they climbed the stairs, she said, "You heard Father. Are you really looking forward to having Dan stay at the house?"

"Are you?" Cosy countered.

They both paused, staring at one another.

"Why should I care one way or the other?" Rosalind said at last, continuing up the steps.

"I try to please Father," Cosy told her as they reached the second floor and turned to the left, toward the west wing.

"Father seems to want you to please Dan." Rosalind's tone was tart. "Do you always obey Father to the letter?"

Cosy hesitated before saying, "I try to."

Rosalind gave her a dark look. "My advice to you is to beware of Daniel Rackham. He's not what he seems to be—believe me."

Cosy stopped beside a closed door. "I'll tell you the truth. I care nothing for Dan; but if our father wants me to be friendly to him, I see no harm in obeying." She reached for the knob and opened the door. "This is the gray room."

Entering the room, Rosalind's impression was of silver, rather than gray, from the eagle mounted over the mirror to the metallic threads in the curtains. With walls paneled in maple, the room seemed designed for a man.

"A good choice," she told Cosy.

"It's not my favorite room, but I thought it suitable."

"Which is your favorite?" Rosalind asked curiously.

"My own room. Would you like to see it?"

"By all means."

Cosy's room was in the east wing, as Rosalind's was. Instead of double windows, though, this bedroom had only a single one. Beside the window was a French door leading to a small balcony.

"How charming," Rosalind said.

"The only other room with a balcony is in the west wing. I would have given it to you but—" Cosy paused and looked away from Rosalind before adding "—I thought maybe you'd like to have a room near me."

Rosalind stared at her in surprise.

"And there's another reason," Cosy added—reluctantly, Rosalind thought. "You know Father sleeps in the west wing. Not often, but once in a while, he has a special guest stay at the house and he always gives her the room next to his, the one with the balcony."

For a moment Rosalind groped for her sister's meaning, and then comprehension flooded through her. Hadn't Aunt Rhoda described Jephthah Collins as a man with a penchant for the ladies?

"You mean our father entertains his fancy women here?" she asked, shocked.

"Fancy women?" Cosy echoed. "I'm not certain what that means. It's always the same person, a widow who lives on a farm a few miles away. She's pleasant enough, but there's nothing very fancy about her."

Though relieved that their father didn't intend to insult her by parading women-no-better-than-they-should-be in front of her, Rosalind found a new worry. "Do you think Father intends to marry this widow?"

Cosy shook her head. "I overheard him tell her he'd never marry again, that marriage only led to trouble."

It certainly had in her father's case, Rosalind told herself. But at least she needn't have to face the problem of a stepmother any time soon. One unexpected half-sister was more than enough to cope with.

As if aware of Rosalind's last thought, Cosy said, "Dan calls us Snow White and Rose Red, like the sisters in the fairy tale. I've been trying to remember how the story goes."

"Something about a bear that turns into a handsome prince," Rosalind said after a moment's reflection. "As I recall, one sister marries the prince and the other marries his brother."

Does Dan have a brother? The thought popped into Rosalind's head unbidden and she immediately tried to quash it. Dan was certainly no prince and, even if he were, she had absolutely no interest in marrying him. None whatsoever.

"I may never marry." Cosy's voice was sad.

Glancing at her, Rosalind noticed she was staring out the window, so she looked, too. There was nothing to see but a stand of pines.

"Why on earth not?" she asked Cosy.

"I fear Father and I will never agree on who would be a proper husband for me."

"Maybe he intends Dan to be that man." Rosalind tried to ignore her prick of displeasure at the idea.

Cosy shook her head. "He told me Dan was a nomad, not the marrying kind. But even if Dan weren't, he isn't the man I'd choose." She smiled faintly. "And, if he were, it would be no use because Dan prefers you."

To her dismay, Rosalind flushed. "Why do you say such a thing?" she asked crossly. "I have no interest in him.

How did we get on the subject of Dan, anyway? I've heard quite enough about him for one day."

She swung away from the window and crossed the room, glancing around in an effort to learn more about Cosy. "How bare your dressing table is," she commented. "Nary a lotion or a cream. In fact, your room scarcely looks lived in. Why you don't even have a Bible on the stand beside your bed! Don't you read the Bible?" Belatedly it occurred to her that perhaps Cosy had never learned to read and she chided herself for asking.

"Miss Genette, my teacher, didn't have me read the Bible," Cosy said.

"Aunt Rhoda made me read a Bible verse every day," Rosalind told Cosy. "That's how I discovered that our father's name—Jephthah—is from the Bible."

"Father's name is in the Bible?" Cosy echoed.

Rosalind nodded. "Come into my room and I'll show you."

Her small white Bible opened by itself to the Book of Judges. Holding it, Rosalind sat on her bed, motioning to Cosy to sit next to her. "Here's the part about Jephthah," she said, pointing. "I used to read these verses over and over to myself when I lived with my aunt in Boston. You see, she told me my father was dead; I never knew he was alive until after she died." She began to read aloud:

"And Jephthah made a vow to the Lord . . ."

Rosalind continued reading the story of Jephthah's promise of a burnt offering to God of whoever first met him at the door of his house when he returned home. And how, though he was upset when that person was his daughter, "her father . . . did with her according to his vow which he had made."

Cosy remained silent for long moments, finally saying,

"Jephthah had no choice. He had to keep a promise made to God."

Rosalind frowned. "I've always thought it a horrid tale. How perfectly terrible to burn one's own child as a sacrifice! What kind of a God would want that?"

Cosy shrugged. "Who can know what God would want?"

Having expected Cosy to be as upset as she'd been when she'd first read the story—she still felt a thrill of horror when confronted by the verses—Rosalind stared at her in confusion mixed with disappointment.

"I'd have run away if I'd been the Biblical Jephthah's daughter," she said. "No one is going to use me as a burnt offering!"

"In the very old days," Cosy said slowly, "the People sometimes burned and then ate their enemies to absorb the braveness and virtue of a foe."

"Ugh, how ghastly. Do you mean the Chippewa actually practiced cannibalism?"

"The Hurons did, anyway," Cosy said. "I learned from Miss Genette that in 1629 they boiled and ate Etienne Brule, the first white man to explore Lake Superior. Like you, my teacher was shocked at this, but she didn't understand that the Hurons would never have eaten him if they hadn't admired his courage."

Rosalind stared at her sister in consternation. "It's terrible whatever their reason. I don't want to hear any more. How could you bear to live with heathen Indians for six years?"

She might have felt somewhat superior to her half-sister after learning Cosy was not only part-Indian but illegitimate besides; but, because they were the same age, she'd thought of Cosy as more or less like herself in many ways and had been willing to extend a tentative hand of friendship. How wrong she'd been!

Cosy was not like her, not at all. On the surface Cosy might seem like a polite, quiet young girl; but underneath she was really as savage as any Indian.

And, perhaps, as dangerous.

Eight

When Rosalind woke the next morning, the thought that Daniel Rackham was only a corridor away from her gave her an unexpected frisson of pleasurable anticipation. No matter how hard she tried to convince herself he meant nothing to her, she failed. Rising, she hurried through her toilette, taking pains to look her best.

When she came down to breakfast, she found Dan in the dining room with Cosy and her father. He glanced up, saw her and smiled in his lopsided way. Her breath caught and a strange warmth spread along her abdomen and into her loins, unsettling her. This inner surge of heat was quite beyond her control. Such a thing had never happened to her before. What did it mean?

The feeling had nothing to do with love, of that Rosalind was positive. Love was sweet kisses and gentle caresses, not this disturbing sensation of a fire blazing somewhere inside her. Why ever had she imagined it would be thrilling to have Dan so close at hand? As it was, with him gazing at her so intently, she could hardly swallow a bite of food. She wished he were a million miles away from her.

"I've found a way to keep Dan close by until the weather improves," her father said. "I've discovered he's a dab hand with explosives; and since Appleton, at the mine location, needs an explosive expert, Dan will be staying there temporarily to help out."

Instead of being delighted to hear Dan would be removed from her immediate vicinity, Rosalind's spirits plummeted. She remained mute while Cosy asked questions about what he'd be doing in the mine.

Later that morning, as Dan was carrying some of his belongings to the stable where Jim had readied his horse, Rosalind, muffled in her gray cloak against the damp chill, drifted across his path, intending it to appear to be a chance meeting. She'd meant to say something light and frothy, a casual farewell to show him she didn't care whether or not she ever saw him again; but when she looked into his brown eyes, she found herself speechless.

"Will you miss me?" he asked.

Rosalind realized beyond any shadow of a doubt that she would miss him terribly, but she knew she'd rather die than admit it. Tossing her head, she said, "Why should I?"

Somewhat to her surprise, he didn't smile and make the joking response she'd come to expect from him. Instead, he reached to her and traced the outline of her lips with his forefinger, making her heart race.

"Rose Red," he murmured. "In the fairy tale, the prince's brother wins Rose Red. I have no brother."

She remembered Cosy saying Dan had called the two of them Snow White and Rose Red and mentioning that the prince married Snow White. At the time she'd wondered if Dan had a brother.

Gathering her wits, she threw off the spell he'd cast and said tartly, "I knew you were in disguise, but I wasn't aware you were a prince."

Dan threw back his head and laughed. "You don't know the half of it, my sweet Rosalind."

"I'm not your sweet anything!" she cried. "And I shan't miss you, not for one minute. Goodbye—and good riddance." She whirled around to stalk away but was foiled by his sudden grip on her arm.

"The right words are *au revoir,*" he told her, turning her to face him again. "Whether either of us wants it or not, we damn well are going to meet again."

And not only meet, Dan told himself as he looked into her blue eyes, as beautiful and treacherous as Lake Superior. He couldn't trust her, that was a given, plus the fact her father had made it clear his Boston daughter was off limits to the likes of Daniel Rackham. None of that mattered. He wanted her and nothing could prevent him from going after what he wanted.

Later, riding away from the house toward the mine location, Dan shook his head ruefully. Life would be one hell of a lot simpler; not to mention much safer, if he played by the rules.

Though Jephthah Collins had set no-trespassing signs around Rosalind where Dan was concerned, he seemed to be quite willing to allow Dan to amuse himself with Cosy. He didn't believe old Jephthah would go as far as to permit him to bed the girl, but he could be wrong. Cosy was a tasty morsel—so why wasn't he tempted? Why risk an uproar and, worse, a failure of his mission, over his lust for the wrong daughter?

Dan smiled wryly. Could a leopard change his spots? Not since he'd been a small boy had anyone ever told him what he could and could not do and held him to it. He thrived on challenge, and Rosalind would certainly be one. He knew she hadn't yet admitted to herself that she wanted him and he was also aware she'd fight her own urges to the bitter end. She might be hooked, but reeling her in would prove tricky. Which, of course, made any prize all the more worth winning.

Not that he intended to marry her. Marriage was for men content to be tamed and caged, not for the likes of him. He meant to, and he damn well would, roam free forever.

As he rode on, he began to whistle, gradually realizing he'd chosen the tune Rosalind had played last night, "Black Is The Color Of My True Love's Hair." Like his. He grinned, wondering if she understood how transparent she was to him. His smile faded as it occurred to him that Cosy's hair was as dark as his. Though Cosy, unlike her sister, was anything but transparent, he could tell she had little interest in him as a possible lover. Even if he tried to win her over, he doubted that changing her mind about him would prove easy. So why didn't he find Cosy a challenge?

For the first time since he'd impulsively kissed Rosalind aboard the *Phoenix,* it occurred to him that she might not be the only one who'd gotten hooked on that bloody boat. A moment later he shook his head. Nonsense! Rosalind was a mere chit of a girl; he was a man of experience. No untried miss of eighteen could possibly be more than a temporary diversion to him. Hell, he could take her or leave her. But, since he *had* to lay hands on that sunken gold to succeed in his mission, he couldn't very well leave the area. He had to stay around, so why not amuse himself with pretty Rosalind?

Looking at it another way, paying court to her against her father's wishes might serve another purpose: It might well distract old Jephthah from Daniel Rackham's real goal.

Dan began to whistle again, well content. And this time the tune was "Dixie."

With Dan away, the days dragged for Rosalind. She

watched the countryside gradually turn green, trees un-
curling their leaves, buttercups and cowslips budding in the
fields by the river. Courting birds chased one another,
swooping over her head when she ventured outside during
the days when the sun shone. Unfortunately the sun's
warmth was often countered by the chill north wind.

I don't miss Dan, she insisted to herself. He means nothing to me. Absolutely nothing. He's arrogant, forward, and,
worst of all, an enemy. A Reb.

Yes, he was certainly all of those things. But then why
did this looked-forward-to spring seem so dull? Why didn't
she rejoice in his absence and let herself enjoy the company
of the ladies who called on her and invited her to tea?

"In Boston, it's summer by now," she complained to her
father near the end of June as she sat with him and Cosy
at the dinner table.

He smiled at her. "Haven't you heard that the Upper
Peninsula has only two seasons—winter and the Fourth of
July? Come to think of it, the Fourth's next week. Ojibway
goes all out to celebrate—a parade, races, games, picnic
tables by the river, and the target-shooting contest I've won
for two years running. You'll have a grand time." Jephthah
inclined his head toward Cosy. "Won't she?"

Cosy smiled and nodded, her dark eyes sparkling.

Since Cosy didn't often look so animated, Rosalind decided her sister believed there was something special about
the celebration. Or perhaps Cosy expected to see someone
special there. Who could it be? She seemed as uninterested
as Rosalind was in any of the young men in Ojibway.

With the weather improving, Rosalind thought, chances
were Dan might return in time for the celebration. For a
moment her spirits lifted until it struck her that Dan could
be the special one Cosy wanted to see.

"What do you like best about the celebration?" she asked Cosy.

"The games and races," her sister answered. "What fun they are to watch!"

Jephthah frowned. "Games are all very well, but don't let me catch you hobnobbing with any of those damn Indians."

"Indians?" Rosalind echoed, glancing from her father to Cosy and back.

"The People play a swimming game," Cosy said. "I used to join in when I lived in their village."

"That's past for you and don't you forget it," Jephthah warned.

"Yes, Father."

"The trouble with those damn Indians is they'd rather play games than work. There's not an Indian in this land you can count on to be a dependable worker." Jephthah shook his head. "The men are worthless in the mines."

"The People see no reason to take so much copper from under the ground," Cosy said. "They think it will anger the Kitchi Manitou."

"Superstitious nonsense! The truth is they'd rather sit around doing nothing than put in a day's work."

Cosy opened her mouth, seemed to think better of it, and subsided without further protest. Rosalind eyed her appraisingly. Was it possible her sister had a lover among the Indians? Likely she'd deny it if asked outright, but Rosalind meant to watch her closely during the Fourth of July celebration and see if she gave herself away.

As if in anticipation of the Fourth, July began with warm weather at last, the sun blazing in an almost cloudless sky, the breeze from the west soft and benign. The Fourth dawned fair and warm.

Rosalind chose a blue glacé silk gown, a straw bonnet decorated with pink silk roses, and a parasol that matched her gown. She'd grown so accustomed to Cosy helping her dress that she hadn't gotten around to pursuing her quest for her own maid. Cosy could be so mild and accommodating that time and again she found herself forgetting her sister's savage background.

Cosy wore a pale-green gown that brought out the unusual color of her eyes and an off-the-face spoon bonnet.

"What, no parasol?" Rosalind asked.

"I like the sun."

"But your complexion! You'll turn as brown as an—" Rosalind caught back "Indian" at the last moment. "Really," she scolded to cover her near mistake, "you ought to take more care of your looks. Unmarried young ladies are judged by their attractiveness as much as their accomplishments, you know."

Cosy's lips curled into her secret smile, annoying Rosalind and causing her to renew her vow to discover what it was her sister kept hidden.

All Ojibway had turned out to celebrate, Rosalind decided when they reached town—not only the townspeople but the Indians from upriver. She tried not to stare at the Chippewa men and women in their blue cloth or deerskin leggings and tunics, the clothes colorfully ornamented with dyed porcupine quills and beads.

"Did you dress like that when you lived with them?" Rosalind whispered to Cosy, who nodded.

As they passed the Bigelow House, Jephthah was hailed by a group of men who stood talking by the hotel door. When they invited him to join them, he hesitated, looking at Rosalind and Cosy.

Rosalind smiled at him. "Do join your friends, Father,"

she urged. "I see Mrs. Dorset and her daughter walking toward the river. If you're worried about Cosy and me being unescorted, we can join the Dorsets."

"That seems like a good plan," he said. "I *would* like to spend a few minutes with these gentlemen."

Rosalind took Cosy's arm and hurried her toward the Dorsets, slowing as they came up behind the plump matron and her young daughter. "Just in case Father is watching us," she whispered to Cosy, "we'll pretend to be with them for awhile, but actually we won't let the Dorsets see us."

Cosy's conspiratorial nod made her realize her sister was as eager to escape from their father as she was. It was far more exciting to be on their own. She smiled at Cosy, feeling a link between them.

With so many people strolling through the town, they soon intermingled with the crowd and Rosalind, certain they were hidden from their father's sight, veered away from the Dorsets.

"What shall we look at first?" she asked Cosy.

Cosy turned to face the river. "The swimming games. See, they're beginning."

They edged closer to the river bank where seven Indian men, stripped of most of their clothes, were poised to dive into the water. Why they were practically naked! Rosalind was torn between staring and averting her gaze from the smooth, brown male bodies clad only in loincloths. Aunt Rhoda would have had an attack of nerves on the spot, but Rosalind found herself unwillingly fascinated by the men's near-nakedness.

A glance at Cosy revealed that all her sister's attention was focused on the nearest Indian brave. Did she know him? Rosalind scanned him quickly, feeling a reluctant admiration. In her eyes, no Indian was truly handsome; but she could see that Cosy might think he was. He was obviously the finest specimen among the seven men.

"What's his name?" she whispered.

Without taking her gaze from him, Cosy murmured, "Black Water."

Evidently hearing the murmur, the man glanced over his shoulder. He didn't smile when he saw Cosy, but Rosalind noticed that his expression brightened.

As one by one the men dived into the river, Cosy pushed her way through the throng to stand on the very brink of the bank. Rosalind remained where she was, trying to make up her mind whether to tease Cosy about Black Water— what peculiar names Indians had—or keep quiet and see what else she might learn.

A voice spoke softly into her ear. "Have you missed me?" Dan asked.

She whirled, tingling with excitement, and found him looking down at her with a glow in his brown eyes that heated her blood.

"I hoped—that is, I thought you might return today," she said breathlessly.

His arm slid about her waist as if to shield her from the press of the people around them. Because of the crowd, it was impossible to move away from him, she told herself, uneasily aware she ought not to be enjoying his touch.

"What I mean is," she went on, trying to recover her equanimity, "it would have been a shame if you'd missed the celebration."

His crooked smile made her heart beat faster. "I'm most interested in celebrating," he murmured, "but not in this mob. The day is too lovely to spend watching games that mean nothing to me. I expect you're not particularly interested in watching Indians swim, either. Shall we find a less-crowded spot?"

Before she had a chance to agree or disagree, he began leading her through the throng, away from the river.

"Cosy—" she started to say.

"Cosy is perfectly capable of looking after herself."

"But Father might be displeased if I—if you and I—"

"Actually, you look rather pale," Dan said. "Are you, perhaps, feeling a bit faint? I'm sure your father wouldn't object if I took you to a quieter spot until you're quite recovered."

One of Aunt Rhoda's warnings surfaced in Rosalind's mind. "Men are lustful animals, all of them. Not a one can be trusted."

She glanced up at Dan and the look in his eyes took her breath away. What did her aunt, a spinster all her life, know of men? She doubted if Aunt Rhoda's blood had ever turned to liquid fire in her veins the way hers was doing at this very moment. If she paid attention to an old maid's warnings, likely she'd be a spinster all her life, too.

"I—I am rather warm," she admitted. "It's stifling among all these people."

Without further delay, his arm still about her waist, Dan swept her on until they were free of the crowd, urging her onward until they reached a buggy. He handed her up, unhitched the horse, and climbed in beside her.

"Where are we going?" she asked, wondering belatedly if she were being indiscreet.

One of his crooked smiles was his only answer. When he turned the horse onto the narrow lane leading to the river bluff, she realized where they were heading. "This is the way home!"

"Certainly the coolest spot on a warm afternoon, you

must agree. We'll have some tea and you can play for me afterwards if you like. You'll sing your plaintive songs of love betrayed to me and I'll—"

"Mrs. Howard and Hilda have the day off," she objected. "Even Jim does. There's no one at the house."

He raised his eyebrows. "Surely you know how to prepare tea."

"Yes, but . . ." Her words trailed away as she contemplated the inadvisability of going to the house with Dan.

"But you're afraid of me," he suggested. "Is that it?"

Rosalind bristled. "Why should I be? I wasn't afraid of you aboard the *Phoenix;* why should I start fearing you now?"

"No reason, no reason at all."

She eyed him as sternly as she could manage. "I really *don't* trust you, though. How can I when I don't even know who you are?"

"Who else but Daniel Rackham?"

"I think you have another identity, Major—"

"Hush," he said, leaning over and kissing her, his free hand caressing her nape. His lips, soft at first, pressed harder, forcing her own apart. His tongue slipped between her lips, kindling the warmth deep within her into a blaze.

When he let her go, she gasped for breath, everything forgotten but his nearness and the tumult inside her. When he halted the horse, she saw they were in front of the house. He leaped down, hitched the horse, scooped her into his arms, and carried her up the steps to the porch.

"Whatever are you doing?" she cried, laughing. "Put me down!"

He did, catching her to him and kissing her long and hard, then holding her close to his side while he opened the door, not letting her go even after they entered.

She pushed her hands against his chest. "You mustn't."

He released her only to reach up and unfasten her bonnet. "You're a lovely little rose," he murmured, his hand caressing her blond curls. "This should be all the gold a man ever needs."

Thrilled, her knees weak, she tried to compose herself. Surely there was no harm in a kiss or two was there? She yearned to have him hold her close again, to feel the excitement of his lips on hers. But was that wise?

Confused, unsure of herself, she needed time to understand what was happening to her, needed a few minutes alone. "I—I'm going to—to tidy up," she stammered, pulling away and rushing toward the stairs. "I'll be down shortly," she flung over her shoulder.

Her heart pounding in her ears, Rosalind dashed up the steps and along the corridor to her bedroom. Opening her door, she stepped into her room; but when she tried to close the door behind her, she met resistance and she turned to see why.

"Oh!" she gasped, staring at Dan. She hadn't dreamed he'd follow her.

"I've never seen your room," he said, edging past her, ignoring her shocked surprise. He gave the door a kick with his heel so that it slammed shut, closing them in together.

"You shouldn't be in here," she protested, backing away from him. "You must leave!"

"A few minutes ago you boasted that you weren't afraid of me. Have you changed your mind?"

She stared at him, at his glowing eyes, his crooked smile, his broad shoulders. This was no Reginald Morley, afraid of wounding a young woman's tender sensibilities, nor a Jacob Thompson to be put off with a kiss on the cheek.

To her dismay, she realized she was glad he wasn't easily discouraged.

"You don't really want me to leave," he murmured, reaching for her and drawing her unresisting into his arms.

Drowning in the flood of sensations within her, she whispered, "Please . . ."

"Please what?" he asked huskily against her lips, then gave her no chance to answer.

Her dim awareness that she shouldn't allow him to stay, shouldn't let herself be bemused by his caresses, was blanketed by a haze of desire. As his mouth trailed from her lips along her throat, adding fuel to the blaze consuming her, she understood it made no difference what his real name might be or what kind of man he was. His caressing hands moved over her, unbuttoning her gown, pushing aside her undergarments until his mouth was against the bare flesh of her breasts. She moaned.

"I've wanted you ever since you defied me on that damned boat," he said hoarsely, stripping off her gown and yanking her free of the hoop.

He flung away his shirt, lifted her onto the bed, and eased down next to her. His chest was quite unlike the smooth bronzeness of the Indian men she'd seen at the river. His skin was white where the sun hadn't touched him, and black hair curled between his nipples. Seeing him partially undressed excited her far more than the almost-complete nudity of the Indians.

Moments later she was in his arms, and the indescribable wonder of his bare chest against her aching breasts made her cry out softly.

"My beautiful Rose," he whispered, "my sweet and lovely Rose, tell me you want me, too."

"Yes," she breathed, not knowing or caring what she was

agreeing to, aware only that she wanted more and more of the wondrous pleasure only Dan could give her. "Oh, yes."

His lips closed over hers, his tongue exploring her mouth, making her cling to him in a frenzy of need. When he tasted her breasts again, she arched against him, gasping, her fingers tangled in his hair.

"Dan," she begged. "Please, Dan . . ."

His hand slid up under her shift, caressing her inner thighs until she thought she'd die of pleasure. When he suddenly stopped, his body tensing, she moaned in protest.

"Listen," he ordered.

She opened her eyes, abruptly jerked from her daze of passion by the muted clang of metal on metal. Someone was knocking at the front door.

Nine

Rosalind sat up in panic, crossing her arms across her bare breasts. Dan swore and rose from the bed, pulling his clothes on in haste. She watched him, wide-eyed.

"Who can it be?" she whispered. "Everyone's at the Fourth of July celebration."

"Evidently not quite everyone," Dan muttered as he fastened his shirt. "Whoever it is knows someone's at home because I left the horse and buggy in front of the house. I'll answer the door and say you're resting."

Rosalind nodded, mortified at her nakedness.

To her relief, Dan didn't so much as glance at her while he finished dressing. As soon as he left the room, she slid off the bed and rearranged her undergarments, flushing in shame as she did. Whatever could she have been thinking of to allow Dan into her room, let him take off her gown and . . .

Were such intimacies permitted in the marriage bed? Quite probably, she decided. The liberties she'd allowed Dan might be reprehensible because she was a maiden, but if they were married . . . Rosalind sighed. They were not. How could she possibly marry him? She didn't even know exactly what name she'd be assuming. Would she be Mrs. Rackham? Or Mrs. Eaton?

Shaking her head, she picked up her discarded gown

from the floor. Sadly wrinkled—she'd have to choose another before venturing from her room. Who could possibly have come calling? Neither Cosy nor her father would have knocked, and she didn't think it could be any of the celebrating villagers. Who, then?

She stepped into the hoop, then chose a lavender gown from her wardrobe, struggling with the buttons and hoping she'd managed them all. As she arranged her disordered hair, she noticed how pink-faced her mirror image was. Her eyes, too, had a telltale glow, a glow she knew was the result of Dan's lovemaking. Would he notice?

She supposed she should thank God she'd been saved from her own lack of judgment by the unexpected caller but, in a way, she found herself resenting the rescue.

As she descended the steps, she heard voices from the parlor, Dan's and another man's. She frowned as she reached the entry, thinking she'd heard that other voice somewhere before but unable to identify it. Pausing in the doorway of the parlor, she stared in surprise, her fingers coming to her lips.

"Ah, there you are, Rosalind," Dan said, managing to sound quite like her father. "I trust you've recovered from your indisposition?"

"Rosalind," the second man said, "do forgive me for not notifying you ahead of time, but the chance to visit Ojibway came unexpectedly and I couldn't resist."

"Mr. Thompson—Jacob," she managed to say, coming into the room. "I'm happy to see you again." She flicked a glance at Dan, but he wasn't looking at her.

"I first sought you in town," Jacob said, "but when I failed to find you at the celebration, I asked where your father lived and—"

"It was so hot in town," Rosalind interrupted. "The

crowds—" She allowed her words to trail off and did her best to look fatigued.

"You're still flushed," Jacob said, earning himself a swift glance from Dan. "I do hope I'm not keeping you from resting."

"No, no, I feel much better. Won't you have some refreshment? I'll make tea."

"Perhaps Mr. Thompson would prefer brandy," Dan said. "Or whiskey. Jephthah has an excellent stock, sir, and I know were he here he'd offer you your choice." Without waiting for an answer, Dan crossed to the liquor cupboard.

"I do believe we have some cheese biscuits," Rosalind said. "If you'll excuse me, I'll fetch a tray."

Jacob Thompson, of all people, she said to herself as she hastened from the room. Though he'd seemed quite taken with her aboard the *Pewabic,* she'd considered it no more than a shipboard flirtation. She'd nearly forgotten his promise to call on her. And what a time he'd picked to call!

". . . business associate of Jephthah's," Dan was saying when she returned with the tray of biscuits. "I'm here for the summer."

For the summer. The words echoed in Rosalind's head as she gazed at Dan, ignoring Jacob. Dan wouldn't be staying in Ojibway. She'd known from the beginning he was here only temporarily, but now she realized how short the time would actually be. July. August. Two months. Then he'd be gone. Without her? She drew in her breath, remembering how her father had warned her that Dan wasn't the marrying kind.

"I understand you're a lawyer, Mr. Thompson," Dan said, swirling the brandy in his glass.

Rosalind glanced at Jacob. His glass was on the table

next to him, and it didn't look to her as though he'd sampled any of its contents. He lacked several inches of Dan's height, but he was good looking enough with his curling chestnut hair and light-brown eyes. If she'd never met Dan, perhaps she might have been attracted to him.

The front door opened and closed. After a moment Cosy entered the parlor. "Rosalind!" she cried. "Are you all right? When you disappeared so suddenly I worried that something had happened to you."

"I found the crowd oppressive," Rosalind said. "Is Father with you?"

"No, I haven't seen him. I came straight home, hoping you were here." Cosy glanced at Dan and Jacob.

Gesturing toward Jacob, Rosalind said, "This is Mr. Thompson. I believe I mentioned meeting him aboard the *Pewabic*. He's visiting from Houghton. Jacob, this is my half-sister, Coesius."

Jacob bowed slightly. "Delighted to meet you, Miss Collins. I wasn't aware Rosalind had a sister."

Cosy nodded politely.

Rosalind smiled. "Having a sister was a surprise—a pleasant one, of course—to both Cosy and me. Until my arrival, neither of us knew the other existed."

Jacob's left eyebrow rose slightly, but he didn't comment.

"Shall we toast these two lovely ladies?" Dan asked, raising his glass.

Searching for another topic of discussion, Rosalind said, "While we were aboard the boat, Jacob, I feel sure you mentioned that you played the piano. Can I tempt you to try the lovely spinet we have in our music room?"

"I'd much rather listen to you sing," Jacob said. "I haven't forgotten the song you favored us with on the *Pewabic*."

" 'Jeanie,' I think," she said. "Let's go into the music room. I'll play it and we'll all sing."

"If you're certain you feel up to it," Jacob told her.

"Oh, I believe Rosalind is quite recovered," Dan drawled.

Cosy was still puzzling over Dan's remark as she watched her sister sit on the stool, open the lid of the piano, and begin to play. It wasn't as much his words as the way he'd said them. As though he and Rosalind shared a secret.

". . . floating like a vapor on the summer air . . ." Rosalind sang.

Her clear, high voice was joined by Dan's lower tones as he came to stand beside the piano. Mr. Thompson didn't sing with them. Instead, he eyed Cosy, who was hovering in the doorway to the music room, as if wondering why she didn't come in.

Cosy hesitated, then entered and crossed to the window, telling herself she wasn't envious of her sister's ability to coax music from the piano. It was more that she felt awkward standing by the piano knowing nothing of the kind of music Rosalind played and none of the words to the songs.

Mr. Thompson walked over to her. "Don't you care to sing?" he asked.

"I don't know how."

"I'm not very good, either." He smiled, a smile that was more than polite, not a mere flash of teeth; he smiled at her as though he meant it. She didn't drop her habitual caution, but she warmed to this stranger with the red-brown hair and mustache and eyes the color of a fawn's coat.

"Coesius is an interesting name," he said. "Latin. Let's see—cat's eyes? Yes, without a doubt, because yours are definitely green."

Except for her father, he was the only person she'd ever

met who recognized where her name came from. "You're right about my name," she said, "but I'm usually called Cosy."

"I'm Jacob," he said. "Another name with a meaning. Every name has one, you know."

She nodded. "Among the People, a name is given to you because you've earned it in some way. The name is fitted to the person."

His eyes grew bright with interest. "By the People, I assume you mean the Chippewa. They have the right idea about names. We, on the other hand, must grow into our names willy-nilly. Take mine for instance."

"Jacob," she said, the name on her tongue for the first time. She liked the feel of it, so she repeated the word. "Jacob. What does it mean?"

"The supplanter. From the Biblical story of Esau and Jacob."

"I'm not familiar with the Bible," she admitted reluctantly.

"They were brothers, and Jacob stole Esau's birthright," he said. "Jacob wasn't a particularly admirable person, although God seemed to favor him despite his faults."

"Is the name Daniel from the Bible, too?"

He nodded. "It means God is my judge." He glanced over at Dan, singing with Rosalind at the piano. "The Biblical Daniel was an interpreter of dreams."

"Rosalind means rose," Cosy said. "Our father calls her Rosie."

"Your father's name means God opens," Jacob told her. "I looked it up after I met Rosalind on the boat."

Cosy pushed aside the memory of her sister telling her how the Biblical Jephthah sacrificed his own daughter. Recalling the words Rosalind had read from the Bible left her uncomfortable. "You know the Bible well," she said to Jacob.

"All of man's pettiness as well as his greatness is set forth in the Bible. Nothing that people do should surprise you after you've read through it."

Cosy thought over what he'd said. Was it true? Not having read the Bible at all, she had no way of knowing. Jacob talked to her differently than any man she'd ever met, not trying to flirt or tease. Deciding she liked him, she offered him a real smile, like the one he'd given her.

He blinked, his expression changing, a new look in his eyes. Admiration? When she found herself hoping it was, she blushed. "What dreams did Daniel interpret?" she asked quickly, hoping to distract Jacob so he wouldn't notice her flushed face.

"I believe he predicted the downfall of the king of Babylon."

"The People believe dreams come from the spirit and so every dream has a meaning," she said. "Some dreams are medicine dreams—true dreams warning of what will come."

"You know a great deal about the Chippewa," he said.

"I was taught by a medicine woman."

" ' . . . far, far away . . .' " Dan and Rosalind sang. " 'That's where my heart is turning ever . . .' "

"Mr. Rackham tells me he's staying at your house," Jacob said. "He's not from these parts, then?"

"I'm not certain where his home is," Cosy admitted.

"Perhaps he comes from the East, as I do?"

It seemed to Cosy that Jacob was overly curious about Dan. Was it because he saw Dan as a rival for Rosalind's attention?

"I have no idea."

Jacob smiled disarmingly. "I don't mean to pry. As an attorney, I've become so used to asking for information that I forget myself socially." He looked straight into Cosy's eyes as he spoke.

Cosy shifted her gaze away from him, recalling Hungry Moon's warning: "Beware the man who stares unblinkingly at you while he swears to the truth, for his tongue is truly forked."

"I've offended you," Jacob murmured.

"No, Mr. Thompson, not at all."

"Won't you please call me Jacob? I hope we can be friends because you're a most unusual young woman, Coesius Collins, and I'd like to know you better."

She couldn't help but be pleased. Before she could answer, the music stopped and they both looked toward the piano.

"It's your turn, Jacob," Rosalind said, rising from the stool. "If you don't come here immediately, I'll suspect you really can't play a note!"

Jacob walked slowly to the spinet and sat on the stool. His long fingers touched the keys gently and the melody began the same way—gentle and soft, the notes rising like iridescent bubbles to drift in the air. The sound was unlike the tinkling songs Rosalind played, and Cosy listened in amazement. It hadn't occurred to her there could be such a difference. She drifted closer, fascinated.

"Jacob is a classicist," Rosalind said, waving her hand. "Far above me. I'm sure my simple tunes bore him." Glancing at Dan, she murmured. "Do they bore you, too?"

"Not yet," he replied, seemingly amused when she pouted.

Cosy couldn't miss the current passing between Dan and Rosalind. Her sister looked exceptionally pretty, with her cheeks pinker than usual and a sparkle in her eyes. The lavender gown she wore set off the gold of her hair.

Lavender? Cosy frowned. Surely Rosalind had worn a blue gown today.

Jacob stopped playing abruptly and stood up. "I'm sorry if I've annoyed you," he said to Rosalind.

She made a face at him. "Don't be so stuffy. I quite envy your musical ability." Turning to Dan, she said, "Jacob and I did enjoy our trip together on the *Pewabic*. What a shame you missed the boat."

"I'd forgotten you'd planned to sail on the *Pewabic,* Mr. Rackham," Jacob said. "How generous of you to give up your berth to Miss Collins."

"I never could resist a lady in distress," Dan said.

"Interestingly enough," Jacob said, "I came over from Houghton today on the *Pewabic*. "I was told she'd carried a cannon, guns, and ammunition to Sault Ste. Marie from downstate."

Dan raised his eyebrows. "Surely they don't expect an Indian uprising."

"There are rumors that England intends to attack the United States from Canadian bases to help the Confederates," Jacob said. "Michigan has copper mines, and the South is in dire need of copper."

"But we're not at war with England," Rosalind protested.

Jacob shrugged. "It's been an uneasy peace for years."

Rosalind turned to Dan. "Is this true about being attacked from Canada?" she demanded. "Is that why—"

"Is that why the cannon was sent to the Soo?" Dan finished for her. "I'll tell you what I think. Michigan *is* being attacked—by nerves. England has too many problems in Europe to get into our war."

"It's possible you're right," Jacob said. "Still, there's no harm in being prepared."

Cosy, standing quietly aside observing the others, had the feeling that what wasn't being said was as important as the words they spoke, though she had no idea what those unspoken words might be.

"I'm happy I found you at home," Jacob said to Rosalind. "It was more than I deserved after coming without notice. I'm staying at the Bigelow House for a few days. I hope you'll be kind enough to let me call again tomorrow."

Rosalind smiled and held out her hand to him. "Perhaps you'll join us for dinner tomorrow," she suggested.

"Thank you, I'd like to." Jacob bowed over Rosalind's hand and released it.

Since Rosalind showed no inclination to show him out, Cosy stepped forward and walked with him into the entry.

When they reached the front door, Jacob took her hand, surprising her. He held her hand lightly, but she sensed a hidden strength. His fingers, curling around hers, were long and supple.

"I'm happy we've met, Miss Collins."

"Cosy," she said. "How can I call you Jacob otherwise?"

"Isn't it strange," he said softly, seemingly as much to himself as to her.

"What?" she asked when he didn't continue.

"How well your hand fits into mine."

She gazed at their linked hands, quite aware she should have pulled away moments ago. But she liked the feel of his fingers pressing gently against hers, holding her without effort, ready to release her if she wished. Shocked by her realization of how much she liked being touched by Jacob Thompson, she flushed, easing her hand from his.

"Have I upset you?" he asked.

"Yes!" she blurted, then fought to recover her poise. "I mean, no. No, of course not."

"Since I'm sure you must know, maybe you'll be willing to tell me how the Chippewa say goodbye."

"We—that is, the People—don't have words for hello or goodbye. When it's time to leave, they just go."

Jacob smiled wryly. "And it *is* time, isn't it? So I'll make my departure with no farewell."

Cosy closed the door after him and leaned against it, reluctant to return to the music room. Alone, she could retrieve from her memory every word Jacob had said to her and think about them. He'd told her it was strange how well their hands fit together, but what was stranger to her was how comfortable she'd felt with him.

He didn't make her catch her breath or cause her heart to pound the way Black Water did, but she was already looking forward to tomorrow, when she'd see Jacob again.

Cosy walked slowly toward the music room, her thoughts shifting to her sister. Was it her fault Rosalind had left the celebration? Had she felt deserted?

I didn't mean to leave her behind at the river, Cosy told herself. It was wrong of me to be so eager to see Black Water that I forgot all else. I'll have to apologize to her.

She wondered when Dan had returned. Had he and Jacob arrived at the house together? And why had Rosalind changed her dress?

As she neared the parlor, Dan's voice, taut with anger as he spoke to Rosalind, made her pause.

"I suppose you thought it was clever to drop those hints to Jacob Thompson. You're no fool; why must you behave like one? What do you know about him? He says he's a lawyer, but what a man claims to be and what he really is aren't necessarily the same."

"You ought to know," Rosalind snapped. "And I intend to go on saying what I want to whom I wish."

"It's *not* a game." The chill in his voice made Cosy's eyes widen.

"Yet you don't trust me with the truth, do you?"

"I've never met a woman I trusted."

"I certainly don't trust *you!*" Rosalind spoke angrily but her voice trembled.

"Which makes us even."

"I hate you!" Rosalind cried. "I've loathed you from the moment I first set eyes on you climbing over the rail of that boat. You—you—Blackbeard!"

Dan laughed. "Beard? Me? I don't even have a mustache. Maybe you're thinking of your friend Thompson. He has quite a luxuriant mustache."

"Leave Jacob out of this. You know very well what I mean."

"Less than an hour ago you didn't hate me. Quite the contrary, in fact."

"That was a mistake. I won't make the same one twice." Rosalind spoke through her teeth, sounding almost like a spitting cat to Cosy.

"What makes you think I'll give you the chance?" Dan drawled.

"Ohhh!" Rosalind cried. She burst from the parlor in tears, not even noticing Cosy as she rushed across the entry and up the stairs.

A moment later Dan sauntered into the entry, stopping when he saw Cosy. "Your sister's a tad overwrought," he said. "I'm taking a walk." His voice was even enough, but he slammed the front door as he left.

Dan was also, in his own words, a tad overwrought, Cosy thought as she went upstairs.

Rosalind refused to let her in, calling through her closed door in a choked voice that she wanted to be alone. Going to her own room, Cosy stepped onto her small balcony and took a deep breath of the warm July air, smelling the sweetness of the red roses climbing along the fence near the stable.

Though she was troubled by what seemed to be a secret alliance between Dan and her sister, she didn't know how she could help Rosalind—or even whether Rosalind would accept her help if she offered. Closing her eyes, she shut away her worries as well and let herself feel the wonder of the summer day.

Soon the blueberries that grew in the marshes on the other side of the river would be ready to pick, and next the raspberries that grew in the clearings, for this was the Moon of Ripening Berries. A bird trilled, sweet and high, and she tried to identify him by his song. A finch? No, that was wrong. She cocked her head to listen more carefully, and the hoot of an owl startled her. An owl? But it was nowhere near dusk! She opened her eyes and stared toward the pines, certain it was no bird calling.

Moments later, she slipped through the back door. She found, as she'd expected, Black Water waiting among the trees.

"What a risk you're taking coming here when the sun is high," she scolded. "If my father should see you—"

"Your father is with those men who shoot at targets," he said. "Listen."

The crack of rifles drifted from the village.

"I saw you today," he said, "there on the river bank in your fine clothes."

"I was watching you," she admitted.

He put his hand on her shoulder. Though her heart beat faster at his touch, somehow she didn't feel quite the same as she had when they'd met among the pines once before. It had been night then; perhaps she felt safer in the concealing darkness.

"Have you spoken to your father?" he asked.

"He won't listen. His heart is bad toward the People."

Black Water's fingers tightened on her shoulder. "I saw a man leave your house, a man with hair on his face. Has the lynx arrived? And is he the one your father wishes you to marry?"

Was Jacob the lynx in Hungry Moon's dream? Cosy had no idea. "My father hasn't met Jacob Thompson," she told Black Water. Besides, Jacob came to see my sister, not me."

"You said that about the man called Dan. She can't marry two men."

"I think she wants Dan, not Jacob. But Jacob doesn't know it yet."

As Black Water pulled her closer, a jay flew overhead, squawking, and he tensed, letting her go. "Brother Blue Jay sends a warning," he whispered. "Someone comes." A moment later he was gone, melting away into the shadows between the pines.

Cosy stepped hesitantly from the concealment of the trees and paused to look around. She saw no one. Breathing a sigh of relief, she hurried toward the house. Reaching the back door, she put her hand out to turn the knob but, to her surprise, the door opened before she touched it.

"Checking on the owls again?" Dan asked.

Cosy found herself at a loss for words. Pushing past him, she entered the kitchen.

"You met a man in that pine grove, didn't you?" Dan

continued, grasping her arm and turning her to face him. "And the odds are he was an Indian. I assume your father doesn't know."

She swallowed, remaining silent, avoiding his gaze.

Dan smiled. "Shall we bargain? I'm sure you heard your sister arguing with me in the parlor and, Rosalind being as easy to read as a primer, God knows how much more you suspect."

Cosy raised her chin to look him in the eye. "You and my sister have secrets between you."

"Have you mentioned this to your father?"

"No, not yet."

"Then I'll trade my silence for yours. You say nothing about secrets and I won't mention owls. What Jephthah doesn't know won't hurt him."

Slowly, reluctantly, Cosy nodded, not at all sure she was doing the right thing and greatly fearing she'd come to regret her bargain.

Ten

When Jacob Thompson came to the house the following afternoon, Jephthah gathered them all in the parlor, offering whiskey to the men and sherry to Cosy and Rosalind.

"So you're Rosie's lawyer friend from Houghton," Jephthah said. "In practice by yourself, are you?"

"No, not yet," Jacob answered. "At the moment I'm working for the Keweenaw Mining Company."

"Bill Dawson's group," Jephthah said. "You've met Bill, haven't you, Dan?"

"I don't believe I've had the honor."

"Dan's a good man with a fuse if you need a little blasting done," Jephthah told Jacob.

Cosy watched Dan and Jacob survey one another covertly. The People openly pitted one man's strength and skills against another's so each would know who was the stronger and more skilled, but in her father's world she'd discovered this was done more subtly. Jacob seemed as confident and as sure of himself as Dan, making her wonder who would win if they were put to a test.

"Bill's going to need some financing to bring in that new mine of his," Jephthah said to Jacob. "I might be interested, if you'd care to pass the word along."

"I'll do that," Jacob agreed.

"Don't you let Bill get squeezed out by Boston money,"

Jephthah warned. "You take anything from those Massachusetts boys and the first thing you know, you're out on your tail with nothing to show for it and they're millionaires three times over."

Jacob nodded. "Mr. Dawson is aware of the danger."

Turning to Rosalind, Jephthah said, "I don't mean to monopolize your young man, Rosie. Suppose you take him to the music room. I'm sure he'd enjoy hearing you sing."

Rosalind cast a swift glance at Dan, Cosy saw, but then smiled at Jacob and led him away.

"Seems to be a nice young fellow," Jephthah said once they were gone. "Rosie could do worse. He should do well if he keeps his eyes open, especially if he stays with Bill Dawson. There's a lot of potential in that copper property Bill's bought up." Lowering his voice, he continued, "Once we get our hands on the gold, I'd like to take a flyer on its potential. Can't afford to do so until then. What do you think, Dan? Like to join me?"

"I'm no expert on copper lodes."

Jephthah gave him a knowing smile. "I suspect you've already got your own use for your share of the gold."

"Right."

"Appleton told me you never stay in the same place two years running—that true?"

Dan avoided a direct answer, merely saying, "He talks too much."

Jephthah nodded. "I agree he's no one to trust with a secret. But I owe him for putting me in touch with you."

"What Appleton actually told me was that you needed a diver to retrieve copper."

"You wouldn't expect me to tell him the truth, would you? Though it does happen to be true that a boat carrying copper sunk off Fourteen Mile Point about a year ago, so that backs up my story." Jephthah shook his head. "A man would hardly make expenses recovering that copper. Luckily Appleton knows nothing about the *Kaug* or about diving. What he does know is mining; there he's got no match. Where'd you meet up with him, Dan?"

"It might have been in Baltimore. Or maybe New York."

Jephthah chuckled. "All right, don't tell me. I'll get it out of Appleton one of these days."

Rosalind's voice came faintly through the closed door of the music room singing another of her songs about doomed lovers.

"Ah, Rosie has her mother's voice," Jephthah said. "Lovely."

Despite her efforts not to feel jealous, resentment smoldered inside Cosy. Was there nothing about her mother or herself her father could find to praise? Who planned the meals with Mina Howard and saw to it that Hilda got the laundry done and kept the house clean? Who made sure Jim tended to repairs? Who made certain that Jephthah's favorite French brandy was close at hand and in good supply?

Rosalind had yet to lift a finger to help around the house. She'd invited Jacob to dinner, but had she bothered to notify Mina? Or see that there was enough meat to serve?

Cosy sighed inwardly. Though it was true Rosalind paid little attention to her unless she wanted something, she didn't really dislike her sister. Uncaring she might be, but Rosalind really wasn't mean.

"Jealousy burns the spirit," Hungry Moon had warned. "Be aware of your own worth so there is no need to envy another."

In the People's village I was valued for what I could do, Cosy thought. I was encouraged to become a healer—Hungry Moon made me feel that if I worked hard I might someday be as skilled as she was.

But who valued her here in her father's house? A great longing to see her foster mother swept over Cosy. Yet how could she violate her father's order not to visit the People's village?

Jephthah rose and stretched. "A walk alone before dinner is what I need." He winked at Dan. "I'm sure you don't mind being left behind with Cosy."

Cosy lowered her gaze, not wanting her father to read the knowledge in her eyes. Did he think she didn't know where he went on his afternoon walks? Did he actually believe she didn't realize that the Widow Carmondy had supplanted Mrs. Ludlow and that his walks took him to Maybelle Carmondy's small white house near the Episcopal church?

Dan had risen when her father did and, once he left, Dan began to prowl restlessly around the parlor. "I notice Jephthah didn't ask if you minded being left alone with me," he said finally.

Cosy shrugged. "My father assumes I'll do as he wishes."

Dan stopped in front of her chair, gazing down at her. "But you don't always, do you?"

"I try."

"Hasn't anyone ever told you the road to hell is paved with good intentions? On the other hand, I suspect you prefer forest paths to paved roads. Forest paths and those who use them."

Not wanting to be drawn into talking about Black Water, Cosy changed the subject by asking, "Shall we join my sister and Jacob?"

Dan's eyebrows rose. "Jacob? Not Mr. Thompson?"

Cosy flushed, eliciting a laugh from Dan. He reached a hand to her. "Since I take it you prefer not to be alone with me, allow me to escort you into the music room."

" 'Making our hearts in their sadness rejoice . . .' " Rosalind was singing as they entered. She glanced up, saw Dan, and stopped playing.

"You're just in time to listen to Jacob," she said, getting up from the stool.

Moments later, Jacob's fingers came down hard on the keys and crashing chords startled Cosy. The notes pounded at her, throbbing into her ears as she watched Jacob's fingers flash over the keys. The music poured over her in great waves of sound, making her feel a rising anticipation, as though she were preparing for a cataclysmic event.

Sometimes the men's chanting while the drums beat at the People's village affected her in a similar way, bringing her the understanding she was part of a greater whole.

When he finished, Jacob sat with bowed head.

"I felt what you played," she said after a moment, impulsively holding out her hand to him.

"So did I," he said, swiveling to look at her, grasping her hand and bringing it to his lips, his mustache soft on the back of her hand. His lips warmed more than her hand; their touch warmed her heart as well.

As he released her and stood, Cosy suddenly realized they were alone in the music room. Rosalind and Dan had disappeared. How impolite of Rosalind after Jacob had come from Houghton to call on her.

"My sister—" she began.

Jacob waved his hand dismissively. "You're here with me, aren't you?"

"Yes, but Rosalind is the one you came to see."

His fawn-brown eyes held hers. "Yesterday, maybe."

Cosy's breath caught. Could Jacob really be telling her he preferred her company to Rosalind's?

"I want to know all about you," he said. "Tell me everything."

She gazed at him in amazement. Most men preferred to talk about themselves.

When she didn't immediately answer, he said, "To begin with, why were you taught by an Indian medicine woman?"

"My mother was half-Indian," she said. "After she died, my father had to raise me alone and for a few years I lived at the Anishinabe—Chippewa—village upriver." She sighed. "I sometimes think I never should have left."

"Why did you?"

"My father came for me, saying it was time I learned his ways."

"The result being a beautiful young woman with every advantage—knowledge of the wilds as well as of civilization, wealth, intelligence, love—"

"Love?" she echoed.

"Your father's. And perhaps a young man's?"

Cosy bit her lip as Black Water's image flashed before her.

"I've upset you."

She shook her head. "It's only that Father doesn't approve of the People."

"And the one who loves you is an Indian brave. I see."

But did he truly understand? How could he? She wondered at herself for speaking of private matters to this man she hardly knew. When she began exposing her innermost thoughts to strangers, it was past time for her to visit Hungry Moon. If only she could find a way!

"I've never seen an Indian encampment," Jacob said. "I

hope you'll be kind enough to take me to the one upriver sometime."

"I don't know." Her tone was troubled. Jacob could have no idea that he was asking her to share a part of her life with him, a private part she'd never shared with anyone.

"I, too, am partly of another people," he told her.

Startled, she stared at him.

"Not Indian," he went on. "My mother's father was a Jew. She named me Jacob after him."

"A Jew?" Cosy asked. "I don't understand what that is."

He blinked, then smiled at her. "I forget you're not a Bible reader and have been isolated here in the northland. Jewish people are—" He paused. "To be brief, I'll just say that in many places the Jews aren't any more highly regarded than the Indians. Even being partly Jewish can put a man beyond the pale."

"Half-breed," Cosy murmured. "A hateful word."

"Definitely. Although the word isn't used for a part-Jew. I don't know why. So you see we have something in common, you and I. We share a bond."

Both reached out at the same time and their hands linked. "Even without knowing this, I felt you were a friend," Cosy said. "Now I know you are."

"A friend," Jacob repeated. "Yes, I suppose that's the right word to begin with."

To begin with? What did he mean? Before she could ask him, Mina Howard appeared in the doorway, causing Cosy to pull her hand free.

"Excuse me, miss," Mina said, "but I need to talk to you."

Cosy glanced at Jacob, who promptly said, "I'll amuse myself at the piano."

As she left with Mina, he began playing something light

and carefree, reminding her of butterflies flitting over summer blooms. How wonderful to have a talent that could brighten another's heart.

"It's Hilda," Mina said as Cosy followed her toward the kitchen. "She's crying and carrying on and she won't tell me what's wrong."

"Have you seen my sister?" Cosy asked, realizing that Rosalind and Dan weren't anywhere in sight.

"She went for a walk with Mr. Rackham," Mina said.

Hoping they'd have the sense to return before her father did, Cosy walked into the kitchen where Hilda, crouched on a stool with her face buried in her hands, sobbed brokenly. Jim stood near the back door, a cup of coffee in his hand. Cosy drew up a chair beside Hilda and sat down. Taking a handkerchief from the pocket of her dress, she put an arm around Hilda's shoulders.

"Look at me, Hilda," she ordered, her tone kindly but firm. She had to repeat the words before Hilda dropped her hands and raised her tear-stained face.

"Take this." Cosy proffered the handkerchief. Hilda grasped it and began mopping at her eyes.

"Mina and I want to help you," Cosy said, "but we can't unless you tell us what's the matter."

"I daresn't tell," Hilda mumbled.

"You must."

"Said he'd kill me."

"Who said?"

Hilda shook her head, sobs shuddering through her.

"Reckon *I* can guess," Jim said. "Must be that no-good bastard—'scuse me, miss—her ma married. He's a mean varmint, even when he's sober."

"Is Jim right? Is it your stepfather?" Cozy asked.

"He hurt me," Hilda cried. "He beat me till I don't fight him no more."

Cosy didn't fully understand what Hilda meant until Mina muttered, "Raped her."

Crouching beside Hilda, Mina touched the girl's abdomen. "You got something in there?"

Hilda nodded, wailing anew.

"Someone oughta blast a few holes in the son-of-a-bitch," Jim said harshly.

Mina straightened, shooting Jim a narrow-eyed look. "Why don't you arrange it?"

He frowned, then smiled grimly. "Hilda's a Finn, ain't she? Happens I know a few Finlanders." Turning, he ducked outside.

Cosy rose, wondering if she ought to go after him. Surely he didn't intend to shoot the man in cold blood!

As if reading her thoughts, Mina said. "Don't worry—Jim's no fool. You never heard what Finns do when a man rapes one of their women? They tie him to a tree and use their knives to clean out his crotch. They'll take care of him. Now it's up to you to cure Hilda."

"Cure her?" Cosy didn't understand.

"There's medicine to get rid of what that black heart planted inside her. Hungry Moon will know what to use. You can get it from her."

Mina was right about Hungry Moon's knowledge, and there was no question that Hilda must be helped. "I'll try," Cosy said, "but my father's forbidden me to go to the village."

Mina smiled slyly. "We'll find a way. What he don't know won't hurt him." She turned to Hilda. "Time for you to stop that blubbering," she said, "so we can get on with dinner."

* * *

The following week, the two-masted sloop Jephthah had chartered arrived at the Ojibway harbor crewed by a tan-skinned captain and two sailors whose skin was a very dark brown. Cosy had never seen the like.

"They're Negroes from the Caribbean," her father told her. "Captain Marcos is a mulatto—that means part Negro. They were my crew when I first located the *Kaug* and, so I persuaded my cousins in the islands to send the same three men this time. The fewer who know what we're up to, the better."

So Captain Marcos was a half-breed, like Jacob and her-self, Cosy thought, wondering if he found the term as dis-tasteful as she did. He was a tall, taciturn man who wore a beard, a perpetual scowl, and a long-bladed knife at his waist. She doubted that many would dare to call him a half-breed.

Stocking the boat with the equipment Dan had specified occupied her father. She could count on his being at the docks most of every day.

"This is your chance to go to Hungry Moon," Mina told Cosy. "If your father comes home while you're gone, I'll tell him you're visiting a woman-friend in town."

Cosy found it easy enough to slip away carrying her doeskins and moccasins in a bundle. Once in the woods, she changed into them, reveling in the freedom of An-ishinabe clothes. She hurried along the trail, aware she had four miles to cover before reaching the village.

When the deep woods, lush with summer growth, closed around her, she breathed deeply, inhaling the scent of decay as well as growth. What died contributed to what would grow, that was the way of the earth and of everything that lived.

Her heart was light as she sped along the trail, each beat saying *home, going home.* For wasn't the Anishinabe village her true home, the home of her spirit?

To her right the river flowed, massive and deep, on its way to Kitchigami. She knew from what she'd been taught by Louella Genette that Kitchigami, Lake Superior, was one of the five Great Lakes that drained into the St. Lawrence River and thence into the Atlantic Ocean—the Great Salt Water that Hungry Moon had told her of. Once the ancestors of the Anishinabe had lived by the Great Salt Water but had been driven westward by Iroquois, snake enemies, until they reached the shores of Kitchigami.

Sometimes she felt that she was divided into two parts— one Anishinabe, like her mother; the other white, like her father—and that the two sides of her could never meld into one. Either she must give up the People's ways completely or turn her back on the ways of her father, for the two did not mesh.

Brother Blue Jay flew ahead of her for a time, warning of her coming, but his calls stopped as he reached the edge of his territory. Each jay, she knew, had his own territory and fought any other bird that dared to challenge his claim. Animals, too, set boundaries and repelled invaders. But, like the People, birds and animals didn't claim to own a part of the woods; they merely claimed it for a time and then moved on.

"No one owns the earth," Hungry Moon had taught her. "We are a part of the earth and the earth is a part of us."

Yet Jephthah Collins owned the land his house was built on. He felt that land belonged to him and, according to the laws of the whites, he did own it.

Who was right?

A chipmunk darted across Cosy's path and dived into the hollow end of a windfall. The chipmunk's quick motion startled a rabbit who'd been frozen into a protective crouch beside the trail, and it leaped into the underbrush in frantic zigzag hops.

"I don't hunt you, Brother Rabbit," Cosy murmured in the People's tongue. "And I bring no harm to you, Sister Chipmunk."

The woods changed from trees that lost their leaves when cold came to trees who kept their needles, tall pines whose branches filtered the light of Father Sun. She increased her pace, weaving in and out between the trees in the fragrant gloom of the forest, the brown carpet soft under her moccasins.

Once she'd been so accustomed to traveling along the People's paths that she didn't tire easily, but living in her father's house had softened her. She was only two-thirds of the way to the village, and already her breath came faster and her heart beat more often.

Black Water, she thought, could run the few miles between the village to her house in half the time she was taking without even beginning to tire. Though her errand had nothing to do with him, she couldn't help but hope he might be there.

It still puzzled her why she'd confessed her secret to Jacob, letting him know that she yearned for a man of the People. It was true Dan might suspect she did, but she hadn't told him and she never would. Dan was not her friend. Was Jacob? Could she ever truly trust a white man to be her friend?

The faint smell of skunk made her grimace. Something had startled Brother Skunk into spraying his pungent perfume, and the odor traveled far. She was glad it was no closer. Animals usually avoided him as they did Brother Porcupine with his bristly quills, but there were always younglings who had to learn by bitter experience.

Porcupine. *Kaug.* Her father's sunken treasure boat. Would it prove as treacherous to tackle as the animal it was named for?

The village was on the west side of the river; she was on the east side. So, as she approached, she searched the east bank and was happy to find a canoe she could use to paddle across. The village dogs greeted her with warning barks that subsided once they caught her scent, and it warmed her heart to think they still remembered her smell.

Before she disembarked, a tall woman appeared among the curious children drawn to the bank to stare at the new arrival.

"Hungry Moon!" Cosy cried, leaping from the canoe and flinging herself at the older woman.

Hungry Moon hugged her close. "I dreamed my white owlet was coming," she said, "though I didn't expect you to be alone. A lynx was with you in my dream."

Lynx? Cosy frowned. Could she possibly mean Jacob?

"Come to my lodge and we will talk," Hungry Moon said.

A girl was coming out of the wigwam as they approached, and Cosy recognized her as Spotted Fawn, younger than she by several winters but now blossoming into womanhood. Cosy smiled, saying, "How you've grown!"

Spotted Fawn smiled in return. "It's good to see you, White Owl." Her smile faltered and faded. "Have you come to stay?"

Cosy concealed her surprise. The girl obviously didn't

want her to remain in the village. Why? They'd never been enemies. "I live with my father now," she answered, noting Spotted Fawn's relief at her words.

"Spotted Fawn gathers plants for me," Hungry Moon said as she led Cosy around the wigwam to where a sitting platform had been built in the shade.

A pang pierced Cosy's heart as she realized what that implied. Spotted Fawn had taken her place helping Hungry Moon. Was she also learning to be a medicine woman?

As if in answer, Hungry Moon said, "She's quick to learn. Though she hasn't the same gift for healing as you, her blood runs true. She will become a good medicine woman."

Feeling as bereft as a deserted child, Cosy swallowed the lump in her throat, blinking back tears. She must not be selfish. The village needed Hungry Moon's skills; she must pass them on to a successor, and White Owl could no longer be her choice.

"I've come to ask a favor," she said when she could speak, going on to explain to Hungry Moon what had happened to Hilda.

Hungry Moon remained silent for a time. "I understand that such a child would not be welcomed by the mother," she said at last, "and, if born, would condemn both itself and the mother to a life of misery. Because this is true, I'll help. The plants you will use are powerful and poisonous. Hilda may be very sick, and it's possible she will die. See that she knows this."

Cosy nodded, then listened carefully as Hungry Moon told her how to prepare the concoction to give Hilda.

"Something other than Hilda troubles you," Hungry Moon said when she finished.

"I—I've met Black Water in the pine grove by my father's house. We have done nothing wrong but—" She paused. "My father's heart is bad toward men of the People," she said, "but we wish to marry, Black Water and I."

"Black Water is not for you and you are not for him." Hungry Moon's voice was sad. "He knows this to be true. You must also accept the truth."

Cosy shook her head. "He's the only man I want for a husband."

"He is not for you," Hungry Moon repeated.

"If I can convince my father of Black Water's worth, I don't understand why he and I can't marry."

"The reason lies within you. If you search your heart and can't find the truth, then you must try once again to have your vision dream."

When she had lived in the village, four times she'd tried and failed to have the vision dream that was supposed to come to boys and to girls before they became men and women. Four times she'd fasted for two suns and two sleeps in a tree deep in the woods, apart from everyone, but the dream hadn't come to her.

"I'm no longer a girl," she told Hungry Moon.

"But you're still a maiden. You must try once more."

"Four is the spirit number, and I've fasted four times."

"It's harder for those with mixed blood. Don't give up. You must dream your spirit animal so he can guide you on the path you must take." She laid her hand on Cosy's head, stroking her hair. "Few paths are easy and smooth, my little owlet, child of my heart."

Instead of warmth from the treasured caress, a chill ran along Cosy's spine, a creeping dread of what lay in wait for her along the path she didn't want to follow.

Eleven

Cosy, having changed back into her petticoats and gown in the woods, carried the rolled bundle of her doeskins under her arm as she slipped in through the back door.

In the kitchen, Mina pulled the bundle away from her, saying, "Your father's here. He asked for you and I said you were gathering wildflowers to decorate the dinner table. Hilda's out now picking some so we won't be caught in a lie. Did you get what was necessary?"

At Cosy's nod, Mina sighed with relief. "I knew Hungry Moon wouldn't deny you. But we can talk later. You'd best go in to your father."

In the library, Cosy found not only her father but Dan and Rosalind as well, all standing around an opened crate. As she entered, Dan was lifting out something round and metallic. He set it carefully on the floor and turned back to the crate.

Catching sight of her, Jephthah said, "Ah, Cosy. You're just in time to see Dan's diving suit."

She watched Dan pull out a strange-looking garment which he arranged on the floor beneath what Cosy realized must be the diving helmet. Staring down at it, she felt a chill invade her spirit. "Mishibezo," she whispered, unable to control a shudder.

Dan, kneeling beside his equipment, looked up with a frown. "What did you say?"

"Pay no attention to her, Dan," Jephthah urged, scowling at Cosy.

"But what *is* Mishibezo?" Rosalind asked, looking at Cosy.

Cosy had to swallow before words would come. "A monster. The evil under the water."

Rosalind laughed. "Don't be silly. It's only a diving suit and helmet. You don't really believe in evil monsters, do you?"

"Of course not!" Jephthah was emphatic. "Cosy was filled with nonsense by that Indian medicine woman. She's learned better since." Glaring at Cosy, he said, "There'll be no more talk of evil or monsters, do you understand?"

Cosy nodded, wishing she could flee from the room. No one understood, and her father wouldn't allow her to try to explain. She knew the diving equipment was not a monster, but she also knew the strange fear that had settled into her when she saw it was a warning of evil to come, a warning connected with the suit and helmet. And with Mishibezo.

Rosalind watched Cosy edge back until she stood some distance from Dan's equipment. How could her sister cling to the heathen superstitions she'd learned in that Indian village? She hoped Dan hadn't been annoyed by Cosy's childish behavior.

"That helmet looks terribly heavy," she said to Dan.

"It's a clumsy device, but I don't notice the weight underwater," he told her. "I wouldn't consider diving without the helmet and the suit. Some nasty things have happened to men who've tried to go down deep without equipment."

"If you don't mind my asking," Jephthah put in, "how did you get into the business?"

"I never resent questions," Dan assured him. "I just don't answer some of them." He grinned. "We divers guard our secrets."

"You seem to have more secrets than most men," Jephthah commented, but without rancor.

If her father only knew! Rosalind thought.

"Will you take me on the boat with you?" Rosalind asked her father. "I'd like to see how everything works."

Jephthah glanced at Dan. "It's up to him."

"Come along if you like," Dan said. "You, too, Cosy. That way you can be sure it's only me inside this thing and not some monster from the deep."

Rosalind, eyeing Dan covertly, wondered why he'd invited Cosy when he hadn't invited her. She glanced at her sister, Cosy had put distance between herself and the diving equipment. Her expression, though, was calm, showing none of the fear that had been in her voice when she spoke of Mishibezo, whatever that was.

"Sailors are a superstitious lot," Jephthah said. "I know a lot of them believe women on board bring bad luck."

Dan looked up. "You're paying them, aren't you? What do their superstitions matter?" His gaze settled on Rosalind. "Come to think of it, though, bad luck and some women often *do* go together."

The following day Cosy fasted, trying not to reveal what she was doing. But at dinner her father noticed her playing with the food on her plate rather than eating.

"What's the matter?" he asked.

"I don't feel hungry," Cosy said, relieved that she could

speak at least a partial truth. Not eating all day had made her feel a bit queasy.

"You're not sickening for something, are you?" he asked.

She shook her head. "Haven't you said yourself that I'm as healthy as a horse?"

"That's true enough. Never could bear to be around a female that swooned over trifles."

"I think it's safe to say neither of your daughters seems to be the swooning type," Dan said, earning himself a sharp look from Rosalind.

After dinner, Cosy excused herself, saying she had some household duties to discuss with Mrs. Howard.

"When will you prepare the medicine for Hilda?" Mina asked when she reached the kitchen.

Cosy took in Hilda's pallor and her frightened eyes. "You're certain you want to take the medicine?" she asked the girl.

Hilda nodded, her face twisting with hatred. Putting a hand on her stomach, she muttered, "It ain't mine—it's his."

"You know the medicine might make you sick. Maybe so sick you won't recover."

"Mina told me. Can't be worse'n what *he* done to me."

Taking Cosy aside, Mina whispered, "I've been bringing Hilda with me to my place at night so that snake can't get at her. She believes he's put a monster inside her and she says she'll kill herself before she'll birth it."

Cosy took a deep breath, her heart heavy with pity for poor Hilda. Dangerous as the medicine might be, it did offer a way out for Hilda, a chance to live. If she did nothing, the girl might give way to despair and take her own life, as she'd threatened to do. For Hilda's sake she must not delay any longer.

"Don't eat anything after you get up in the morning," she told Hilda. "I'll give you the medicine when you get here."

Later, as she waited in her room until she could be sure everyone slept, Cosy firmly put aside her concern over Hilda. Tonight of all nights she must free her mind from worry, but doing so was not easy and her thoughts were still in turmoil when she finally heard complete silence fall over the house. It was time.

Dressed in her doeskins, she crept down the back stairs, quietly let herself out the back door, and hurried to the pine grove. She'd chosen the tree earlier, a sturdy mountain ash that grew in a tiny clearing amidst the evergreens. Reaching for the lowest limb, she swung herself up into the tree and settled as comfortably as possible on a wide branch, her back to the trunk.

The ash had already shed the white petals of its flowers, though it was too soon to see or feel the tiny nibs that would turn into clusters of red berries at the end of summer. Her father had told her once that the mountain ash was also called a rowan tree. More importantly, Hungry Moon had taught her it was a spirit tree. She had never before chosen to climb a mountain ash to seek her vision dream.

"Visions come to those with quiet minds," Hungry Moon had said.

The night was anything but quiet. How was it possible to shut away the love calls of the frogs and the insects who searched the night for a mating partner? Below her she heard the faint scurries of small animals hunting for food, using the darkness to conceal themselves from the fox and weasel and owl.

I will not listen, she told herself, closing her eyes and wishing she could close her ears as well. I am White Owl, she said silently in Anishinabe. I am one of the People. I belong to the earth that Father Sun warms, the earth that Grandmother Moon shines her silver light upon, the earth that offers us all that is necessary to live. Like the plants and the animals, like the rocks and the soil underfoot, I am part of the earth, I belong to the earth.

As she repeated the words over and over under her breath, the night sounds gradually faded. She no longer felt the gnawing of her empty stomach; she was no longer aware of the tree's rough bark under her hands or the cool breath of the breeze as it passed through the branches of the ash. She was suspended in a timeless place.

The piercing cry of a lynx, frighteningly near, startled her into opening her eyes. Her breath caught. Dark as the night was, she could clearly see the beast crouched on a limb slightly above her. Instead of being the usual spotted brown with golden eyes, this lynx was as white as the first snow of winter and its luminous green eyes stared into hers.

Hear me, healer whose blood is mixed. The words entered her heart rather than her ears. *Hold fast to your healing; it is the path you must follow.*

Its green gaze held hers a heartbeat longer, and then the white lynx vanished completely.

At first she didn't realize what had happened, then tremors of awe tingled through her as she understood she hadn't been visited by a real animal but by a spirit lynx. *Her* spirit lynx. She'd had her vision dream.

Tears of joy in her eyes, she climbed down from the tree and made her way back to the house, scarcely noticing that the sky was already turning light, heralding the rise of Father Sun. I *am* a healer, she marveled.

At dawn, in the kitchen with Hilda and Mina, she sprinkled four pinches of the powdered leaves and roots Hungry

Moon had given her into a pan containing a small amount of boiling water. Leaving the pan on the stove, she stirred the simmering brew until it was well mixed, then poured the concoction into a cup and handed it to Hilda, cautioning her that the liquid was hot and might taste bitter.

Hilda downed the dose quickly. "It's gonna work, ain't it?" she asked, her voice trembling with anxiety.

"Yes," Cosy replied confidently, buoyed by the assurance her vision dream had given her. Though Hungry Moon had cautioned that two doses one sun apart might be necessary, somehow Cosy knew that Hilda would only need the one.

Hilda pounded her stomach with her fists, muttering, "Fork-tailed devil."

"No need to hurt yourself," Mina admonished Hilda. "Didn't you hear Miss Cosy tell you the medicine would work? Stop fretting and help me with the chores before it begins to act on you."

Anticipating the need Hilda would have for a private, hidden spot, Mina, Cosy knew, had already laid an old blanket on the floor in a far corner of the pantry and set a chamber pot and a basin of water near the blanket.

"Come fetch me if I'm needed," she told Mina. "I'll be in my room."

Once in bed, she fell asleep almost before she pulled the covers over her.

White Owl, perched on the upper limb of a pine, watched the white spirit lynx spring to the ground from a branch below her into the path of another lynx, one whose spotted coat was a deep reddish-brown.

You will help the healer, the white spirit lynx said.

How? the other asked.

The secret lies within you. Only you can set her feet on her true path.

I will try to find the secret, the spotted lynx said, though I do not know what it is.

The spirit lynx rose into the air like smoke and vanished and the other sprang into the night, also disappearing.

Cosy woke abruptly to find Rosalind shaking her shoulder. "I thought you'd never rouse," her sister said. "You didn't appear at breakfast, and we ate over an hour ago. Before he left with Dan for the docks, Father asked me to see if you were ill."

Rubbing her eyes, Cosy sat up in bed, clutching at the shards of her dream, putting them away for safekeeping until she had time to study their meaning. "I'm quite well. I merely overslept," she said. "I'll be down shortly."

Cosy had planned to dress quickly and descend the back stairs to see how Hilda was faring before joining her sister, but she had no chance to do so because Rosalind lingered in her room, stepping onto the balcony while she washed and slipped into her undergarments. She was putting on a green-checked gingham that required no hoop when her sister came back into the room.

"Do let me fasten your gown for you," Rosalind said, not waiting for an answer before lending a helping hand. "Did you know Dan and Father are having the crew take them out onto the lake this morning?"

"Is Dan going to dive?" Cosy asked, recalling with an inward shudder the equipment he'd uncrated the previous afternoon.

"Just a test dive he says—not to the *Kaug*, but in shallower water. I wanted to go along, but Father said not until tomorrow." She grimaced. "I think he means to prepare the crew for our appearance. What silly beliefs sailors have! Of course Father's crew are all Negroes, and everyone knows how superstitious *they* are."

Cosy, having had her own beliefs mocked by her sister, was tempted to say, "As superstitious as Indians, you mean?" but she managed to hold her tongue. She didn't wish to start a quarrel with Rosalind.

After she was ready to go downstairs, Rosalind followed her from the room, trailing her like a shadow as she descended the back stairs. In the kitchen, Mina was removing a pan of rolls from the oven and Hilda was nowhere in sight. A faint moan came from behind the closed pantry door. Seeing Rosalind's puzzled frown, Cosy realized she'd heard the moan, too, and would have to be distracted.

Breaking off two of the hot rolls, for she was starving, Cosy said, "Do stroll around the grounds with me, Rosalind."

Rosalind stared at her. "Now? Before you've eaten?"

Cosy held up the rolls. "I'll nibble on these while we walk."

Shrugging, Rosalind said, "If that's what you wish."

Cosy led the way to the back door, opening it and letting Rosalind exit first. Catching Mina's eye, she gestured toward the pantry and Mina nodded, indicating the medicine was working.

"Well?" Rosalind challenged as she and Cosy began to circle the house. "I assume you invited me on this walk to discuss something of importance. What is it?"

Since that hadn't been her purpose, Cosy was taken aback. She bit into a roll as she tried to think how to answer, forcing herself not to wolf down the rest of the tasty, warm bread.

"It's about the Fourth of July, isn't it?" Rosalind asked. "I've known all along you suspected me."

Cosy blinked in surprise.

"You needn't pretend," Rosalind continued. "What if I

did come back to the house with Dan? As goggle-eyed as you were over that naked savage, I'm amazed you even noticed I was gone."

Stung by Rosalind's contemptuous tone, Cosy blurted, "I don't care what you and Dan are up to! But Father wouldn't approve of . . ."

Rosalind stopped walking and faced Cosy. "Don't you dare bring up what Father might or might not approve of when you're as guilty as I am. What about you and Black Water?"

Cosy could find no answer.

The two sisters stared at one another in silence for some moments before Rosalind smiled wryly and said, "Maybe deep down you and I aren't as different as we think."

It was a new idea to Cosy and, as they began walking again, she wondered if her sister might not be right. "But what about Jacob Thompson?" she asked after a time.

"Do you mean how do I feel about Jacob?" Rosalind waved her hand airily. "I enjoy his company, so why should I discourage him? Nowhere is it written that a lady can't be interested in two gentlemen at the same time."

Cosy felt an odd pang. Did Rosalind speak the truth? Was her sister as attracted to Jacob as she was Dan? If so, it shouldn't make the slightest difference to Cosy and yet, somehow, Cosy felt troubled.

"Aren't you excited about going on the boat tomorrow?" Rosalind asked.

"Tomorrow?" Cosy echoed.

"Yes, of course. I can't wait to watch Dan dive. I should think it would be frightening to shut oneself into that suit and helmet, but he isn't a bit afraid. He claims he finds it exhilarating to explore the deep."

"Dan is brave."

Rosalind shot her a calculating look. "I suppose you can't help but admire him."

Courage was always to be admired, Cosy thought but didn't say so, not wishing to have her sister mistake her words. It was plain that Rosalind was jealous of Dan and wouldn't believe her if she denied any interest in him as a man even though it was the truth.

And Jacob? a voice inside her asked. Would you be telling the truth if you denied any interest in Jacob as a man? Not wishing to examine that question, Cosy bit into the second roll, savoring the sweet, yeasty flavor.

"Those sailors from the Caribbean Sea are sinister-looking creatures," Rosalind said. "But then sailors often are. I've seen other rough-and-tumble seamen in Boston. These men Father hired must be capable or Father wouldn't have asked for them a second time."

"I remember the first time Father went after the *Kaug,*" Cosy said. "He didn't use a diver who wore a suit and helmet that time, just a diver like the men of the People." There'd been more to that episode, she knew, but her father had never told her exactly what had happened.

"You mean he used an Indian diver?"

Cosy shook her head. "No, the man was from one of the Caribbean islands like the others."

"Now that he's got Dan, Father's certain to succeed," Rosalind said.

Cosy might have agreed if she hadn't had that premonition of evil when she had first seen the diving equipment.

When they returned to the house, Cosy finally managed to be rid of Rosalind's company by telling her she'd promised to help in the kitchen.

"Honestly, you spoil those servants by doing their chores for them," her sister complained, but made no effort to follow her to the kitchen, opting instead to drift into the music room.

Cosy found the pantry door open and Mina inside with Hilda, who was on her knees trying to clean herself off.

"It's done," Mina said. "What was inside came out all of a piece into the chamber pot, and she's not bleeding over-much."

"I feel awful sick," Hilda moaned.

"Likely the medicine will make her vomit for a time," Cosy said to Mina. "You'd better take her to your place and stay with her until you're sure she can be left alone. I can manage here."

Mina nodded and helped Hilda from the pantry. After they'd left the house, Cosy carried what had been expelled into the pine grove where she dug a hole with a gardening fork and buried it. After filling in the hole, she carefully strewed brown needles back over the dirt, then dragged a nearby rotting log until the end covered the tiny grave, protecting it.

"Kitchi Manitou," Cosy intoned, "Great Spirit, this unformed being who could not live will nourish the earth to which it belongs, the earth we will all one day nourish. Kitchi Manitou, heed me, for its spirit is too unformed to travel the Sky Path. Heed me and allow this blighted spirit to return to you, where it belongs."

As she rose from her crouch by the log, a flash of white on a branch above caught her eye, but when she looked there was nothing to be seen. Nevertheless, she was certain her spirit lynx had been with her and her heart lightened, knowing this was a sign Kitchi Manitou had heard her plea.

* * *

When the four of them boarded the sloop the following day, the water of the lake was like glass. The sun shone hot, and hardly enough breeze blew to push the boat westward toward the humped outline of the Porcupine Mountains.

Rosalind imagined the sailboat moved like a great sluggish fish and decided the name on the bow—*Sturgeon*—was most appropriate. When she mentioned this to Captain Marcos, he merely grunted.

Annoyed by his rudeness, she avoided him after that and tried to ignore the other two crew-members. Were they always so sullen or was it due to their belief that women aboard brought bad luck?

Joining her father, who stood with Cosy and Dan beside the crate containing the diving equipment, she mentioned how taciturn the captain seemed to be.

"Captain Marcos didn't want you and Cosy aboard," Jephthah said, speaking in a low tone. "After what happened when he was here before, he doesn't want to risk any more trouble."

"Trouble?" Dan repeated.

"I told you we lost the diver."

"So you did. Mind explaining exactly what happened?"

Jephthah glanced over his shoulder and lowered his voice still more. "As you know, he didn't use any equipment but he was experienced, though he complained about the cold water. Superior never does warm up. Still, he had no real trouble and, just before the storm hit, he brought up the first load of gold. We had to run for shelter then.

"Christ, that was some blow. The waves crested at ten feet or more; I never saw the lake so angry. Three boats went down with all hands. We waited the weather out in port."

"And then?" Dan prodded when Jephthah fell silent.

"Once the lake quieted—two days after the storm, as I recall—he dived and came back up almost immediately to report the *Kaug* had shifted position and disappeared. The bottom sloped sharply, and he figured that the storm caused her to slide down the slope into much deeper water. I asked him to take a look down there. He dived—and never came up."

Shocked, Rosalind asked, "Not ever?"

"Superior's a deep, cold lake," Jephthah said, "and she doesn't always give up the dead."

"Diving into the deeps is damn dangerous without equipment," Dan said. "If he's still down there, it could be I'll come upon what's left of him."

Rosalind shuddered and grasped Cosy's hand, noticing her sister seemed as shaken as she was.

A few minutes later, Captain Marcos ordered the anchor lowered. Jephthah nodded his approval. "Smack dab on target. Marcos is first-rate."

"Today's only a reconnaissance dive," Dan said as he fitted himself into the suit with Jephthah's aid. "I'll try to locate the *Kaug* and discover how she's lying so that the next time I go down I can zero in on the gold." He grinned at Rosalind adding, "wish me luck," just before her father lowered the helmet over his head.

Rosalind tensed as his face disappeared behind the metal, reappearing in a distorted image through the glass of the faceplate. Cosy's fingers tightened on hers as she made a tiny sound of distress.

While Dan, in his suit and helmet, clomped away from them to the rail, Rosalind stared at the air hose snaking along the deck, chilled to realize Dan's life depended on what seemed to her an extremely flimsy device.

She'd anticipated being excited while she watched Dan dive. How wrong she'd been! She was so terrified for him that it was all she could do not to run after him and beg him not to dive—not that he could hear her, shut inside that grotesque helmet.

The larger of the two black crewmen helped Dan over the rail and onto the ladder on the boat's hull. Holding tight to Cosy's hand, Rosalind edged closer, determined, despite her increasing apprehension, to watch every movement Dan made.

Slowly he descended the ladder into the barely moving water until there was nothing left to see except bubbles rising from where he'd vanished into the lake. Would he ever rise from those cold waters?

No longer able to contain her fear for him, Rosalind turned away from the rail and flung herself, sobbing, into Cosy's arms.

Twelve

"Pull yourself together, Rosie." Jephthah's voice held a note of warning that cut short her weeping. As she eased away from Cosy and groped for her handkerchief to dry her tears, her father added, "If I'd known you intended to carry on like this, I'd have left you home."

"I—I'm sorry," Rosalind said, dabbing at her wet cheeks. "I didn't realize watching Dan dive would frighten me."

"Dan knows what he's doing," Jephthah said gruffly, watching her with narrowed eyes.

To avoid his gaze, Rosalind turned to stare, with mixed dread and fascination, at the winch—a large spool wound with heavy rope—that would pull Dan up when he signaled. Now, though, it kept unwinding as he dropped deeper and deeper. What was it like under the waters of this cold lake?

"Black Water dives into the depths without equipment," Cosy said from beside her.

Though she spoke softly, Jephthah heard her. "Black Water?" he repeated. "I suppose he's one of the braves from the Indian village."

"He's the finest diver in their village," Cosy told him.

Rosalind was surprised to hear an unfamiliar note of defiance in her sister's voice. Cosy almost never disagreed with their father, obeying him without question.

Jephthah snorted. "There's no man alive who can go down to where the *Kaug* now rests without suiting up. You don't understand, Cosy. The deeper the water, the more pressure it exerts. If a man without protection dives deep enough, he'll get the life squeezed out of him. Your Black Water wouldn't last five minutes in these depths."

"He wouldn't dive under the shadow of Kaugwudja anyway," Cosy said. "Evil dwells in Kitchigami where the mountains creep into the water."

"For the love of God use English!" Jephthah snapped. "I've warned you enough times to leave heathen ways and heathen words behind."

"What I meant was the People believe an evil spirit lives in Lake Superior where the Porcupine Mountains cast their shadow," Cosy said.

Jephthah turned to Rosalind. "You must see what influence you can exert on your sister. I hesitate to send her to Father Dunne for spiritual instruction—he'd be shocked at this spouting of pagan nonsense."

"Surely you don't really believe in such things as evil Indian spirits," Rosalind said to her sister. "There are no such spirits, you know. God watches over us and there's but one God."

"I've been told God is a spirit who is Three-in-One."

"Yes, but that's not the same," Rosalind insisted. "You must let Father Dunne explain about God; he can do so far better than I. And you must promise not to shock him with Indian superstitions. You don't want your immortal soul in danger, do you?"

Cosy's look was puzzled. "I don't understand."

"If you don't believe in God and do as He wishes," Rosalind explained patiently, "your soul can't enter heaven."

"But there *is* an evil spirit who mocks God." Cosy turned to her father. "You said so yourself. The Devil. Satan."

Jephthah cleared his throat. "Yes, well, perhaps we'd best let the matter rest until the priest can enlighten you properly. In the meantime—" Jephthah paused and placed his hands on Cosy's shoulders "—I want no more talk of Indian lore or Indian men. Is that clear?"

"Yes, Father." Cosy's voice could barely be heard.

Rosalind quashed her impulse to put an arm around her sister, fearing Cosy would stiffen, rejecting her sympathy. She's not like me, Rosalind thought. She's so very different. How can we ever be close?

When Jephthah went aft to speak to Captain Marcos, Rosalind moved closer to Cosy, murmuring, "Doesn't it seem to you that Dan's been underwater for a long time?"

"I don't know how long he needs to search for the *Kaug,*" Cosy said. "But I'm sure he's all right."

Rosalind stared at her. "How can you be sure?"

Cosy shrugged. "Dan isn't a man who runs heedlessly into danger."

How do you know? Rosalind thought indignantly. You weren't on the *Phoenix* when he climbed aboard as a pirate, risking his neck to take over the boat. You don't have the slightest idea what Dan's really like.

Gazing down into the silvery water, Rosalind tried to convince herself that nothing bad would happen to Dan, that he'd surface soon, the helmet would be lifted from his head, and he'd smile at her, the same wonderful lopsided smile she'd first seen aboard the *Phoenix*.

Time dragged, making her feel as though hours passed before Dan gave the signal to be pulled up. For long, agonizing minutes she watched the winch become thick with rope once again before his helmet finally broke through the surface. She was on pins and needles by the time the crewman named Tarse helped him up the ladder, over the rail, and into the boat.

As his helmet was lifted off his head, she began to move toward him, but before she could take more than two steps, Cosy grasped her arm, holding her firmly. "No," she murmured.

Furious, Rosalind fought to pull free.

"Wait," Cosy warned in a whisper. "Don't anger Father further by showing so clearly how you feel about Dan."

Rosalind, brought abruptly to her senses, gaped at her sister. Whether she wanted to acknowledge it or not, there was value in Cosy's advice. Father would have to be carefully brought around to accepting the fact that she cared for Dan. It wouldn't do to thrust it in his face, especially where others would see. Also it might not be such a good idea to make Dan aware of her feelings.

"How did it go?" Jephthah asked Dan.

"Nothing definite," Dan answered, wiping his face with a towel. "I'll dive again tomorrow."

Jephthah's glance flicked from Tarse to Regg, the other crewman. He cupped his hands and called to Captain Marcos, "Head her in."

His gaze settled on Rosalind and he said, "You'll stay at home from now on."

She didn't protest. Waiting at home could be no worse. She really didn't want to watch again while Dan disappeared into the cold water of Lake Superior.

"I don't like the weather," Captain Marcos said, approaching Jephthah. "The east wind, she has a bad name on this lake, and she blows from the east now."

"Has the glass fallen?" Jephthah asked.

The captain shook his head.

"As long as it stays steady, we'll sail tomorrow." Jephthah clapped the captain on the shoulder. "You sailors have as many superstitions as the Indians. There's not a cloud in the sky, my friend, and the bad wind you speak of is no more than a gentle breeze."

Captain Marcos shrugged. "If you say we go, we go." But Rosalind thought he didn't look happy about it.

After returning to the house, Jephthah called for a meeting with Cosy, Rosalind, and Dan in the library. "Now that there are no extra ears around," he said to Dan, "what exactly did you find?"

"I have her located. As your last diver reported, the bottom slopes sharply, not only once but twice. And the *Kaug*'s at the lowest level she can reach without dropping into hell."

"Into hell?" Jephthah scowled. "That seems an odd way to put it."

"I found part of what may be your unlucky diver. Or perhaps one of the *Kaug*'s unfortunate passengers. A skull caught between two shattered planks on what I took to be the stern of the *Kaug*."

As Rosalind grimaced, she heard Cosy make a small sound of distress.

Jephthah dismissed the skull without comment. "What about the gold?"

Dan shook his head. "The boat's broken up into bits and pieces. I'll be damn lucky to find those boxes of gold right off."

"Damn it, man, I need the money. I've sunk everything into the Nonpareil, and you know yourself that last vein was a dud."

"Take it easy, Jephthah. I didn't say I wouldn't be able to find the gold, merely that it'll be tricky and may take

longer than we planned. I'm not a man who gives up easily."

"Do you mean you'll be diving time after time?"
Rosalind asked, her voice betraying her fear despite her
effort to speak calmly.

Dan raised his eyebrows at her.

"But it's dangerous!" she cried.

"Now, Rosie," Jephthah chided, "we've had enough fool-
ishness from you and your sister for one day. I'm sorry I
permitted the two of you to come along."

"I'm quite safe," Dan assured Rosalind. "I take as few
chances as possible."

"It seems so risky—so far down there with only one
rope and one air line. What would happen if—" She broke
off, unable to voice her anxiety.

"I'm always careful. Nothing will happen," Dan said
firmly. He stood and stretched. "I think I'll take a stroll
before dinner, Jephthah, and get the stale air out of my
lungs. We can discuss tomorrow's dive later this evening."

"Whatever you want," Jephthah agreed.

Rosalind slipped from the library ahead of Dan. Without
pausing to cover her head or search for a parasol, she
hurried to the kitchen and out the back door into the sun-
dappled afternoon. When Dan strode from the house minutes later, she was waiting near the front door. He paused
when he saw her, frowning.

"I thought I'd walk with you," she said uncertainly, seeing his expression. She'd counted on being welcomed.

"My intention was to walk into town," he said. "Alone."

"Oh."

He smiled at her. "On the other hand, we might stroll
into the pine grove, you and I." He offered his arm.

Rosalind glanced toward the huge pines that towered

high above the house. She'd thought they might walk through the field between the house and the river bluff, not into the woods. She really didn't care for the darkness under the trees and had been avoiding the pine grove since her arrival.

Still, among the pines they'd be hidden from view; no one in the house could see them. She glanced sideways at Dan and what she saw in his eyes made her heart beat faster and faster.

Should she go with him? The same desire that glowed in his eyes beat in her blood, urging her on, making it all but impossible to refuse. She took his arm.

The ground under the trees was mounded with dead pine needles, making Rosalind stumble. Dan caught her, then eased his arm around her waist.

"I thought today that you were never going to come up," she confessed as they slowly threaded their way between the trees. "Like that diver from the Caribbean."

"Would you really care?" he asked, his arm tightening.

Since she was still wearing the riding costume she'd chosen for the boat, a skirt with no hoop, the increased pressure caused her hip to brush against his, making her breath catch. "I couldn't bear it if anything happened to you!"

"I don't dive unless I'm quite certain nothing will," he assured her. "Your concern is sweet but misplaced."

Pine-scented gloom enclosed them, with but an occasional shaft of sunlight slanting through the thick branches overhead. Dan paused, glanced around them and seemed to listen for a moment. She heard nothing other than the soft song of the summer breeze in the pine boughs.

A moment later he turned her to face him and then moved his hands to her shoulders. Gazing deeply into her eyes, he said, "I've been waiting."

She could hardly speak for the wild tumult within her. "Waiting?" she breathed.

"Waiting for you to want me as I want you." Dan drew her to him and lowered his head until his next words were whispered against her mouth. *"Do* you want me, Rosalind?"

Intoxicated by his touch, by his musky male scent, and by the teasing promise of his lips so close to hers, she barely managed to whisper, "Yes, oh yes."

His mouth closed over hers and she gave herself up to the magic of his kiss, a man's kiss, deliciously deep and hot, not at all like the fumbling closed-mouth kisses she'd gotten from boys. Their kisses had scarcely stirred her, whereas Dan's made her tingle from head to toe, igniting a fire deep inside her.

She clung to him, relishing the thickness of his dark hair under her fingers, wanting the kiss to go on forever while at the same time she yearned for more than kisses. She gasped with pleasure when his hand closed over her breast and she swayed against him, her knees growing weaker by the minute.

He eased her down onto the springy brown needles, unfastened her jacket, undid the lace ties of her undergarments, and put his mouth to her bared breast, making her moan as the flames inside her blazed hotter. She wanted, she desperately wanted—what did she want? Her naked breasts against his bare chest? Oh, yes, flesh against flesh, she longed to feel that wondrous thrill again.

When he took off his shirt, she threaded her fingers through the hair on his chest, exulting because she had the right to touch him, touch him anywhere, as much as she wanted. How could she ever tire of touching him?

His caresses grew bolder, finding the moist warmth between her legs and stroking until she was aquiver with need. "Please," she begged, her voice no more than a husky whisper.

"What do you want?" he asked hoarsely, his warm breath teasing her ear.

She couldn't tell him what she needed because she didn't know, but she knew only Dan could quench the flames that threatened to consume her. "You," she breathed.

When he finished removing the last of her clothes and rose, naked, above her, she reached for him eagerly, eager to be in his arms, nestled close, riding a tide of bliss. Part of him, hard and probing, touched her ready moistness and she opened to him, accepting. She wasn't at all prepared for a sudden burning pressure that hurt enough to make her cry out.

He caught her cry in his mouth, kissing her, murmuring soothingly, "It's all right, my sweet; you're all right. I won't hurt you."

As she slipped under the spell of his kisses and caresses once more, she found she no longer felt any discomfort. Soon she was overtaken with an urge to move her hips against him and, when she did, he thrust deeper into her. An inexplicable throbbing began inside her, creating waves of pleasure so intense she thought she might die of it.

She moaned again and again, clutching him, gasping his name as she involuntarily matched his driving rhythm until the waves crested and flung her out of herself into a marvelous place she'd never been. As in a dream, she heard Dan give a hoarse cry, felt his body spasm and then relax.

When she returned to awareness, she found herself on her back. Dan, beside her, was raised on one elbow, gazing down at her. She smiled languorously, too replete to move or speak.

He offered his crooked grin in return. "I hope that was what you wanted," he murmured. "*I* certainly did."

"Dan," she whispered, not answering, merely enjoying the sound of his name. "Oh, Dan . . ."

He bent his head and brushed his lips over hers. "You're even sweeter than I imagined," he told her. "But we'd best get dressed before we're discovered. For all I know, that blasted lawyer may be back in town and on his way to call on you again."

She didn't want to think of Jacob, of all people. Or anyone else besides Dan. Nor did she have any desire to dress. When Dan got to his feet, she openly stared, no longer too shy to look directly at his nakedness and, strangely, not minding her own.

Noticing her interest, he said, "Have you ever seen a man's body?"

She shook her head as her gaze fastened on that part of him that had given her so much pleasure. She blinked in disbelief when it seemed to change before her eyes, unexpectedly growing larger.

Dan chuckled. "See what you do to me?" He reached down, grasped her hand and pulled her up. "Get dressed, my sweet," he ordered. "Otherwise—"

"Otherwise, what?" she murmured, her fingers caressing his cheek.

"Otherwise I'll wind up making love to you all over again and chances are we'll get caught in the act by your father. We both know he wouldn't be pleased."

Rosalind bit her lip. Making love was what Dan called it, but she realized now he hadn't once told her he loved her.

"Do—do you love me?" she asked without thinking, regretting her words as soon as they were said.

He didn't reply immediately. She'd started to turn away,

tears stinging her eyes, when he finally put a finger under her chin and forced her to look at him.

"Don't cry," he begged. "The truth is I do love you as much as I've ever loved any woman. But—" His voice trailed off.

"But you're not a marrying man," she finished, blinking away the tears. "In my heart I knew that. Only I hoped—" She paused and shook her head. Turning from him, she began to dress.

"Loving someone, wanting to hold her, to caress her, doesn't mean a man wants to marry," Dan said from behind her. "It doesn't necessarily mean it for a woman either."

"I—I love you," she said, able to admit it only because she wasn't facing him. "I've never loved a man before and I hoped, that is I thought, when love came to me it would lead to marriage."

"I know," he said, regret edging his words. "I know."

When she was completely dressed, her hair smoothed as best she could without a brush, she turned to him. He stood before her, a lock of his dark hair falling carelessly over his forehead, as handsome a man as she ever expected to see, and, for an instant, she felt as though her heart might burst with mingled love and pain.

He reached to tuck a stray curl behind her ear. "From the neck down you're the epitome of respectability once more," he said. "But your face gives you away." He ran a caressing finger along her cheek to the corner of her mouth. "You still have the charming but telltale blush of passion."

Rosalind put her hands to her flushed face. She must look like a veritable wanton! How could she possibly return to the house?

"We'll walk across the field when we leave the woods,"

Dan said, as though reading her mind. "The sun and the wind will account for your pink cheeks."

Rosalind stepped away from him, feeling suddenly dispirited. How easily Dan could calculate what must be done to keep their secret. From long practice with other women? She quelled the impulse to accuse him, not wishing to reveal her uncertainty.

Saying nothing, she laid her hand on his arm and allowed him to lead her from under the shadow of the trees toward the sunlit meadow. Dan breathed deeply, flinging back his head as he released the air in a sigh.

"I feel wonderful!" he told her.

Rosalind sighed inwardly, wanting to believe it was because of her, because they'd made love, but no longer sure how much she meant to him.

"I find diving exhilarating," he told her. "But afterwards I sometimes get the strangest sensation, as though I'm about to suffocate, which is odd because I never feel that way inside the suit."

Chilled to the bone by his words, Rosalind removed her hand from his arm. "Is that why you took me into the woods?"

He laughed and caught her hand, turning her toward him with her back to the house. "Rosalind, my sweet, you are an innocent. Don't you realize I'd never need an excuse to make love to you? Don't you understand how enticing you are with your rosy lips and lovely body?" He ran a forefinger lightly over the curve of her breast.

Rosalind caught her breath as desire flared within her at his touch. Despite her annoyance, despite the fact they could be clearly seen from the house, it was all she could do not to fling herself into his arms and beg him to make love to her all over again.

Gazing into Dan's eyes, she saw her own need reflected in his, and a triumphant realization dawned. He was as trapped by her as she was by him!

"Come along," he said, looking away. "We'll walk to the river bluff before we return to the house."

As they passed through the field, Rosalind picked a daisy from the many blooming around them, plucking the white petals off one by one until only the yellow center remained.

"Aren't you going to reveal the decision?" Dan asked.

She slanted him a haughty smile. "It's a secret."

If only the daisy could be right, she thought. *He loves me,* the last petal had proclaimed. He'd said he did but qualified it. Dan Rackham was not the marrying kind.

A sudden thought took her breath away. How could she have forgotten what she knew about him? Could it be Daniel Rackham couldn't marry because Major Eaton already had a wife?

"You—you aren't married, are you?" she blurted out.

"Good Lord, no!" He seemed genuinely amazed at her question.

"Not even in your other life?" she persisted.

"What other life? As far as I know I'm only living one."

"I meant about the piracy and your other name. Your real name."

He gave an exasperated snort. "How many times do I have to tell you that Daniel Rackham *is* my real name? As for the episode with the *Phoenix,* it's part of the past and I never look back."

A premonitory shiver ran along her spine. Would she one day be Dan's past? No, she refused to believe it. Dan was hers, no matter who he was or what he'd done. She wouldn't allow him to discard her, no matter what she had to do to prevent him. Never!

Thirteen

The breeze blew strong over the river as Rosalind stood on the bluff beside Dan gazing down at the brown water and across it to the cultivated fields and apple orchards on the low bank of the other side. Forested hills rose behind the farms.

"The wind's shifted to the west," Dan said. "That ought to make Captain Marcos happy."

Even though she realized his change of subject was meant to distract her from any further discussion of the *Phoenix,* she couldn't help her sudden spurt of anxiety when she thought about his diving tomorrow.

"I hope you find that stupid old gold first thing in the morning," she cried. "Once it's hauled aboard the *Sturgeon,* there'll be no need for you to dive again." As she spoke, she stared apprehensively beyond the buildings of the town to the cold blue of Lake Superior.

Dan chuckled. "I thought only Cosy believed in the evil spirit of the lake."

Rosalind scowled at him. "You know very well I don't hold with Indian superstitions. But I can't help worrying that something might happen to the rope that connects you to the boat. Or to your air-supply line." She shuddered. "I refuse to watch you dive again."

"A sensible decision, considering how you feel." He took

her arm and turned her away from the bluff. "We'd best start back to the house."

She raised her eyebrows. "Are you afraid of my father?"

"I fear no man. But I see no point in antagonizing Jephthah unnecessarily."

Though admitting to herself there was wisdom in what he said, it wasn't what Rosalind wanted to hear. "Father wouldn't care if you went walking with Cosy," she said. "I fail to see what difference it makes to him."

"Where you're concerned, Jephthah prefers your friend Jacob Thompson."

"I'm not my father. And Jacob isn't you."

"You're single-minded, I see." He begin guiding her toward the house. "My father warned me about girls like you."

She smiled at him. "And my father warned me about men like you."

"Then perhaps we're both in trouble."

If I have anything to do with it, *you* definitely are, she thought. I don't care who you are as long as you're mine, and I *won't* let you leave me after the gold is ashore.

"Cosy cares nothing for you," she said. "Father has no idea how stubborn she can be. He'll never make her accept any man as a husband except the one she chooses."

"He doesn't expect Cosy to marry me."

"Then what *does* he expect?"

Dan offered his crooked smile. "How about friendship?"

Rosalind sniffed. "I suspect Father knows very well you're not the kind of man who wants friendship from a woman. I've come to believe that the only reason he married my mother was because she wouldn't make love with him otherwise. Obviously Cosy's mother felt differently. Maybe Father thinks Cosy will behave in the same wanton way as her mother did. But I doubt she's any more like her mother than I am like mine."

Noticing Dan was gazing at her in some surprise, she asked, "What's wrong?"

"You're more perceptive than I thought."

"Women have to be," she said tartly. "We have few-enough weapons."

They entered the house by the rear door, passing through the kitchen where the housekeeper stirred the contents of a pot on the stove. She glanced at them, then quickly away.

As they left the kitchen, Rosalind whispered, "She doesn't like me, that Mrs. Howard."

Dan shook his head. "Mrs. Howard is a dour woman who never smiles at anyone. You're carrying your mind-reading ability too far, my sweet."

Rosalind shrugged, unconvinced. They reached the foyer and, before she started upstairs, she touched Dan's hand, reluctant to leave him. He pressed her fingers, released them, and turned away.

In her room Rosalind tidied her gown, dislodging a few pine needles she'd not noticed. After brushing her hair, she twisted it up into a French knot, allowing one curl to escape down her back, all the while remembering what had happened in the pine grove. She descended the stairs and, still bemused, drifted into the music room where she sat at the piano and let her fingers wander over the keys while continuing to think of Dan. When he held her, nothing else mattered. If only she could be in his arms forever . . .

"What's that you're playing?" Jephthah asked from behind her.

Startled, Rosalind hit a discord, then realized she'd been playing an Irish tune she'd learned from Janet Morley. She flushed, not looking at her father.

"Go on with the song, don't let me interrupt," Jephthah insisted. "Sing the words, why don't you?"

Sing the words to this song? Sing, "My Danny boy, I love you so," with her father standing beside her?

"I—you startled me," she stammered. "I've forgotten what I was playing."

"I'm glad you've returned from your walk," Jephthah said after a short silence. "I've been wanting to talk to you about the party."

"Party?" she echoed, turning on the stool to face him. "What party?"

"Haven't I mentioned having a party before? I plan to invite your Houghton friend, Jacob Thompson, as well as a number of folks you've met here in Ojibway. You'd best begin planning right away since the party should be soon— next week, if possible. I expect you and Cosy will need new gowns and such."

"Yes, of course. A party sounds exciting. But next week? When did you decide on having it so soon?"

"This afternoon," Jephthah said meaningfully. "While you were on your walk."

The good weather held for three days during which Cosy remained at home with Rosalind while Jephthah and Dan sailed on the *Sturgeon*. Dan dived each day, but by the end of the third day he still hadn't located the gold. Perhaps, Cosy thought, Mishibezo was hiding it from them.

Meanwhile, she and her sister were having gowns made for the coming party. Hers was to be of white satin, the design simple. She'd decided to wear the jet necklace that had been her mother's, and the dressmaker had found jet buttons to trim the gown.

Cosy sighed and stared at the rain slashing against the parlor windows. Her father brooded in the library, drinking brandy and chafing because Dan couldn't dive until the weather improved. Rosalind was in her room reading poetry. Dan had gone out earlier and, though Cosy thought she'd heard him return, he was nowhere to be seen.

She was relieved that Hilda had improved enough to return to work, seemingly in better spirits. Apparently her stepfather had rather suddenly left town.

When a knock came at the front door, Cosy called to Hilda that she'd answer it. When she swung the door open and saw Jacob standing on the porch, her heart lifted.

"Please come in," she urged, smiling at him.

He paused in the entry to take off his hat, water dripping onto the floor from its crown. "I had business in town, so I thought I'd take a chance on your being home—and Rosalind, too, of course."

"Won't you come into the library? My father will welcome you, I know. I'll tell Rosalind you're here."

Jacob's gaze held hers. "I haven't forgotten our last conversation."

"I haven't either," she admitted, wondering if his eyes were truly fawn in color. Weren't they more the shade of maple sugar?

His hand brushed against hers, whether by accident or design she wasn't certain, but the brief contact warmed her.

"I shouldn't ask you but I will," he said. "Are you glad to see me, Cosy?"

She nodded, suddenly shy. "I'll ask Rosalind to come down," she said, turning toward the stairs.

Hurrying along the hall to her sister's room, she decided that, if she were Rosalind, she'd pay more attention to Jacob and less to Dan. She tapped on the door once, twice, three times. There was no answer. Was her sister asleep? Easing the door open, she peered in.

"Rosalind?" she called softly.

Receiving no response, she slipped inside. The room was empty. Where could her sister be? She wasn't downstairs, and obviously she hadn't gone for a walk in the rain. Returning to the corridor, she called, "Rosalind?" In vain.

Is it possible she's in my bedroom? Cosy asked herself.

When she looked into her room and then the other empty room in the east wing, she found no one. That left the west wing, where the men slept, and the attic. Aware her sister disliked the attic because she feared the spiders that spun their webs there, Cosy was left facing an unwelcome possibility. She hadn't seen Dan and she couldn't find Rosalind. Were they together?

Cosy shook her head. Rosalind wouldn't!

Or would she?

Making up her mind, Cosy walked slowly to the men's wing. Opening the door of the empty room next to her father's, she called, "Rosalind?" After doing the same at her father's door, again without success, she crossed the hall and called her sister's name into the unused bedroom beside Dan's, then glided back toward the stairs, not stopping at Dan's room. As she reached the top of the stairs, she heard a door open and glanced around.

"Did you want me?" Dan asked, standing in his doorway in his shirtsleeves and breeches. His feet were bare and his hair tousled.

"No, I'm looking for Rosalind," Cosy said. "Jacob Thompson's here to see her."

Dan muttered something she didn't quite catch, then said, "Have you tried her room?"

"She's not there."

"Here's my suggestion. You go down and entertain Mr. Thompson and I'll find Rosalind."

"But—" she began.

"Be a good girl, Cosy, and do as I say."

Realizing his solution was the only way for all of them to save face, she nodded. As she descended the stairs, she tried to tell herself her sister could be visiting Dan's room on some errand—to sew a button on his shirt or to return something she'd borrowed from him. But she knew better. Rosalind and Dan were together because they were lovers. How bold they were to use Dan's bedroom—what a chance they took!

Father would be furious if he found out. Cosy would do her best to keep their secret.

Entering the library, she could look at neither her father nor Jacob as she said, "Rosalind was resting. She'll be down soon." Lying was difficult; the words seemed to stick in her throat.

"I've persuaded Jacob to stay over until the party," Jephthah said jovially. "With empty bedrooms upstairs, it's foolish for him to remain at the Bigelow House when he'll be far more comfortable here."

"I'll see the room next to Dan's is ready," she said, aware of the reason he'd invited Jacob to stay and knowing it was too late for such a ploy to be successful. Rosalind was in love with Dan; she had no interest in Jacob.

"Has Dawson hit a promising vein yet?" Jephthah asked Jacob.

Cosy lingered, telling herself it was because she was curious to hear what her father planned to do about the new mine and not because of any particular interest in Jacob.

Jacob shook his head. "It's too early to tell. All the indications point to the copper being there, though."

Jephthah smiled wryly. "Many a man who depended on indications has wound up with empty pockets."

"I don't deny that. But, as I mentioned, it's early days yet. Have you given up the idea of putting money in?"

"I'm still interested but not quite ready to act. I hear Owen Chamberlain's staying at the Bigelow. I imagine that's what brought you to Ojibway."

"As a matter of fact, yes."

Jephthah frowned. "I warned you about that Eastern money. Chamberlain's from Boston, as I'm sure you know."

"Mr. Dawson needs cash," Jacob said. "Eastern money pays the bills as well as any other kind."

"Easterners are greedy connivers!" Jephthah spat the words. "Me, now, I'd only want a share of the profits, but those Boston boys are never satisfied until they own everything you've got, including the shirt off your back. Ask Dawson to hang on for another month before committing himself."

"I'll tell him," Jacob agreed, "but I can't guarantee what he'll do."

Rosalind appeared in the doorway, cheeks pink, eyes bright. "Why, Jacob," she murmured, "what a pleasant surprise."

Jephthah beamed. Turning to Jacob, he said, "No need for you to traipse about in the rain. Jim'll take the wagon down and pick up your bag from the hotel."

"Thank you, sir."

"Are you staying at the house, Jacob?" Rosalind asked.

"Your father is most persuasive." Jacob smiled at Rosalind.

Cosy told herself she didn't mind if his smile for her

sister was as genuine as the smile he'd given her. After all, it was really Rosalind he'd come to see, wasn't it? Rosalind was especially pretty in a blue afternoon dress the color of her eyes. It wasn't the gown she'd had on earlier, but Jacob couldn't know that and Father wouldn't notice.

Rosalind's glance kept straying to the open door, Cosy noticed, realizing her sister must be waiting for Dan to appear.

"I believe I'll ride into town with Jim," Jephthah said. "There's someone I want to see."

"Will you be back for dinner?" Cosy asked, wondering if her father planned to visit Widow Carmondy. When he did, he often stayed late.

"I should be back in an hour, give or take a few minutes. Has anyone seen Dan?"

After a moment, Cosy said, "I think he's in his room."

Jephthah hesitated, then said, "Might as well let him rest while he can. This rain won't last forever." He strode from the library.

"Do come into the music room," Rosalind said to Jacob.

Cosy watched him follow her sister without so much as a backward glance and assured herself she didn't care. Marching to the kitchen, she told Mina there'd be a guest for dinner, then hurried upstairs to make sure everything was in order in the room Jacob would be using. She met Dan in the hallway.

"Who went out?" he asked.

"Father—he'll be back in an hour. He's invited Jacob to stay at the house for a few days."

Dan shrugged. "It's Jephthah's house. Did he say where he was headed?"

Cosy shook her head.

"I hope he's not planning to collar Captain Marcos. The

captain's got a knife-edged temper even in good weather."
Dan started past her.

"Are you going to marry Rosalind?" she blurted out.

Dan paused, eyebrows raised. "Marriage must be the
foremost thought in every young lady's mind, since they
seem to talk of nothing else. Why do you ask?"

Cosy twisted her hands together, uncomfortable under his
sardonic gaze, wishing she hadn't spoken. But since she
had, she refused to back down. "You know very well why."

"Men like me don't marry, as I believe your father
warned the pair of you." He flashed a grin and continued
toward the stairs.

*If Dan doesn't want to marry her, why doesn't he leave
her alone?* Cosy asked herself indignantly as she straightened the coverlet on the bed Jacob would be using. *Dan
is taking advantage of my sister. Black Water would never
do that to me; he's a far more honorable man than Dan.
Didn't Black Water ask me to marry him without so much
as a kiss between us? If only Father could be persuaded . . .*

Without her willing it, her thoughts drifted from Black
Water to Jacob. *Is he an honorable man?* she wondered.
She finishing tidying the room and, as she went back
downstairs, she heard Rosalind playing the piano and singing:

" 'If at last you cannot love me
Do not weep, I understand . . .' "

The words seemed to hang in the air. *Cannot love me.*
Was Rosalind assuring Dan she understood?

When she entered the music room she saw Jacob at the
piano watching Rosalind while Dan stood by the window
gazing outside. At last Rosalind stopped singing and her
fingers dropped from the keys.

"Evening red," Dan said.

"I beg your pardon?" Jacob responded.

Dan gestured at the window and Cosy saw that the clouds obscuring the late afternoon sky were streaked with scarlet.

"The rain has stopped," he said. "Evening red and morning gray will send the sailor on his way."

"Are you planning a sail on the lake?" Jacob asked.

"You might call it that," Dan said.

The front door slammed, startling them all. "Dan!" Jephthah shouted. "Where the hell are you?"

Dan strode from the music room with Cosy trailing behind him. Jephthah stood in the entry. "The most hellish bad luck," he growled as soon as he saw Dan. "Tarse got drunk, got in a tavern brawl, and got skewered."

"Is Tarse dead?" Cosy asked with concern.

"Might as well be," her father muttered. "Dr. Blake sewed him up—for what that's worth. Tarse is flat on his back, too weak to even open his eyes. Doc says most of Tarse's blood soaked into the saloon floor and he'll be lucky to survive. Those islanders are used to rum, not the rot-gut forty-rod they serve in the U.P."

"I won't dive without someone on the pumps who knows what he's doing," Dan said.

"I've been helping Tarse," Jephthah said. "I've learned enough to take his place. The problem is that Marcos won't sail without two crewmen and I'm damned if I want some idler from the docks on that boat, someone who'd blab our secret all over town."

"So we don't go out." Dan spoke flatly.

Jephthah slammed his fist against the newel post. "Damn it, we have to!"

"Keep your voice down," Dan cautioned. "We'll figure out something."

In the gloomy silence, Cosy glanced from one man to the other, wondering if she dared speak. "I know a man you can trust," she ventured finally.

"Who?" Both men spoke at once.

"His name is Black Water," Cosy said.

"No!" Jephthah's voice was harsh with anger. "How many times have I warned you—"

"Hold on, Jephthah," Dan broke in. "If Cosy says this Black Water can be trusted, maybe we ought to consider him."

"Never saw an Indian yet who'd turn in a decent day's work. Besides, he wouldn't come. Too scared of Cosy's evil lake spirit."

"Black Water will come if I ask him," Cosy insisted.

"Does he know anything about boats?"

"Only canoes. But he's quick to learn and he's not one to give away secrets."

"What choice do we have?" Dan asked Jephthah. "Captain Marcos won't sail without two crewmen and you refuse to let any man from town on the boat." He half-smiled, giving a slight motion of his head toward the music room. "Of course we could shanghai Jacob."

"A lawyer? Never!" Jephthah glanced over his shoulder and lowered his voice. "I told him you're diving for copper, and I sure as hell don't want him to know about the gold."

"You don't trust lawyers, I see."

"He's a fine man," Jephthah said. "He'll make Rosie a good husband. She'll need someone steady if she's as much like Cecily as I think she is."

"But you don't want him in on the gold," Dan said.

"I'd rather risk the damn Indian." Jephthah turned to Cosy. "I suppose he lives upriver."

She nodded, trying to dampen her excitement. "I can go to the People's village early tomorrow morning."

"Not alone, you won't," her father growled.

"No harm could possibly come to me there," Cosy said indignantly.

Jephthah scowled. "You need to rest for the dive, Dan," he said, "so it's up to me. I hoped I'd never have to see that miserable Indian camp again, but—"

"Pardon me, sir," Jacob said, coming into the entry. "I didn't mean to listen, but I couldn't help overhearing you mention the Indian camp just now. If you're making a trip there, I'd certainly like to come along. As I mentioned to Cosy, I've never been to one."

Jephthah eyed Jacob speculatively. "Interested in Indian camps, are you? That's more than I am." He glanced at Cosy, back at Jacob, then at Cosy again and nodded to her. "Since he's so eager to make the trip, I'll send Jacob along to keep an eye on you."

Though she'd longed to go alone, Cosy was surprised to discover she had no objection to her father's decision. In fact, she was pleased.

At dawn the next morning, Cosy met Jacob in the kitchen and they slipped quietly from the house. "Is that what you wore when you lived with the Chippewa?" Jacob asked, as he eyed her doeskins and braided hair with interest. When she nodded, he added, "The clothes become you."

"They're more comfortable than what I wear in my father's house," Cosy admitted.

"I can't imagine myself in buckskins," Jacob said, "but I've always had a secret yen to wear them."

Cosy glanced at his flannel shirt and his town trousers

and boots. The shirt was the color of blueberries and showed off his red-brown hair and mustache to great advantage. "The People would call you Ishcoda, Fire Hair," she told him.

"Would they really?" he asked, obviously pleased.

"Why do you wish to visit them?" she asked as they cut across the field toward the woods along the river.

"Perhaps because I'm a Jew," he said. "Do you know that you're the first person in years to whom I've revealed my ancestry? No one thinks of me as a Jew because I was taught from an early age not to advertise the fact that my mother's people were Jewish."

"My father doesn't know?"

Jacob shook his head.

About to insist that she didn't think it would make any difference to her father, Cosy hesitated. He disliked Indians, maybe he didn't care for Jews, either. She'd never heard him mention them, one way or the other.

"Are the Jews so very different?" she asked.

"Yes and no. As human beings, we're all essentially the same. The problem comes from religion—how we worship God."

Cosy shrugged. "There's only one Great Spirit for all."

He nodded. "Unfortunately, people view Him in different ways. Those who believe one way mistrust the views of those who believe in another." He paused to glance up at a squawking jay.

"Brother Blue Jay warns of our coming," she said as the trees closed around them. Moistness rose from the ground and droplets of water flicked from the undergrowth as they passed.

"I'm more of a city man than a woodsman," Jacob admitted. "Set me down in any city and I could find my way around, but I fear I'd soon be lost in these woods if I were alone."

"All you have to do is follow this trail. See the sign?" she pointed to bent saplings and inconspicuous blazes cut on the bark of trees. She turned to look at him. "I think I could find my way in almost any woods near where the People have a village but I'd be lost in a city."

"It's possible for you to learn about cities," he said, "just as I'm learning about this wilderness."

"I'm not sure I'd want to."

"Maybe someday I can change your mind."

Cosy pondered his words, uncertain what he meant by them. Jacob remained silent, and they hiked on in single file without speaking, Cosy in the lead. When at last they came to a small beach along the river and paused for a brief rest, both were damp from the wet woods.

"Beautiful," Jacob murmured as they stood side by side.

Looking across the expanse of rushing water to where the spreading branches of maples hung over the river along the far bank, Cosy nodded her agreement. All but hidden under the maple leaves, a bear fished in the shallows. Muk-wah was the People's name for the river. She turned to tell Jacob this and point out the bear.

Jacob, she found, was looking not at their surroundings but at her. His gaze trapped hers, and the glow deep in his eyes made her breath catch.

Slowly almost reluctantly it seemed to her, he bent his head until his mouth brushed against hers. "If I kiss you properly," he murmured, his warm breath caressing her lips, "I'll never let you go."

Fourteen

Jacob brushed Cosy's lips with his once more, wanting to deepen the kiss and fully taste her sweetness. He longed to hold her, to feel the soft curve of her breasts under his hands, to make her completely his—all the while aware it was an impossible desire. He had too much at risk. What he wanted at this moment, what he so desperately needed, he couldn't have; he could allow nothing to deflect him from the course he must follow.

Exerting strength of will he didn't know he possessed, he took a deep breath, straightened, and took several steps away from her, putting her beyond his reach. He turned from the bewilderment in her lovely green eyes, knowing he couldn't tell her the truth and not wishing to lie. There should never be lies between Cosy and him.

While he searched for words, his gaze fell on the paw and hoof prints outlined in the mud of the river beach and he grasped at the chance to speak of something besides his own behavior.

"Wild animals must come here to drink," he said. "I recognize deer tracks, but I'm not sure of the others."

For a moment Cosy didn't reply, then she bent to study the ground. "Rabbit here," she said pointing. "Bear. Weasel. Lynx."

"I'm impressed."

"I don't read signs as well as most of the People," she said and sighed. "I sometimes feel that I'm trapped between them and my father, neither one thing nor the other."

He wished he dared pull her into his arms and try to comfort her but, if he touched her, he'd forget everything else but Cosy. Why the hell did he have to find her now, of all times? And why her, for that matter? Why not Rosalind or any one of the other young women he knew? The questions were unanswerable. Fate played havoc with human lives.

"I like you just as you are," he said. Like didn't even approach his feelings for her, but he dared offer her nothing warmer.

Her smile didn't reach her eyes. "It's time to go," was all she said.

They plunged back into the woods, following a barely perceptible trail. To distract himself from brooding over Cosy, Jacob kept a sharp lookout for blaze marks and other trail signs. They traveled in silence. She set a fast pace, a man's pace, one more remarkable feature of this woman he already admired far too much for his peace of mind.

Eventually her pace slowed, meaning, he hoped, that they were nearing the camp. As much as he hated to admit it, his feet hurt, since the boots he wore were made for city streets, not the wilderness. They emerged from the woods into a clearing beside the river, which was narrower here than near Ojibway. A cluster of bark-covered wigwams were scattered among the trees on the opposite side of the water. He saw a half-grown boy paddling a canoe toward the bank where they stood.

"Eagle Feather's coming to ferry us to the village."

Jacob stared at the canoe, already more than half way across. "How did he know we were coming?"

"My foster mother, Hungry Moon, must have dreamed." He frowned. "Dreamed we were coming, you mean?"

Cosy nodded, her attention on the canoe. Gliding to the water's edge, she greeted the Indian boy in what Jacob knew must be the Chippewa tongue. Eagle Feather replied in the same language, then beached the canoe before glancing at Jacob.

Warned by Cosy that he must kneel rather than sit in the canoe, Jacob climbed into the middle, leaving Eagle Feather in the bow and Cosy in the stern to paddle across to the village. How graceful her movements were! He found himself staring at her, bemused, unable to look away.

What did she think of him? Here in the woods he felt like a fish out of water. Men were supposed to be the trail breakers and the rowers of boats, but he'd done neither. While he could argue a case in court or handle a sailboat with the best of them, he'd never broken a trail or paddled a canoe in his life. If he'd foolishly insisted on being the leader of this expedition, they'd still be wandering around in the woods.

Jacob tried to tamp his urge to show off in some way for Cosy, to let her know he had skills, different though they might be from those of the Indians. He *was* a crack shot, but that had nothing to do with here and now. There's no need to compete, he muttered under his breath. Whether Cosy admires you or not is of no concern.

He failed to convince himself.

As Eagle Feather beached the canoe, Cosy looked in vain for her foster mother. The boy had said Hungry Moon told him to meet them, so why wasn't she waiting? What was wrong? Disturbed, momentarily forgetting Jacob, Cosy jumped from the canoe and ran toward her foster mother's lodge.

She'd almost reached it when the flap lifted and Hungry Moon appeared, moving slower than she usually did. As the older woman came fully into the sunlight, Cosy checked her rush to embrace her foster mother, staring in shock at the change she saw.

It had been less than a moon since she had last been here—how could Hungry Moon have ailed this much in so short a time? Or had she been blind and not seen the change before?

"Mother, you've been ill," she said, the words choking her as she embraced the older woman.

Hungry Moon gave her a brief hug and then put her firmly away. "You are welcome, my white owl," she said. "You and your friend."

Belatedly, Cosy became aware that Jacob stood behind her and motioned for him to join them.

"You are still my little owlet," Hungry Moon said, "looking at me with eyes round and big. Know that my dreams have shown me the way I must travel and that I've made my peace with what will be. You must not sadden yourself with useless grieving."

Blinking back the tears her foster mother had warned her not to shed, Cosy said, "This is my friend Jacob, whose name means he who comes after." In English she told Jacob, "This is my foster mother, who is called Hungry Moon."

"I'm grateful to be allowed to visit you," Jacob said.

"You are welcome." Hungry Moon spoke in English. "Before I met you, I dreamed of your coming. In my dream you were Bezo, the Lynx, powerful and dangerous."

After pondering her own dream, Cosy had decided the spotted lynx in it must be Jacob, even though she didn't understand how he could possibly help her become a healer.

She saw, though, that Jacob was completely taken aback by Hungry Moon's words.

Wishing to speak privately with Hungry Moon, Cosy said to Jacob, "I'll explain later." Turning to her foster mother she said, "Perhaps Eagle Feather could show Jacob around the village while we talk."

Hungry Moon gestured to the boy, ordering him to guide Jacob. When the two women were alone, Hungry Moon led the way to the seating platforms.

"You bring trouble to the village," she chided Cosy when they were comfortable.

Cosy was astounded. "Jacob?"

"Jacob is a man with a good heart. The lynx only kills from hunger or to protect himself. I don't mean him; I mean *you*. Why have you come?"

"To see you. Why didn't you let me know you were ill?"

"Letting you know would change nothing."

"But I want to be with you. To help you."

Hungry Moon shook her head. "Even if your father would let you stay in our village, you couldn't help me. And I'm not alone. As I've told you, Spotted Fawn lives in my lodge."

Rebuked, Cosy fell silent.

"What's your other reason for coming here?" Hungry Moon asked after a time.

"I came to tell Black Water that my father has work for him," Cosy admitted.

"Work that you have arranged?"

"No! A man was hurt and my father needs someone to take his place."

"So you gave him Black Water's name."

"I wanted my father to have a chance to see what a fine man Black Water is," she confessed.

"I will ask Black Water and hear what he wishes to do," Hungry Moon said. "You have no need to speak to him. I tell you again there is no future for you with Black Water. You must let him go from your heart."

"I'm a woman and should be free to make my own choice," Cosy argued. "If my father approves of Black Water—"

"You're a woman, but freedom isn't always possible for women, whether they be of the People or not. Nor are men always free to do as they will. Listen to my words for they are dream words and therefore true: You cannot marry Black Water. It is not to be."

"We love one another," Cosy protested. "I want to marry him and live here again. We'd be happy; I know we would."

"What is to happen can't be changed." Hungry Moon's voice was sad.

"Have you seen, then, what is to be for me?"

Hungry Moon didn't speak immediately and when she did, she closed her eyes. "I have seen only that the white owl leaves the river and the pines and flies where my dreams do not follow."

Cosy had no idea what this could mean. "Will you tell me what is ahead for Black Water?" she asked finally.

Opening her eyes, Hungry Moon said, "Even if I had dreamed of him, it is harmful to speak of what is to be for another."

"She never dreams of me." Black Water eased around the side of the wigwam and stood before the women with his arms folded across his chest. He scowled at Cosy. "Why have you brought this white man with hair on his face into the village?"

"Jacob means no harm," she said, rising from the platform. "I came to ask you to return with us—with me. My father needs a man who keeps secrets, a man who is not afraid of the water. I told him you were that man and so he wants you to work aboard a boat with sails."

Black Water's scowl faded, but he remained somber. "Where does the boat journey?" he asked.

"By the mountains, by Kaugwudja. There the man named Dan dives to recover gold from a sunken boat. He wears a covering to protect him from the deep water. You'd help the dark-skinned man who steers the ship."

"And your father?"

"He'll be on the boat. When he sees how strong and brave you are, I hope he'll change his mind about men of the People."

Black Water smiled. "I'll go on this boat with sails. For you."

"I knew you wouldn't refuse!" Cosy's impulse to throw her arms around him faltered when she noticed Hungry Moon's frown.

"Danger lies within Kaugwudja's shadow," the older woman said.

"Not for white men," Black Water countered. "I'll be on a white man's boat."

"It is not good," Hungry Moon insisted. "Be warned."

"I hear," Black Water acknowledged. Turning to Cosy, he asked, "Who is this Jacob?"

"A friend of my sister's, as I told you before. They met on the boat bringing her to Kitchigami."

"Your sister loves another," Black Water said. "I've seen her share her blanket with another in the pine grove by your father's house."

Though surprised that Black Water had seen them, his words didn't shock Cosy for she'd known in her heart that Rosalind and Dan were lovers. "There's need to hurry," she told him. "My father wants the boat to sail today, while the weather is good."

"We'll use my canoe," Black Water said. "Meet me at the river bank."

Cosy watched him as he strode away. When she turned to Hungry Moon again, she saw Jacob standing beside the seating platform with moccasins on his feet and his boots slung over his shoulder by their laces.

"That, I take it, is Black Water," he said.

"He is well named," Hungry Moon replied in English before Cosy could speak, "for there's a darkness within him."

"No!" Cosy cried.

"You see him as you wish to see him," Hungry Moon told her in the People's tongue. "You look at Black Water with the admiring eyes of the little girl you once were. I say again, he is not for you."

"Every man and every woman carries at least one secret within them," Jacob said, "a secret hidden from all eyes."

"You're wise for a man so young," Hungry Moon said, peering closely at him.

"Wise enough to trade for moccasins, at any rate," Jacob said. "Eagle Feather thought my clasp knife was a fair exchange, but I think I got the best of the bargain."

Ignoring his talk of trading, Hungry Moon said, "I see you carry a secret, man-who-is-a-lynx, a secret that burdens your heart."

Cosy stared at her foster mother.

"I was warned you were a medicine woman," Jacob said, bowing slightly to Hungry Moon.

Cosy glanced from one to the other. Clearly Jacob accepted what her foster mother had said about him. From courtesy or because it was true? Before she'd made up her mind which to believe, Hungry Moon rose slowly from the platform and hugged her.

Putting her arms around the older woman reminded Cosy of how thin her foster mother had grown, and her heart grew heavy with apprehension for she knew Hungry Moon was dying. "I'll come back to see you as soon as I can," she promised.

Smiling faintly, Hungry Moon freed herself and stepped back. "Dream of me instead."

Swallowing against the lump in her throat, Cosy turned away and hurried toward the river with Jacob at her side. They found Black Water waiting beside his canoe.

No one spoke as the canoe sped swiftly downstream. Soon they neared the small river beach and Black Water steered toward it, pulling the craft to shore.

"We'll walk from here," he told Cosy in the People's tongue as they climbed out. "Under the bluff there's no place for the canoe." But when she started along the path, he caught her arm, detaining her.

Cosy glanced at him, noting he looked disturbed. "Would you mind going on alone?" she asked Jacob. "I'm sure you can find your way from here."

Jacob nodded. As he walked past them he said, "And I'm sure you can find me if I do get lost."

After he vanished into the trees, Cosy turned to Black Water. "What is it?"

"The boat with many sails," he said. "Is this boat called *Nahma?*"

In her mind Cosy saw the black letters painted on the sloop's wooden hull. "The *Sturgeon,*" she said in English. Switching to the People's tongue she added, "The white men have named the boat *Sturgeon*—their word for Nahma."

"And you told me Dan is the man who dives. Is it not true Hungry Moon dreamed of him as a fox?"

"It's true," she agreed, wondering what was bothering Black Water.

"I, too, have dreamed," he said. "I dreamed of danger, but I didn't understand the dream until now. I will speak to Dan about my dream."

"Can you tell me?"

"You weren't in the dream. The fox is the one I must warn."

Realizing he'd told her all he intended to, Cosy said, "I hope he'll listen. White men's ears are often closed to what the People say."

Black Water shrugged as if it made little difference to him whether Dan listened to his dream warning or not.

"We must hurry and join Jacob," she said, aware all three of them had to arrive at the house together so as not to risk her father's ire. If he thought she'd spent time alone with Black Water, he'd be furious.

"I don't like your being with Jacob," Black Water said. "Don't bring him to our village again."

Ready to argue that Jacob was perfectly harmless, Cosy held back. Harmless was not the right word for a lynx. Nor was it the right word for that brief kiss Jacob had given her at the river beach. As she remembered it, she could almost feel the soft caress of his lips and the way her heart had pounded when she'd thought he meant to pull her into his arms. Was it relief or disappointment she'd felt when he had not?

Abruptly turning from Black Water, she started up the trail, repeating, "We must hurry," over her shoulder.

When the three of them reached the house, they found Dan and Jephthah impatiently awaiting their arrival. Taking

Black Water in tow, they set off for the dock, leaving Jacob and Cosy behind with Rosalind.

"Very interesting what your father is doing," Jacob said as they were finishing a lunch of sliced venison heart, peas, and tiny new potatoes. "But it seems to me it's hardly worth his time and money. Will he really be able to raise enough copper from that sunken boat to do more than cover his expenses?"

Rosalind's fork clattered onto her plate as she hastily covered her ears with her hands. "Don't speak of it, I beg you," she cried. "Diving is so terribly dangerous that it frightens me to think of Dan down there under the water."

"I'm sorry," Jacob said soothingly. "I won't mention the subject again."

Cosy eyed Jacob curiously, seeing him in a new light since Hungry Moon's mention of his secret. What or whom did the secret involve? Her father? Was he suspicious of what her father was doing? Had he brought up the diving because he didn't really believe it was copper Dan dived for and hoped to learn more from either her or Rosalind?

After the meal, Rosalind chatted with Jacob for a while, leading him into the music room. However, it was apparent she didn't feel like singing or playing the piano. Cosy knew her sister's mind was elsewhere. She refused a walk, finally excusing herself "for a rest."

After she'd left them alone in the music room, Jacob said to Cosy, "Perhaps you'd like to rest, too. That was a rather long hike we took this morning."

"I'm not tired." She felt almost as distracted as Rosalind in her worry about what might be happening aboard the *Sturgeon*. Dreams were not to be taken lightly and, though Black Water hadn't given any details, his dream had upset him enough that he meant to warn Dan.

"I've had visions of myself living in the forest as a man of nature," Jacob said, turning her attention fully to him.

"Visions?" she repeated. "A vision dream, you mean?"

He shook his head. "No, more of a daydream, where you play with various fancies that intrigue you. Living as the Indians do has always been a favorite daydream of mine. At the Chippewa village today I admired the craftsmanship that went into the making of the canoes and the wigwams." He glanced down at his feet, still clad in moccasins. "Remarkable how comfortable these moccasins are. And the intricate quillwork is superb, as were the decorations on your doeskin dress and leggings."

She no longer wore these, having changed as soon as she had entered the house into the kind of gown her father preferred, but she hadn't removed her moccasins. "I dyed the porcupine quills for my clothes and made the designs myself," she said proudly.

"You're a woman of many talents, Cosy." Jacob rose from the window seat and walked toward the piano, leaning against it as he turned to face her. "The Chippewa people, both men and women are magnificent physical specimens with a grace of movement it's a pleasure to watch. But I realized today that I couldn't live among them, not in a none-too-clean village overrun with dogs, a village whose children are dirty and naked and—" Seeing the outraged expression on her face, he paused.

"I don't mean to offend you, though I realize I am," he said. "I could have told you only what I admired about the Chippewa, but I have this compulsion to be honest with you. I want no untruth between us. I believe you wouldn't lie to me, and I shan't to you. The reason I'm mentioning what's wrong with the village is because of your yearning to return there to live. You can't because you're not the same young girl who left the village several years ago. Despite your love for Black Water, I don't believe you'd be happy living there as his wife."

"How dare you say such a thing?" she cried, leaning forward in her chair. "How can you possibly understand how I feel?"

"If Black Water loves you, why doesn't he try to become a part of your world rather than making you a part of his?"

"I'm already a part of his world." Anger simmered in her words. "I belong with the People."

"He's a fine-looking man," Jacob went on, his calmness infuriating her. "He seems intelligent as well. Isn't there a possibility that Black Water—"

Cosy spoke through her teeth as she forced herself not to shout at him. "White people hate Indians. They call Indians lazy and say they won't work. They don't realize the People aren't interested in money or working for another person for wages. The People work for themselves and share with the villagers they live among—the men by hunting and fishing and the women by harvesting plants and making clothes from the skins of the animals that are eaten for food."

Jacob nodded. "I don't argue against that way of life— for the Chippewa. But you're not really one of them, Cosy. You said yourself that you belong to your father's world as much as to theirs. Remember that less than half your life was spent with the Indians."

She sprang to her feet. "I won't listen to another word!"

His brown eyes narrowed with anger. "That's because you don't want to hear the truth. Yet in your heart you know it *is* the truth."

She rushed toward him, her hands clenched into fists, seething, determined to pound at him until he stopped.

When she struck out, Jacob caught her wrists and yanked her to him, holding her fast while bringing his lips down on hers in a bruising, punishing kiss.

As she struggled to free herself, the heat of his kiss seared through her, sapping her strength, urging her to respond instead of fight. Despite her resolve not to give in, her rage seeped away bit by bit, leaving a frightening desire in its place.

Suddenly he released her, pushing her away from him. He swung around, sat on the piano stool, and brought his hands down onto the keys in loud, crashing chords, creating as violent a sound as the great war drums made.

Cosy stared at him for a moment, confused by the storm within her, then turned and ran from the room, his thunderous music following her up the stairs and into her room.

After a restless night, Cosy rose before dawn. By the time sunrise streaked red across the sky, she was dressed in a gown with no hoop. After pulling on her Zouave jacket, she tied her straw bonnet firmly and stalked down the stairs. She hesitated as she approached the library but took a deep breath and continued on into the room.

"I'm going with you on the *Sturgeon*," she announced.

Her father sighed. "Cosy, you know that we agreed you girls would stay home."

"I promise not to say a word about any superstition of the People," she said. "And Rosalind's not coming. She doesn't care to watch the diving."

"Captain Marcos won't be happy. He didn't like having you aboard the first time."

"If I'm not here," Cosy pointed out, "Jacob and Rosalind will have a chance to be alone. When I'm here, Jacob feels he has to be polite and entertain me, so I thought I'd go with you on the boat." She wondered at herself speaking so smoothly when she was well aware that Rosalind had no interest in being alone with Jacob. As for Jacob—but, no, she refused to let what had happened between them enter her mind.

"Yes, I see what you mean," Jephthah said. "Very well." He fixed her with a steely gaze. "But don't think I'm not aware of your private reason for wanting to be on that boat. You must give me your promise not to talk to Black Water—not one word—or you stay home."

"You have my promise," she said quickly. At least he hadn't told her that she couldn't look at Black Water.

Dan, who'd entered the library as they talked, followed Cosy when she left the room.

"Your Indian friend warned me about a dream he had," Dan said when they reached the entry. "Something about a fish and a fox being swallowed by a porcupine. I had trouble following him but I gathered it was bad medicine."

"He dreamed of danger," Cosy said. "You're the fox."

Dan raised his eyebrows. "A fox, am I? While I might agree with that, I can't swallow the rest. The Chippewa certainly are a calamity-minded group. All I've heard from you—and now from Black Water—are predictions of doom. I'll make my own luck, thanks just the same."

Cosy, watching him return to the library, felt her heart grow heavy with foreboding. Black Water had said nothing about a porcupine to her and she was sure he'd had no idea the sunken boat, *Kaug,* was named after one. Yet a porcupine had been in his dream with the sturgeon and the fox. If he'd had a true dream, and she feared it was one, dreadful danger lay ahead.

Fifteen

Captain Marcos, Regg, and Black Water were already aboard the *Sturgeon* when Cosy arrived with Dan and her father. The captain scowled at Cosy but said nothing. She looked away from him, gazing at the sun rising above the narrow band of clouds along the horizon. Otherwise, the sky was clear. The early morning air was mild, promising a pleasantly warm day.

Seagulls circled the sloop as it eased from the harbor, their cries plaintive to her ears. The lake itself was calm, almost glassy. Noticing her father and Dan walking away from her, she trailed after them, fearing if she didn't stay close to her father he might think she was seeking Black Water's attention. She'd looked at Black Water when she first stepped aboard, but he'd given her one quick glance and turned away.

She passed two boxes stacked one above the other near the small cabin and, to her surprise, saw XXX lettered on the side. When she'd seen similarly marked boxes at the Nonpareil Mine, her father had told her they contained the dynamite used for blasting underground rock to free the copper.

"Why do you need dynamite here?" she asked Dan, who was running his fingers carefully along the air hose.

"To clear away the debris," he said. "I can't get at the

gold because of the way the wreck settled in that deep cleft after the storm."

"Does dynamite explode underwater?"

He nodded. "They've been using it in England for underwater blasting for years. An English diver who trained under Colonel Pasley of the Royal Engineers taught me the technique. Pasley was an expert, one of the first men to use a closed diving suit." He gestured at his own suit. "Pretty much like this one."

"Could there be something wrong with that air hose?" she asked.

He shook his head. "Before every dive I always check every piece of my equipment myself. Rule One is never to dive with any part of your gear in questionable condition."

Cosy could well understand his caution. "But couldn't you be pulled up quickly enough to survive even if air stopped coming through the hose?" she asked.

"Yes, I could be pulled up, but it's not that simple. If a diver happens to be very deep when the hose breaks, his entire body gets squeezed—and that's the end of him."

"Squeezed?" she echoed.

"I've explained that water has pressure and the deeper you are, the greater the pressure. The air inside the suit and the helmet keep the diver from feeling the water pressure; but if the air is lost, the pressure can crush the diver to death. It's called the 'squeeze.' "

Cosy grimaced. "How can you keep diving when you know that might happen?"

Dan paused to look at her. "I don't take risks. Unless all my equipment is in top condition, I don't go down. And I never dive without a knowledgeable man, one I can trust, manning the pump and towline. Your father, in this case."

Cosy nodded, easing away from him to stand at the rail.

She wished she hadn't asked so many questions since now she had a specific horror to imagine happening under Kitchigami's blue water. When a shadow skimmed across the boat, she looked up, noting that small white clouds had appeared to scud across the sky. One of them had momentarily blocked the sun.

"Rain," Captain Marcos muttered from close behind her.

Startled, she turned to face him. His dark eyes were narrowed, but any other expression was hidden by his curly black beard.

"The clouds, they make shadows on the water," he said. "Means bad weather."

Cosy sniffed the air, trying to gauge its dampness as Hungry Moon could do. Was it going to rain? She couldn't be sure.

"If a storm is brewing, shouldn't we turn back?" she asked.

Captain Marcos grunted. *"Poderoso caballero es Don Dinero."*

"I don't understand."

"Is Spanish saying. Means *Señor* Money is one very strong man."

"Señor Money?" she repeated, still puzzled.

He shrugged. "Your father will wait for water to pour from the heavens before he'll give up. *Porque?* Why?" He made a sweeping gesture over the rail toward the water. *"El Dorado* calls. Gold."

Scowling, he took a step toward her. "Better no woman on my boat. *Maldito.* Not good. Already Tarse, he is much hurt. Better you stay home."

Cosy swallowed. "I will after this," she promised, wishing her back weren't against the rail so she could escape from the captain's anger.

"No birds follow us," he muttered, shaking his head. *"Muy mal.* Very bad." To her great relief, he moved away from her.

Turning to face the lake once again, Cosy glanced around, belatedly realizing that she'd seen no gulls since they'd cleared the harbor. Hungry Moon had taught her that birds fly inland before a storm. Yet the clouds were still small and white, not gray and heavy with rain or the ominous copper color that heralded the most violent of storms. With the sun shining so brightly, it was difficult to believe in Captain Marcos's dire prediction.

She glanced toward Black Water, wondering what he thought about the weather but not daring to ask him lest she break her word to her father. But he could hardly object to her watching Black Water, whose grace of movement as he worked was pleasing to her.

Recalling what Jacob had said about the People's village, she frowned. It might be true that the encampment could be cleaner, and it *was* true about the many dogs. But what Jacob didn't realize was that, in a bad winter, the dogs were a source of food for the People. No doubt he'd be horrified if she told him. Jacob didn't understand. He was like all other whites; he would never understand.

"Get out of the way, Cosy," her father ordered. "Dan's ready to dive."

She obeyed quickly, hurrying to stand near her father and watch as Dan climbed over the rail, down the ladder into the water, down and down until she could no longer see the top of his helmet. Did he worry about what could go wrong, she wondered, or were all his thoughts of the *Kaug* and freeing the gold buried somewhere inside her?

Dan had ignored Black Water's dream, not believing he could be in danger. Was the danger only to the fox, Dan, or to all aboard the *Sturgeon?* Cosy hadn't thought to ask Black Water if he knew. Breathing in dampness, she glanced hurriedly up at the sky. The clouds, though still white, had thickened. And wasn't there a smudge of darkness along the horizon? She edged closer to her father, who was intent on the air pump and the rope unwinding from the spool.

"Father?" she said hesitantly.

"Don't bother me, Cosy." His voice was impatient.

Taking another look at the horizon, she tried again. "I think a storm's coming, Father."

"You and that crepe-hanger Marcos. Damn it, we're not heading in until Dan has a chance to set off that dynamite charge. Hell, the sun's still shining; there's plenty of time."

Cosy started to protest, then thought the better of it, aware anything she might say would only annoy her father further. She retreated, staring anxiously at the increasing grayness on the horizon, the low line of clouds dark with rain. Who knew how soon they'd roll up the sky? All who lived near Kitchigami learned to fear the lake's sudden squalls. Why wouldn't her father listen to her?

Though she was half-afraid of him, she approached Captain Marcos. "A storm *is* coming," she said.

He gestured toward her father. "Tell him, not me."

"I did, but—" She paused and sighed.

Captain Marcos merely grunted. The dark-skinned Regg met her gaze, rolling his eyes as if agreeing with her but saying without words that he could do nothing. With only Black Water left to appeal to, she hesitated before taking a deep breath and walking purposefully toward him. "The weather—" she began in the People's tongue.

"Don't tell me," he said bitterly. "I'm not the captain and I'm not your father. I'm just a paid worker."

Biting her lip, Cosy returned to her father's side. "Please look at the sky," she begged. "I'm worried."

"I've seen the clouds. I know we're in for some rain. Dan's not ready to come up yet."

"Dan's under the water!" she cried. "He doesn't know what's happening up here. He can't even see the sky. If he could—"

"I know what I'm doing," Jephthah insisted. "We'll have time to run for the harbor after Dan has set the charges. We're less than four miles out."

The dark mass of clouds climbed higher. Cosy divided her attention between the sky and her father, whose unsmiling face had taken on a grim look that frightened her.

Finally, Captain Marcos stomped over to them. "Signal the diver," he ordered Jephthah. *"Pronto!"*

"All right, damn it!" Jephthah yanked hard on the rope—once, twice, three times—the agreed signal that Dan was about to be raised.

The captain stepped to the rail and stared into the water. "He comes up, yes?"

"I'm waiting for his answering signal."

Captain Marcos glared at him. "No more waiting. Pull him up!"

Jephthah began turning the winch handle, grunting with strain, and slowly the thick rope began to wind around the spool. "Black Water," he called, "I need some help here."

When Black Water put his hands on the handle, adding his strength to Jephthah's, the rope tautened but no longer coiled onto the spool.

"Stop!" Jephthah ordered Black Water. "Hold the rope as it is." He wiped sweat off his forehead with the back of his hand.

"What's the matter?" Cosy asked.

"Damn rope must have snagged on something down there, because we can't budge it. We'll have to wait for Dan to free the rope before we can pull him up."

"But what if he doesn't know it's caught?" Cosy asked.

"Wait and we all drown." Captain Marcos pointed to the north where angry blue-black clouds roiled.

"What the hell do you want me to do?" Jephthah shouted, glaring at the captain. "Cut the rope and leave him to die?"

Captain Marcos gestured toward the distant shoreline. "The storm, she'll blow us on those rocks when she hits, then we all die. One or all, you got to choose."

Cosy gasped in horror at his words. She stared uncomprehendingly at Black Water as he stripped to his breechclout. Belatedly realizing what he meant to do, she cried "No!" as he leaped onto the rail.

Black Water's dive was perfect. He hit the water cleanly and disappeared. Cosy held her breath, clutching the rail with both hands as she anxiously watched the ruffled water. After an eternity his head broke the surface many yards from the boat.

"Come back!" she called. "Come back!"

His dark head slid under the water once more.

"Good," Captain Marcos said, "he follows the rope. *Valiente,* a brave man."

A fierce pride in Black Water mixed with Cosy's fear for him. He'd seen what had to be done and had had the courage to do it. But would he be able to dive deep enough? Surely the rope must be snagged on the wreckage of the *Kaug,* and Dan had said the boat lay in a cleft too deep to reach without the protection of a suit.

Black Water's head rose above the surface again, this time farther away, and then went under. Clouds clutched at the sun with dark tentacles and the sails filled with the freshening wind, making the *Sturgeon* tug at her anchor. Waves slapped against the hull, rocking the boat.

"No time left," Captain Marcos warned.

Cosy turned on him furiously. "You can't leave them both to drown. What kind of a man are you?"

"A man who wishes to live, *señorita*. The storm, she comes fast." He strode to the anchor chain.

"Wait!" Jephthah's voice was thick with strain as he called to the captain. "The rope's loose. I'm pulling him up."

The captain paused, his hand on the anchor hoist. Regg rushed to help Jephthah turn the handle, and the rope coiled around and around the spool. Cosy's bonnet blew off her head, while the wind whipped her hair about her face.

At last the metal helmet broke through the surface, and Dan grabbed for the rope ladder. Jephthah reached to help him while Regg rushed to aid the captain in hoisting the anchor. Dan was safe.

But where was Black Water?

Cosy ran to clutch at the captain's arm. "No, don't raise the anchor," she begged. "Wait for Black Water."

Captain Marcos shrugged off her hand without replying and thrust her away from him so violently that she stumbled, almost falling. She rushed to her father, now helping Dan remove the helmet.

"Make the captain listen," she pleaded. "He mustn't leave Black Water behind. He can't!"

"Cosy, I can't do anything about it," Jephthah said.

Feeling the ship lift and move despite the fact the anchor was still being hoisted, Cosy drew in her breath and, as wind-blown rain slanted across the deck, staggered to the rail to search the roiling waters. She could see nothing.

Waves splashed high, drenching her, and tears ran down her cheeks to mingle with the rain lashing the boat. Frantically, she tore off her jacket and bent to unbutton her boots.

Strong arms jerked her upright, holding her firmly despite her struggle to free herself. "Let me go!" she sobbed. "I'm a good swimmer; I'll find him."

"Stop it!" Dan spoke into her ear, his grip tightening. "Don't be an idiot. No one can survive in those seas."

"Black Water won't drown," she sobbed. "He won't; he won't. He's a strong swimmer. Tell the captain to turn back—please!"

"He couldn't turn back if he tried," Dan said, urging her away from the rail and toward the cabin. "The boat's being driven shoreward by the wind. It'll take all his skill as well as some luck to hit the harbor entrance."

Through her misery and desperation, Cosy became aware that Dan still wore his suit. She longed to rend it from him, tear it into a thousand pieces and toss them into the teeth of the storm. Why had her father sought the gold? Why had he hired Dan to help him search for it? Better that the gold should lie hidden in the depths of Kitchigami forever.

Yet the fault really lay with her. She was the one who'd given her father Black Water's name; she was the one who'd traveled to the village and persuaded him to board the *Sturgeon.*

For you, Black Water had told her.

Sobs racked her as she realized she and she alone was guilty of letting him die. For her.

Wrapped in her father's coat, she huddled inside the small cabin with Dan and Jephthah while the wind raged and the boat shuddered through the angry waves.

"Marcos is taking a hell of a chance leaving the sails up," Jephthah muttered.

"If we don't make the harbor, we're done for anyway," Dan said. "Either we get there fast or not at all."

From where it lay on the deck, Dan's diving helmet stared up at her with its glassy eye as though Mishibezo himself were inside it. She shuddered and turned her face away.

"What went wrong down there?" Jephthah asked Dan. "Did the Indian reach you?"

Dan shook his head. "I never saw him. What I did notice was some commotion in the water above me. When I realized someone was diving, I knew I must be in trouble. The dynamite was partially fused but I left it and started back immediately, checking the air hose and the rope as I went. A piece of debris had shifted, and I found the rope wedged between it and a rock. It took me several minutes to work the rope loose, and then I signaled."

"Black Water saved your life," Cosy whispered, not looking at either man.

"Yes," Dan agreed, "I know that."

"We left him to die," she said dully. "I killed him."

"Come, Cosy, that's ridiculous," Jephthah protested. "Black Water dived into the lake of his own free will. No one forced him."

"He loved me," she said. "He came aboard the *Sturgeon* only because I asked him. He came despite his dream of—"

A horrendous crash cut off her words.

"The forward mast," Jephthah said. "I knew it would go." He ducked out of the cabin, returning moments later, grinning. "We made it! Damned if that surly black devil didn't bring us safely into the harbor."

The five of them waited out the worst of the storm in a

dock warehouse with the wind tearing at the roof and the rain smashing against the walls. Water ran under the closed door to pool at their feet. Cosy shivered in her sodden garments, her wet hair plastered against her head.

Captain Marcos crossed himself. "By God's grace we live," he said.

Cosy thought of Black Water adrift in the howling storm and knew he couldn't possibly survive, no matter how exceptional a swimmer he was. She wept for him, making no effort to wipe away her tears.

"Ah, the Indian," Captain Marcos said, evidently noting her distress. *"Valiente*—a good man. But the sea, she has no favorites. Good, bad, she takes them as she will."

Cosy wasn't comforted by his words, nor by the arm her father wrapped around her. She felt as though nothing would ever comfort her.

"If there'd been a way to save him," Dan told her, "I would have tried."

Cosy didn't reply.

"Do you think the charge might have gone off?" Jephthah asked Dan.

He shrugged. "It's possible. Who knows?"

They don't care about Black Water, she told herself. None of them. To them he's merely an Indian. No one cares about him except me.

When at last they reached home, Mina Howard took charge of Cosy, stripping off her wet clothes, toweling her hair dry, and putting her into a warm flannel nightgown before tucking her into bed while Rosalind hovered nearby, wringing her hands. Exhausted, Cosy plunged almost at once into a deep well of sleep, only to rouse some hours later to darkness and to grief. She rose and went to her window where a moon just past full gleamed into the room.

Outside, it bathed the pines in silver light. Small scudding clouds raced across the moon's face from time to time, briefly obscuring it, but the storm was over.

Cosy's heart weighed so heavy in her chest that it hurt to breathe. She sighed, turning from the window and leaving her room. Downstairs, she huddled on the window seat in the music room, gazing at the moonlight's silver trail along the river. A spirit trail.

"May the Great Spirit guide you safely to the Sky Path," she murmured.

Four days would Black Water's spirit travel before it came to the land of shadows. Four times would the fires be lit for him to show him the way.

She rose, plucked a copper holder containing a fat white candle from the marble-topped table, lit the candle with one of the matches kept in the drawer, and placed candle and holder on the sill of the window facing the river.

Surely Black Water's spirit would follow the river to the People's village before leaving on the long journey to the land of shadows, and her candle would light his way. Gazing at the tiny flame, she tried to picture him in her mind.

"Cosy."

Startled, she gasped, whirling to see Dan beside her.

"Are you all right?" he asked.

"I couldn't sleep," she said evasively.

"Nor could I. I feel responsible somehow for Black Water's death."

"You aren't at fault. I am."

"I'll never forget how you stood by the rail with the rain drenching you, ready to dive into that seething lake to rescue the man you loved. In a way, I hated to stop you, but of course, I couldn't let you plunge to your death."

She hadn't thought about dying, only of saving Black

Water. It would, she realized now, have been impossible. If Dan hadn't stopped her, she would have drowned.

"He was a brave man," Dan said, "diving at the risk of his own life to try to rescue me."

"I can't really believe Black Water's gone," she murmured.

"He must have drowned. No one could survive in those waters."

She knew Dan was right, but it was difficult to accept death. "This candle," she said, "is to light the darkness, for his spirit."

"You're shivering," Dan said. "You ought to go back to your room."

Any chill she felt was of the spirit. "What can it be like to leave one's body behind and travel the long journey to the Sky Path?"

Dan took a deep breath. Looking over her head into the moon-silvered night beyond the window, he said, "I think once you die, nothing matters. Only the living care about duty or honor or love."

Cosy sighed. "Black Water loved me. He wanted us to marry. Father was against it. Even Jacob said I wouldn't be happy in the People's village." Tears she couldn't shed burned her eyes. "He was wrong!"

Dan's gaze shifted to her. "What business is it of Jacob Thompson's whom you marry? I don't trust that man, Cosy. I didn't like him staying in this house, and I'm damn glad he went back to the Bigelow House before the storm. I hope to hell he remains there. Beware of him."

She stared up at Dan in confusion. Though she was angry with Jacob, her anger had nothing to do with whether she trusted him or not. What did Dan think she ought to beware of? He couldn't know that Jacob had kissed her.

"You'll catch a chill sitting here," Dan said. Reaching down, he grasped her hand and pulled her to her feet. "I'll see you to your room."

At her door, he bent and kissed her on the forehead. "Try to sleep," he murmured before leaving her.

Once in bed, Cosy closed her eyes, expecting Black Water's image to appear. Instead, what she saw was Jacob's face, troubled and yearning, the way he'd looked after they'd kissed at the river beach.

No! she told herself. Banish him! Jacob means nothing to you. Black Water was the man you loved, not Jacob. Black Water, whom you'll mourn forever.

When at last sleep's dark embrace claimed her, she dreamed of traveling above the earth with her white spirit lynx. Far and long they drifted under the moon, at last coming to rest in a forest glade where she lay curled against the lynx for warmth and comfort. Under the moon's pale light she snuggled close, stroking its soft fur, knowing this was where she belonged. Only then did she realize the lynx was no longer white but a dappled red-brown, not her spirit lynx, but the other . . .

She woke with Jacob's name on her lips.

Sixteen

When, two days later, Cosy was faced with attending the dinner party her father had planned, she hadn't the heart for it. "I don't wish to be there," Cosy told her father at breakfast.

He frowned at her. "Nonsense. It'll do you a world of good to see a few people. It's too bad Black Water drowned, but that's no reason to shut yourself away from everyone."

"I'd rather be excused," she persisted.

"You *will* attend," he told her in a tone that brooked no argument.

Since she had no choice, that evening Cosy, with help from Hilda, donned her new gown. Her mother's jet beads contrasted sharply with the elegant sweep of white satin, their darkness glittering against her skin as well as the soft shimmer of the dress. She pulled her hair back from her face and caught it with black combs high on her head as waves rippled down her back. It was not at all stylish, but the effect suited the gown.

Hilda drew in her breath, staring wide-eyed. "I swear to God you're as beautiful as a bride."

Gazing at her mirror image, Cosy smiled sadly. A bride, when there was no longer any man she cared to marry?

"You don't look nothing like yourself," Hilda added.

Made uneasy by Hilda's words, Cosy studied herself. It

did seem as though the familiar Cosy had hidden some-
where, leaving behind a haughty stranger as a replacement.
Perhaps the old Cosy was lost forever. Like Black Water.
Sighing, she turned away from the mirror.

"Very handsome, Cosy," her father said when she joined
him in the parlor.

Dan rose and bowed. "You should always dress in
white," he told her. "It's particularly suited to you."

Rosalind, approaching the parlor, heard Dan's remark to
Cosy and her mouth tightened. She had to admit that her
sister was striking, but the gown was certainly not made
in the current style and the stark contrast of the jet beads
and buttons with the white satin was unsettling.

Her own gown had been copied from a fashion magazine
she'd brought from Boston. The upper skirt was of a pale
rose tulle over an overskirt of rose silk crossed by bands
of wine velvet repeated at the bodice's low neckline. A
quilled border finished the hem. Her rose-amethyst teardrop
necklace matched the pale rose of the gown to perfection.
If she did say so herself, she looked prettier than she ever
had before.

Yet knowing how well she looked did little to boost her
confidence. If only she hadn't seen Dan coming from
Cosy's room two nights before. The discovery had gnawed
at her ever since. What had he and Cosy been doing? She
greatly feared she knew.

Oblivious to the knock at the front door, she took a deep
breath, forced a smile, and swept into the parlor where she
twirled to show off the gown.

"My beautiful Rosie," Jephthah murmured.

Her father's admiration was not what she needed. Tilting
her head, she glanced at Dan through her eyelashes.

"I'm struck speechless," he said. "A vision of roses."

Was he making fun of her? Determined not to reveal how she felt, Rosalind clung to her smile. "What do you think, Cosy?" she asked.

"I've never seen you look lovelier." Cosy sounded sincere, but Rosalind couldn't decide whether or not to believe her.

Jacob's arrival in the parlor was a welcome relief. He glanced from one sister to the other and shook his head. "Snow White and Rose Red," he said. "Two fairy-tale princesses. Cosy, you've achieved an elegance that royalty might well envy; and Rosalind, your beauty rivals any rose that ever bloomed."

Rosalind pretended pleasure while she examined Jacob's words to try to discover if she'd come out ahead or behind. No more than even, she told herself. But it didn't really matter, because she didn't care whether or not Jacob found her beautiful. Dan was the only man who mattered.

Was it possible Dan had shared Cosy's bed? Lain with her sister as he had with her? Kissed Cosy and caressed her? Rosalind thrust the disturbing thought aside and smiled up at Jacob. Seeing admiration in his light brown eyes, she wondered if he meant only to flirt with her as he had aboard the *Pewabic* or whether his feelings for her had grown warmer since then.

She flashed a quick look at Dan, who was talking with her father. Two could play at Dan's game. Placing her hand on Jacob's arm, she murmured, "I do hope you are to be my dinner partner this evening. Since you moved back to the hotel, we've scarcely seen you."

"Not by my choice, I assure you," Jacob said. "I am a working man, you know, and duty comes before pleasure. I sincerely regret that duty also will take me back to Houghton tomorrow."

Rosalind pretended to pout. "So soon? I'm beginning to believe you don't care for our company."

"Your belief is misplaced. If business hadn't interfered, you would have seen so much of me that you'd have been relieved to hear I was departing on the morning boat."

Rosalind hoped Dan had heard every word of her conversation with Jacob. "Do tell me you plan to return shortly," she cooed to Jacob.

"You have my word," he assured her. "I can barely tear myself away as it is." He paused and glanced at the others. "I heard about the drowning. Your sister seems sadly affected by the loss."

Rosalind examined Cosy's face. Smooth and cold, only the mournful droop to her mouth conveyed any emotion. But if Cosy had loved that Indian brave so much, why would she allow Dan to make love to her? If she had. If he had. Why else, though, would he visit her room at such an hour?

Other guests began to arrive, diverting her. All through dinner Rosalind laughed and flirted with Jacob and the other male guests, but her heart wasn't in it. She had no real sense of what they said or what she replied, because her attention was fixed on Dan. She watched him covertly, miserably wondering if he preferred Cosy to her.

I'll confront him with what he did, she told herself as she sipped yet another glass of wine, not caring that her head was already spinning dizzily.

After the meal ended and the men rejoined the ladies, Jephthah insisted she play for their guests.

"Oh, not first," she said. "Jacob must be first. I insist." Despite her father's frown, she refused to back down, aware she was in no condition to sit at the piano. Not so much because of the wine but because her nerves were on edge. She *had* to confront Dan soon.

When Jacob began playing, Rosalind stood by the piano for a few moments, then slipped away and sought out Dan, grasping his arm and urging him from the music room, careless of who might see them.

"This is unwise," Dan muttered as they passed the parlor where some of the guests had lingered to talk.

"I don't care." She struggled to keep her voice low. "I must talk to you."

He glanced around, shrugged, and followed her into the entry. She'd planned to make use of the library, but the sound of men's voices coming from inside the room made her veer away toward the stairs.

Dan halted, staring at her, eyebrows raised. She tugged at his arm. Her room was the only place she could be sure of privacy.

"Have you lost your mind?" Dan asked. Grasping her hand, he pulled her with him to the front door, opened it, and led her outside. "This gives us the excuse you needed—fresh air, feeble though it might be. If we were caught upstairs, no excuse would be possible, as you very well know. Now just what the hell is so important it can't wait?"

She jerked her hand free and stared up at him in the light of the waning moon. "Why were you in bed with Cosy?" she demanded.

He said nothing, gazing down at her with an expression she couldn't read in the pale light.

"Answer me!" she cried, her head spinning. "I know you were in her room because I saw you come out."

"You've had too much wine," he told her coldly.

Tears filled her eyes. "Don't you love me?" she asked, choking on the words. "Don't you love me at all?"

"Of course I do." He reached for her, pulling her close. "You know I do."

Clinging to him, she tried to convince herself he meant what he said. "But if you love me, why were you with Cosy?" she wailed.

"She watched Black Water drown. She needed comfort."

"Oh!" Rosalind wrenched away and struck at him, but he caught her wrist. "I hate you!" she cried.

Dan yanked her to him, holding her so she couldn't move. "I didn't promise you fidelity. As a matter of fact, my love, no promises were exchanged by us. For all I know, you may have offered the charming Mr. Thompson your favors. You certainly seemed friendly enough tonight."

Rosalind listened in indignation mixed with confusion. Was Dan jealous? How dare he be jealous after making love to her sister? But had he really admitted to that?

"After all," Dan went on, "I wasn't aboard the *Pewabic*. How do I know what you and Jacob Thompson might have—"

"Shut up!" Her voice rose. "You know you were the first man I ever—" She broke off. "You *know* you were. You're beastly. You don't love me; you don't even know what love is; you aren't worth—"

He cut her off by kissing her and, though she writhed and twisted to free herself, he held her fast. She tried to keep her anger alive, but the heated passion of his kiss made her forget everything other than her need for him. When he finally released her, she was trembling so much that she had to clutch at him to stay on her feet.

"We can't stay here; we're sure to be missed," he said. "Since you're not fit to rejoin the party, I'd best take you around to the kitchen door and get Hilda to help you upstairs and into bed."

"Dan," she pleaded, staring up at him, as dizzy from his nearness as she was from the wine.

He gripped her shoulders, holding her away from him. "Don't ever question me again, Rosalind. I am what I am. Either accept me or forget me, but don't ask me to explain what I do. It's not that I don't love you—never think I don't." He bent and brushed his lips over hers so tenderly she thought she might swoon. Then, with his arm around her waist, he led her toward the back of the house.

Rosalind awoke the next morning with a throbbing headache, a most unpleasant taste in her mouth, and the realization that Dan would never tell her exactly what was between him and Cosy. If anything. She managed to crawl from the bed and wash. Then, uncomfortable with summoning Hilda—good heavens, what must the girl think of her after last night?—she dressed herself and went downstairs just as the clock on the landing struck twelve.

Mrs. Howard made her a cup of tea and offered her dry toast, saying, "You'll feel better if you eat this."

The last thing Rosalind wanted was food, but she decided the housekeeper might know what she was talking about. She sat at the kitchen table and choked down the toast. Then, carrying her second cup of tea, she wandered from the kitchen, wondering where everyone was. She found Cosy in the music room, staring out at the river.

"Where are father and Dan?" Rosalind asked as she sat in a chair beside the piano. "Surely, Dan doesn't plan to dive again. Not after—" She broke off, belatedly remembering about Black Water.

"Before he left last night, Jacob asked me to say goodbye to you," Cosy said, instead of giving her a direct answer. "He planned to catch the *Leeland* this morning."

Rosalind sighed. "I meant to go down and see him off but I woke too late."

"He knew you weren't feeling well. Dan told us Hilda had helped you to your room."

"I'm afraid I drank too much wine," Rosalind admitted, putting a hand to her head. "I had no idea overindulgence could make one feel so awful the next day."

"If you'd like, I'll fix you a tisane," Cosy offered.

Rosalind was about to agree when she remembered that it was likely to be some strange Indian remedy. She finished the last swallow of tea and set her cup and saucer on a nearby table. "Thank you, but I think not," she said.

"Father and Dan probably did see Jacob off," Cosy said. "They left for the docks early to watch the new mast being fitted onto the *Sturgeon*." Her voice turned fierce. "I wish she'd sunk like the *Kaug*, sunk so deep no one could ever find her."

Rosalind, listening to her sister's bitter words, couldn't help wondering if Cosy also wished she and their father and Dan, plus the boat's crew, had gone down with the *Sturgeon* and drowned like Black Water.

"I hope Dan won't dive again," she said, her thoughts fixed on him. "I can't imagine why he'd want to after what happened during the storm."

"Señor Money," Cosy muttered.

Rosalind was taken aback. "Who?"

"I meant that Dan and Father believe recovering the gold comes before all else."

After a short silence, Rosalind said, "I'm sorry about Black Water."

Cosy didn't reply immediately. When she did speak, her voice had regained its usual calm. "Jacob said he'd be back again near the end of August."

"How nice," Rosalind said listlessly.

"I've noticed you don't seem to care for Jacob's company, though you sometimes pretend to."

Rosalind shrugged, not feeling well enough to wax indignant over what was none of her sister's affair.

Cosy rose from the window seat and crossed to Rosalind's chair, looking down at her. "The truth is you're not interested in Jacob because you're in love with Dan. Do you think you're being fair in not telling Jacob?"

Rosalind stared at her in total disbelief. How dare Cosy say such things to her? "What do you care?" she snapped, her head throbbing painfully as she got to her feet to face her sister.

"I wouldn't like to see Jacob hurt."

"You're a fine one to talk! Enticing Dan to your room on the very same night you lost your Indian lover."

Cosy blinked, seemingly at a loss.

"I saw Dan leave your room." Rosalind spat the words at her.

"But he—I—" Cosy hesitated. "You're mistaken," she finished.

"I suppose you expect me to believe he was comforting you."

"Yes, he was."

"Damn you, Dan's mine!" Rosalind cried, her anger at the pair of them erupting. "Mine! I'm warning you here and now to keep away from him. I won't be responsible for what may happen if you get in my way."

Cosy turned without a word and stalked from the music room.

In the days that followed, the two were polite to one another, but the breach between them remained. As July gave way to the sometimes sultry heat of August, the *Stur-*

geon was repaired and Tarse recovered enough to return to work. To Rosalind's dismay, Dan resumed diving despite her protests.

Cosy's strange expression, *Señor* Money, echoed in Rosalind's head. Was gold worth risking death? Both her father and Dan certainly believed it was.

Rosalind tried to ignore her fears for Dan's safety, accepting several invitations to afternoon teas and musical soirees. Each time she planned to go, though, a bout of sickness intervened.

"Summer complaint," Jephthah told her after she was more-or-less recovered from her third attack. "My grandmother used to dose us with sulfur and molasses each spring to avoid it."

Rosalind grimaced. "Aunt Rhoda had a more palatable remedy. She used spices and cinnamon bark, but I'm not sure how she made it up."

A week later, Rosalind took to her bed, again suffering from nausea and vomiting. Cosy came to her room and offered her medicine, saying, "This is a tea made from raspberry leaves and blackberry root. Hungry Moon cured many of the children at the People's village with this same infusion."

After staring suspiciously at the cup Cosy held, Rosalind shook her head. "I'm not an Indian child."

"But I'm sure this will help you."

Glancing toward the open door of her bedroom, Rosalind lowered her voice. "How do I know what you might give me? You've never wanted me here."

Cosy stared at her, aghast. "You can't believe I'd harm you!"

Rosalind shrugged. "I don't know what you might do

to get me out of the way. You're not like me; you're half-savage. Go away. Leave me alone."

When Cosy did as she asked, Rosalind fretted. She wasn't accustomed to being ill—Aunt Rhoda had often marveled at her good health. But now it seemed she was tired much of the time, besides her bouts of vomiting. Worst of all, since she seldom felt able to join the others for dinner, she saw very little of Dan.

August was half over by the time Rosalind recovered enough to be up and about most of the time, though she lacked the energy to accept social engagements. This left her with no one for company during the day except Cosy. Since she didn't care to talk to her sister, Rosalind grew bored. She was sitting in the parlor embroidering one sunny afternoon when she saw Cosy pass by the open door, tying on her bonnet.

Dropping her fancy work, Rosalind sprang to her feet, crying, "Wait! Where are you going?"

Cosy paused and replied, "For a short walk."

"I'll go with you."

"If you like."

After collecting her hat, gloves, and a parasol, Rosalind followed her sister out the front door. Cosy crossed the drive, skirting the stable, obviously heading for the river bluff. As they neared the stable, Rosalind noticed a man emerging from the dark interior. When he saw her, he ducked his head and hurried away, keeping his back turned toward her.

Rosalind frowned. The man was not Jim but a stranger. And yet—hadn't she seen him somewhere before? "Who is that?" she asked Cosy, nodding toward him.

"I don't know," Cosy replied without much interest. "Perhaps a friend of Jim's."

Rosalind might have dismissed the incident as trivial except for the man's furtive behavior. For some reason he'd tried to avoid them. Or was it only her? Why? Because he was afraid she'd recognize him? She made up her mind to question Jim when she and Cosy returned from their walk.

"I'm glad you're feeling better," Cosy said.

"So am I," Rosalind told her. During her unwilling sojourn in bed she'd decided to cast aside her suspicions about Dan and her sister and accept their explanation that he'd been merely comforting Cosy that night, preferring to believe he hadn't made love to her. On the other hand, she wasn't going to admit this to either of them.

Searching for conciliatory words, she said, "I know Black Water's death left a scar. I regret that I haven't been more sympathetic."

"He died bravely," Cosy said.

"And he saved Dan's life, so Father tells me."

Cosy nodded.

"Did you really love Black Water so very much?"

"He wanted to marry me," Cosy said. "I think we would have been happy together if Father had ever agreed to the marriage."

Rosalind glanced at her curiously. "You really wouldn't have gone against Father's wishes to marry the man you loved?"

Cosy sighed. "I didn't, did I? And now it's too late."

Moved, Rosalind laid her hand on Cosy's arm. "I'm sorry you lost your chance for happiness."

Cosy stopped, turning to look at her. "I don't think you'd allow Father's disapproval to stop *you.*"

Rosalind's lips curled into a smile. "You're right. If the man I love asked me to be his wife, nothing would or could prevent me from agreeing. But—" She paused and shook her head, her smile fading. Cosy knew as well as she did that Dan wasn't a marrying man.

"I believe Dan loves you," Cosy said as they walked on.

Her sister might be speaking the truth as she saw it. Rosalind couldn't be sure, but she fervently hoped Cosy's belief was correct.

On the way back to the house, Rosalind stopped at the stables, telling Cosy she wanted to speak to Jim. Waiting until after her sister had walked on, Rosalind sought out the handyman.

"I saw a man here earlier," she said to Jim. "A friend of yours?"

"Nope."

"What did he want, then?" she asked.

Jim glanced up from the board he was sawing. "Nothing much."

With frustration, she watched him resume his work. Jim could be difficult. At first she'd thought he didn't like her specifically; but on further acquaintance, she'd decided his dislike wasn't personal since it included most, if not all, women. As she tried to think of a way to pry information from him, it suddenly occurred to her where she'd seen the stranger's face before and she drew in her breath sharply. He'd been on the *Phoenix*. He was the man who'd addressed Dan as Major Eaton.

"He was asking you about Mr. Rackham, wasn't he?" she accused Jim.

"Maybe," Jim admitted.

"I insist you tell me what he said."

Jim shrugged. "Wanted me to deliver a message is all."

"What message?" Her voice quivered with eagerness.

He glanced at her again, then turned his head and spat

tobacco juice the other way. "I'll be telling Mr. Rackham that."

Wheedle as she would, Jim refused to say another word and she finally gave up. Returning to the house, she could hardly wait to confront Dan when he and her Father returned this evening. The man was presumably his confederate and friend, here in Ojibway to meet with Dan—or was it Major Eaton?

"Did Jim tell you who the man was?" Cosy asked when she came into the house.

Taken aback—she hadn't revealed that she'd meant to ask the handyman about the stranger—Rosalind shook her head. "Jim isn't much of a talker."

Cosy smiled in agreement. "He has a good heart, though. And he'd do anything for Father."

The men came home very late that evening, missing dinner. Jephthah entered first, throwing the door open wide and shouting, "We've done it, damned if we haven't!"

Dan followed him in, grinning. Both men weaved on their feet, making Rosalind realize they'd stopped at the Bigelow House for a few drinks.

Jephthah looked all around, then put a finger to his lips in an exaggerated gesture of secrecy. "C'mon to the library, li'l Rosie. You, too, Cosy. Can't take a chance."

When they'd gathered in the library with the door closed, Jephthah swaggered into the middle of the room. "Told you I knew where it was, didn't I?" he boasted.

"Smartest man in the country," Dan avowed.

"And I got me the best damn diver in the world," Jephthah crowed.

"Does this mean you've finally found the gold?" Rosalind asked him.

" 'Course we did. Right there in the *Kaug*."

"Where is it?" Rosalind asked, relieved to think that Dan wouldn't have to dive any more.

"Safe enough," her father said. "Dan's rigged up a special cage to hold it."

"Are you're saying the gold is still down there on the bottom of the lake?" Cosy asked.

Jephthah nodded. "Going back tomorrow to haul it aboard." He peered owlishly at her, then turned to Dan. "She doesn't want to celebrate," he said sadly. "My li'l girl's not happy for me. My own daughter."

"I'm glad you have your desire close at hand," Cosy said.

"How 'bout you, Rosie?" he demanded, swinging around to stare at her. Before she could answer, he shook his head. " 'Nother long-faced gal," he said to Dan. "What's the matter with 'em?"

"Didn't want us to find the gold," Dan suggested.

Jephthah laughed. " 'Fraid you'd leave is more like it." He shook his finger at Rosalind. "Saw you making eyes at Dan. Can't have that. Dan's a travelin' man. Always travelin' on. Right, Dan?"

" 'S'right," Dan said. "Places to go. Things to do."

Rosalind, furious with the pair of them and at the same time worried about Dan because he wasn't through diving after all, glared from one to the other.

"Wouldn't you like something to eat, Father?" Cosy asked. "Dan? Mrs. Howard has kept your dinner warm."

Jephthah shook his head. "Gonna have 'nother drink."

While her father searched for his brandy bottle, Rosalind edged closer to Dan. "Has Jim spoken to you?" she whispered.

Dan blinked at her. "Jim?"

"Ssh," she warned. She didn't care if Cosy heard her,

but her father mustn't. "I'm going into the music room. Join me when you get the chance."

"What's that, Rosie?" Jephthah asked, turning to her, bottle in hand.

"I said I was going to play the piano," she told him.

Alone in the music room, she sat on the stool and stared at the piano keys. Traveling on. Places to go. She gritted her teeth and began to play.

" '. . . and we'll all drink stone wine when Johnny comes marching home,' " she sang, banging out the march furiously.

"What's this about Jim?" Dan spoke into her ear and she misplayed a chord, startled by his nearness. She hadn't heard him come in.

"Don't stop," he ordered. "Go on playing."

She glanced at him, realizing his speech was no longer slurred. Her father hadn't been feigning intoxication but Dan must have been. Why had he pretended? Was he always playing a role?

Obediently she went on with the music. "Jim has a message for you," she said. "From a man I've seen before."

"What man?" he demanded. "And where's Jim?"

"I don't know the man's name," she said, "but he spoke to Major Eaton aboard the *Phoenix*. As for Jim, quite likely he's gone home for the night."

"Christ! I'll have to find Jim right away." He strode toward the door, pausing momentarily to add, "Tell your father I went for a walk."

She nodded, allowing the song to trail off as soon as Dan disappeared from her view. By the time she rose and returned to the library, Dan was nowhere in sight. She found Cosy arranging a pillow behind Jephthah's head to prevent it from lolling sideways as he slumped in his chair.

"He's had too much to drink," Cosy said. "Chances are he'll sleep here all night. I'll fetch him a quilt."

"Dan's gone out," Rosalind said. "He thought a walk might clear his head."

"Do you mind very much?" Cosy asked.

"Mind?"

"About Dan's leaving now that the gold's been found."

"He hasn't gone yet," Rosalind said grimly.

Cosy gazed at her for a moment but said nothing more before leaving the room.

Dan intends to go without me, Rosalind told herself as she climbed the stairs to her room. He doesn't intend to marry me; he never did. Tears pricked her eyes, and she blinked them back. Crying wouldn't help. What would, if anything?

Seventeen

Finding his way at night by the glimmering light of the moon was second nature to Dan. He was tired for he'd worked hard today—diving was never easy—and it would have taken less effort to saddle a horse than hike into town, but a man on foot is less conspicuous than one on horseback. Above all, Dan meant to remain as inconspicuous as possible. As he climbed the hill leading to Jephthah's house, he nodded with satisfaction. He was no more than a dive away from accomplishing what he'd set out to do. And just in time for Hawkins's arrival.

As for Jephthah, he didn't feel he was cheating the man. Without a diver there'd be no gold, and Dan knew he was the best diver to be found in this country. He might have equals across the Atlantic, but none here. Dan chuckled. Jephthah would never realize exactly how good a diver he was.

Tomorrow night he and Hal Hawkins would row out and recover what he'd stashed away under the lake's cold, concealing waters. His bonus. No one knew how much gold the *Kaug* had carried, not even Jephthah, so there was little risk to him, even though he was aware Jephthah didn't quite trust him. Which was fair enough—he didn't altogether trust Jephthah Collins either.

The way he'd arranged things, both he and Jephthah would come out ahead. And his extra share would be used for a better cause than investing in a chancy copper mine. A few days more, and he'd be wiping the mud of the Upper Peninsula from his heels, leaving without regrets.

Dan frowned. Well, maybe one. Rosalind had gotten under his skin in a way no other woman ever had. Pretty as she was, it wasn't her looks that intrigued him as much as her daring spirit. Her refusal to be cowed had attracted him from the first. Not to mention her eager response to his lovemaking. Untutored as she was in the art, she possessed a fiery passion that could drive a man wild. He grimaced as he felt his body respond to the mere memory of their last fervid embrace.

Damn the girl! She'd be difficult to forget.

Wrapped in her gray cloak and crouched on the ground behind the lilac bush near the front door, Rosalind started at the eerie cry that seemed to float toward her on the night breeze. Telling herself firmly it was no more than an owl, she still couldn't prevent a shiver. How could Cosy ever have tolerated living in a primitive Indian camp where she was so close to creatures of the outdoors? While Rosalind was aware owls wouldn't harm her, their mournful hoots were disturbing.

The night had grown progressively cooler as she waited behind the bushes, determined to intercept Dan before he reentered the house. She wrapped the cloak closer about her, trying to ignore the metallic taste of nausea rising in her throat.

Gold was metallic, too, she thought. And wouldn't dead men's gold be unlucky? Hadn't it already been? Besides the crew of the ill-fated *Kaug*, there'd been the unknown diver from the Caribbean who'd never risen from his last dive and Cosy's friend Black Water, whose body hadn't been recovered either. All dead. Even if Dan returned from his final dive after retrieving the gold, would misfortune follow him and her father, too?

Or would the misfortune be hers when Dan left Ojibway and she never saw him again?

Footsteps! Rosalind shifted to peer cautiously between the branches of the lilac bushes. In the pale light of the lowering moon, she saw a man approaching and knew it was Dan, for no other man walked with such assurance. She rose and slipped around the bushes to confront him.

"What the hell?" he swore, stopping abruptly. "Rosalind?"

"I waited for you. Did you see that man?"

"Keep your voice down," he warned.

"All right. But did you?"

His "yes" was reluctant.

"What did he want? Are they after you?"

"Who? What do you mean?"

"The Union Army," she said with some exasperation. "Whoever it is they send to hunt down spies. How should I know who that might be?"

He chuckled. "No one's after me."

"Then why is that man from the *Phoenix* here?"

"That's my business, love, not yours."

She hadn't expected him to tell her, but she'd reached her own conclusions during her long wait. "If the Union Army's not after you, then the message must have been that the Rebs want you to try again. I'm right, aren't I?"

"Ssh!" he cautioned. "Windows are open. Let's get farther away from the house."

Rosalind waited until they reached the other side of the barberry hedge before saying, "Last week I heard you and

Father talking about some Confederate proposal to exchange prisoners."

"So we did."

When he didn't go on, she resisted the impulse to punch
him on the arm. "You must think I'm exceedingly stupid,"
she snapped. "If General Grant has refused to exchange
prisoners again, as he refused last April, then it stands to
reason that your Rebel friends are planning another attempt
to free the Johnson Island Confederate prisoners. Just as
you tried to do last May when you pirated the *Phoenix.*"

"Your imagination is most colorful."

"I'm right," she insisted. "You won't admit it, but I'm
sure of it. Why else would that man come seeking you?"

Dan didn't answer.

Rosalind took a deep breath. "You ought to know by
now I'd never give you away. At least tell me if you're
going off with that man."

"I'm not finished with my responsibility to your father,"
he said.

"You will be soon. What then?" She tried to see his
expression, but the moon was too low to cast enough light.
"You'll be caught," she said desperately. "Caught and
hanged. I heard them talking about what happens to spies."

"I've never been caught. I won't be."

"There's always a first time. It's bad enough that you're
leaving me behind, but I can't bear to think you might die."
She stumbled over the last word.

"Stop worrying about what hasn't happened," he said.
"Because it won't happen. And I haven't left yet." He
reached to pull her into his arms. "We still have tonight."

"I want to be with you always," she whispered.

"Nothing is for always," Dan told her. "Nothing lasts."

Rosalind thought her heart would break at the sadness

in his voice, but then his lips came down on hers and the fire only he could ignite flared within her and she melted into his embrace.

Her eager response inflamed him. He had to have her now. Tonight. God knew, this might be the last time. Tasting her sweetness, feeling the soft warmth of her body pressed against him, he regretted more than ever that he must leave her. But he had no choice. In time she'd forget him and, in the end, she'd be better off without him. As for him, he didn't need anyone but himself. That's the way it always had been and the way it always would be.

Releasing her, he led her toward the pine grove, one arm holding her close to his side. In the scented darkness under the trees, he spread her cape on the ground for her to lie on, his desire spinning out of control when he discovered she wore only her nightgown underneath.

"You little minx, you knew what would happen," he accused as he shed his clothes and pulled her down onto the cape with him.

"I knew what I wanted to happen," she murmured, twining her fingers in his chest hair before sliding her hand lower.

He caught her wrist, aware he was closer to the edge than she realized. "Whatever became of the sweet, innocent girl I met on the *Phoenix?*" he teased.

"Oh, sir, I fear I was changed forever after my ravishment by a bold pirate," she said with mock dismay, snuggling against him.

Dan chuckled as he dipped his head to kiss her, his hands closing around her breasts, full and taut, her nipples already swollen with need. He relished her moan of delight. There was nothing he'd rather do than pleasure Rosalind.

Somewhere in the pine grove an owl hooted four times, momentarily distracting him, reminding him of how Black

Water had once summoned Cosy to a lover's meeting in this same grove and now never would again. His arms tightened around Rosalind.

She's mine, he told himself. Mine and mine alone.

Driven by the need to possess her utterly, he plunged inside her and, urged on by the erotic movement of her hips, thrust hard and fast, mindless with desire, feeling her match his rhythm, hearing her gasp his name, her voice rising higher as she spiraled to fulfillment.

He joined her at the peak with a shout of "Mine!" then, clinging together, they tumbled over the edge.

Rosalind, resting her head against Dan's chest, listened to the steady beat of his heart, smiling to herself as she recalled what he'd cried at the climax of their lovemaking. *Mine.*

It was true, she'd always be his, forever and ever. Her smile faded as she realized that, though he'd been totally hers during the time they'd made love, she had no assurance he really *was* hers in the same sense that she was his.

Nothing lasts, he'd said. That could only mean he intended to go off without her.

She sat up abruptly and slammed her fist hard against his shoulder. "Don't you dare leave me!" she cried, beating her fists against his chest. "I won't let you leave me!"

Cosy woke with a start to find Mina Howard standing beside her bed. "What is it?" she said, hurriedly rising, realizing from the room's dim light that it was barely dawn.

"When I came to work, I met a boy with a message for you from Hungry Moon," Mina said. "He waits by the river beach with a canoe. You must go to her." She glided from the room.

Retrieving her doeskins from the back of the wardrobe, Cosy dressed quickly and eased quietly down the back stairs. Mina was waiting in the kitchen with a packet of bread and cheese for her to eat on the way.

"Thank you," Cosy said, her hand on the doorknob.

"Wait. I have something to say," Mina told her. "Your sister's been ill lately."

Cosy nodded impatiently, eager to be off.

"She also has had no blood flow for two moons," Mina added significantly.

Hungry Moon had taught Cosy how to recognize many signs and symptoms, so she understood immediately what Mina was saying. Rosalind was pregnant. And there could be no doubt the child she carried within her was Dan's.

"You'll have to tell her what's wrong with her," Mina said. "She doesn't know. It's not too late to—" She didn't finish, but she didn't need to. What had worked for Hilda might also work for Rosalind.

"We'll talk about it later," Cosy promised and left the house, putting her new worry over her sister aside in her anxiety about her foster mother.

At the river beach, she found young Eagle Feather waiting with a canoe. Though it was upstream, with both of them paddling, they soon arrived at the village. Hungry Moon was not waiting to greet her, but Cosy, her heart filled with dread, hadn't expected her to be. She jumped from the canoe and rushed toward her foster mother's lodge, only to be intercepted by a young girl.

"She lies beneath the trees," the girl said.

Cosy eyed her, not quite recognizing the plump face. Then yet again . . . "Silver Willow?" she questioned.

The girl ducked her head, smiling shyly. "Yes, I'm Hungry Moon's helper," she said softly. "She needs two of us,

for she is very sick." Silver Willow led the way toward a
stand of young birch.

"Hungry Moon likes to be where the trees watch over
her," she said. "Last night she dreamed, and so she sent
for you. Spotted Fawn and I have been watching but I found
you first, even though I'm younger." She smiled proudly.

Silver Willow could be no more than nine, at the most,
while Spotted Fawn must have seen at least sixteen winters.
Old enough to marry.

Hungry Moon lay on a reed platform beneath the guard-
ian trees, Spotted Fawn at her side. "Leave us," the old
woman whispered to the girl.

When she was alone with Hungry Moon, Cosy knelt
beside the platform, afraid to touch her foster mother lest
she inadvertently cause pain. The hand of death lay clearly
on the stick-thin old woman's face. Only her dark eyes still
glowed with life. Her skin had the yellowish tinge of fatal
sickness.

"I have come," Cosy said softly. "You dreamed and you
sent for me and I am here."

Hungry Moon lifted a feeble hand, and Cosy grasped it
gently. "We will not meet again until the time comes when
we both are in the land of the spirits." Hungry Moon's
voice was surprisingly strong.

Recognizing she was about to be given a final command
from the dying woman, an order she must carry out, Cosy
swallowed her grief and asked, "What would you have me
do?"

"You know Spotted Fawn has taken your place," Hungry
Moon said.

Tears welled in Cosy's eyes.

"Don't cry, my Koko, for you can't be replaced in my
heart," the dying woman assured her. "There you will al-

ways be my own white owlet. But your way is no longer with the People, and we must have a medicine woman."

"I should have stayed with you," Cosy mourned. "Here is the only true happiness."

"No. Your future lies elsewhere. A future where danger stalks your path. I warn you again that you must tread warily, trusting in no one."

"I heed your words."

"I do not fully understand my dream of the lynx and the wolf," Hungry Moon went on. "I only know they will meet and oppose one another and, when they do, you will be in deadly peril. Be careful."

"I will try to avoid danger."

"There is more. I need your promise you will do as I ask. You must promise without knowing what it is I ask of you."

"I will do anything you tell me," Cosy replied without hesitation. "I promise."

Hungry Moon closed her eyes briefly and when she opened them again Cosy flinched at the pain she saw there. "Where is the medicine to ease you?" she asked.

"The pain I feel is not mine, it is yours," Hungry Moon told her. "You have promised me, and I shall watch from the Spirit World to hold you to your vow."

"I have promised," Cosy repeated.

Hungry Moon sighed. "He is not dead," she whispered. "Black Water lives."

Cosy gaped at her, the name hanging between them.

"He recovers his strength with the others of his Wolf totem who live in the village over the mountains to the west, where the storm left him."

Scarcely able to believe what she was hearing, Cosy

didn't at first connect Black Water's miraculous deliverance from death with the promise she'd made to Hungry Moon.

"What you tell me gladdens my heart," she said.

"We're all happy he lives," Hungry Moon told her. "Especially Spotted Fawn, for she will be his wife."

"But I love him!" Cosy cried.

"You accepted his death. There is no true bond of the spirit between you and Black Water or you would have known he was alive."

Cosy had no answer; Hungry Moon spoke the truth. "How is it that he lives?" she asked at last.

"I have heard that in the midst of the storm there was a great uprush of water from the bottom of Kitchigami. Wood long drowned was spewed forth and he caught hold of a piece of this medicine wood and it kept him afloat."

The dynamite? Cosy wondered. Had part of the *Kaug* been blown up by Dan's partially fused charge? Was this what had saved Black Water?

"Soon Black Water will return to our village and claim Spotted Fawn as his wife." Hungry Moon spoke fiercely, though pain showed deep in her eyes. "I have dreamed this and know it for the truth. You must loosen your hold on him; you must let go so Black Water can live in peace with himself and with Spotted Fawn."

"I have promised you," Cosy's voice broke and tears spilled from her eyes. How painful it was to discover he still lived and yet could never be hers.

Hungry Moon squeezed her fingers and released her hand. "Now you must leave me."

Cosy pressed her cheek briefly to Hungry Moon's gaunt one. "I wish I could stay."

"When you leave this time in body you must also leave in spirit," her foster mother warned. "Your life here is of the past and you have another path to follow. Do not try to cling to what cannot be."

Cosy blinked away her tears. "I heed your words though I do not see where my path leads."

"Dream," Hungry Moon said. "You will be shown." She closed her eyes.

Since there was no more to be said, Cosy reluctantly turned and walked slowly toward the river. She found the two girls waiting at the edge of the grove. "Please send a message to me when she—" Unable to go on, she gestured with her head toward where Hungry Moon lay among the birches.

Spotted Fawn touched her hand gently. "I will do as you ask, but I think you will know long before my message reaches you."

Cosy spent the return canoe trip sunk in misery. Losing Hungry Moon to death would be hard to bear; but much of her distress came from her realization that she, herself, had forfeited her right to Black Water by giving up so easily, by believing him dead when nothing within her had felt him die. He lived but she'd never see him again for she'd made a death promise to Hungry Moon and a death promise could never be broken.

She left the canoe at the river beach, waved to Eagle Feather and hurried along the trail toward home. The woods were hot and breathless, buzzing with black deer flies, the kind that bit and left raised welts that itched. When she reached the meadow, she broke into a run, eager to get away from the flies.

Her father met her at the back door. "Where have you been?" he demanded. "And what the hell are you doing in that damned Indian dress?"

"Hungry Moon is dying," she said. "I went to see her for the last time."

"You defied me by going to the Indian camp alone and without my permission?" He glared at her. "Go to your room and take off those squaw clothes immediately. I don't ever want to see you wearing them again. Do you hear? I'm leaving for the docks now, and I expect you to be here and dressed like a civilized lady when I return."

"Yes, Father." Cosy fled up the back stairs and shut herself into her room.

He never seemed to find her an obedient, loving daughter, and yet she did love him and she tried to do what he asked. A lump rose in her throat. Didn't he understand that sometimes he was unreasonable? How could she possibly have not hurried to Hungry Moon's side?

Sighing, she peeled off the doeskins and hid them in a far corner of her wardrobe. Pouring water from the pitcher into the basin, she washed the itching bites, then pulled on an old white muslin dress that required no hoop or crinoline and wrapped her braids around her head, pinning them into place.

Someone rapped at her door. "Come in," she called.

A white-faced Rosalind entered on unsteady feet and clung to the back of the first chair she reached. "I'm so sick," she whimpered. "I couldn't stop vomiting and then Hilda—she was helping me—said a terrible thing. Oh, Cosy, it can't be true. What am I going to do?"

Cosy, putting an arm around her waist, led Rosalind to the bed and helped her to lie down, propping a pillow under her head.

"What's Father going to say?" Rosalind moaned.

Cosy, understanding that Hilda, having just been through the first few months of a pregnancy herself, must have realized what was wrong with Rosalind, said, "No one's going to tell Father about the baby."

Rosalind gasped. "Don't say it out loud; please, don't. Maybe that's not what's wrong with me."

"I think quite probably it is," Cosy said. "Have you told Dan yet?"

Rosalind sat up. "Heavens no!"

"So no one knows except the four of us."

"Four?"

Cosy nodded. "If Hilda guessed, Mina Howard surely has," she said, skirting the truth.

"Neither of them like me," Rosalind wailed. "They'll tell Father."

"They aren't fools. They know he'd be furious about it, and they're not eager to put him into a rage. Louella Genette once told me that in the old days kings sometimes cut off the heads of messengers who brought them bad news, and I've often thought that if Father had lived in those days he might have done exactly that, though he might have regretted it afterward. In any case, Hilda's afraid of Father and Mina keeps her own counsel no matter what."

"But what am I going to do?"

"The first thing is to tell Dan. After all, he's the father."

"But he's gone with Father. Dan's diving again today." Tears filled her eyes. "What if something happens to him?"

Cosy eased her back down on the bed. "Nothing will. Rest now; and when Dan comes back this evening, you can arrange to be alone with him for a few minutes."

Rosalind wiped her eyes with a lace-edged handkerchief and gazed up at Cosy. "Do you think he'll marry me? He'll have to, won't he?"

"More than likely."

"You must think I'm a wicked wanton," Rosalind said.

"Why? Because you fell in love with Dan?" Cosy shook her head. "You did nothing shameful. Please, try to rest."

Rosalind sighed and closed her eyes. A short while later, Cosy saw her sister was asleep. She tiptoed from the room, closing the door behind her. Hearing a noise from Rosalind's room, she walked along the hall, looked in, and saw Hilda changing the bed sheets.

"Didn't mean to say it," Hilda mumbled when she noticed Cosy. "It just sort of come out by itself. I won't never say nothing about it again. Not to nobody."

"Good," Cosy said. "That's wise of you."

Returning to her bedmaking, Hilda reached to fluff up a pillow and knocked a book off the nightstand. Cosy retrieved it, glancing at a paper that had fallen from the book, a paper that Rosalind had scribbled on. "Miss Rosalind Collins," she'd written. And, underneath, "Mrs. Daniel Rackham. Rosalind Rackham." Then, "Major and Mrs. Eaton? Rosalind Eaton?"

Cosy stared at the question marks, wondering who Major Eaton could be. Rosalind had never mentioned him. Perhaps he was someone her sister had met on the trip from Detroit to Ojibway, the way she'd met Jacob. She slid the paper back into the book and replaced it on the night stand.

Rosalind, in Cosy's bed, was still asleep when Jephthah came home that evening. Alone.

"Where's Dan?" Cosy asked her father.

"He said he had some business in town and wouldn't be back until late," Jephthah said. "I expect he's going to celebrate." He rubbed his hands together, smiling. "We got all the gold, Cosy. Hauled it up today. If I hadn't overdone the celebrating last night, I might have stayed in town with Dan; but I admit I'm bushed." He looked around. "Where's Rosie?"

"She's resting. She didn't feel well earlier, so she won't be having dinner with us tonight. I'll take her up some chicken broth later."

"Nothing seriously wrong with her, is there?" Jephthah asked with concern.

Cosy shook her head. "Rosalind will be fine." It wasn't quite a lie. Once she married Dan, her sister's problem would be solved.

Dinner went well. Mina's venison stew was a favorite of her father's, and he was elated because they'd finally accomplished what they'd set out to do. He seemed to have completely forgotten his anger at Cosy and, although she would have liked to have told him Black Water was alive, she decided this wasn't the time.

"Going to turn in early tonight," Jephthah said to her shortly after they'd eaten. "You be sure and take good care of Rosie."

"I will, Father."

Cosy carried a tray of broth and toast up to her room, woke Rosalind, and persuaded her to eat. Rosalind, relieved when she found she was able to keep the food down, thanked her.

"I've said some rather nasty things to you," she said as Cosy helped her return to her own room. "I'm sorry. I really would like to be friends."

"We *are* friends," Cosy assured her.

"Stay and talk to me," Rosalind begged. "I don't want to be alone."

Cosy assisted her out of her clothes and into a night-gown. As she was brushing Rosalind's hair, her sister asked, "Do you read poetry?"

"Sometimes," Cosy replied.

"A poet named Giles Fletcher wrote some lines I memorized because they seemed so true:

'Love is the blossom where there blows

Everything that lives or grows . . .' "

After she finished, Rosalind gazed expectantly at Cosy.

"Very true," Cosy agreed. "Without love, what is life?" Despite herself, her words came out bleak with pain.

Rosalind didn't seem to notice. "Exactly the way I feel," she said.

The clock on the landing struck nine.

"Are you sure Father didn't say what time Dan would be home?" Rosalind asked, not for the first time.

"Late was all he said," Cosy repeated patiently. "Dan had business to attend to."

Rosalind frowned, muttering as much to herself as to Cosy, "I'm afraid it has something to do with that man."

The man they'd seen with Jim? Cosy wondered. Why was her sister so troubled about him?

"I know they hauled up the gold," Rosalind said suddenly, "but what did they do with it once they had it?"

"Father said it's locked in the town-bank vault."

"All of it? Or just Father's share?"

Cosy blinked. "I didn't think to ask him that."

Rosalind whirled around, knocking the brush from Cosy's grasp as she clutched at Cosy's hands. "He isn't coming back," she cried. "Dan's not coming back! Oh, Cosy, what am I going to do?"

Eighteen

Since she could say nothing to help staunch Rosalind's woeful sobs, Cosy finally brought her a small glass of Mina's raspberry wine and insisted she drink it. Eventually the tears stopped and she was able to persuade Rosalind to get into bed.

"I can't sleep," Rosalind said piteously. "I'll never be able to sleep again. Please, don't leave me alone, Cosy."

Cosy sat in the rocker beside Rosalind's bed. "My foster mother used to sing a song to me, a lullaby of the People, when I couldn't sleep," she said. "Shall I sing it to you?"

"Whatever you wish," Rosalind said with a sigh.

Cosy crooned the words as she remembered Hungry Moon doing, blinking back tears. Never again in this world would she see Hungry Moon.

"What does the song mean?" Rosalind asked when she finished. "Can you sing it in English?"

Translating the words from the People's tongue took Cosy's mind away from her foster mother's impending death.

" 'Sleep, my little one,' " she crooned.

> " 'Outside our lodge the owl calls
> But I will keep you safe from harm.
> Outside our lodge the wind blows cold

But I will keep you safe and warm.
Sleep, my little one, I am here,
I am here beside you, I watch over you,
Sleep, little one, sleep . . .' "

"I don't recall anyone ever singing a lullaby to me before," Rosalind said drowsily. "Not ever."

Saddened by her sister's words, Cosy repeated the simple song, singing softly, first in English, then in the People's tongue. When she finished, she glanced at Rosalind and saw she'd fallen asleep.

After leaving the room as quietly as she could, Cosy went downstairs. All was in darkness except for the glow of the two wall lamps in the entry. Mina and Hilda had left for the night and her father had, as he'd said he meant to, retired early. She drifted into the music room where she touched one key of the piano, listening as the lonely note rose into the air and disappeared.

She would never, she thought, be able to play Rosalind's plaintive love songs, or to sing as sweetly as her sister. But she didn't really care. If she ever did learn how to coax music from the piano, she'd want to play like Jacob, play music that demanded you listen, music that showed pictures without the need for words.

She glided to the open window and gazed toward the river, but the night was overcast so she could not see the water. The faint aroma of the pines wafted on the breeze and the frogs peeped insistently. Far off, an animal howled. A wolf? She shook her head. No, what she'd heard was a dog. When she found herself continuing to listen, she asked herself why. What was she waiting to hear? Certainly not a dog or even a wolf. What?

And then her heart leaped within her breast when she

heard what she hadn't known she was listening for—the plaintive hooting of an owl. Cosy rushed from the house and ran toward the pine grove. Halfway there, she saw the dark figure of a man and flung herself at him, crying his name.

"Black Water!"

Strong arms held her, but she realized immediately they were not the right arms and she freed herself.

"Cosy," Dan's voice said.

"I heard an owl," she said.

"I heard the owl, too," he replied, "and it *was* an owl. Black Water's dead. You must have realized he couldn't be calling you."

"Black Water lives!" she cried. "I discovered today that he was washed ashore."

"No one could have survived that storm," Dan argued.

"I think your dynamite must have gone off and blasted wood from the *Kaug* up from the bottom. He clung to the wood and survived."

"I'll be damned. I'm relieved to hear he didn't drown." Dan touched Cosy's shoulder. "I'm sorry to disappoint you by not being Black Water, but I'm glad you're here because you can do me a favor. I see the house is dark. Is everyone in bed?"

"Father and Rosalind both are, yes." She took a deep breath, striving to calm herself.

Not only had she been wrong about the owl's call, but she'd broken her promise to Hungry Moon by running to meet Black Water—never mind that he was nowhere near and so she hadn't actually met him. In her heart she'd violated her solemn vow. Shame gripped her with fierce talons.

"Cosy?" Dan asked, making her realize she'd missed what he said. "Are you listening to me?"

"I'm sorry."

"I'm leaving tonight and I need to collect some of my belongings from the house. Could you—"

"Leaving?" she repeated, her guilt temporarily forgotten as she remembered poor Rosalind's predicament. "You can't leave!"

"I can and I am."

"But Rosalind—"

"Never mind Rosalind."

"You'll have to mind her. She's carrying your child."

The silence lasted so long the tree frogs began to call again.

"You're certain?" Dan's tone was grim.

"From all her early signs, I'm quite sure."

"Damn! I knew I shouldn't have come back for my things. If I'd gone with Hawkins after we retrieved the—" He broke off abruptly.

"Surely you don't intend to go off and leave her to face this problem alone," Cosy said indignantly.

"Not now. Damn it, I can't do that to Rosalind. I wish to hell you hadn't told me. It changes plans I can't afford to have altered."

Cosy's ire rose. "You talk as though you resent what's happened, when you know very well you're at least as much to blame as she is. Don't you have any feeling for Rosalind at all?"

"Be quiet, Cosy. How and what I feel is no concern of yours. I do care for Rosalind or I damn well wouldn't hang around. She can't be far along—maybe I can talk her out of having the baby. You once told me you were learning to be a medicine woman. There must an Indian remedy that would rid her of the child."

"I don't know if Rosalind would agree. There are such remedies, but they're dangerous and she might die."

Dan's sigh seemed to come from the soles of his feet. "I hate like hell to marry her."

"What a thing to say!"

"You know I'm not the marrying kind. Rosalind would be more unhappy as my wife than she'd be if I left right now."

Cosy put her hand on his arm. "You can't go. Rosalind would be a ruined woman, and the child would have no father. No name."

My father took me, Cosy thought suddenly, *even though he wasn't really married to my mother. He took me and gave me his name and tried to raise me as best he could. I must always remember he didn't have to; he could easily have abandoned me.*

"Don't worry, Cosy; I'll do what's expected of me," Dan muttered.

"Why were you leaving so secretly? Without even telling my father."

"That's my business. And if you keep your mouth shut, you can avoid upsetting Rosalind and your father with what only you and I know."

They walked slowly back to the house, neither touching nor speaking. As they reached the back door, Cosy said, "When will you see Rosalind?"

"Leave well enough alone," he advised. "I'll do what I must in my own way and at my own time."

At least I had enough sense to give Hawkins half the gold we retrieved tonight, Dan told himself as he wearily climbed the stairs. *He'll get it to Beall. They can start things moving without me, and I'll do my damnedest to arrive in time for the fireworks.*

With that settled as much to his satisfaction as was possible, he set his mind to the immediate problem. Rosalind.
He found himself smiling, though wryly. The little minx
had outsmarted him. There was no honorable way out of
the muddle except to marry her; and, unfortunately, except
for a few transgressions here and there, he was essentially
an honorable man.

There'd be compensations—he doubted he'd ever tire of
Rosalind—but he didn't expect to enjoy marriage. Nor
would she find it the paradise that, being a woman, she
undoubtedly looked forward to. Wedded bliss was a mis-
nomer . . .

Dan and Rosalind's wedding date was set several weeks
ahead, bringing it into September. By then Captain Marcos
and his crew had been paid and had sailed off in the *Sturgeon*. And Jephthah's initial outrage at Dan and Rosalind's
forthcoming marriage had settled into a begrudging accep-
tance.

By the time the fall rains began, invitations had been
sent out and the gowns were ready. Rosalind had insisted
hers not be pure white but an ivory silk.

"This way I won't feel like a complete hypocrite," she
confessed to Cosy. "Anyway, people will count months as
they always do and everyone will know when the baby is
born that I wasn't entitled to wear white. Then I can remember that I chose ivory and hold my head up."

Though Cosy thought there was very little difference
between white and ivory, she didn't say so. Rosalind's happiness had a brittleness that she didn't want to risk shattering. She hadn't uttered the slightest protest when
Rosalind chose both the color of the gown she was to

wear—blue—and the style, a far fussier one than she pre
ferred.

The wedding day was overcast and cool, but the rain
held off. St. Patrick's was filled with flowers and wedding
guests. Among them, Cosy saw Jacob Thompson and won
dered what he thought of Rosalind's marriage. His gaze
met hers, and he smiled so warmly that her heart lifted
making her realize how much she'd missed him. Seeing
Jacob always brightened the day. She hoped they'd have a
chance to talk.

Dan was elegant in his dark coat and striped trousers
He stood by the altar rail, wearing a continuous smile with
the little twist of lip caused by the scar and, in general
acted as though he couldn't be happier.

Jephthah, when he took Rosalind's arm to lead her up
the aisle, looked every inch the proud father. Cosy in her
place beside the rail, listened to Father Dunne intone the
words of the marriage sacrament and wondered how happy
Rosalind and Dan would be as wife and husband. As Mr
and Mrs. Daniel Rackham.

The strange name she'd seen on the paper in her sister's
room flashed into her mind. Major Eaton. Whoever he'd
been, Rosalind would never be Mrs. Eaton.

The reception was held at the house, with Mina and
Hilda assisted by two village girls hired for the occasion
Some of the guests had already arrived by the time Cosy
reached home, but Mina reported that everything was going
well and she didn't need Cosy's help.

As Cosy threaded through the throng of guests, she heard
a woman say to Rosalind, "Well, my dear, the sun wasn't
actually shining, but the rain did hold off. That's some
thing."

"Happy is the bride the sun shines on," a man's voice murmured into Cosy's ear. She turned and saw Jacob.

"But it doesn't say how the bride will feel if it neither rains nor shines," he added. To her dismay, his voice sounded blurry. She knew Jacob wasn't much of a drinker, but it seemed he'd had too much to drink today.

"Do you think I should warn her?" Jacob asked gravely.

"Warn who?"

"Why—the bride. Tell her to beware. No sun and no rain. Ambiguous." He stumbled over the last word.

"No, Jacob," Cosy said firmly. "I don't think you should talk to Rosalind right now."

He shook his head. "Solemn duty."

Glancing at the bride, Rosalind saw that her sister was watching Jacob nervously, apparently having overheard some of what he was saying. I can't let Jacob make a fool of himself in front of all these people, she thought. Nor can I allow him to ruin Rosalind's wedding.

"Gonna tell the bridegroom just what I think about him, too," Jacob muttered darkly.

"Jacob," Cosy said hastily, taking his arm, "I feel the need for some fresh air. Please escort me outside."

He stared at her, blinking, seeming not to recognize her.

"You do know me, don't you?" she asked. "I'm Cosy."

He nodded slowly. "Could never forget Rosalind's savage sister. I'll take you to the forest where you belong."

Rosalind smiled at yet another acquaintance who had wished "the best to a lovely bride." Her cheeks felt stiff, and she wondered if her smile looked as false as it felt. Though she'd been free during the past week of those pernicious spells of vomiting, smells tended to nauseate her and most of the men wafted whiskey fumes into her face when they spoke to her.

She glanced around for Dan and saw he'd also noticed that Jacob Thompson was talking wildly from too much drinking. Cosy had taken Jacob's arm and, thank heaven, was leading him through the guests toward the front door. Poor Jacob. No doubt he was upset over her marriage. But she'd never been the slightest bit in love with him, whatever he might have felt for her.

Cosy seemed to be having some difficulty in maneuvering Jacob outside and Rosalind breathed a sigh of relief when Cosy succeeded and they disappeared from her view. Again she looked for Dan and saw he was edging toward the door. Was he going after Cosy and Jacob?

She wished she knew what Dan felt. At first she hadn't been able to couldn't contain her happiness when he had asked her to marry him, but then she had discovered Cosy had told him about the baby. After that, the joy had seeped away, drop by drop, until Rosalind had begun to wonder if she should have somehow found the courage to refuse to marry him and let him leave Ojibway without her.

But she couldn't. She loved him. And besides, now that she was carrying Dan's child, her father would have insisted Dan marry her even if she'd been brave enough to release him.

She kept an eye on Dan, who smiled and spoke to the guests around him as he inched ever closer to the door. Eventually he reached it and, without as much as a glance at her, slipped outside. He needs a breath of air, she tried to tell herself, but had to blink back tears at being left behind.

As though drawn by an invisible cord, Rosalind, too, drifted in the direction of the front door, smiling, always smiling, saying thank you, being polite.

"I don't know when I've seen a prettier bride," a matron in gold satin told her.

"Or a more dashing groom," a younger woman in a blue-lace overdress said wistfully.

Dashing described Dan perfectly, Rosalind thought. He was a man everyone noticed. And when he touched her, she forgot that anyone else existed. But did he reciprocate her feelings? Did he love her at all? She'd seen desire in his eyes when he'd held her, but was that love?

Finally easing away from the two women, Rosalind whipped through the door onto the porch where she shivered in the chill gray afternoon. Where had Cosy and Jacob gone? Had Dan followed them?

As soon as Jacob was outside, he freed his arm from Cosy's and grasped her hand instead, hurrying her toward the pine grove.

"Wait!" she cried, pulling back

"I'm not drunk, but I am in a hurry," he said. "Don't slow us down." To her surprise he spoke briskly, his words clear and crisp.

She obeyed, wondering why he'd feigned being the worse for drink and what he meant to do now.

"I thought you'd never get around to leading me out of the house," he said as they stepped under the interlaced branches of the trees.

"Didn't you mean what you said about Rosalind?" she asked in confusion as he halted and turned to face her.

Jacob looked at her sternly. "Don't you know better than to believe I was jealous? I certainly don't envy her marrying that bastard. And I wouldn't choose to be in his place."

"Then why pretend?"

"Because I wanted to establish that I was drunk." He turned and peered through the gloom as though fearing they'd been followed. Lowering his voice, he said, "Has Rosalind told you anything unusual about Daniel Rackham?"

Cosy shook her head, unsure what Jacob was getting at.

"Has she ever mentioned any particular reason why she sailed from Detroit on the *Pewabic?* "

The name on the piece of paper popped into Cosy's head and she said, "No, none. But I've been wondering if there were a Major Eaton on the *Pewabic.* "

Jacob's hands clamped down hard on her shoulders. "Where did you hear that name?" he demanded.

Though taken aback by his intensity, she told him why she'd asked. "But why does it matter?" she said. "What's wrong, Jacob? Please tell me."

"I can't. It's—" He paused, listening, so she listened as well and heard the crunch of pine needles under someone's foot.

Before she could say or do anything, Jacob pulled her into his arms and kissed her, hard and thoroughly. She found herself responding eagerly, fitting herself into his embrace as though she belonged there.

Before she quite lost all sense of time and place, it struck her that the reason Jacob was kissing her must be because he wanted to mislead whoever he thought had followed them. She stiffened, angrily struggling to free herself.

Rosalind left the porch, skirted the house and gazed toward the pine grove. She was just in time to see a man slip among the trees. Dan? She hoisted the skirts of her wedding gown and began to run. When, out of breath, she reached the pines, she plunged into the grove, heedless of her clothes.

The first thing she saw was Jacob Thompson, on his back, blood trickling from one corner of his mouth. Dan stood over him, holding Cosy around the waist. Her dark hair had come free of its pins to blow across her face in the damp wind. For a long moment Dan and Cosy gaped at her, then Cosy jerked away from Dan and dropped to her knees beside Jacob.

You can't fool me, sister mine, Rosalind thought bitterly. I saw you.

"What's going on?" she asked.

"Isn't it obvious?" Dan asked, gesturing toward Jacob. "Your devoted Mr. Thompson had too much to drink and, since he lost one sister, he tried to console himself with the other."

"So you rushed out to *comfort* Cosy yet once again, is that it?" Rosalind's voice rose with spite and rage. "Were you afraid Jacob might usurp your privileges?"

"You're not making sense, Rosalind," Dan said calmly. "As a matter of fact, I feared Cosy might have trouble with him and I came out to help her. I was right."

"It seems to me Jacob's the one who needs help," Cosy said tartly, frowning up at them.

Rosalind ignored her, staring straight at Dan. "You left me, left me on our wedding day, to chase after Cosy." Tears gathered in her eyes and spilled onto her cheeks. "We've been married only a few hours, and you couldn't even—" Sobs choked off her words.

Dan stepped around Jacob and took her into his arms. "Come back to the house with me," he urged. "Don't work yourself into a passion over nothing."

Nothing! She hit his chest with her clenched fist, and he caught her wrists, rendering her helpless.

"You don't love me," she sobbed.

"I married you." The coolness in his voice chilled her. "Stop behaving like a goose." He began urging her away from Cosy and Jacob.

She resisted. "I hate you!" she cried. "I hate you, Daniel Rackham Ea—"

His hand closed fast and hard over her mouth, making her bite her lip. He propelled her across the brown needles so rapidly her feet scarcely touched the ground.

When they were halfway to the house he halted, held her away from him, and glared down at her. "As my wife, I expect you to keep your mouth shut about certain things." She'd never heard him speak so icily. "What's past is past, and that includes the *Phoenix*. As for Cosy, you have absolutely no reason to be jealous of her. Try to keep in mind that I may not have planned on marriage but we *are* married."

Rosalind gazed at the ground, tasting the blood on her bitten lip, ashamed to look at him. No matter how upset she'd been, she should never have blurted out the name Eaton. Thank God he'd cut her off. The last thing in the world she wanted was to get Dan in trouble.

"I'm sorry," she whispered.

"Are you?" He tipped her chin up to look into her eyes.

"No matter what, I'll never mention anything about the past again," she said fervently. "I'd die if anything happened to you. Please don't be angry with me."

"I'm not angry."

"You are. You've turned as cold as the weather." She shivered.

"You *are* a little goose, running outside without a shawl.

That can't be good for you in your condition." Putting an arm around her, he helped her the rest of the way, sweeping her into his arms and carrying her up the steps and into the house so that they made a dramatic entrance.

"The bride tried to get away, but I caught her and persuaded her to return," he said with an easy laugh. "I think we'd best be off before she changes her mind again."

People crowded onto the porch as she and Dan hurried hand in hand down the steps and along the drive to where the horse and buggy waited. They were going no farther than the Bigelow House, but that was far enough for privacy. She could hardly wait to get away from the well-wishers and be alone with Dan. The rain began as they started down the hill in the buggy, falling harder and harder until the road became a sea of mud.

The rain's not an omen, Rosalind told herself. The sun may not have shined on our wedding, but neither did it rain. Until now.

They were given the finest suite in the Bigelow House. "Is there anything you'd like?" Dan asked once they were inside the rooms. "Something to eat? A small glass of sherry?"

Rosalind shook her head.

"I'm going downstairs for a few minutes," he told her. "I'll be back by the time you've changed."

"Changed?"

"Into clothes more appropriate than your wedding gown." He smiled. "Come, Rosalind, you know what I mean."

"I—yes." Her voice quivered.

He looked at her quizzically and said, "You're sure you wouldn't care for the sherry?"

"No, I'd rather not." She didn't add that she was afraid the wine might nauseate her.

He kissed her on the forehead and left the room.

Rosalind took a deep breath, glancing around the sitting room, elegantly decorated in blue and gold with a rose-sprigged carpet. She recalled her first night in Ojibway, nearly five months ago, spent in this same hotel. She'd been a girl then, nervous about meeting her father.

Now she was a married woman, expecting her first child all too soon. And she was nervous about being alone with her husband. What had possessed her to rail at him like a shrew? She shook her head and walked into the bedroom where she found their clothes had been unpacked and placed in the wardrobe, a huge carved mahogany affair. She reached in and took out a pale-pink nightgown with deeper pink satin roses across the bodice. The material was thin and cool under her fingers, and a frisson of excitement passed over her as she realized Dan would feel this gown with his hands, as well as her body warm underneath.

She had to struggle to undo her gown, but she managed. Removing the rest of her clothes, she slipped the nightgown over her head. Pattering to the mirrored dressing table in her pink satin slippers, she sat down and brushed her hair until the curls rippled down her back. Standing, she examined her image critically. Was she thicker in the waist yet? Pregnant women always looked so ungainly. She turned sideways, frowning. The shape of her breasts were clearly visible under the thin silk of the gown, and her frown faded. Surely her breasts were fuller, but she didn't mind that.

The sound of Dan's key turning in the lock startled her. She turned to face the bedroom doorway, her hands clasped between her breasts, suddenly shy.

"Ah," he said, "the maiden surprised."

"You're making fun of me."

"No, not really. You're very lovely, Rosalind, very desirable."

He hadn't said he loved her, but she put it from her mind and took a step toward him. He lifted her into his arms and carried her to the bed, lowering her gently onto it. He bent and kissed her, then flung off his clothes, showing little heed where they fell.

How strong he was and how beautiful to look at! Seeing the evidence of his need for her made her heart pound. By the time he pulled off her nightgown, she was aflame with her need for him.

"The lamps are still lit," she murmured when he reached for her.

"Who wants to make love in the dark and miss seeing you?" he teased.

When he kissed her, she clung to him, hardly able to believe that now they could make love at any time they chose. "Oh, Dan," she whispered against his lips, "I could do this forever."

His arms tightened around her. "So could I."

As his hands caressed her, she wondered for a brief instant if, had she never met Dan, another man might have made her feel the same wonderful inner fire. She dismissed the notion immediately. Only Dan could evoke such deep, desperate yearning; only Dan's lovemaking would satisfy her every desire.

When at last they joined together and, moving as one, rose higher and higher, she all but swooned from the final pleasure he brought to her.

Later, when he lay beside her, she turned, wanting to pour out her feelings, but his eyes were closed and she could tell from his breathing that he'd fallen asleep.

"I love you," she whispered, but he gave no sign he heard and she turned away, staring at the Worthington stove on its square of zinc.

One of Aunt Rhoda's axioms slipped into her mind. "Men take what they want from a woman and then leave her. They're selfish. Uncaring."

But Dan gave, too. The exquisite delirium that raced through her when they made love was his gift to her. He seemed to take care that she enjoyed their lovemaking.

Was that love?

She turned back to him and reached a hesitant finger to trace the scar near his mouth. His lips twitched. She leaned over and kissed him and his eyes opened.

"Where did you get that scar?" she asked.

"Fighting," he said tersely.

"In the war?"

"No."

"Tell me," she cajoled.

He raised up on one elbow and frowned at her. "In a brawl. The other man's ring raked me before I clobbered him. Never felt it until I saw the blood. Not very dashing, you see. No military heroism."

"Were you a soldier? Are you one?"

"No to both questions."

"But—" She paused, not daring to mention the "Major" that went with Eaton. He'd told her firmly that was a closed subject.

He lay back down and stared up at the ceiling. "I'm not the man you should have chosen," he said. "Poor Rosalind—it won't be easy for you."

Nineteen

The next morning Rosalind woke alone to a gray dimness. The lamps were no longer lit, but a faint glow came from the crack around the door of the stove and the room was warm, so she knew the fire hadn't gone out. Dan must have risen to tend it. She hadn't heard him. Where was he now?

"Dan?" she called softly. No one answered

She rose and donned the pink robe that matched her discarded nightgown, thrust her feet into the satin slippers, and hurried into the sitting room.

Dan, fully dressed, sat in a chair by the window staring down at the waking town.

"Is something wrong?" she asked.

For a long moment she thought he intended to remain silent, but finally he turned to her.

"I've reneged on a commitment, something I've never done before." His voice was bleak. "I gave my word. I may not be a gentleman, but I keep my promises."

She greatly feared she knew what he meant, and despair settled over her like a shroud.

He reached and grasped her hand. "Would you be upset if I went away without you for a few weeks, maybe a month?"

"This has something to do with those Confederate prisoners on Johnson Island, doesn't it?" she accused. "That man I saw aboard the *Phoenix,* the one who gave Jim a message for you, he brought word another attempt was to be made, didn't he? And you mean to lead it, I suppose."

"I promised," he said.

"Are you a Reb, then?"

He shook his head.

She stared at him in disbelief. "You certainly must sympathize strongly with their cause. First, you pirated the *Phoenix* when you tried to free those Rebel prisoners in May; now you intend to try again, and yet you expect me to believe you're neither a soldier nor a Reb. What are you, then?"

"I'm a man who gives full value for his hire," he said. "A man who keeps his promises."

"That's why you were so eager to bring up the gold for my father, isn't it? You wanted to use your share of the gold to finance another escape attempt. You've intended all along to return to Lake Erie and those Rebel spies you've been working with." She put her hands on her hips and glared at him. "You claim you don't break your promises— what about the promise you made to me?"

"Obviously I didn't expect to wind up with a wife," he responded. "I certainly can't take you with me."

"If I can't go, you can't. I don't care what you told those Rebs; the only thing important to me is that we exchanged vows where you promised to cherish me and care for me. Isn't that more important? What if you're killed? Or caught and hanged?"

"The baby would have my name," he pointed out.

"What do I care about the baby?" she cried. "It's you I want—alive, not dead. You can't go!"

He rose to face her. "Rosalind, you're becoming overwrought. You don't seem to understand that—"

"Every time I try to tell you how I feel, you insist I'm overwrought. As for understanding, you're the one who doesn't understand. You're the one who thinks everything else is more important than love." Her voice rose. "Don't I matter? Don't I matter at all?"

He pulled her to him, holding her by force when she tried to get away. "You damn little vixen," he muttered. "Since you insist, I'll show you what matters."

Though she struggled and fought, his hard, demanding kisses and his intimate caresses excited her, blurring her anger, invading her with a sweet languor that made her forget everything but the thrill of his lovemaking. She would never, she realized, be able to resist him. And at the moment, she didn't care . . .

Later in the day, when Rosalind returned with Dan to her father's house, they found Jacob waiting in the parlor.

"I couldn't return to Houghton without apologizing to you," he said to Rosalind. "I'm heartily ashamed of my behavior at the reception yesterday."

"You had too much to drink," Dan said. "It could happen to anyone. I'm sorry I had to deck you, but—"

Jacob held up his hand. "My fault entirely." He touched his jaw gingerly.

"I'm not angry with you, Jacob," Rosalind said.

"If anyone's put out with you, it'll be Cosy," Dan told Jacob. "You were a bit rough with her."

"Cosy has kindly forgiven me," Jacob said.

Jephthah came into the parlor. "Thought I heard Dan's voice," he said. "Jacob and I have been doing some talking, and the result is I'm off to Houghton with him on tomorrow morning's boat. I don't mean to waste any more time in getting my share of Dawson's new mine."

"That's quite a coincidence," Dan said, "since I plan to be on the boat, too."

Rosalind tensed at his words. After making love to her this morning, he'd insisted he had no choice but to keep his word; he couldn't live with himself if he didn't. She'd finally accepted that nothing she could say or do would prevent him, so she'd stopped arguing. But that didn't mean she had to be happy with his decision.

"Are you thinking of investing in the mine, too?" Jacob asked Dan.

Dan shook his head. "I've some old business I need to clear up in Detroit before Rosalind and I make any plans for the future. I'll be returning as soon as possible."

Rosalind had been doing some quick thinking. "If Father is going to Houghton, perhaps I'll take the boat that far and say goodbye to you there, Dan."

Jephthah nodded. "Sounds like a good idea. It'll be a nice little outing for you, Rosie, and Cosy can come along as well. It's been quite awhile since she's had a chance to go anywhere, and she'll be company for you on the trip back."

Rosalind didn't care to have Cosy along but she could hardly say so to her father, so she smiled and nodded, then glanced at Dan to see how he was taking her announcement.

He met her gaze and shrugged. "Quite a party," he said flatly.

Rosalind noticed for the first time that Cosy was standing in the doorway to the parlor. She wondered how long her sister had been there.

"Mrs. Howard has a room ready for you and Dan," Cosy

said to Rosalind. "Hilda's already moved your belongings. Would you like to go up now?"

Rosalind really wanted Dan to come upstairs with her, but he was talking to her father and, since they'd already had one bitter disagreement at the hotel, she didn't care to risk annoying Dan by interrupting.

"Yes, I think I would like to rest for a bit," she told Cosy.

"Since I'm about to leave, I'll say goodbye to you, Rosalind," Jacob put in.

His words caught Jephthah's attention. Breaking off his conversation with Dan, he turned to Jacob. "Nonsense, I insist you stay for dinner. Dan and I have a bit of business to discuss, then the three of us will have a spot of brandy." He gestured toward the music room. "You might like to exercise your fingers on the piano."

Cosy followed Rosalind from the parlor and up the stairs to the spare bedroom that was to be shared by Mr. and Mrs. Rackham. Rosalind relished the sound of those words—Mr. and Mrs. Rackham—and repeated them silently.

"Shall I bring you some tea?" Cosy asked, pausing in the doorway.

"I think not, thank you," Rosalind said politely.

"I overheard what Father said about us all catching the morning boat to Houghton," Cosy said, "but I wasn't quite certain I understood everything. Is Dan going on past Houghton?"

"He has business in Detroit," Rosalind said, a bit sharply. It was none of Cosy's affair what Dan did. Because she was annoyed, she added, "I confess to being surprised you forgave Jacob so easily for his behavior yesterday. After all, you were the victim, weren't you?"

"I don't believe he meant to insult me. Since you've brought up the incident, though, I do have something to say." Cozy took a deep breath and let it out slowly. "You made some accusations then about Dan and me that weren't true. Dan has never cared for me; it's you he loves. Put any other thought from your mind. My foster mother used to tell me that jealousy is a slow poison."

Rosalind was outraged. "Are you accusing me of being jealous?" she demanded. "I certainly am *not* jealous of you. What an idea!"

Cosy merely looked at her in silence until Rosalind turned her back to her, saying, "I'd like to be alone." When she looked around, Cosy was gone and the door was closed.

As Cosy, upset over Rosalind's behavior, slowly descended the stairs, she heard the thundering of Jacob's music and paused to listen, finding herself more disturbed than ever. The music seemed ominous, a promise of violence to come. When she reached the entry, she saw that the library door was closed; evidently her father and Dan were closeted in there. She stood indecisively for a moment, then made her way to the music room.

Jacob didn't appear to notice her as she slipped inside, so she was surprised when he took his hands off the keys, looked at her, and rose. "I was hoping you'd join me," he said.

Cosy eyed him uneasily. She still didn't understand why Jacob had allowed Dan to hit him yesterday without any attempt to either defend himself or strike back. And she was annoyed at herself for responding, even for a minute, to his kiss. He'd used that embrace, not because he'd wanted to kiss her, but for reasons of his own.

"I know I behaved abominably yesterday, but I'm not at liberty to explain why," he told her as though in answer to her confusion. Holding out his hand, he reached toward her. Before she realized she meant to, she offered him her hand in return. He grasped it before she could change her mind.

"Join me on the window seat," he said, drawing her with him.

Though she sat as far away from him as possible on the small seat, he kept her hand in his.

"You didn't have too much to drink," she said accusingly, "and you didn't really want to kiss me."

"You're right—and wrong." He leaned toward her, gazing into her eyes. "Wanting to kiss you has become a chronic condition on my part, and yesterday was no exception. Have you no magic medicine to cure me?" He brought her hand to his mouth, brushing his lips across the back. Then he turned her palm toward him and an amazed thrill knifed through her as she felt the warmth of his tongue against her skin.

Cosy drew in her breath. "Why did you do that?" she asked, finding she could barely whisper the words.

"Because I needed to taste you." He leaned closer and ran his tongue lightly over her lips. "Mmm. Delightful. Unforgettable." There was a disturbing hoarseness to his voice.

Cosy, aware of a strange stirring deep inside her, not only was powerless to move away but yearned to edge closer. She didn't love Jacob. Why did he affect her in these disturbing ways?

Jacob's lips touched hers, the kiss gentle at first until, with a groan, he pulled her into his arms, his kiss deepening until it seemed to take possession of not only her mouth but her entire body. She clung to him, responding to his passion with her own, offering, taking.

He raised his head to gaze at her, closing his eyes momentarily as though in pain, then gripped her shoulders and held her away from him. "I thought I could control myself," he said with that same unsettling husky rasp in his voice. "I was wrong. I don't have the right, Cosy, not now, not yet."

She was turning his words over in her mind when she heard her father's voice so clearly she knew he must have come out of the library. Jacob rose from the window seat and walked to the piano. By the time her father reached the door of the music room, Jacob was playing and, to Cosy's amazement, singing what sounded like one of her sister's melancholy love songs:

> " 'How can I bear to leave thee,
> One parting kiss I give thee;
> And then whate'er befalls me,
> I go where honor calls me . . .' "

"What the devil are you playing?" Jephthah asked, apparently as surprised as she.

Jacob stopped, closed the lid of the piano, and got to his feet. "A melody called 'The Soldier's Lament,' " he said, "about a young man off to war bidding his true love farewell. I understand it's quite popular with the troops."

"No doubt," Jephthah said dryly. "Come along, and we'll have that brandy."

Aware she wasn't included in the invitation, Cosy remained on the window seat, watching Jacob as he followed her father from the room. Soldier's lament or not, she felt Jacob had directed the song at her. But why? He was going nowhere but back to Houghton and she'd be on the same boat with him. In any case, she was certainly not his true love.

* * *

When the five of them reached the docks early the next morning, the *Detroit* was waiting. She was a sidewheeler with a freshly painted octagonal pilot house. The white paint set off the shining brass fittings, making the boat gleam in the late September sun as the captain eased her from the Ojibway harbor into Kitchigami.

Cosy feared she might not enjoy the trip since her last experience aboard a boat had been on the *Sturgeon* in the terrible storm where Black Water had been left to drown.

She stood at the rail eyeing the white clouds scudding across the bright blue of the autumn sky. They were small and not at all threatening. The breeze blew fresh and cold from the west. Nothing in the day augered ill. She gathered her shawl closer about her against the chill, her spirits rising.

"A fair morning, good sailing weather," Jacob said as he came up to stand beside her.

"We're fortunate," she told him. "The entire month of September can be cold and rainy."

"Maybe we're experiencing an Indian Summer."

Cosy shook her head. "Next moon, Falling Leaf Moon, is the time for that. After the weather's been so cold and dreary that you've given up hope, October offers warm sun and clear skies."

"This is my first autumn in the Upper Peninsula."

"I've never lived elsewhere."

"That's part of your charm," he told her. "But I think you once said you'd like to see more of the world."

"Oh, yes. I've studied maps and I know the world is very large, with oceans and other continents. Even Michigan is a big state, with two peninsulas."

"Have you ever been to Houghton before?" he asked.

"Not since I was a child. I lived there for a time with Father, but I'm afraid I don't remember much about it. We moved many times when I was small."

"It's remarkable how, without a wife, he managed to raise such an accomplished young woman."

"My father has always been good to me," she said slowly. "But Hungry Moon and, later, Miss Genette taught me much of what I know." She sighed. "Now Hungry Moon is dying and I can't be with her."

"I'm sorry. But life goes forward, Cosy, not backward."

She frowned at him. "Why do you keep insisting that if I lived at the People's village I'd be traveling backward? It wouldn't be like that, not at all."

"I was there," he said. "The living conditions at the Chippewa village might not have bothered you as a child, but they would now. You'd have difficulty adjusting and, in the end, might not succeed. You've become part of another world, one that has as much or more to offer as the Indian way of life."

She shook her head. "You don't understand."

"You've just told me you'd like to travel and see more of the world. I've noticed how much reading and music seem to fascinate you. These are all things you'd have to forego if you returned."

"I wouldn't care," she said stubbornly.

"You say Hungry Moon is dying. When she's gone, what is there for you in the Indian village? I've heard Black Water is alive, after all. Would you marry him? Bear his children? Become, to all intents and purposes, just another Chippewa squaw?"

"I've been trained to heal," she countered. "Hungry Moon taught me."

"You told me she chose another girl to replace you. What of her—will this girl step aside, give up her role as medicine woman for you?"

Spotted Fawn's face appeared before Cosy, her dark eyes unfriendly. No, Spotted Fawn would not willingly give up her position as the tribe's medicine woman. Nor would she be willing to relinquish Black Water.

"I could live with the People and be happy," Cosy said, but her words no longer carried conviction, not even to her. Jacob angered her. Why must he force her to view things in ways she didn't wish to?

"Why not try to be a healer in my world, which is your world, too, this world we both live in?"

She gazed at him in astonishment. "You have doctors," she said finally. "I'm not a doctor."

"No, but only because you haven't been trained as one. Doctors are scarce in the Upper Peninsula, you know. Think of the good you might do."

"It's not possible for me to learn to be a doctor," she said. "Even if it were possible, I'm not certain I could do good. The People honor their medicine women, but would my Father's people honor a woman who was a doctor? I don't think so."

Jacob shrugged. "Honor can be earned."

"There you are." Jephthah spoke heartily, coming up alongside them. "A fine, brisk day. May our business go as well as the weather."

"Bill Dawson's looking forward to having you as a partner," Jacob told him.

"You haven't met Bill yet, Cosy." Jephthah said. "You'll like him."

Jacob raised his eyebrows but didn't comment.

"Smile a few times at old Bill," Jephthah said to Cosy, "and you'll have him wrapped around your little finger."

Jacob frowned. "I agree that Bill's a fine man, and I get along very well with him. But—" He paused and glanced at Cosy before going on. "Do you know him very well, sir?"

"I've known him a few years, but he's more of an acquaintance than a friend," Jephthah replied. "Why?"

"In that case, my advice to your daughter is to keep her smiles to herself. Bill has a somewhat unsavory reputation with the ladies."

"I don't worry about Cosy," Jephthah said. "She's learned how to take care of herself."

If it weren't a glare Jacob shot at her father, it was the next thing to it, Cosy thought. She hoped the two men wouldn't get into an argument.

"I'd best go and see if Rosalind needs anything," she said hastily, hoping her absence might cool Jacob down.

"I wouldn't bother her," Jephthah advised. "She prefers to be alone with her new husband, never mind what Dan might wish. Rosie wanted him; and now that she's got him, she'll just have to learn what she's landed herself with."

Cosy gazed at her father in some amazement. He'd never had anything but praise for Rosalind, managing even to take the news of her pregnancy without chastising her, though he fumed at everyone else.

"There's no accounting for the vagaries of women," Jephthah went on. "I like Dan, but he's a wanderer and that makes a bad husband. I ought to know; I used to roam in my younger days myself. Rosie's mother, poor Cecily, tried to follow along and she wasn't strong enough to survive." He sighed and shook his head. "Rosie's in for some heartaches."

"I think I'll walk along the deck and leave you two to talk business," Cosy said, wanting to be by herself.

As she left them, her mind was on what her father had said about smiling at Bill Dawson, for she remembered how, months before, her father had told her to smile at Daniel Rackham. She hadn't wanted to smile at Dan and, from Jacob's description, she was certain she wouldn't care to smile at Bill Dawson, either. What did her father expect of her? Was she a sacrifice as the daughter of the Biblical Jephthah had been?

Cosy shook her head, deciding she was being fanciful. All Father wanted was for her to help him in his business dealings by being friendly to the men he happened to be working with. He'd never once suggested she be more than friendly. It occurred to her that Jacob had not been included in the men she was to smile at. But, of course, that was because Father had expected Jacob to be interested in Rosalind. As he had been.

Or had he? Recalling Jacob's peculiar behavior at the wedding, she wondered anew what game he'd been playing. Why had he asked her what she knew about Rosalind's journey before she boarded the *Pewabic?* She'd known nothing, of course, but she *had* told him about Rosalind writing Major and Mrs. Eaton on that paper. Was that significant? But how could it be?

I shan't worry over it, she told herself, it has nothing to do with me. The reminder of Jacob's behavior at the wedding, though, brought troubling thoughts about Rosalind's accusations. How can she possibly believe there's anything between Dan and me? Cosy wondered.

But, as Hungry Moon had told her, jealousy needed no reasons since it was a poison in the mind of the jealous person. Cosy hoped the poison in Rosalind's head would vanish after Dan left for Detroit. She and her sister had begun to be friends before Rosalind's marriage to Dan—could they be again?

Cosy paused to stare at Kitchigami's blue water, noticing a smudge near the horizon that she knew would turn into a boat or an island when they came closer. Will I ever marry? she wondered. She'd always hoped Black Water would be her husband, but that was not to be. Who else would want to marry her? And if someone did, would she wish to marry him?

Her mind fixed stubbornly on Jacob. The more she tried to dislodge him from her thoughts, the more he occupied them. She didn't love him—why did he haunt her in this way? Why did she recall his kisses so vividly and with such yearning?

In an effort to distance herself from Jacob, she deliberately concentrated on the spot near the horizon, watching it grow larger, grow into land, an island—no, two islets, close together. There were many small islands near the shore of the Keweenaw Peninsula, Cosy knew, and the *Detroit* was traveling fairly close to them.

The People considered islands to be the home of spirits. In Kitchigami, near Kaugwudja, lay the Great Spirit's Island, where she'd never been. Women didn't accompany the men there when they made offerings of tobacco to Kitchi Manitou—except for Hungry Moon.

Because she was a respected medicine woman, Hungry Moon had much freedom and was treated differently than were the other women in the People's village. Ordinary squaws, Jacob had called those other women. If she could marry Black Water, would she resent being treated like one of those ordinary women? As nothing special when she had always been special, chosen by Hungry Moon to follow her on the medicine path? For the first time she wondered if Jacob might not be right.

He'd suggested she could be a healer in the world of the white man. Could she? Cosy shook her head. Her father would never agree and, besides, she'd have no idea how to go about such a thing. And yet there'd been her dream about her spirit lynx advising the red-brown lynx she thought of as Jacob that he was to help her. How? she wondered.

Because the sun began to touch her differently, Cosy realized the boat was turning and she came out of her reverie. They must be rounding the tip of the Keweenaw Peninsula. She saw it in her mind's eye as the map showed it—a finger of land sticking into Kitchigami. The *Detroit* must steam up one side, round the tip, and sail along the other side before reaching the channel to Portage Lake and Houghton.

She began to walk on and was dismayed to find a man following her, a stranger. She didn't care for the way he stared at her. Eventually she rushed away, searching for her father and Jacob, miserably wondering if something about her had suggested she might welcome the man's approach. Her father was alone, and she remained near him until the evening meal was served.

The food was excellent, freshly caught lake trout finished off with apple pie.

"Ten to one they're Ojibway apples," Jephthah said to those at their table. "The fellow across the river from my place has to fight off the bears to grow his apples. One night he shot three of those black rascals in an hour. Bears like apples as much as people do. Can't blame 'em. His apples are the best I ever tasted."

After they finished eating, some of the passengers settled into card playing, inveigling Jacob into the game. Dan had disappeared and Cosy tried to talk to Rosalind, but her sister gave such short replies that she gave up. Seeing that the strange man who'd tried to accost her was a player in the card game, Cosy decided it was safe enough to venture onto the deck.

The twilight had deepened into real darkness; gone were the long summer evenings when the sky stayed light until ten o'clock or later. Cosy strolled along the deck, her shawl close about her to ward off the chilly night breeze. When she rounded the stern, she saw a dark figure standing by the rail and hesitated, not wishing to have another unpleasant encounter.

"Hello, Cosy," the man said, and she realized with relief that he was Dan. "I haven't spoken to you all day," he added.

She heard the slurring of his words. He'd been drinking.

"Your sister doesn't want me to go," he said plaintively. "Matter of honor, but women don't understand honor. Maybe you do, 'cause you think like an Indian. They know about honor."

"Yes, the People respect honor," Cosy said cautiously. "I think maybe Rosalind does, too, but she doesn't want you to leave her behind."

Dan snorted. "No place for a woman, not where I'm headed, and she knows it."

Cosy remained silent, not certain she should be alone with Dan. She wasn't afraid of him, even though he'd been drinking, but she feared Rosalind might misinterpret this chance evening meeting.

"Another thing," Dan said after a time. "You like the bastard, I can tell; but be careful, li'l sister-in-law, 'cause I don't trust him."

Unlikely as it seemed, Dan must mean Jacob. She couldn't decide if defending Jacob was wise, so she said nothing. It was always better not to antagonize a man who'd had too much to drink.

"I think I'll walk on," she murmured after a suitable pause.

When she started to move away, Dan grasped her arm and pulled her back so she was against the rail. "He's dangerous," Dan insisted. "Don't know why exactly. I can sense danger ahead, though. Always could. Be careful."

Cosy tried to ease away from him without an overt struggle, but he tightened his grip. "Do let me go, Dan," she said quietly but firmly. "I've heard your warning."

His hands moved to her shoulders and he stared down at her, the light from the waxing moon revealing his somber expression. With her back to the rail, Cosy was helpless to free herself.

"You heard but you won't listen," he muttered. "Women never do. Told Rosie I'd make a rotten husband; she paid no heed."

Cosy heard a gasp, then the sound of running feet, but Dan's body prevented her from catching even a glimpse of who fled. "Let me go!" she hissed, fearing the worst. "If that was Rosalind, she's sure to misinterpret what she saw."

Dan released her and turned to look. Cosy stepped around him to peer along the deck, but there was no one in sight. "You'd best go find Rosalind," she said.

He stumbled, recovered, and strode unsteadily away. Left alone, Cosy leaned against the rail, watching as clouds drifted across the moon before passing on, allowing silver light to trail across the water. Stars glimmered in the sky, so far away and yet seemingly close enough to touch.

Before there were people in the world, Hungry Moon had told her, there were animals who could talk and change shape. In those early days, Star Dancers lived on the Moon.

Neither animals nor humans, they had lived forever, dancing nightly across the sky from star to star. One night, a star fell to earth with one of them clinging to it and the others were so unhappy that they fell, too, and became mortal. Then there were no more Star Dancers.

"That is why," Hungry Moon had added, "we have all looked up at the stars at night and felt the pull within, the bond linking us with the sky."

Suddenly the stars blinked out, one by one, and Cosy was left in impenetrable darkness. Then an image of an osprey filled her vision, wings beating, whirling to dive for prey. But this osprey dived not for fish but at a white owl who flew below, not seeing the danger. Cosy ached to cry a warning to the owl. She could not.

But *I'm* the white owl, she thought. I'm Koko, Hungry Moon's white owlet, and Hungry Moon has sent me an urgent message. But who is the osprey?

The first time Hungry Moon had dreamed of the osprey was when Rosalind came to Ojibway.

Rosalind.

Danger.

The darkness vanished as suddenly as it had come. Cosy smelled the scent of roses and caught a glimpse of the stars overhead at the same time that she realized she was no longer merely leaning against the boat rail but being tipped over it. Before she could try to save herself, unseen hands thrust at her, shoving, and she was falling, falling, falling . . .

Twenty

Cosy gasped with shock as she plunged into the water and it closed over her head. She fought her way to the surface where, choking and coughing, she gulped air before sinking again, drawn down by the weight of her clothing. She tore at the buttons of her clothes underwater, struggling frantically to shed her wet garments. Rising again, she tried to tread water as she strove to pull off her skirt, but the chill of Kitchigami numbed her fingers, making her clumsy.

The lake, which had seemed calm from the boat deck, slapped waves in her face. Panic clutched at her. Was Mishibezo reaching up from the bottom to seize her? The water monster had been cheated of Black Water so he'd be hungry for another victim. What could save her from his evil clutches?

She heard a splash. Moments later a voice cried, "Cosy!"

Or had she imagined the call?

"Help me!" she cried, choking as she went under again. Sputtering and gasping, she came to the surface once more.

"Cosy, keep shouting so I can find you," a man's voice called. Jacob's voice.

"I'm here," she cried through the darkness, struggling to stay afloat. "Here!"

After what seemed an eternity, she saw Jacob's head in

the water. As he swam toward her, she noticed he was clutching a life preserver which he thrust at her. She grasped the ring, holding one side while Jacob held the other. After taking a few moments to catch her breath, she used her free hand to unfasten her outer, then her inner skirt. She slipped them off with relief.

"I can swim now," she said.

"Swim where?" Jacob asked bleakly.

Looking around, Cosy saw the lights of the *Detroit* growing smaller and smaller. The boat was leaving them behind. She tipped her head back to look at the moon, then turned her face toward where she knew the shore must be.

"Swim toward the land," she said.

"Miles away," he told her. "Too far."

"There are islands between us and the mainland."

"We'll have to hope to find one," he said. "Which way?"

She pointed and they swam in that direction, each holding to a side of the ring. When exhaustion slowed them, they floated until a chilling numbness creeping into her bones warned Cosy they dared not rest.

"We must keep swimming," she said, her teeth chattering so hard she could hardly get the words out.

"Damn, this is a cold lake," Jacob muttered.

Then they ceased wasting breath on words and swam. The moon rose higher in the sky, spilling its silver across the water. Time ceased to have meaning, there was only the chill water and the endless struggle to survive. Eventually Jacob said something but, though Cosy heard the words, she was too exhausted to understand their meaning.

"Land," he repeated. "Land ahead."

Only then did she see the dark mass rising in front of them. There was no shallow water as they approached, no beach, nothing but rocks. Cosy laboriously pulled herself up onto the rocks and collapsed. She heard Jacob's ragged breathing beside her.

Eventually she recovered enough strength to feel the familiar prickly resilience of old pine needles under her hands. Shivering uncontrollably, she huddled against Jacob, but he was as wet and chilled as she and gave no warmth. She'd never been so cold in her life.

"My guess is we're on an island," Jacob said, rising. "We can't rest. There's no way to build a fire here; we have to keep moving to get warm."

"Pine branches," she said through her chattering teeth. "Make a blanket."

"No," he said. "Come on, stand up."

Once on her feet, Cosy discovered that, despite her numbness and the fact she'd lost both shoes, she could walk. The moon glinted on the water to her right and, by its light, she saw the dark silhouettes of pines to her left. She'd started to turn her head when she realized she'd also seen something else beyond the rocks where they came ashore.

Halting, she pointed and whispered, "Canoes." Grasping Jacob's hand, she led him to where three canoes were pulled up above the water line on a tiny beach between the rocks.

"Chippewa village?" Jacob asked in a low tone.

Cosy raised her head to sniff the night breeze, discovering the scent of smoke mixed with the odor of pine. But where were the other smells of a village—cooking, hides drying? And why were no dogs barking to warn of strangers? "I'm not sure," she said. "I do smell smoke."

"We need that fire. Which way?"

When she showed him, Jacob tried to hurry her along; but she kept pulling back, her uneasiness forcing her to a halt when they were but a few yards into the pines.

"What's wrong?" he asked.

"Ssh." She spoke into his ear. "I fear this may be something other than a village of the People. We must be careful."

"You mean these Indians might not be friendly?"

"If this is what I think, quite possibly not," she whispered. "We must go back to the shore. Hurry."

Jacob obeyed without argument; but to her alerted awareness, he made far too much noise scuffling through the pine needles as well as trampling on and snapping brittle twigs. She feared what might happen if those who'd lit the fire heard them.

Leaning close, Jacob whispered, "Who are they? Enemies of your people?"

"No. Mides—medicine men—having their Midewewin ceremonies. Taboo to those who don't belong." She froze, listening. Was someone following them? "We'd best take one of the canoes and leave this place as quickly as possible."

They fled toward the shore, heedless of noise, and had almost reached the canoes when strong hands jerked Cosy off her feet and pinioned her arms behind her. Jacob's startled curse told her that he, too, had been trapped.

"Don't fight," she called to him. Then, quickly, she switched to the People's tongue.

"Help me," she begged her captor, still unseen for he was behind her. "My enemy sought to give my spirit to Mishibezo. I have sworn to avenge the wrong. Aid me, my brothers of the People. I, Koko, ask this of you."

She waited a moment. There was silence.

"Help also the friend who rescued me from Kitchigami's cold water," Cosy went on. "Though he is white, he has saved my life and I ask your help for him in his need. I, Koko, request this."

Did the arms that gripped her slacken their hold a trifle?

She spoke again. "I am cold. My body shakes with Kitchigami's chill. My spirit, too, is cold with the knowledge my enemy wishes me to die. I am Koko from the banks of the Mukwah River, the river called Ojibway by the whites. I am Koko from the lodge of Hungry Moon of the Loon totem, from the place near where the great chief Konteka once dwelt."

She waited, aware that others had joined the two who held her and Jacob captive.

"It is true you are wet and cold," a man's voice said, speaking the People's tongue.

"It is true," she agreed.

"Have you a canoe?" the same voice inquired.

"Had I a canoe, I wouldn't need help," Cosy replied. "The boat I sailed on was one which walked on the water and carried many people."

"You have an enemy on that white man's boat?"

"I have. I was pushed into the water to drown or to be eaten by Mishibezo. My friend dived in after me, and the Great Spirit guided us to this spot where there were those of my people to help me."

"Your friend is a white man," the voice said.

"Yes, I have said so."

"You are from Hungry Moon's lodge?" a woman's voice asked.

"It is true."

"I know of her," the woman said. "She is Medicine Woman to the people of her village."

"Her spirit readies itself for the long journey on the Sky

Path," Cosy replied. "Had I heeded her warning, I would have known of my enemy sooner."

After a moment, the woman spoke again. "I have decided," she told Cosy. "I will help you."

"Death to the trespassers," the man snarled.

"She is of the People," the woman argued, "and she comes from a Medicine Woman's lodge. I, Red Grass, say she will live."

There was a long nerve-wracking silence before the man said, "Lame Wolf will take them to our village. I, Great Heron, have spoken."

Cosy's captor immediately began to urge her along ahead of him. "They're taking us to their village," she called to Jacob. "Don't resist."

They reached the shore and, their wrists bound behind then with thongs, were thrust into a canoe. As the oarsman paddled away from the island, Jacob said to her, "How do we know he's not going to dump us in the water?"

"Great Heron said we'd be taken to their village and so I believe we will be."

"Apparently you think only the white man speaks with forked tongue."

"Men of the People also lie at times. But had Great Heron intended to kill us, we'd be dead by now. We're safe enough until Great Heron confers with the other Mides about our fate."

"In other words we're only temporarily safe."

"Yes. Great Heron delayed killing us only because Red Grass, who is also a Mide, insisted on helping us—I think because she knows of Hungry Moon." Cosy sighed. "How I wish Hungry Moon were here. She'd know what to do."

"I still don't understand why they'd want to harm you

if you've persuaded them that you're a woman of the People."

"I told you. We stumbled into a secret medicine society gathering. Some members of this society seek only to heal, but others do evil."

They lapsed into silence and, exhausted, Cosy found herself drifting into sleep despite their precarious situation. She had only a confused impression of arriving at the village and being taken to a lodge where she collapsed on a mat by the fire.

Cosy awoke to early daylight and the familiar smell of pine resin mixed with smoke. She blinked and sat up, gathering a blanket around her.

Two women sat on mats nearby, their eyes fixed on her as they sewed. One was an older woman, the other scarcely more than a girl, perhaps the daughter of the older woman. Jacob was not in the wigwam. Cosy swallowed her anxiety about him and set about establishing herself as one of them.

"I am called Koko," Cosy said in the People's tongue. "I am grateful you have allowed me to share your lodge."

They continued to stare until finally the older one set aside the moccasin she was beading and rose. "You are not of the People," she said, "and yet you speak as one of us."

"My mother belonged to the People," Cosy said. "I lived in Hungry Moon's lodge on the Mukwah River."

"I am Cloudy Dawn," the woman said. "I have heard of that village."

"I have no proper clothes," Cosy told her, encouraged because the woman had offered her name. She dropped the blanket to show her undergarments. "My dress was lost in Kitchigami."

"We have only deerskin," Cloudy Dawn said.

"Long did I wear the tunic, skirt, and leggings of skin," Cosy assured her. "My feet are accustomed to the soft hold of moccasins."

The young woman rose and approached Cosy. Crouching, she hesitantly fingered the lace of the camisole Cosy wore, obviously admiring the garment. "I am Wind Song," she said shyly.

Cosy smiled at her. "I will gladly trade these garments I wear for real clothes, People's clothes," she offered.

Wind Song gave her a pleased smile and glanced hopefully at the older woman, who frowned but did not forbid the exchange.

Soon Cosy was dressed in doeskins with moccasins on her feet, her hair braided and bound back, held in place with a fillet of wood.

"Now I see your mother in the bones of your face," Cloudy Dawn admitted. "It is true she was of the People."

Only then did Cosy think it was safe to try to discover Jacob's whereabouts. She began in the People's roundabout manner. "This lodge, where I am, is yours," Cosy said. "Do you share it with a man?"

"I share it with my husband, Great Heron. He is the chief of the village."

"I have met your husband. Where does the man who was with me lodge?" Cosy asked.

"He rests in the wigwam of Lame Wolf," Cloudy Dawn said.

"I have also met Lame Wolf," Cosy told her. "Can you tell me when your husband will return to the village?"

"I cannot be sure," Cloudy Dawn said, glancing at the younger woman. A flicker of fear crossed Wind Song's face. She turned away, resumed her seat on the mat, and bent her head over her sewing.

Did Wind Song fear Great Heron's return? Cosy wondered why, for she'd assumed the girl was his daughter.

Cloudy Dawn eased down beside the girl and picked up the partly beaded moccasin she'd been working on. Cosy knew the women would now be reluctant to speak and she thought it was related somehow to the fact she'd asked about Great Heron's return. She must find Jacob and see if he were all right.

After a few moments, Cosy decided the best approach was a direct one. "I shall seek the man who is my friend," she announced. "I must know if he is well." Lifting the flap, she stepped outside.

Neither woman made any move to stop her, nor did they give her directions. Relieved to have gotten this far without trouble, Cosy looked around. The day was overcast with a hint of rain in the air. A cool breeze touched her face and went on to rustle the leaves of the maple behind Cloudy Dawn's lodge. Scarlet and gold leaves fell in a brilliant shower.

Cosy set off, walking warily among the lodges, counting. Twenty, a good-sized village. Children running between the wigwams paused to stare at her. Several dogs approached, more curious than belligerent. She ignored them as they sniffed at her and soon they lost interest.

Glancing at the children, she chose a boy nearly as tall as she was and asked, "Where is the lodge where Lame Wolf dwells?"

The boy gaped at her, then pointed.

She nodded her thanks before hurrying toward the wigwam he'd indicated. Stopping before the closed flap, she announced in the People's tongue, "I have come to visit my friend."

After a moment the flap twitched aside and she saw the face of the man who had been her captor last night, Lame

Wolf. "You should not be here," he snarled. "Go back to the women."

"I will speak with my friend, first," she insisted, refusing to be intimidated.

"Great Heron will decide what you will do." Lame Wolf's eyes were cold and hard.

"Great Heron is not here," she said. "I wish to see my friend who rests within your lodge."

"Go back to the women," he repeated, scowling.

Realizing this man would never let her inside his lodge, she called out, "Jacob! Are you all right?"

"Bastard's got me tied." Jacob's words were muffled.

Lame Wolf thrust himself from the wigwam and lunged at Cosy. She jerked back, crying, "Do not touch me! You have no right. And by what right do you bind my friend?"

"You, too, will be bound if you do not obey." He glared at her but made no further move to approach. "When Great Heron returns at sunset, you and your friend will die."

Frightened, Cosy retreated to Cloudy Dawn's lodge. Jacob, who'd already risked his life to save hers, was tied and helpless. Somehow she must find a way to save him as well as herself. But how?

She entered the wigwam and found only Wind Song inside, still sewing.

"I don't like Lame Wolf's hospitality," Cosy said, sitting on a mat next to the girl. "My friend is being mistreated. He is bound hand and foot."

Wind Song glanced at her, then away, without speaking.

"Is it true, as Lame Wolf claims," Cosy asked, "that when Great Heron returns both my friend and I will die?"

Wind Song bit her lip. "It is taboo."

"The ceremonies, you mean? But we saw nothing. Why would your father, Great Heron, wish to kill us?"

"He is *not* my father!" The words burst from the girl. Then her voice dropped and she spoke so softly Cosy could scarcely hear her. "He is cruel. His heart is filled with evil."

"But you live in his lodge."

"I am married to his son," Wind Song said, "and when Great Heron is not present, I help Cloudy Dawn. I don't live here; I would not!"

"There has been trouble between you and Great Heron," Cosy said, stating the obvious in the hope that she could learn something that might help her and Jacob.

"Great Heron speaks lies! His son and I have been married sixteen moons and, because I do not yet carry a child, Great Heron insists the reason I'm barren must be that I'm unfaithful to my husband. I would never be unfaithful!" Wind Song gazed pleadingly at Cosy. "Never!"

"I believe you. Most wives are allowed at least twenty-four moons to conceive before anyone mentions barrenness," Cosy said.

"Not him! Great Heron has me watched to see if I go to a lover. Even my husband is beginning to mistrust me. Soon he will reject me, and then I'll be an outcast." Tears filled Wind Song's eyes.

"What turned your husband's father's heart against you?" Cosy asked.

Wind Song bowed her head. "He caught me once in the forest and tried to force himself upon me, but I fought him and escaped. He's been angry ever since."

"Why did you not tell your husband of this outrage?"

"At first I feared to say anything, and now it's too late. Who'd believe me, a barren wife accused of being unfaithful?"

"I believe you," Cosy said. "And I'll help you by telling you the roots you must gather and how to prepare them to cure your barrenness. Know that I was trained to be a Medicine Woman."

Wind Song stared at her, hope dawning in her eyes.

"I will help you," Cosy said, "but in return you must help me."

"Yes!"

"Then find where the star root grows, the blue flag, and the blacksnake root. Gather and dry these roots, four of each, for at least seven suns before chopping and mixing them together. Steep that in water another seven suns, and pour off the liquid. Drink twelve drops, no more, of this each sun, starting from the time your blood flow stops and ceasing when you miss your next blood time, for you will be with child."

Wind Song regarded her with awe.

"Remember to talk to the plants when you gather their roots, telling them why you need a part of them. There's also a special chant you must memorize and say while you chop and mix the roots." Cosy recited the chant, and Wind Song repeated it until Cosy was satisfied she'd learned each word.

"Success is yours if you follow exactly what I've told you," she said. "I will make one more suggestion. Take into your lodge, to live with you and your husband, one of the respected old widowed women of the village and see to it that she is always with you when you are not with your husband so that it becomes impossible to accuse you of unfaithfulness."

"I will do as you say."

"Good." Cosy took a deep breath. "Now you must help me. My friend, the man tied in Lame Wolf's lodge, must be freed before Great Heron returns at sunset. He must have moccasins to travel fast and quietly. We will also need food, a knife, and a blanket. Can you find a way to obtain these things for me and to free him?"

"The moccasins, the knife, the blanket, and the food are easy," Wind Song said, "but freeing the white man is not."

"Think of how you might lure Lame Wolf from his lodge for a short time. If you can do that, I'll creep in and cut my friend's bonds."

Wind Song frowned in thought, then her brow cleared and she smiled grimly. "Lame Wolf is the man Great Heron has set to watch me," she said. "He will certainly trail after me if he believes I go to meet a lover. I'll take pleasure in fooling him."

Some time later, from her place of concealment behind a rack on which a deerskin was stretched to dry, Cosy watched as Wind Song crept stealthily past the side of Lame Wolf's wigwam. At first Cosy feared the girl was being too obvious and held her breath when Lame Wolf, seated in front of his lodge, turned his head to watch her. He glanced quickly around, then rose and drifted in her wake.

Fervently hoping that he'd truly taken the bait and wasn't merely pretending to follow Wind Song, meaning to circle back to see why he was being lured away, Cosy dashed from behind the drying deerskin, attracting the attention of two small girls before she ducked inside Lame Wolf's wigwam. She could only pray they wouldn't sound an alarm.

She found Jacob lying on the ground, his hands and feet bound behind him. "Don't speak," she whispered as she quickly slashed through the thongs with the knife Wind Song had given her.

Jacob groaned as he sat up. His boots were gone, lost in the lake. She slipped moccasins over his feet, relieved that they fit, and helped him stand. "Can you walk?" she whispered, knowing his arms and legs must be numb from being bound.

He nodded.

The same two little girls who'd watched Cosy enter were waiting when she emerged with Jacob. Though she saw no one else, dozens of eyes could be on them. Lame Wolf, she knew, was the real danger. All she could do was pin her faith on Wind Song's ability to lead him astray.

"This way," she told Jacob, and he stumbled along behind her as she led the way toward the woods, following Wind Song's directions toward a river that would take them to a village by a lake.

"Those who live by Torch Lake hate Great Heron and the Mides," Wind Song had assured her. "They will help you reach Houghton."

If Lame Wolf didn't overtake them before they reached the Torch Lake village, Cosy thought apprehensively. The only weapon they had was one knife, while he would be armed with a bow and arrows or, perhaps, a gun.

At least Jacob's stiffness seemed to be easing, enabling him to pick up speed.

"The entire village will be after us," he said.

"No," she told him. "This is a Mide matter, and so the villagers won't interfere. And the only Mide in the village until the rest of them return at sunset is Lame Wolf, the man who tied you."

Jacob grimaced. *"That* bastard. How did you manage to rescue me?"

"I bargained with Wind Song, a favor for a favor. She lured Lame Wolf away from the lodge."

It took them some time to reach the river bank and, when they did, a fine, misty rain began. "Where are we headed?" Jacob asked.

"Wind Song said we were two sleeps from Houghton on foot. If we follow this river to Torch Lake, we'll find another village of the People, a friendly village. She thinks we may be able to buy a canoe there. Do you have any money?"

"Lame Wolf didn't undress me," Jacob said, "so he didn't find my money belt. I have money. But what makes you so sure the Indians at Torch Lake will welcome us?"

"They hate and fear the Mides. I think they'll help once I tell them what happened to us at the hands of Great Heron."

They skirted a cedar swamp, sometimes sinking in mud to their ankles. Finally Cosy called a halt and they ate some of the dried meat Wind Song had given her, quenching their thirst from the river.

"I've never met any woman like you," Jacob said as they once again hurried along the river, as near the bank as they could manage. "Beautiful, feminine, as brave as any man, and not afraid to show your intelligence." He peered along their back trail. "Unfortunately, none of those excellent qualities are any match for a man with a gun."

Her heart sank. "Are you sure Lame Wolf has a gun? I didn't see one in his lodge."

"If he doesn't, I feel sure someone in that village must have a rifle they'll lend to a man with strong medicine power such as you claim a Mide has."

She knew Jacob was right. She was also aware that, though they had a head start, Lame Wolf would soon find and follow the trail they'd left and could also outpace them.

Apparently Jacob's thoughts matched hers, because he suddenly halted. "We can't outrun a bullet," he said, "so we'll have to be cleverer than Lame Wolf. We'll set a trap."

"He'll be cautious," she warned.

"There's a way to entice him into losing his caution," Jacob insisted. "We'll use you as bait."

Twenty-one

As they stood in a small burned-over glade in the dense pine forest, Jacob drew Cosy into his arms. "God knows I hate to risk you," he said. "If we had the time and equipment, I'd dig a pitfall; but we have neither. So Lame Wolf will have to be enticed into a deadfall trap."

She looked directly into his eyes, knowing their chances of escaping Lame Wolf were slim even with a deadfall. "Enticed by me," she said. "I'll do my best."

Giving her a quick hug, he released her. He pointed to where a huge white pine, its trunk scorched and burned by lightning, lay on the ground, fireweed springing up around it. "First, gather branches," he said.

As Cosy did so, she fretted over Jacob's plan. The People used deadfalls to trap animals, but Lame Wolf was far cleverer than any animal. Did they have a chance?

Bringing an armful of dead branches to where Jacob knelt by the fallen pine, she saw he was using the knife Wind Song had given them, cutting strips from the buckskin food pouch to tie the makeshift trap together. When he'd finished, they strewed the dead branches about to look as natural as possible. Cosy studied the result doubtfully. She could see the deadfall—surely Lame Wolf would, too.

"Now lie on the ground ahead of the trap—right here," Jacob ordered.

When she did, he asked her to turn on her side and carefully propped a heavy log over her legs so it appeared she was caught underneath.

"He won't be fooled," she whispered, afraid Lame Wolf might be close enough to hear if she spoke aloud. "He'll suspect a trap when he doesn't see you."

"He *will* see me," Jacob whispered back. "I'll seem to be trying to lift this log off you. It would help if you moaned and cried."

If Lame Wolf did have a rifle and chose to shoot first, they couldn't possibly escape. But, since he was a warrior of the People, Cosy thought he'd try to prove his courage rather than taking the easy way. Lying helpless under the log, she had no choice but to wait and see if she were right.

Her heart thudded in her chest as she began to moan. "Oh," she cried, "it hurts so—help me!"

"I'm doing all I can," Jacob answered loudly, "but since that fall I took, I can hardly use my right hand."

"Oh-h-h," she moaned, the very real fear she felt entering her voice.

"Cosy, I'm trying. Are you all right? Cosy!" Jacob's tone carried a convincing urgency. Even if Lame Wolf understood no English, he would hear the desperation.

Cosy wondered if Jacob were as apprehensive as she was. Men seldom admitted to feeling fear. "Please!" she cried. "Oh-h-h . . ."

I can't keep this up much longer, she thought. I can't bear to lie under this log, waiting for the roar of a gun. Or the silent, swift flight of an arrow.

With a shriek that stopped Cosy's breath, Lame Wolf leaped from the shelter of the trees, hurling himself at Jacob. For a heart-stopping moment, she thought he was going to miss the deadfall trap entirely.

Then his right foot tripped the hidden trigger, springing the trap, and the heavy pine branch fell, striking his shoulder and throwing him off balance. The rifle he carried thudded to the ground. His momentum kept him going. Reeling and stumbling, he crashed into the log propped above Cosy's legs, toppling it so the log's full weight rested on her, with Lame Wolf on top of the log. She screamed in pain and terror.

Jacob flung himself on the warrior, jerking him off the log. They both fell, then scrambled to their feet. Lame Wolf reached for his knife; but Jacob grappled with him, trying to pin his arms. Cosy struggled to free herself, but the log held her down firmly.

Lame Wolf broke away from Jacob and freed his knife. "Get the gun!" Jacob shouted to her, but she couldn't move; she was trapped.

With horror she watched Lame Wolf raise the knife and slash at Jacob and saw the red stain of blood cover Jacob's shirt.

Jacob staggered back. Recovering, he yanked his own knife from his belt and circled the warrior warily, searching for an opening. Cosy watched helplessly, the pain in her left leg forgotten. Fear gripped her as Jacob stumbled. She searched the ground nearby for something to throw to distract Lame Wolf. There was nothing. She wrenched at a jagged branch on the log that pinned her legs but couldn't move it. Still the men circled each other, Jacob seeming to waver. From loss of blood?

The wolf and the lynx, Cosy thought, recalling Hungry Moon's puzzling dream. An unequal fight had they been animals, because a wolf depended on the pack to some extent while a lynx was a solitary creature, an efficient killer on his own. Even wounded, a lynx should be able to finish a single wolf. Unfortunately, only in Hungry Moon's dream was Jacob a lynx . . .

Still, hadn't her own vision dream summoned a white lynx as her spirit animal? Could she call on the white lynx to aid her and Jacob? Drawing in a deep breath, Cosy let the sound of a lynx scream gather in her mind. Opening her mouth, she cried out in the nearly human, high-pitched, terrifying squall of a hunting lynx.

Startled, Lame Wolf half-turned. Jacob leaped forward and buried his knife deep in the warrior's chest, then jumped clear. Lame Wolf took a step, put a hand to his chest, and toppled to the ground. Jacob approached him warily, standing over his fallen adversary for long moments before dropping to one knee.

"Is he dead?" Cosy asked.

Jacob's head jerked up as though he were surprised by the sound of her voice. "Yes," he said grimly.

"I'm trapped under the log," she said.

He sprang to his feet, strained to lift the log, then triumphantly flung it aside, freeing her. Cosy ran her fingers over the bones in her legs but could feel no break. Relieved, she tried to stand, leaning on Jacob, only to find the pain in her left ankle so severe that tears came to her eyes. She blinked them away, forcing herself to stay upright.

Gritting her teeth against the pain, she turned her attention to Jacob, saying, "Let me look at your shoulder."

He glanced in some surprise at his blood-soaked shirt, lifting a hand to his shoulder. He winced as he touched it.

"Come closer so I can see," she ordered, sinking down onto the log, no longer able to tolerate the pain of standing.

Jacob knelt beside her, and very gently she pulled his shirt aside to expose his right shoulder. Lame Wolf's knife had gone through the flesh between Jacob's shoulder and his neck. Blood had clotted across the slash and she was careful not to disturb this lest the bleeding begin anew. Since the bleeding *had* stopped and Jacob was able to use his arm normally, the wound was probably not serious and should heal quickly if kept clean. She eased the shirt back into place.

"How are you?" Jacob asked, his gaze following hers to her left ankle, which was already swollen and discolored. He shook his head. "You can't walk on that."

"We have to go on," she said. "We must be safely inside the Torch Lake village by the time Great Heron and the other Mides return to their village."

"Sunset," Jacob muttered, glancing at the sun, which was already lowering. He looked around. Gesturing toward the rifle Lame Wolf had dropped on the ground, he asked, "How about trying that as a crutch?"

With the stock resting under her arm, the rifle proved to be a fair makeshift crutch, enabling Cosy to hobble slowly along beside Jacob as they followed the river. The sun was far down the sky when the welcome scent of cooking fires told her they were nearing the Torch Lake village. Soon dogs rushed toward them, snarling and barking, followed by three men and several half-grown boys.

Cosy told her tale as succinctly as possible—the near drowning, crawling ashore on an island where a Midewewin ceremony was being held, capture, escape, the pursuit by a hostile Mide.

The village chief, a massive old man named Tall Hemlock, shook his head. "Our brothers to the east are tainted by evil. We no longer trade with them or exchange women for wives. You are welcome to take refuge with us."

"We are grateful," Cosy told him, trying to ignore her throbbing ankle as she leaned on Jacob. "It's possible, though, that Great Heron may follow us here and cause trouble for you."

Tall Hemlock drew himself impressively erect. "He would not dare attack me! Our village is smaller, our people fewer, but we are strong and quick and not steeped in the ways of wrongness. Death awaits Great Heron should he trespass here."

Cosy and Jacob followed the chief and the others toward the ten wigwams grouped near the lake shore, were shown to Tall Hemlock's lodge and made welcome there. His wife, Blue Lake, bound Cosy's leg with healing roots and bark and poulticed Jacob's wound. After sharing rabbit stew with the chief and his wife, Cosy and Jacob lay down to sleep side by side on reed mats next to the fire.

Jacob reached to her and grasped her hand, holding it in his. Warmed and comforted by his touch, she closed her eyes.

Cosy woke to a lessened darkness, a hint that dawn was near. At first she thought someone in the lodge had called her name, but then she realized the voice she heard was in her head. An image of Hungry Moon shimmered in the air above her, not frail and weak as when she'd last visited her foster mother but strong and vital as in earlier days.

"I see you are safe, my Koko," Hungry Moon's voice said, "and so my spirit can begin its journey. Help others, as you were taught to do. Learn all ways of healing and live your life with joy and courage. Do not mourn; one day we will meet again in the place where there is no grief or sorrow."

The voice ceased, the vision slowly faded. Tears sprang into Cosy's eyes.

"What's the matter?" Jacob asked from beside her.

"Hungry Moon's spirit came to me," Cosy said brokenly. "She's dead."

He pulled her close to him and she wept against his chest until she fell into a troubled sleep. She woke in his arms to the twittering of birds perched on the roof of the wigwam. Blue Lake was stirring the embers of the fire, coaxing them into flame as she added dry twigs.

Cosy sat up, remembering her vision. But she had no time to grieve; she and Jacob were only temporarily safe, and they must hurry on their way.

"Do the People say, 'Good morning?' " Jacob asked. "Or is that unspoken, like hello and goodbye?"

She saw he was smiling at her and almost gave way to a sudden strange impulse to lean down and kiss him.

"It *is* a good morning," he went on, sitting up. "We're both alive, against the odds. A trifle battered, maybe, but mending. At least I am. How about you?"

Cosy rose, putting her weight on her uninjured ankle and carefully shifting part of it to the other. To her relief, though there was some pain, it was bearable. "Better," she said.

An hour later she stood with Tall Hemlock, a dozen children, and several dogs at the lake shore while Jacob loaded supplies into the canoe the chief had insisted on giving them, refusing payment.

"You made me a gift of the rifle," he'd said. "I will remember you warmly in the cold days of winter when the gun brings us food."

As Cosy eased into the canoe, Tall Hemlock said, "Your spirit is one with ours, Koko. May you and your friend go safely and may the Great Spirit speed your journey."

She paddled into the lake along with Jacob, instructing him gently in the People's way of handling canoes. He was quick to learn and so, as they headed west following Tall

Hemlock's advice, she was able to turn her attention to watching for landmarks to guide them. First would be the rock shaped like a bear standing on his hind legs.

"I know you didn't fall overboard from the *Detroit*," Jacob said after a time. "You were pushed."

Cosy glanced at him and nodded. "By Rosalind. I didn't see her, but I smelled her perfume. Jealousy truly does poison the heart."

"Rosalind wasn't the only one who saw you in Dan's arms. I was on deck, too."

Cosy stiffened. "I was *not* in his arms!"

"It certainly looked like—" Jacob broke off. "We agreed once not to lie to one another, so I believe you. But even if he had been holding you, there was no excuse for Rosalind's attempting to drown you."

"When we were captured on the island, I told Great Heron my enemy had tried to kill me and I must avenge the wrong done to me."

"And do you intend to?"

She didn't reply, unsure how she felt toward her half-sister. "My foster mother taught me that those with poisoned hearts harm themselves as much as they do others," she said at last.

"That's not really an answer."

"When I see Rosalind again, I'll know what to do," Cosy said.

"Life with the man she chose may not be a happy one," Jacob said. "Perhaps the melancholy love songs she favored were a recognition deep in her heart that her lover would cause her pain. As I recall, one of them spoke of love being lonely. I found that particularly sad."

Cosy repeated the line of the song, one of her sister's

plaintive love laments: " 'For love is ever lonely, love is ever untrue . . .' "

"It doesn't have to be that way," Jacob said.

She paused in her paddling to give him a long look. What did he mean? Was he referring to Rosalind and Dan? Or to someone else?

Meeting her gaze, he smiled at her. "In my opinion, there's one problem with canoes—the paddlers must kneel too far apart."

Jacob watched Cosy's puzzled expression change as she realized what he meant. She flushed and looked away from him. "There's the first landmark," she said, pointing.

He saw the rock shaped like a standing bear and glanced up at the sun, high in the heavens. About noon. His right shoulder had begun to ache, and he knew the pain would worsen as they paddled on. He'd also seen Cosy wince when she'd shifted position and was aware her ankle must be hurting her. Chances were they wouldn't be able to keep up the pace they'd set this morning; they'd be lucky to reach Tall Hemlock's second landmark, a lone dead pine on a point, much before sunset.

That meant spending a night camping along the lake shore. Safe enough, he decided, if they didn't light a fire. A canoe left no trail to be followed; and so, if Great Heron was in pursuit, he'd have no idea where to look for them.

Cosy would be alone with him in their night's camp. The thought sent a sudden surge of desire through Jacob, and he tried to quell it in vain. No, he told himself. You can't take advantage of her. You don't have the right.

But he sure as hell had the need to make her his, a need that threatened to become a permanent ache. She was so lovely and she felt so right in his arms, as though she belonged there. Belonged to him.

Unfortunately, duty came first, and there could be no question of that, not with his country at war.

"You sang part of a sad love song to me once," Cosy said as though reading his thoughts. " 'The Soldier's Farewell,' about leaving because honor calls."

"I remember. Do the Chippewa have such songs?"

She didn't answer immediately, her gaze fixed on the water. He was both startled and pleased when she began to sing in a low, quavering voice. Though he couldn't understand the Chippewa words, the anguish and sorrow of the song came through clearly.

"Will you sing it in English for me?" he asked.

"The melody is meant for the People's tongue, so I don't think I can; but I'll try to tell you what the English words would be. She began slowly, obviously translating from one language to the other as she went along:

> "It is time for you to depart
> I will not weep for you
> I will wait.
> If you do not return
> I will not weep for you
> I will die."

An unexpected ache gripped Jacob's throat, preventing him from speaking for a minute or two. No matter how differently humans live or how differently they speak and believe, he told himself, when it comes to love, we're much the same.

"It's a beautiful, heartbreaking song," he said at last.

Cosy didn't look at him; neither did she speak. There was only the soft swish of their paddles and the occasional splash as a fish jumped from the water to lunge at a low-flying insect.

Jacob knew he would treasure the memory of this moment for as long as he lived—the clean lines of the birch-bark canoe, the sun's glimmer on the blue water, here and there along the shore the scarlet of maples and the gold of oaks and birches brilliant among the green of the pines. But most of all, the woman sharing the canoe with him. Her dark hair caught into a thick braid, her cat-green eyes, the high cheekbones of her face, the fascinating faint duskiness of her skin, and her lithe, sweetly curved body combined to make her the loveliest woman he'd ever seen.

"We won't reach the channel before dark," Cosy said, breaking his reverie.

"I agree."

"If we try to push ourselves to go on much farther," she said, "your wound may start to bleed again."

"I'm entirely willing to pull into shore and set up a night's camp," he told her. "We'll be safe enough."

She gazed at him gravely. "Will we?"

He was about to argue that Great Heron couldn't possibly follow their trail past Tall Hemlock's village when he realized she might not be referring to possible pursuit by the Mides. And he doubted that she was worried about animals attacking them. That left him. Since he couldn't honestly assure her she'd be safe from him, he held his tongue.

Unexpectedly, she smiled. "I see you keep your word."

That puzzled him until he remembered his promise to always be honest with her, and then he chuckled at her cleverness.

Cosy looked away from him, her gaze sweeping the shoreline. "There," she pointed.

On a slender point extending into the lake, Jacob saw

the landmark pine that Tall Hemlock had described. A burned and fallen pine had proved to be their salvation yesterday. Deciding this second dead pine was a favorable omen, he said, "We'll camp near that point."

Cosy nodded. "A good choice." As they paddled toward shore, she said, "Didn't you once tell me you were not a woodsman but a city man, born and bred? Yet you've obviously had experience with deadfall traps and you mentioned pitfalls as well. Does learning to become a lawyer include such things?"

Jacob met her inquiring gaze. "My education as an attorney had nothing to do with such knowledge. I've been specially trained to construct traps as well as other useful devices of a kind not generally needed by city lawyers." He couldn't very well tell her who'd trained him or why, so he added, "The reason doesn't matter."

She questioned him no further, but Jacob remained troubled. He'd tried from the beginning to be honest with Cosy, but had he really kept to his promise? True, he hadn't lied outright; but he certainly had lied by omission. And would continue to.

By the time they reached shore, his shoulder throbbed with pain, making it difficult to use both arms as he helped Cosy pull the canoe ashore and then, though they'd met no other lake travelers, drag it behind nearby bushes to conceal it.

She pointed to an upthrust rock a few yards away and said, "If we camp here, this will shield us from the wind while we sleep."

They placed their gear—three blankets and a food pouch—at the base of the rock. Cosy removed her moccasins and sat on the bank of the small stream near the rock to soak her left ankle in the rushing water. Jacob spread one of the blankets on the ground and stretched out on it, watching her. She not only had eyes like a cat but a cat's flowing grace. No man, he told himself, could look at Cosy and not want her. After a time, she turned and gestured to him to join her.

When he sat beside her, she eased his shirt off his shoulder and bathed his knife wound with the cold water from the stream. "It's healing well," she said.

She was so temptingly close to him that it took all the willpower he possessed not to pull her into his arms. When night fell and they lay side by side on the blankets, he knew he'd be even more tempted. Could he resist? He knew he wouldn't want to.

"Am I hurting you?" she asked.

"If you mean my shoulder," he said, "no."

Her eyes widened. "But what else—" She broke off. Moving her hand from his shoulder to his cheek, she asked, "What troubles you, Jacob?"

With a groan he turned his head so his mouth touched her palm. As he licked droplets of water from her skin, his left hand rose to cradle the back of her head and he heard the soft sound of her drawing in her breath. Of protest? Of surrender? He searched her face, and joy mingled with his desire when he saw his own longing mirrored there.

He meant his kiss to be gentle; but his passion, banked for so long, broke through, and his mouth came down hard on hers in a fervent, demanding kiss. When he felt her eager response, he wrapped his arms tightly around her, the sweet taste of her going to his head like wine.

At last his lips left hers to travel along her throat and down until he encountered the laced thongs of her tunic. His hand rose to untie them, but then he paused and pulled back, gazing into her eyes. "Cosy, I want you," he said, the words rasping in his throat. "Do you know what that means? What I mean?"

"No," she whispered. "Tell me. Show me."

Her answer added fuel to the fiery need consuming him. He got to his feet, pulling her up with him, guiding her toward the blanket spread on the ground. "Will you lie with me here?" he asked.

She glanced uncertainly at the spread blanket, then at him, but didn't reply.

"Once we're lying side by side," he said, "I'll tell you what I mean. Show you. If you want me to stop, I will; but you'll have to say so right away. Later on may be too late."

Without speaking, she eased herself onto the blanket until she lay on her back. He dropped down beside her, lying on his side, facing her. With his forefinger, he traced the outline of her lips. "When I kiss you," he murmured, "I enjoy tasting your mouth."

"Yes," she said shyly. "I like tasting you, too."

"I'll taste more of you," he told her softly as he leaned toward her and ran his tongue over her lips, probing gently until she opened her mouth, offering him entry. He kissed her deeply, fighting with himself to keep control of his ever-mounting need.

While he kissed her, he untied the thongs of her tunic and unlaced the front. His hand slipped inside and touched her breast, and she moaned when his thumb caressed her nipple. He pushed the tunic aside, trailing kisses along her throat and down until his mouth closed over her nipple.

Her "Oh!" was a breath of surprised pleasure, and her hands stroked his hair, holding his head to her breasts as he tasted first one, then the other. He paused for a moment and removed her tunic, gazing at the round softness of her breasts with their peaked nipples in delighted appreciation.

"You have a lovely body," he murmured as his hands caressed her.

A moment later he had his shirt off and was pulling her close, savoring the feel of her breasts against his bare chest. "Besides tasting you," he whispered in her ear, "I enjoy touching you. Every part of you."

She pulled slightly away. "Be careful of your wound," she murmured.

"With you in my arms, nothing can hurt me," he said.

Reassured, Cosy snuggled closer to Jacob, her senses alert as her nipples brushed across the hair on his chest. How wonderful it felt to lie flesh to flesh with him. She didn't want him to ever stop kissing and caressing her. Her entire body was aflame; and deep inside her, there was a strange new throbbing as something seemed to uncoil like a tendril reaching toward the sun.

And the sun was Jacob.

"Do you want me to stop?" he asked, his warm breath in her ear exciting her.

"No," she murmured. "Oh, no."

"If I go on, I may not be able to stop," he warned.

"Go on," she urged, finding herself longing to touch and caress him as he was touching and caressing her. She ran her hands over his back and down until she came to the cloth of his trousers. How smooth his skin was despite the strong muscles she knew lay beneath.

He pulled away and she made a sound of protest. "We still have too many clothes on," he told her, the rasp in his voice making her shiver with anticipation.

He pulled off her moccasins, then reached under her skirt to untie her leggings, his hand lingering on her thigh, then touching her where no man ever had touched her, sending sudden hot pleasure coursing through her. His continued caresses made her gasp, and she was hardly aware of him removing her leggings, then her skirt.

He left her momentarily to shed his moccasins and trousers, and she saw a naked man's body for the first time. Since small children of the People went unclothed in the summer, she was well aware of the difference between boys and girls; but looking at Jacob took her breath away.

He pulled her close and resumed his intimate caresses, making her helpless with a longing that was pleasurable and, at the same time, urgent, demanding something more. She slipped her hand between them and touched his thrusting manhood, needing to feel as well as see.

"Ah, God, Cosy," he gasped. He took her hand away, eased her onto her back, and rose over her.

When his hardness probed at her moist softness, a piercing joy shot through her. She suddenly knew exactly what she longed for and she opened to him, welcoming his thrust, needing him, wanting him.

Loving him.

Twenty-two

If there is such a thing as a paradise on earth, Jacob told himself as he lay on the blanket with Cosy in his arms, I'm in it. Overhead, the lowering sun slanted through the branches of the surrounding pines; the brook gurgled and sang as it rippled past, and the aromatic odor of the evergreens mingled with Cosy's own unique scent. As he well knew, she was the key to his paradise.

In the aftermath of the shattering intensity of their lovemaking, he was temporarily at peace, more so than he could ever recall being, and at the same time anticipating the promise of the coming night alone with Cosy.

"Did you know I wanted you from the moment I set eyes on you?" he asked. "You were the most beautiful and unusual woman I'd ever met. Or ever expected to meet."

She tipped her head to look at him. "What you told me was that you wanted us to be friends."

"I thought that was safer to admit to, as well as being at least part of the truth. We are friends, aren't we?"

Her answer was somewhat hesitant. "We are."

He brushed his fingers lightly over her cheek, marveling at its soft smoothness. "Friends who've become lovers."

She turned her head and kissed his fingers, the warmth of her lips kindling a spark of renewed desire. He drew her closer, reaching under the blanket he'd drawn over them to caress the enticing curve of her hip.

"I thought at first you came to our house to visit Rosalind," she said, snuggling against him.

It had never been the reason, merely the excuse, but he couldn't reveal that truth. "After that first time, it was you I came to visit," he told her. Which was no lie. He'd returned as much to see her as in the line of duty.

"You weren't easy to understand," she said.

"I tried to conceal my feelings. Partly because you often mentioned how much you cared for Black Water, making me jealous of a man I'd never met."

"I've always admired Black Water. I thought I loved him."

He pulled back a little, rising on one elbow. "You thought?" he echoed.

She considered. "I *did* love him in a way."

"And now?"

"I no longer regret that he and I can never marry."

He had the impression she was choosing her words carefully. Why shouldn't she? And why should he feel disappointed in her answer? What, after all, had he told her? What could he tell her?

A line from "The Soldier's Lament" circled in his mind, repeating over and over: "Farewell, farewell, my own true love, farewell . . ."

Because he knew he'd have to leave her, the truth of the words saddened him.

Telling himself that the time for leaving had not yet come, he lifted her and eased her over until she lay on top of him, her soft warmth banishing any other thought from his mind. When her lips found his, making him realize she was as eager to begin making love again as he was, elation thrummed through him.

She would never belong to Black Water. Or to any other man. She was his and his alone.

Suddenly she sat up, straddling his thighs. She flung off the covering blanket, stared down a moment at what was revealed, then ran her fingers over his thrusting manhood, caressing him until he groaned in pleasure and caught her hand.

"Why do you stop me again as you did before?" she asked.

He pulled her down so they both lay on their sides and murmured against her lips, "Much as I enjoy what you're doing, I want to share the lovemaking with you."

He tried to go slowly, trying to make it last, but kissing and caressing her drove him wild with need and when she arched against him, moaning, he eased inside her. A thrust of her hips buried him deep within, and then they moved together in perfect rhythm. Her final cry of complete abandonment was echoed by his.

They rested, rose, and splashed in the stream, then dressed and ate the dried meat and berries Tall Hemlock's wife had given them. Jacob's final look at the lake as night closed in showed no canoes on its darkening waters. Reassured, he lay down beside Cosy on the blanket, took her hand in his and immediately fell asleep.

Cosy, with Jacob beside her, had never felt so warm and protected. She knew she'd found her true love, the man her heart would always belong to. Her feeling for Black Water had been a girl's attachment to an admired warrior; she'd been thrilled and excited when he'd taken notice of her. And she understood now that Black Water would have expected her to be exactly what Jacob had said—a wife of the People. Not exactly her husband's servant but not an equal, either.

What she felt for Jacob was entirely different. As he'd said, he'd been her friend before they became lovers and he was still her friend, a man she could trust and depend on. A man she could talk to, who valued her intelligence. A man who believed she could be a healer no matter what world she lived in.

But Black Water *had* asked her to be his wife, and Jacob hadn't mentioned marriage. Or love.

If she hadn't been so tired, this omission might have caused her more concern. As it was, she fell asleep while turning the matter over in her mind.

She woke before dawn in Jacob's arms. In the darkness they made love slowly and sweetly before sleep claimed them again.

The squawk of a blue jay jerked her awake at sunrise. She jumped to her feet, looking around to see what had alarmed the jay. Searching the trees for the bird, she spotted him flitting from one tree to another near the creek. Looking at the ground, her gaze fell on a fat porcupine waddling along the bank. She breathed a sigh of relief and turned to Jacob, who was just sitting up, yawning.

She smiled. Whatever training he may have had in setting traps evidently hadn't included learning how birds and animals could warn of danger.

As they quickly washed in the creek, the morning almost as chilly as the water, Cosy's thoughts kept returning to their nearly fatal encounter with Lame Wolf. Something about what had happened troubled her. They dressed hurriedly, chewing on the last of the dried meat as they rolled up the blankets.

"You killed Lame Wolf," she said suddenly, still on her knees.

Jacob, obviously taken aback, got to his feet before replying, "It was kill or be killed."

"I know you had to kill him." She rose and faced him. "That's not what I mean. I've just realized that he isn't the first man you've killed."

Jacob folded his arms across his chest. "What makes you think that?"

"Because you behaved as a seasoned warrior would. After you freed me from the log, you pulled the knife from Lame Wolf's chest, thrust the blade into the earth to cleanse it, and took that knife along with us."

"I thought we might need it."

"You'd already retrieved Lame Wolf's knife," she pointed out, "so we had one."

"In my opinion, two knives are better than one."

She gazed at him levelly. "In my opinion, you don't wish to explain why a city man who knows nothing of the woods is also a warrior. Men who go to war, soldiers, learn to kill. Are you a soldier, Jacob?"

"I can't answer that question, Cosy. Come, it's time we were off." He turned and strode toward the lake.

She followed slowly, her thoughts troubled. Jacob had always been honest with her, or so she believed, but now she knew he had secrets he didn't intend to share with her. Recalling some of the odd questions he'd asked her about Rosalind in the past and his peculiar behavior when Rosalind and Dan were married, she bit her lip. She was aware Dan had his own secrets, some of which Rosalind shared with him. Was there some connection between Jacob and Dan? She carried her worry with her into the canoe.

The day was clear, the air warming as the sun climbed

the sky, glittering on the water of the lake while they paddled along. Jacob didn't speak and, since she had nothing to say to him, she remained silent, her heart troubled.

"Didn't Tall Hemlock mention red rocks as a landmark to show us the channel leading to Portage Lake?" Jacob asked at last.

"Yes. I haven't yet seen that landmark."

"Once we reach the channel we won't be far from Houghton. I wish—" He broke off.

"What do you wish?" she asked.

"I wish we'd never reach the damn town!"

She waited for him to go on, but he didn't explain his outburst or say anything else and they continued to skim over the water in silence. The sun had risen to its highest point when Cosy stopped paddling and, shielding her eyes against the glare as she peered to the north, cried, "I see a sail! A boat!"

Jacob turned to look. "You're right. She's a sloop. And there—" he pointed "—are the red rocks. The sloop must be near the channel entrance." He put his hands to his mouth and shouted, "Ahoy, the boat!" then waved a paddle in the air.

After repeated calls from Jacob, the sloop turned and began to tack toward their canoe. Voices shouted across the water, and soon a line was thrown, caught by Jacob, and made fast. With the canoe in tow, the boat turned and sailed toward the channel again. The rest of the trip into Houghton seemed miraculously quick.

Once the sloop docked, eager hands helped them from the canoe. When they stood on the wharf, one of the crew glanced from Cosy to Jacob and said, "Thought at first you both was Injuns till we seen your red hair, mister."

Cosy realized that, because of the way she was dressed, the man still thought she was.

"We were lost overboard off the *Detroit* two nights ago," Jacob told them.

"Heard about that," a dock worker put in, coming closer. "They figured you was drownded for sure. But here you are. Ain't that something?"

"How'd you do it?" the crewman asked.

Jacob gave a brief account of their rescue by Indians, making it seem as though the Torch Lake villagers had found them and offered the canoe. Turning to Cosy, he added, "This is Miss Collins. Do any of you know where her father, Jephthah Collins, might be staying in Houghton?"

"Heard tell some people from the *Detroit* was staying at the Copper Inn," the dock worker said.

Jacob hired a buggy and they drove to the inn, only to find no sign of Jephthah, though he was registered there.

"How about a Mr. and Mrs. Daniel Rackham?" Jacob asked the desk clerk.

The clerk, eyeing Jacob's wrinkled and dirty clothes, said, "No," adding a belated and reluctant, "sir," obviously hoping to be rid of them as soon as possible.

Anger rising—the clerk had dismissed her with a glance and a sniff—Cosy spoke up. "Falling overboard from the *Detroit* was a most harrowing experience for us. Surely you can be more helpful."

The clerk's eyes widened and he leaned forward. "Off the *Detroit?* And you survived?"

"Do we look like ghosts?" Jacob snapped.

"I did hear there was a woman taken off the *Detroit* and brought to Dr. Adams's place," the clerk offered.

Jacob and Cosy stared at each other. "Rosalind?" she whispered. Had something happened to her sister?

He turned to the clerk. "Where does Dr. Adams live?"

"He's got a place next to his house where he takes care of real sick patients," the clerk said. "Sort of like a hospital, you might say. It ain't far from here."

Dr. Adams's so-called hospital was a small frame building with one door and two windows. When the door opened to their knock, Cosy almost gagged on the foul stench that poured forth.

"My God!" Jacob exclaimed, grimacing.

The middle-aged, graying woman standing in the doorway gazed at them tiredly. "You want to see somebody here?" she asked. Beyond her Cosy noticed three beds, all occupied, lined up in a row.

"Rosalind—that is, Mrs. Daniel Rackham," Cosy said. "Is she here?"

"Rosalind?" the woman repeated. "She's gone."

Cosy stared at her. "You mean—" She broke off, unable to continue. Was this woman saying Rosalind was dead? Her head whirling dizzily, she staggered against Jacob, and then everything turned black.

"She's coming around," a woman's voice said, so faint and far away that Cosy had to struggle to hear. At the same time she was aware of a sharp, aromatic odor in her nose that seemed to seep into her skull.

She opened her eyes to find herself draped across Jacob's arm with him on one knee, holding her.

"Are you all right?" he asked worriedly. "Rosalind isn't dead; you misunderstood."

"Help me up, please," she said.

Jacob rose, setting her on her feet but keeping his arm

around her waist while Cosy shook her head to try to clear away the fumes.

"Spirits of ammonia," the woman said. "Brings a person out of a faint every time."

"Is Rosalind all right?" Cosy asked.

The woman shrugged. "She was bleeding like a stuck pig when they took her away from here. I warned them they'd do her no good moving her, but the young man had the nerve to tell me this place wasn't fit for animals, much less human beings." She sniffed indignantly. "I'm as clean as the next nurse, but I'm all alone here day and night without any help. What do they expect?"

"Where was Rosalind taken?" Jacob asked.

"The older man seemed to think he knew a better place. Humph! Not in this town. Dr. Adams is a good man, not a drunken quack like some I could mention."

"Where did they go?" Jacob demanded, annoyance edging his voice.

The woman drew herself up. "How should I know? !f you've no business here, kindly get off my doorstep." As soon as they did, Jacob helping Cosy down the steps, she shut the door sharply behind them.

"What a monster," he said.

"Maybe she's just worn out," Cosy said. Tempted as she was to lean on Jacob, drawing strength from his nearness, she pulled away. "I'm worried about the bleeding she mentioned. Rosalind could be losing her baby. We must find her. You've lived in Houghton; do you have any idea what my father might have meant when he said he was taking Rosalind to a 'better place'?"

Jacob frowned. "I haven't had the need of a doctor so I don't—" He paused. "I wonder, since he used to live in

Houghton, if it's possible your father meant the Bird Woman?"

"Who is she?"

"I've heard she's a healer of some kind. Some people swear by her. She's a widow named Spolarich and she doesn't live far from here."

In answer to Jacob's knock, Mrs. Spolarich opened the door of her white frame house no more than a crack. "Come in quickly," the tiny gray-haired woman told them. "I don't want Gregor to catch a chill."

Once inside, Cosy noticed a small green-and-blue bird with a curved bill perched on the widow's shoulder. She'd never in her life seen such a strange-looking bird.

"Gregor's a parakeet," Mrs. Spolarich said, evidently noticing her surprise. "My late husband, a sea captain, long ago brought me a pair from the Caribbean and, my, how they've thrived." The bird cocked his head to stare with one beady eye at Cosy, and the old woman copied his gesture. "I realize you're not here to listen to my chatter. Are you, by any chance, looking for Mrs. Rackham?"

"She's my sister. Is she here?" Cosy asked.

"She is, and her husband and father as well. Her husband's with her, and your father's waiting in the parlor. You might want to see him first. Right over there." She gestured but didn't accompany them.

Jephthah, sitting in an armchair, gaped at Cosy and Jacob when they walked into the room. Springing to his feet, he rushed to Cosy and wrapped his arms around her. "My little girl," he said brokenly, "I thought I'd lost you."

Cosy clung to her father, tears coming to her eyes. "Jacob saved my life," she said.

Holding her in one arm, Jephthah reached a hand to Jacob. "I'll never be able to repay you for giving me back

my daughter," he said. "Never. I didn't realize how much
she meant to me until—" His voice broke and he cleared
his throat. Hugging Cosy, he said, "I don't suppose I've
been a very good father, have I?"

Cosy hugged him in return. "I love you," she murmured.
Then, stepping back, she asked, "How is Rosalind?"

Jephthah pulled a handkerchief from his pocket and blew
his nose before answering. "She's in Mrs. Spolarich's spare
bedroom. Damn near bled to death in that horror of a
hospital. I remembered the Bird Woman just in time. When
I was living in Houghton a few years back, a miner got
half his leg cut off, blood pouring out. They brought him
to her, and she stopped the bleeding just like that." He
snapped his fingers.

"And she's helped Rosalind?" Cosy asked.

"Your sister will recover." Mrs. Spolarich spoke from
the archway leading into the parlor.

As Cosy turned to look at her, another of the pretty green
birds flew up and perched on the old woman's other shoulder.

"This is Sonya," she said. "Sonya has been keeping
watch over your sister. Come with me now."

Cosy glanced at Jacob, who shook his head, saying, "I'll
stay with your father."

With her eyes closed and her face deathly pale, Rosalind
lay in a bed in a small room off the kitchen. Dan sat in a
chair drawn up to the bed. The bird named Sonya flew off
the old woman's shoulder and perched on the bed's footboard.

When Dan saw Cosy, he rose. "I heard the commotion
out there when you came in. I'm glad you're all right. So
is Rosalind."

Rosalind's eyes opened, and she stared dully at Cosy.

"I've been punished for what I did," she whispered. "I lost my baby."

"I'm sorry about the baby," Cosy told her.

Tears gathered in Rosalind's eyes. "I thought I didn't care about having a baby; but now that it's too late, I do." Her voice broke. Dan reached to take her hand and Rosalind's eyes fluttered shut again.

"She is not yet strong," Mrs. Spolarich said. "She must rest." As she spoke, Gregor fluttered from her shoulder to perch next to Sonya on the footboard. "We will leave them to watch over her," Mrs. Spolarich said.

Dan hesitated, staring at Rosalind's pale face. All the color was gone from her skin so that she seemed as fragile as porcelain.

"Come," Mrs. Spolarich urged. "We will take tea from the samovar while sleep heals her."

Mrs. Spolarich stopped in the kitchen to load a tea cart; and, as Cosy and Dan walked along, he leaned to her and whispered, "Rosalind told me the truth. I'm sorry it happened."

She had no chance to respond before they joined the two men in the parlor. Glancing about, Cosy saw gilded statues and gold-framed religious pictures she hadn't noticed earlier.

"I can't bear to see Rosie looking so ill," Jephthah said.

"She will recover," Mrs. Spolarich repeated, pushing the tea wagon into the room.

"Rosie owes her life to you," he told the old woman.

"Because you had the sense to bring her to me while there was still time," Mrs. Spolarich said. "You must take whatever credit is due, for I cannot. It is a gift that my family carries, but the true power comes from God."

Cosy gazed at her, fascinated. "How do you use this power?" she asked.

Mrs. Spolarich held out her hands. "I touch the person and repeat the Russian words taught to me by my father, for the gift passes male to female and female to male. Then the power flows through me from above and out through my fingers into the person that needs to be healed." She turned the spigot of the samovar, allowing hot tea to run into a glass.

"I call it a miracle," Jephthah said. "Like Cosy being saved from drowning."

"When did you discover Cosy was missing from the *Detroit?*" Jacob asked.

Dan shot him a quick glance. "Rosalind told me. But, because she'd fallen on the deck and was moaning and crying, I didn't immediately understand what she was trying to say."

"Dan sent a deckhand to fetch me," Jephthah put in, "and between us we carried Rosie to a cabin. 'Drowning,' she kept crying, but we couldn't make any sense of it even when she said, 'He went in after her.' I did wonder if she'd actually seen someone go overboard. I knew you could handle Rosie better that either Dan or I, Cosy, so I went to look for you and couldn't find you. I'd been noticing Jacob paying quite a bit of attention to you and, when I didn't see him, either, I figured the two of you had found a private place to be together. Finally, I realized you were both missing. By then, I couldn't convince the captain to turn the boat around and make a search. He said too much time had passed and there was no use. What the hell did happen?"

Without looking at either Jacob or Dan, Cosy said, "I

accidentally fell overboard. Luckily, Jacob saw me fall, grabbed a life preserver, and dived in after me."

"Jacob told me some Indians helped you get to Houghton," Jephthah said, keeping his gaze on Cosy.

As she nodded, she thought she saw doubt in his eyes. Not about what Jacob had said but about her story. He didn't believe her.

In the beginning, she'd wanted to do exactly what she'd told Great Heron—avenge herself on her sister. But poor Rosalind had been punished more than enough. Her only thought now was to spare Rosalind the pain of their father's knowing the truth about what had happened.

Mrs. Spolarich passed the glasses of tea around, each on a saucer with a sugar lump beside the glass. She then offered tiny jam-filled cookies. Cosy found she was ravenous, and it was hard to be polite and take only one or two after eating very little for the past two days. She watched in some amazement as Mrs. Spolarich placed the lump of sugar between her teeth and drank the tea through the lump.

"An old Russian custom," the old woman said when she noticed Cosy's interest. "Very tasty. You should try it."

"No doubt you'll be staying in Houghton with your wife until she recovers," Jacob said to Dan.

Dan glanced at Jacob. "No doubt."

Cosy's skin began to prickle with uneasiness. Why had Jacob asked that question? What did he care whether Dan stayed or not? And why had Dan's answer seemed evasive? She had nearly the same feeling as when she'd watched Jacob and Lame Wolf circling one another with knives drawn—one would win; one would lose, and the loser's life would be at stake.

Dan set down his barely touched glass of tea and rose

from his chair. "Cosy," he said, "would you mind coming
back to Rosalind's bedside with me? When she believed
you'd drowned, she kept repeating that she'd meant to give
you something of hers and regretted that she'd waited until
too late. It slipped my mind until this moment and, of
course, she's been through too much to remember. I'm sure
she'll rest easier if she's able to give it to you now."

Though puzzled, Cosy nodded, rose, and followed him
from the parlor. Why would Rosalind wish to give her
anything after trying to drown her? It made no sense. Dan
must be lying. But why?

Once they reached the room where Rosalind lay sleeping,
Dan pulled Cosy inside, put his fingers to his lips, reached
in his pocket, removed a small green velvet case, and thrust
it into her hand. Then he leaned close and whispered, "I'm
in deadly danger, Cosy. Will you, for Rosalind's sake, help
me get away without anyone knowing?"

Twenty-three

Cosy stared at Dan in consternation. Not as much because he claimed he was in danger—she'd sensed danger—but because he'd asked her to help him for Rosalind's sake. Almost immediately she realized he understood her better than she did herself. Because that was exactly why she *would* help him—despite what her sister had tried to do to her.

Rosalind, lying so still and white in the bed, had suffered more than she had. If her sister lost Dan as well as the baby, she'd not only be devastated but she might well also lose her will to live.

But there was an additional reason, something Dan didn't know. Because of Jacob, Cosy now knew what it was like to love a man with all one's heart, as she believed Rosalind loved Dan.

She suspected Jacob was somehow involved in the danger Dan spoke of and wondered how and why. But she'd already made her decision to help Dan for her sister's sake.

"Promise me one thing," she whispered. "Promise me that you'll come back for Rosalind when you can."

He nodded. "I promise. If I can return, I will."

"There's a back door off the kitchen," she whispered. "Use it. I'll wait a minute or two before returning to the parlor."

He took one last look at Rosalind, sighed, turned away, and eased from the room. Cosy stared down at the green velvet case in her hands, certain that whatever it contained hadn't been meant for her but for Rosalind. She'd committed herself to enact a part, though, so she'd have to keep pretending. Lifting the lid, she peered inside, frowning at the golden bird with an emerald eye—a pin, she realized, one she'd never seen before. She hated lying—how could she be convincing enough to give Dan a head start? And would Jacob ever forgive her if he discovered what she'd done?

"I have noticed you're limping," Mrs. Spolarich said as Cosy walked back into the parlor.

"I hurt my ankle, but it's improving," Cosy told her. She held out the velvet box. "Rosalind asked Dan to stay with her," she said, looking at her father rather than Jacob. "Here's what she wanted me to have."

Her father reached a hand. "Let's see it."

Cosy gave it to him, watching as he opened the box and removed the pin, turning it over in his hands. "A bird of some kind," he said, holding up the ornament. "I suspect Rosie gave it to you because the emerald eye of the bird is the same color as your eyes."

"May I take a look?" Jacob asked.

When Jephthah handed over the pin, Jacob examined it for a long moment and then looked directly at Cosy. "I find it interesting that your sister chose to give you this particular bird," he said.

She swallowed before asking as calmly as she could, "Why should you think so?"

"Do you know what kind of a bird this is?" he asked.

She shook her head. "I'm familiar with the birds in the

Upper Peninsula but not those from other places. Mrs. Spolarich's parakeets are the first I've ever seen."

"This pin represents a bird that doesn't exist anywhere
in the world, a mythical bird," Jacob said. "It's a phoenix."

Phoenix. Cosy gazed at Jacob in confusion, aware the
word held a hidden meaning for him and also feeling that
he expected her to understand its significance. She did not,
though she thought she might have heard the name at some
time or other. She had no idea where or when.

Jacob rose abruptly. "Thank you for the tea," he said to
Mrs. Spolarich. "I must be off. I'll just let myself out your
back door, if you don't mind." Without waiting for a reply,
he strode from the room, dropping the phoenix pin in
Cosy's lap as he passed.

Cosy stared after him, her heart heavy. Because Jacob
was leaving by the back door, she realized he suspected
Dan was no longer in the house and meant to glance into
Rosalind's bedroom to make sure before going after him.
And Jacob certainly must realize she'd helped Dan escape.

"What lit a fire under him?" Jephthah asked.

Cosy took a deep breath. More lies. Would they never
end? "He lives in Houghton, Father. No doubt he's eager
to get home. We had to camp with the Torch Lake villagers,
you know. They offered me a change of clothes but not
Jacob."

Jephthah nodded. "So I noticed. The sooner we get you
out of those buckskins, the happier I'll be. Your belongings
are in my room at the Copper Inn. Dan can stay here with
Rosie, and I'll take you back to—"

"Dan isn't here," she said. "He had to leave, too."

"The hell he did!" Jephthah frowned. "Going to the inn,
was he?"

"I don't believe so. I don't believe he will be returning."

Jephthah was momentarily speechless.

"I think you both could go to the inn and freshen up without having to worry about Rosalind," Mrs. Spolarich said. "She should sleep for some time, and I shall be here to watch over her." The old woman looked at Cosy. "But please do let me look at your ankle before you leave. I'm quite sure I can heal it."

Cosy glanced from her to the scowling Jephthah, who waved his hand. "Let her try," he said. "No point in limping around if she can fix you up."

Leaving Jephthah alone in the parlor, Mrs. Spolarich led Cosy to the kitchen where she asked her to sit on a chair before filling a basin with warm water from the reservoir attached to the black iron range. Five blue and green birds twittered inside a large brass cage hanging near the stove.

"More of my parakeets," Mrs. Spolarich said. "These are young birds, so I don't let them fly free when I have guests. I cage Gregor and Sonya only at night."

She placed the basin on the scoured-clean wood floor in front of Cosy and sat on a stool next to it. After Cosy eased off her left moccasin, she put her foot into the basin of warm water. While it soaked, Mrs. Spolarich washed Cosy's still slightly swollen ankle with a clove-scented soap.

"Now, close your eyes," the old woman ordered, lifting Cosy's foot to the towel on her lap and patting it dry. She placed her hands on either side of the ankle.

Cosy obeyed. After a few moments, she saw a rain of golden fire behind her closed lids, a fire that didn't burn. She knew the healing fire came from the hands of Mrs. Spolarich. At the same time, she seemed to feel something flow from inside her to join the fiery stream. And then she was no longer sitting in the kitchen with her eyes closed but floating in darkness outside her own body.

Brilliant colors lit the darkness—red, green, yellow—colors that shaped into a large bird with a curved bill like those of the parakeets. It flew, wings outstretched, to touch her ankle with soft feathers.

The bird disappeared, and Cosy once more felt the wood of the chair underneath her. "I have finished," Mrs. Spolarich said. "Open your eyes."

"I had a vision of a large, brightly colored bird with a curved bill," Cosy said.

"A parrot, perhaps?" Mrs. Spolarich gestured toward a painting on the far wall.

Cosy glanced at the picture and nodded. "Yes, a parrot."

"My husband painted that. He said he always thought of me when he saw a parrot." She smiled. "In my youth I loved bright clothes."

"Then it was you I saw," Cosy told her. "As a parrot you flew to me, and your wings brushed against my ankle."

"I felt your power as soon as I touched you," Mrs. Spolarich said. "Together, with God's help, we healed you."

Cosy flexed her ankle without pain. She stood, putting her weight on her left foot, and felt not even a twinge. "It's true," she said. "My ankle is healed."

Mrs. Spolarich tipped her head in a bird-like gesture. "You must use the power I sensed within you to heal others. And you must never forget that all ways of healing come from God."

God. Kitchi Manitou, the Great Spirit.

"I hear what you say and I will remember," Cosy promised.

When she returned to the parlor, Cosy convinced her father that Rosalind was safe in Mrs. Spolarich's care. The two of them rode to the Copper Inn in a hired rig.

"I don't understand where Dan's got to," Jephthah com-

plained. "Nor why Jacob left so abruptly. But what trouble
me the most is how you came to fall overboard whe
you've always been as sure-footed as a cat."

"I was carrying my gloves," Cosy improvised, "and on
slipped from my hands and went over the rail but didn'
fall in the water. It landed on a spar. I foolishly leane
over to try to retrieve it and lost my balance."

Perhaps, she thought, the more one told lies, the easie
they became.

Jephthah took her hand, pressing it between both of his
"I couldn't bear to lose you. Thank God Jacob had th
courage to dive overboard to save you. Is there some af
fection between the two of you? I thought he seemed un
usually attentive."

"Jacob and I are friends," she said. Was it still true o
had Jacob turned against her altogether after what she'
done? She feared the worst.

Jephthah patted her hand. "You're nothing like you
mother, Cosy, for all you favor her in looks. You're a goo
girl; you always have been, and I regret how I've treate
you."

"You've always taken care of me," she said.

He sighed. "Maybe so, but I also tried to use you t
further my own plans. And poor Rosie—I deserted her, lef
her to be raised by that prudish old maid aunt of hers.
haven't done right by either of you."

"When Rosalind came to you, you welcomed her," Cos
pointed out. "You made her feel at home. You did wha
you could for both of us. I love you and I'm sure my siste
does, too."

Tears gleamed in his eyes. "I don't deserve your love
When I thought I'd lost you and feared I'd lose Rosie, i
set me to thinking that there's not one woman I ever treate

right in my entire life. Not Cecily, nor your mother, nor the others I used for my own ends and then discarded. Now it's too late to make amends." He shook his head. "I'm a poor excuse for a man."

Cosy realized her father was, at least to some extent, as guilty as he claimed; but, at the same time, it hurt her to see him so downhearted. After a few moments, an idea popped into her head.

"My mother and Rosalind's mother are both dead," she said, "so it is too late. But what about Miss Genette? Louella Genette. I've never forgotten her; she was so kind to me."

Jephthah looked shamefaced. "Pretty damned kind to me, too, if the truth be told."

"She was in love with you." Cosy pulled her hand free and looked earnestly at her father. "I remember how both Louella and I cried when you sent her away, sent her home to Houghton. Does she still live here?"

He shrugged.

"Why not find out?" she challenged. "If she does, you can try to think of a way to return her kindness. Perhaps it's not too late to make amends to Louella Genette."

Jephthah stared at her. "What strange notions you come up with, girl." He was silent the rest of the way to the inn. As he helped her from the buggy, he smiled, then leaned to kiss her on the cheek. "You're worth more than all the gold I recovered from the *Kaug*," he said.

The warmth of her father's words and the knowledge that he truly loved and valued her stayed with Cosy through the time it took to move her belongings from his room to another. But, when she was alone in her room, she could no longer keep Jacob from her thoughts. Instead of washing up and then changing her clothes, she stood by the window hugging herself against an inner chill.

She'd given Jacob her heart. Must she learn to live without one from now on? She hadn't meant to betray him, though she was convinced he must see it that way. How could she not have helped Dan, knowing how desperately her sister loved him? Hadn't Rosalind been punished enough?

If only she could see Jacob and explain. After all, he'd refused to confide in her and so he might be persuaded to listen to her. But even if he did listen, would he understand? She turned from the window and listlessly began to undress but was immediately reminded of how Jacob had undressed her in their camp by the lake. She sighed, closing her eyes as she relived the wonder of their lovemaking.

She could almost feel the soft caress of his mustache as they kissed, the aching pleasure of his lips at her breast, the breathless anticipation of joining together . . .

She could almost feel it, but not quite. Reliving wasn't the same. Wasn't enough. She wanted, she needed Jacob. Did he miss her as much as she missed him? Where was he?

He'd gone after Dan, of course; and Dan had intended to sail to Detroit. Was that still his destination? She shook her head. When she didn't know the reason behind Jacob's pursuit of Dan, how could she have any idea of where either of them might be?

Perhaps Jacob would be hurt when he finally confronted Dan. Even killed. How could she live without him? Cosy tried to blink back her tears, but they came too thick and fast. Refusing to give in, she pulled off her clothes and, with tears streaming down her face, began to wash herself. When she finished, instead of redressing, she pulled on a nightgown and crawled into bed where she sobbed herself into the oblivion of sleep.

A week went by before Mrs. Spolarich thought Rosalind should attempt the trip back to Ojibway. Cosy and Jephthah remained at the inn, Cosy spending her days at her sister's bedside with Jephthah dropping by now and again. What he did during the rest of the time Cosy didn't know, though she knew he'd discussed the mine investment with Bill Dawson and supposed he was following up on that. Jacob, he'd told her, was nowhere to be found; and Dawson was considerably annoyed about it. Jephthah had decided Dan must have gone on to Detroit, though he still couldn't understand why he'd left without saying goodbye.

The day's journey home aboard the steam propeller *Whitefish* was uneventful, with Rosalind resting in a cabin during the voyage. At the house, Cosy helped Mina Howard settle Rosalind into bed, noting with approval the slight tinge of pink in her sister's cheeks. No longer did she look, as Jephthah had put it, "like death warmed over."

As the days passed, she tried to coax Rosalind into getting up and coming downstairs, but her sister only turned her face away in refusal. She spoke as seldom as possible, though she did listen when Cosy read to her.

"What's the matter with her?" Jephthah asked again and again. "If she's better, why won't she get out of bed?"

Cosy had no answer for him.

At the end of their week back home, Jephthah announced to Cosy at dinner that he was meeting the afternoon boat from Houghton. "Ask Mrs. Howard to have one of the bedrooms ready," he added, "because our guest will be staying."

"How long, Father?" Cosy asked, holding her breath, hoping against hope that the guest would be Jacob. If he were coming to visit, it would mean he'd forgiven her.

"It depends on what her answer is," Jephthah said, and Cosy's heart sank. Not Jacob, then.

Recovering, she asked, "Who is it?"

"That's my surprise. By the way, you'd best choose one of the bedrooms in the east wing."

Surprised, Cosy nodded. He'd never invited a woman to stay overnight before without insisting she be given the bedroom next to his. This guest wouldn't even be in his wing.

The following morning, Hilda cleaned the vacant bedroom next to Cosy's. After she'd finished putting fresh linen on the bed and gone off to other duties, Cosy entered the room to place a small bowl of dried rose petals on a stand by the window. A slight noise made her turn toward the doorway, and she was amazed to see Rosalind standing there in her nightgown, holding to the doorframe.

Setting the bowl down, she hurried to her sister. "Are you all right?" she asked.

Rosalind leaned against her. "A bit light-headed," she admitted. "I expect it's from not being on my feet for so long."

"Shall I help you back to bed?"

Rosalind shook her head. "No. But please come to my room with me."

In her room, once Cosy had helped her into her robe and slippers, Rosalind insisted on sitting in a chair. "Do stop fussing over me," Rosalind said, "and sit down yourself. I've taken up too much of everyone's time already."

Cosy obeyed, gazing inquiringly at her sister.

"You haven't told Father what I did to you," Rosalind

said. It was the first she'd mentioned the subject since the afternoon Cosy had arrived at Mrs. Spolarich's.

"I didn't wish to upset him," she said.

Rosalind grimaced. "I wish you weren't so dreadfully thoughtful. I swear it sometimes makes me feel like strangling you." She put her hand to her mouth. "Why do I say such things?"

"There've been times I've felt like strangling *you*," Cosy admitted.

Rosalind leaned forward. "Please, tell me the truth. Have you heard from Dan? Do you know where he is?"

Dan's name hadn't been mentioned between them until this moment. "I'm not likely to hear from him," Cosy said, "and I know Father hasn't. Both of us assumed he went on to Detroit."

Rosalind's face crumpled, tears trickling down her cheeks. "Why wouldn't he listen to me? He'll be killed; I know he will." She gazed piteously at Cosy. "I love him so. I've always loved him, ever since he came aboard the *Phoenix* with those Rebel pirates and kissed me."

Cosy stared at her. "The *Phoenix?*" she echoed. "Pirates?" Belatedly, she understood that Dan must have been involved in last May's attempt to free Rebel prisoners held in Ohio.

Rosalind pulled a handkerchief from her robe, blotted her tears, and blew her nose. "Yes. He called himself Major Eaton at the time. And now he's trying to free those blasted prisoners again." She blinked rapidly, obviously determined not to start crying again. "I'm afraid for him, Cosy. So afraid. If he doesn't get killed trying, he may still be caught. And then they—they'll hang him."

Major Eaton. The words tolled like a death bell in Cosy's

head. She'd been the one who'd mentioned that name to Jacob. What had she done?

"What hurts so terribly," Rosalind said, "is that Dan left without a word to me, as though I didn't matter at all to him. He doesn't love me. He never has. He wouldn't have married me except for the baby." Rosalind's voice broke, but she took a deep breath and went on. "And I lost the baby—the only part of Dan I might have had."

Cosy's heart ached in sympathy as she tried to think of comforting words. Finally, an idea came to her. "Dan left a present for you," she told her sister. "He said to choose the right time to give it to you, and I believe that time has come." Rising, Cosy hurried to her room and pulled the green velvet box from a drawer. She hadn't touched it since replacing the golden bird inside—a gift, she realized now, that Dan had intended to give to his wife to remind her of their first meeting. He must have hoped I'd finally understand whom the pin was really for, she told herself.

"Here," she said, offering the box to Rosalind.

Rosalind looked at the velvet box for a moment before opening the lid. Lifting out the pin, she drew her brows together, then her face cleared and she smiled radiantly. "How like him," she murmured, studying the ornament. "A phoenix, of all things! Our secret." Caressing the bird with her finger, she asked, "Do you think this means he does love me?"

"I've always believed Dan loves you. There was never anything between Dan and me, no matter what you thought."

Keeping her gaze on the phoenix, Rosalind said, "I'm sorry, truly sorry, for what I did. As soon as it happened, I wished I hadn't done it. I must have been out of my

mind. I don't suppose you'll ever forgive me, and I can't
blame you."

"Good came from what happened," Cosy said slowly,
giving her an indirect answer. "It made Father realize how
much we both mean to him." And I learned what it is to
love a man with all my heart, she added silently. Even
though I've lost him, I'll cherish those hours with Jacob
all my life.

Rosalind glanced at her. "Who is this woman guest Father's invited to stay with us?"

"He didn't tell me. But I know he'll be pleased to hear
you may be joining us for dinner while she's here."

"I have no intention of returning to bed, except to rest
or sleep," Rosalind said firmly. "Dan would want me to
regain my strength, and so I must try to do so. This gift
makes me believe that if he lives, he'll find a way to send
for me, even if he's unable to return. You see, the phoenix
is a bird born from its own ashes, a renewal."

Cosy thanked the Great Spirit for helping her understand
that the phoenix was Dan's gift to Rosalind. She also reminded herself to speak to her father before Rosalind appeared wearing it and convince him of the truth.

"Jacob's all right, isn't he?" Rosalind asked. "I know he
rescued you."

"I haven't seen him since the day we reached Houghton,"
Cosy said, "but he was all right then."

Something in her voice must have betrayed her, because
Rosalind's eyes narrowed. "You and Jacob," she said,
thoughtfully. "of course! Why didn't I see it before? Because I was so besotted with Dan, I suppose. But it occurs
to me now that Jacob was very attentive to you when he
visited. And you—" Rosalind paused. "I once thought you
could control your expression so as to give nothing away,

but I see I was wrong. There *is* something between you and Jacob, isn't there?"

Why not admit it? Cosy asked herself. "I love him," she said sadly.

Rosalind smiled. "And he must love you in return. Didn't he risk his life for you?"

"I don't know if he loves me." It was Cosy's turn to blink back tears.

Rosalind sighed. "I know how you feel." She reached a hand to Cosy, who grasped it and, for a moment, they shared a wordless understanding.

Releasing her hand, Rosalind asked, "But what about Black Water? Dan told me he survived the storm after all."

"I thought I loved him, but I was mistaken. He'll marry another."

"You didn't belong at that Indian village anyway. As fond as you are of your foster mother, your place is with Father."

"Hungry Moon is dead," Cosy said sorrowfully.

"How do you know? Did someone from the village bring you a message?"

Cosy shook her head. "I felt her die while Jacob and I were stranded in the woods."

"*Felt* her die? You mean you haven't had word of her death? Or asked anyone?"

"I don't need to." But even as she spoke the words, a tiny snake of doubt slithered through Cosy. Could she be wrong? Was it possible Hungry Moon still lived? She hadn't received word of her death from Spotted Fawn. Of course, she hadn't been home at the time Hungry Moon presumably died to receive such a message . . .

Rosalind shrugged. "Suit yourself. But if she were *my* foster mother, I'd want to be sure." She rose from her chair

d walked to the bed. "That's better. I'm not a bit dizzy
ow. But I *am* tired. Maybe I'll rest for a few hours before
oming down for the evening meal. That is, if you'll help
.e." As Cosy nodded, her sister added, "I must confess
m looking forward to meeting Father's mystery guest."

So was Cosy.

After lunch, Mina took Cosy aside and said, "I think
ou should know there's been someone watching the house
om the pine grove. I haven't seen him, but I know he's
.ere. I told Jim, and he went to look but didn't find anyone
r any sign of a watcher. He thinks I'm imagining things.
m not. I won't name names, but you and I know one man
ho used to haunt that pine grove."

Cosy nodded, aware that Mina meant Black Water. After
aving the kitchen, though, she shook her head. Why would
lack Water come to the grove when there was no longer
ny possibility they'd marry? Besides, if it were Black
Vater, why didn't he give the owl's call? On the other hand,
it weren't Black Water, who could it possibly be?

Today she had no time to look for herself—she might
ee signs that Jim would miss—but she promised herself
he'd go into the grove tomorrow morning and search.

In the late afternoon, when Jephthah ushered his guest
.to the house, at first Cosy thought she'd never before
een the drab-looking woman in the unfashionable brown
ress, her reddish hair pulled to the back of her head in a
ght, hard knot. Then she gazed into the hazel eyes, and
uddenly she smiled.

"Miss Genette!" she cried. "Louella!"

Twenty-four

Louella Genette held out her arms, and Cosy hugged he in delight. Pulling back, she said, "Father didn't tell m *you* were his guest. I'm so happy to see you again. Com I'll show you to your room."

Jephthah nodded. "I'll see you later, Lolly."

Lolly? Cosy glanced at Louella and saw she was blush ing.

"For some reason your father insists on using that frivo lous nickname," she said as she mounted the steps wit Cosy. "When he called me Lolly in front of the childre they were dumbstruck."

"You have children?"

"Five. Six, if I count Falling Leaf—and I should becaus she was no more than fifteen when she came to live wit us." Noticing Cosy's bewildered look, she laughed. "Onc I'm settled into my room, I'll explain."

Jim, efficient as usual, was just placing Louella's bag in the room, having come up the back stairs. He nodde to them and left.

"What a pleasant room this is," Louella said, "and how summery it smells, quite like roses."

"I can ask Hilda to unpack for you," Cosy offered.

"Oh dear me, no, please don't. I'd much prefer to unpac myself, especially if you'll keep me company while I do."

pening the smaller bag, she began removing undergarments and placing them in a drawer of the curly maple resser.

"Your father told me about his other daughter, Rosalind, oming to live with him," Louella said. "How nice for you have the company of a sister." She paused to glance at osy. "Though I imagine it took some getting used to."

Cosy nodded. Louella had always seemed to understand. ow good and familiar it seemed to be with her again after most five years.

As though echoing her thought, Louella said, "We haven't en one another for over four years. I suspect you're wonring how I acquired six children in that time. Especially nce I never married. Your father was certainly taken back by my motley brood."

"You mentioned Falling Leaf," Cosy said. "Is she Anhinabe?"

"Yes. Louis found her starving and half-frozen last winr in a makeshift shelter near his trap line, so naturally he rought her home with him. The poor child had been bused and deserted by a white man—but I'll go into that ter. First things first. After I left Ojibway, I went to stay ith my ill grandmother in Ohio rather than remaining with y father in Houghton. Grandmother Genette had been king in homeless children and so, when she died a few onths after my arrival, I sold her house and brought the oys—Louis, Frank, and Jerry—back to Houghton with me my father's farm. The youngest, Jerry, was only a baby t the time."

Cosy noticed how Louella's tone warmed when she menoned the baby.

"Then a neighboring farmhouse burned," Louella went n, "and the only survivor was an eight-year-old girl. I

took Emily in and, when no one claimed her, I kept he
Then Falling Leaf's baby girl was born, and she made six

"Would you mind if I came in?" Rosalind asked fro
the doorway. "Do excuse my robe, I've been resting."

"My dear girl," Louella said, "I'm so pleased to me
you. Your father has told me so much about his Rosie th
I feel I know you. Do come in and sit down."

"I lived with Miss Genette—Louella—until Father fi
ished building his house," Cosy told Rosalind. "She wa
my friend as well as my teacher. I had no idea she wa
the mystery guest."

"I recall you mentioning her name before," Rosalin
said. "I'm happy you're here, Miss Genette."

"You *must* call me Louella." She paused and looke
from Rosalind to Cosy. "I shall be quite frank with yo
girls. Your father has asked me to marry him."

"How wonderful!" Cosy cried.

"I'm pleased," Rosalind said. "Father needs a wife."

Louella held up her hand. "Thank you, but I haven't y
accepted. I'm not sure I wish to leave Houghton, and
know the older children will refuse to. Most important c
all, I'm by no means as certain as you seem to be th
Jephthah Collins needs me as his wife."

"But you love him!" The words were out before Cos
realized she meant to say them.

Louella's lips tightened. "I may have once thought I di
I don't believe he ever loved me and I doubt that he doe
now." She glanced at herself in the pier glass and sighe
"I never was pretty and I know I've changed for th
worse."

She had changed, Cosy admitted, there was no denyin
it. The Louella she remembered wore bright ribbons in he

urls and was always interested in trying to sew gowns of
ıe latest fashion.

"Miss Genette—Louella—may I make a few simple sug-
estions?" Rosalind's voice was tentative.

"Of course."

"I had a friend in Boston, Janet Morley, who had the
ame kind of extra curly hair that yours appears to be—
ıough yours is a more attractive color. Please don't be
ffended when I say I don't believe pulling such hair into
knot in an effort to tame it is a good solution. Janet and
experimented with her hair—to her mother's horror, I
ıust admit, because we wound up cutting it quite short.
ȷut short hair did become Janet—in fact, she collected her
ırst beau soon after."

Louella's hands fluttered to her head. "I can't be both-
red fiddling with elaborate hair-dos."

"Once short, Janet's hair only required brushing,"
Ɩosalind countered.

"Louella once wore pink ribbons in her curls," Cosy put
ı. "They looked very nice."

"Oh, do let me try," Rosalind begged, rising from the
hair and advancing on Louella, who stood in front of the
ıer glass.

"I must put my dresses in the wardrobe," Louella pro-
ɛsted.

"I'll be happy to do that," Cosy offered, aware that when
ɛr sister was determined on a course of action she was
ıost difficult to dissuade. In this case, she hoped Rosalind
ʳould succeed in transforming this drab-looking woman
ıto the more colorful Louella she remembered.

Outnumbered and perhaps, or so Cosy thought, in her
ɛart wanting to be more attractive, Louella gave in, sitting

on the stool in front of the mirror and allowing Rosalin
to unpin the knot holding her hair skinned back.

By the time her sister had finished cutting, great chunk
of Louella's hair lay scattered on the floor. "We must was
it," Rosalind said, "to bring back the curl."

"Let me," Cosy urged, not wanting Rosalind to tire he
self.

Rosalind agreed, admitting to some fatigue. "I'll rest
bit," she told them, "and then come back in time for yc
to dress for dinner. It's fortunate we're almost the sam
size, Louella, though I'm not quite sure about the shoes

Once Rosalind had left the room, Louella said, "Jephtha
mentioned that your sister hasn't been well. Good heaven
if she's impossible to turn aside when she isn't feelir
herself, what's she like when she's at the top of her form
I can see she plans to remake me from head to toe. Do
have a choice?"

"It would be simpler to let Rosalind have her way," Cos
suggested.

Louella smiled wryly. "You always were a girl mindf
of others' feelings. What you really mean, I feel sure,
that I can hardly look worse."

Since that was close to what Cosy had been thinkin
she remained silent as she prepared to wash Louella's hai
When she had finished and Hilda had swept up the ha
and taken it away, Louella examined herself in the mirro

"Whether I look any better or not," she said, "cuttin
my hair seems to have chopped off a few years as we
because I suddenly feel younger. But I wonder if that's a
to the good?"

Walking to the door, she closed it and turned to Cos
"I want to confide in you," she said. "As a child you coul
be trusted to keep secrets, and so I believe mine will b

afe with you. Jephthah is a talkative man, as I think you
nust realize. Among other things, he told me that your
ister's marriage came about because she was pregnant and
nat he had grave doubts about the man who was forced
o marry her—that was how he put it—ever being a good
usband."

"Yet I think Dan does love Rosalind," Cosy said.

"Perhaps, but where is he? Your father seems to believe
Dan may never return. I feel sorry for your sister, because
was once in her situation, made pregnant by a man I
new didn't want marriage. Unlike Rosalind, I was too
roud to tell him, too proud to have a man who married
ne out of duty."

Remembering Jerry, the baby Louella had brought back
rom Ohio with the two older boys, Cosy added up the
nonths and said, "You're talking about my father, aren't
ou?"

Louella nodded and sighed. "Why has he asked me to
narry him after all these years? Why, after I'd almost forgotten him?"

"Does he know Jerry is his son?"

Louella shook her head. "I didn't tell him. And, because
've adopted all these other children, I'm sure he doesn't
uspect." She gazed unhappily at Cosy. "Jerry's name is
eally Jeremiah, from the Bible, like your father's."

Cosy gave her a puzzled look. "If you haven't told my
ather about the boy, then I don't understand why you seem
o be comparing Rosalind's marriage to Dan to my father's
sking you to marry him. I'm sure you don't believe Father
s offering you marriage from a sense of duty when he
sn't even aware you've borne him a son."

Louella flung her arms wide. "Just look at me! If I
veren't attractive enough for Jephthah years ago, I'm that

much more time-worn now. What can he possibly see me?"

Feeling her way carefully, Cosy asked, "Do you mi telling me what he actually said to you when he proposed'

"First, he went on a bit about how much he admir what I'd done—taking in the children, he meant—and ho courageous I'd been to make my own way in the wor after my father died. But it really wasn't so difficult. M father taught Louis to hunt and trap before he died; an Louis, in turn, has taught Frank. They're seventeen an thirteen now and do as well as any man. Then Falling Le showed me the People's way of growing corn, using fi in the corn hills for fertilizer, as well as how to make map sugar. We turn a fair profit selling both."

Louella sighed again. "Jephthah went on to ask me marry him without a single word of love. I believe he fee sorry for me. How can I say yes?"

Cosy's heart went out to her, but she found no words comfort. She handed Louella a towel so she could dry h hair and, seeking a diversion, said, "Do you still have tho pretty coral beads you used to wear?"

"My mother's, you mean? Yes, I brought them with me

"I hope you'll wear them tonight."

"Cosy, it will take more than coral beads to transfor me; but since you asked me to, I'll wear them."

Later, when Rosalind returned with the gown she'd ch sen for Louella, Cosy was pleased to see it was almo exactly the same shade of coral as the beads.

"It's very kind of you, but I can't—" Louella began.

"Of course you can," Rosalind said imperiously. "Th color will be perfect with your hair, just wait and see." Sl attacked Louella's hair with a brush, twisting it this wa and that until the pale red curls stood out around Louella's thin face like an aureole.

After encasing Louella with a hoop, Cosy helped Rosalind button her into the coral gown. Fingering the white lace edging the bodice, Louella said, "Can't I insert a fichu? I'm not accustomed to such a low neckline."

"It suits you as it is," Rosalind said firmly, fastening the coral necklace around her throat and smiling at her in the mirror.

Whether pretty or not, Louella looked more like the lively, vivid woman Cosy recalled from the past than the drab creature she'd allowed herself to become.

"I'll wait and go down with you girls after you're dressed," Louella said.

"No!" Cosy and Rosalind spoke in unison.

"I'm sure Father is waiting impatiently for you in the parlor," Rosalind added. "We'll join you in a few minutes." She took Louella's arm, led her to the door, and gave her a gentle push toward the stairs.

Once they were satisfied Louella didn't intend to turn back, Rosalind said, "We'll help each other dress. Do you want to be first?"

Cosy shook her head. "I'd like to see what you've decided to wear." Actually, she hoped she wouldn't have to dissuade her sister from wearing the phoenix pin, because she hadn't yet talked to Jephthah.

She was relieved to find Rosalind had chosen a blue gown with blue accessories. "Why on earth doesn't she want to marry Father?" Rosalind asked as Cosy fastened the back buttons of the gown. "I should think any woman her age would be thrilled to be his wife."

"Louella doesn't believe Father loves her."

"Oh. That does make a difference. I hadn't thought about

it before, but I suppose a woman never gets too old t
wish for love. Well, we've done what we can; the rest i
up to them. When Dan sends for me and Jacob comes t
carry you off as his wife, Father will be all alone, yo
know. He really does need to marry again."

Cosy suppressed a sigh. *Would* Dan send for Rosalind
He'd promised to come back for her, but would he kee
that promise? As for Jacob, she'd broken her promise t
him to be truthful. How could she be sure he'd ever forgiv
her?

Sometime later, they descended the stairs togethe
Rosalind in blue, Cosy in pale yellow. To their surpris
neither Jephthah nor Louella was in the parlor.

"I think I hear voices from the music room," Cosy sai

As they approached the music room, Rosalind put a han
on Cosy's arm, halting her. "The lamp isn't lit," she whis
pered. "Maybe they don't wish to be disturbed."

Cosy started to turn back, but Rosalind prevented he
"It's our duty to find out what's happening," she sai
"Without disturbing them, of course." She crept close
Cosy in her wake, ashamed of eavesdropping but as eage
as her sister to discover what was going on.

"You're even lovelier than you were five years ago,
Jephthah was saying when they came near enough to hea
With some surprise and a touch of embarrassment, Cos
noticed the same husky rasp in her father's voice that Ja
cob's took on when he wanted to make love to her.

"I can't think why I was such a fool as to let you go,
he continued.

"I didn't want to leave you." Louella's voice was so
and warm.

"Tell me you'll never leave me again," he begged.

"Oh, Jephthah," Louella murmured, "do you really love me?"

"Hell, yes, woman!" he roared. "Why else would I ask you to marry me?"

Cosy and Rosalind looked at one another and then fled to the parlor where they collapsed onto the settee, giggling.

"Isn't that just like Father?" Rosalind asked. "Not a romantic bone in his body."

"At least he did manage to admit he loved her," Cosy said. "So she has no excuse to refuse him."

At dinner, they pretended to be surprised when Jephthah proudly announced that Louella had consented to be his wife, and they offered sincere congratulations.

"I believe," Louella said when they finished, "this may be the time to mention plans for my six children."

"Yes, of course, the children," Jephthah said. "As I told you, they're welcome here."

Louella smiled at him. "I know you mean that, but Louis and Frank wouldn't dream of leaving the farm. What I'd like to do is encourage Louis and Falling Leaf to marry—I know they love one another—and deed them the farm, with the proviso that Frank will have a home with them as long as he wishes to stay there. Falling Leaf's daughter will remain with her mother; and so the only children I'll bring into our marriage are Emily, the orphan, and my son, Jerry." She took a deep breath and, her gaze fixed on Jephthah, added, "Actually his name is Jeremiah, and he's not only my natural son but yours as well."

Jephthah stared at her, dumbstruck.

Rosalind, though startled, recovered faster than he did. "How wonderful, Father," she exclaimed. "You're not only acquiring a wife but also the son I'm sure you've always wanted."

Jephthah's quick, smiling glance at Cosy before h
reached for Louella's hand, warmed her heart. Her fathe
hadn't forgotten that what she'd said to him in Houghto
had started him off on the path toward this unexpected an
happy discovery.

The next morning, Cosy awoke from a disturbing drear
where Hungry Moon had seemed to be calling to her bu
though she searched everywhere, Cosy couldn't find he
As she lay quietly, trying to understand what the drear
might mean, her sister's doubting words came back to he

She'd insisted to Rosalind that she knew Hungry Moo
was dead, but why was she so positive? Was her vision a
Tall Hemlock's village true? Might she have interpreted
incorrectly? And why hadn't Spotted Fawn sent word o
the death? If she'd been unable to reach Cosy at the tim
Hungry Moon died, wouldn't the girl have kept trying?

The more she thought about it, the more convinced Cos
became that she might be wrong about her interpretatio
of her vision at Torch Lake. Maybe this recent dream mear
that Hungry Moon, dying at the village, was trying to reac
her.

Making up her mind, she rose and donned her old doe
skins. To set her mind at ease, she'd travel to the villag
and find out the truth. Father, with Louella at hand, wouldn'
miss her; and even if he did, she was determined to go.

In the kitchen, she took the bread and cheese Mina of
fered and explained why she must make the trip.

Mina gestured toward the pine grove. "Will he go wit
you?"

"If you mean Black Water," Cosy said, "I don't thin

he's anywhere near. But I'll look in the pine grove before I go to make certain no one else is hiding there."

From his vantage point, Jacob watched the back door of the Collins house open. Even from this distance, he immediately recognized Cosy. To his dismay, she headed directly toward the pines. When Jim had searched the grove, he hadn't suspected Jacob's presence; but Cosy, because she'd lived with the Chippewa, would be harder, maybe impossible, to fool. He had no choice but to stay where he was; it was too late to move.

He watched her approach, thinking that even when she hurried she retained an easy grace. But why was she wearing Indian garb? The obvious reason was because she intended to go to the Chippewa village. He no longer trusted the obvious. She could be wearing the clothes to make others believe the village was her destination. She was up to something, and he thought he knew what it was—meeting Dan—though he was damned if he knew how Dan had gotten a message through to her.

Perhaps that woman who'd arrived from Houghton the day before had been the courier. An unwitting one, possibly, for he'd taken care to investigate her thoroughly after Jephthah Collins visited her in Houghton. From what he had learned of Louella Genette, it was hard to believe she was a part of any conspiracy. As for Jephthah, he wasn't sure one way or the other. Rosalind would be on Dan's side no matter what. As for Cosy . . . he sighed inwardly. She was the one person he could have sworn he could trust.

He hadn't before considered the possibility Dan might be hiding in the Chippewa village. Dan *had* met Black Water, after all. The more he considered the idea, the more convinced he became. He'd assume that Cosy's reason for

wearing Indian garb *was* the obvious one and that she was
on her way to the village to meet Dan.

He was almost positive Dan hadn't left the Upper Peninsula. Not yet. Not until he was able to bring his wife
with him. Or was it Cosy, instead, that he meant to collect?
Jacob gritted his teeth. He'd kept the Collins house under
observation to no avail. Until now. With Hungry Moon
dead and Black Water about to marry another woman, what
reason could Cosy have to make the trip to the Chippewa
village if not to meet Dan?

She'd reached the pines. In order to follow her, he must
first escape Cosy's notice here in the grove.

The moment Cosy stepped into the gloom under the
trees, she sensed something watching her. Or was it some-
one? She paused, waiting and listening. Though she'd didn't
think it could be Black Water, if it were, he'd show himself.

A small animal, possibly a mouse, rustled in the pine
needles near her feet. She could hear a chickadee calling,
but no blue jay squawked. Whoever or whatever watched
her made no noise or movement and hadn't for some time;
otherwise, Brother Blue Jay would have spotted him by
now and warned those who lived in the grove.

Cosy weighed her chances of finding the watcher against
the time it would take to thoroughly search the grove. She
shook her head, knowing she might make the search and
not find him. Either way, her visit to the village would be
delayed. Whatever or whoever watched had done no harm;
a search could be put off until later today, with Jim to help.
Though not as skilled as a man of the People, Jim was a
fair woodsman and they'd make a good team.

Having made her decision, she turned and left the grove,
hurrying toward the river trail to the village. After she
crossed the field and entered the woods, a blue jay noticed

her and followed overhead for a time, warning of her presence. When she entered a small glade, a covey of ruffed grouse flew up from under her feet, startling her as much as she'd startled them. Later, crossing a small creek, she heard the sharp slap of a beaver's tail giving a warning of her intrusion before he dived to safety.

All the familiar sights and sounds and smells of the autumn woods brought an ache to her throat. Not because she no longer lived with the People but because of what she'd shared in another autumn woods with Jacob. Would she ever see him again? Why must love bring such pain?

When at last she reached the village, there were no canoes on her side of the river and, across the water, the lodges seemed deserted. She called a greeting and eventually four children, along with several dogs, gathered on the opposite bank. Some minutes later Eagle Feather appeared, launched a canoe, and came to get her.

"Where is everyone?" she asked.

"Preparing for celebration," he told her. "The new Medicine Woman is to be initiated at sunset."

Cosy stared at him. "Hungry Moon *is* dead then?"

"She took the Sky Path twenty suns ago. Spotted Fawn sent me with a message, but you were not home."

Cosy counted back. The vision in Tall Hemlock's lodge *had* been a true one. She should never have doubted it. And Spotted Fawn did try to let her know.

"It's a day of celebration," Eagle Feather said. "Before Spotted Fawn is initiated, she is to wed Black Water."

Cosy realized that her heart ached more because Spotted Fawn would become the Medicine Woman than because she would be Black Water's wife. She knew she'd be an intruder at either ceremony.

As Eagle Feather pulled the canoe to the village bank,

Cosy put her hand on his arm and said, "This is not a good day for me to visit. Take me back to the far shore."

"No," Black Water said.

Startled because she hadn't noticed his arrival, Cosy turned to stare at him. He was still a strong, handsome warrior, a man to admire; but her heart no longer pounded like a drum when she looked at him. "I must go home," she said.

"I will paddle you across," Black Water said, wading into the water and gesturing to Eagle Feather, who willingly gave up his place.

Though it was too late for her to object, she said, "This is not a good idea."

"I'm not married yet," he told her.

His words and the tone of his voice disturbed her. With unease, she recalled Hungry Moon's warning of a darkness within Black Water. "Spotted Fawn is a fine young woman," she said firmly, not wishing to reveal her apprehension. "She will make you a good wife."

He didn't reply. Reaching the far side, he beached the canoe. Seeing he intended to come with her, Cosy said, "I'm not afraid to walk the trail by myself. I prefer to."

"I wish to walk with you."

Deciding bluntness was the only way to convince him, she said, "No," and strode away.

He followed.

Since trying to outrun him would be futile, Cosy didn't increase her pace. Instead, she turned on her heel and confronted him. "Go back," she warned. "I don't want your company."

He grasped her arm. "Why did you come to the village?"

"Let go of me."

He paid no heed, repeating, "Why did you come?"

"I dreamed Hungry Moon had died and I had to see if my dream were a true one. Now release me."

"You came to see me," he insisted, his dark eyes gleaming.

Fear pierced through her, arrow-sharp, making her struggle to get away from him. "No!" she cried. "Never!"

"You love me," he muttered, his grip tightening. "You said so."

"I don't, not now."

He dragged her off the trail and through the underbrush to the trees where he shoved her onto the ground and flung himself on top of her.

She fought him, writhing and twisting in an effort to get away. She hit him with her fists and clawed at him with her nails; but he held her down, reaching under her skirt and forcing her legs apart.

"I don't want you!" she screamed. "I will ride the night wind and curse you!"

He laughed. "You have no witch power. And I mean to have you whether you want me or not."

"Stop! Leave me alone!" She realized she'd stopped speaking the People's tongue as if rejecting Black Water's language in her efforts to reject him. "No!" she shrieked. "No, no!"

His weight was suffocating her and she couldn't breathe, but still she struggled, determined to keep fighting. But he had the strength of a warrior. Against him, she was helpless . . .

Twenty-five

One moment a despairing Cosy was pinned and helpless under Black Water and then, so suddenly she couldn't comprehend what had happened, she was free. Pulling down her skirt, she scrambled to her feet, prepared to fight. To her shock, Black Water was grappling with another man.

Jacob!

As she watched, Black Water broke away and reached for his knife. She drew in her breath.

"Try it and you're dead," Jacob warned him, a pistol appearing in his hand.

Black Water held, his gaze fixed on the gun.

"If you want me to shoot him, Cosy, just say the word," Jacob growled.

She never wanted to see Black Water again. Never! But she didn't wish him to die because of what he'd tried to do to her. "No," she said. "Let him go back to the village."

"I don't trust the bastard. He might follow and ambush us."

"Make him give his word not to. Black Water's always been an honorable man." Realizing how ridiculous her words were in view of what had happened, she added lamely, "He was once—or so I thought."

"No man is particularly honorable where women are concerned," Jacob said. "At least not all the time."

"He has a bride waiting in the village." Cosy's voice took on an edge. "This is his wedding day."

"Good God!" Jacob exclaimed. Focusing his attention on Black Water, he snapped, "Your word is good?"

"My word is good," Black Water repeated sullenly, not as much as glancing at Cosy. "I hear what you say. I won't follow."

Jacob gestured toward the village. "Then go."

As Jacob watched Black Water trot off, Cosy hugged herself in a vain effort to control the tremors that had begun coursing through her.

Jacob turned to her, started to speak, then muttered a curse and thrust the pistol into a holster hidden inside his jacket. Pulling her into his arms, he stroked her back, saying soothingly, "You're safe now. Safe with me. I won't let anyone or anything hurt you."

She leaned against him, taking comfort from his warmth and strength, and gradually the tremors eased. When they finally ceased, Cosy stepped back. "This is the second time you've rescued me. I'm grateful you saved me, but I don't understand how you came to be here."

Jacob gazed into her eyes for long moments. "Why are you here?" he asked at last instead of answering.

There was no reason not to tell him. "I began to doubt the truth of my vision at Torch Lake," she said, "when Hungry Moon's spirit came to me after she died. I wondered if I could have been mistaken in believing she was dead. What if I were wrong and she were waiting for me to come to the village to be with her as she died? I had to know."

Cosy shook her head. "I should have trusted my vision. Hungry Moon has been dead many suns. Worse, Black Water misunderstood my reason for coming to the village—

he believed it was to see him. He refused to listen when I told him I no longer loved him. He—" She broke off, unable to go on.

"I still think the bastard deserved to be shot," Jacob said angrily. "He had no right to as much as touch you." He was silent a moment before adding, "You didn't see anyone else at the village?"

Cosy stared at him. What did he mean? She certainly had nothing to hide! "When I called from this side of the river to announce my arrival," she said, "Eagle Feather came and paddled me across. When I asked him about Hungry Moon, he told me she was dead and that a new Medicine Woman was being initiated today. When I heard this, I didn't leave the canoe, asking to be brought back because there was no longer any reason for me to enter the village. Black Water appeared and, though I objected, took Eagle Feather's place and brought me back to this side of the river. I started along the trail, warning him not to follow me, but he refused to listen."

When Jacob didn't immediately reply, she said, "Whom did you think I might see in the village?"

Jacob shrugged. "We'd best be getting along, don't you agree?"

Without a word, she began walking briskly toward home, annoyance mixing with her disappointment. Black Water's attack had terrified her; then Jacob's arrival and his rescue of her had filled her heart with joyous gratitude. If Jacob cared enough to come looking for her, he *must* care for her after all. But his continuing questions and evasion disturbed her. Didn't he trust her?

"You still haven't explained why *you* were on your way to the village," she said tartly.

Jacob looked away from her, back along the path Black

Water had taken. Though she couldn't see the river crossing from this spot, she'd heard the soft swish of paddles before they'd begun walking and knew the warrior was keeping his word.

"They told me at the house you'd just left for the Chippewa village," Jacob said finally, "so I followed, hoping to overtake you."

Cosy thought it over. If Jacob didn't trust her, why should she trust him? No one knew her destination except Mina Howard, and she doubted that Mina would mention it to anyone, Jacob included. But why would Jacob lie? Perhaps someone at the house had seen her dressed in the doeskins as she crossed the meadow, realized where she was going, and told Jacob when he came calling.

"You came to the house to see me?" she asked.

"Why else?"

"I don't know," she said slowly, "but I can no longer believe what you tell me."

"I once believed everything you told me." Jacob's words were edged with bitterness.

Cosy stopped and turned to face him. "At the Bird Woman's house, I helped Dan because of my sister," she said bluntly. "I hated lying to you, but I feared Rosalind might not recover if anything happened to Dan. He told me he was in danger and, though I wasn't sure why at the time, I knew the danger must come from you."

He regarded her coldly. "And just what have you discovered since then about that 'danger'?"

She shook her head. "I promised Rosalind I wouldn't repeat what she told me. I'm still not certain why you pose a threat to Dan."

"In other words, you're on his side, not mine."

"I'm on Rosalind's side!" she cried. "She's my sister!"

"A sister who tried to drown you."

"I've forgiven her. I've learned how terrible love can be."

Jacob blinked. "Terrible? Love?"

She nodded, a lump coming into her throat. "Love pierces the heart like an arrow, and the heart never heals."

He put his hands on her shoulders. "Cosy?"

"Are you asking if I love you?" she demanded. "Yes! And I wish I didn't. I wish I'd never met you!"

"The feeling's mutual," he rasped as he pulled her roughly into his arms, his mouth covering hers in a kiss full of violent passion.

She responded in kind, driven by her pent-up need for him; and they clung together, swaying, striving to be closer, to become a part of one another.

Once he kissed her, Jacob knew nothing else mattered—neither duty nor honor. He loved Cosy beyond all else.

Still holding her, he stepped off the trail. Together they eased to the ground under a maple, its fallen leaves crumbling beneath them as he gathered her to him.

"I want you," he whispered into her ear. "God knows always will."

"The feeling's mutual," she murmured.

He chuckled. "There's no woman like you, Cosy. I love you with all my pierced, miserable heart."

"Jacob," she murmured, "show me again how much you want me."

Urged on by a whirlwind of desire, their coming together was as wild as their surroundings, as natural and as beautiful.

"You have no idea how much I've missed you," Jacob confessed afterwards as they lay naked in each other's arms.

"No more than I've missed you." She sighed and sat up

"I'm sorry I betrayed your trust in Houghton. At the time, I felt I had no choice. Rosalind looked so frail . . ."

He pulled her down next to him. "The betrayal hurt, but what was worse was my jealousy. Like your sister, I couldn't shake the suspicion there was something between you and Dan. I admit that was the other reason I followed you to the Chippewa village. I thought you might be meeting him there."

"Meeting Dan?" She stiffened in his arms, but he held her tightly, preventing her from edging away from him.

"Don't move," he begged. "Hear me out. I think in the back of my mind I knew it was a farfetched notion, but it gave me the excuse to be with you. So I abandoned my post in the pine grove near your house and followed you, refusing to let myself realize that what I really wanted was to hold you like this."

"You were the watcher in the pine grove?"

"I hid in a tree. Jim didn't spot me, and neither did you."

"I would have if I'd taken the time!"

He kissed her, murmuring against her lips. "You're right. Because you were the one who taught me that searchers don't look up."

Momentarily Cosy let herself be beguiled by his kiss, savoring his taste as she felt the slow rise of renewed desire within her. But after a time she pulled away, aware they hadn't completely cleared things between them.

"You hid in the grove to watch for Dan," she said, rising on her elbow to gaze down at him. "Why?"

He sat up. "I think we'd best get dressed and go on while I try to explain as much as I can."

But when they were back on the trail, it was some time before Jacob spoke. "I was on my way to Houghton," he began, "to trace rumors of a Confederate plot to entice

Canada into invading the North and thus help the Rebs
When I reached Detroit, I heard of the failed Rebel attemp
to seize the *Phoenix* and free the prisoners on Johnso
Island. In Detroit, I was given a description of the ring
leader, supposedly a Major Eaton, and told to keep an eye
out for him while I was on my original assignment.

"Aboard the *Pewabic,* I discovered that a man who more
or less fit the description of Eaton had given up his bert
on the boat just before she sailed, presumably out of gal
lantry to a young lady. Your sister. I cultivated her acquain
tance, came to visit her in Ojibway, and whom did I meet
Daniel Rackham. Here was a man who, except for the
absence of a beard, could possibly be Major Eaton. Bu
only possibly. All I could do for the moment was to kee
an eye on him while trying to uncover any clues that woul
point to Eaton and Rackham being one and the same. T
complicate matters, I met you and promptly fell in love.

"Here I was accepting your father's hospitality, wanting
very badly to make love to you, while, because of my
assignment, I had to ask questions and probe for informa
tion. There were times I felt as slimy as a snake. But my
country is at war and it was my duty. I had no choice."

"Are you in the Union Army?"

"Officially, yes, though I seldom wear a uniform."

Cosy bit her lip. "I feared it was like this—Dan on the
side of the Confederates and you on the side of the Union
Enemies. Still, since the effort in May to free the prisoner
failed, what crime is Dan guilty of?"

"We're at war and the penalty for what he did is deat
by hanging. Worse, there's been a second attempt—haven
you heard the news?"

When she shook her head, he said, "I can't say for sur
whether Major Eaton was once again involved, but it fol

lowed a similar pattern. The *Parsons* was pirated, and the men who took her over sailed toward Sandusky. Fortunately, the gun boat guarding the island had been warned and so the attempt once again failed. Those who pirated the *Parsons* fled. Perhaps into Canada, perhaps not."

"What if Dan weren't a part of this second attempt?"

Jacob shrugged. "Why was he so eager to leave his new bride and sail to Detroit if not to take charge of this second pirating?"

Cosy remained silent and troubled, recalling how, in Houghton, she'd made Dan promise he'd return for Rosalind. If he kept that promise, he might well hang.

"You seem upset," Jacob said.

"I can't help thinking how distressed my sister will be if Dan's caught." Surely, she told herself, he'd have enough sense not to come back but, rather, to send for his wife.

"I don't know why Dan grew suspicious of me," Jacob said. "Perhaps I asked one-too-many questions."

"Did you intend to arrest him in the Bird Woman's house?" Cosy asked.

"No, because I didn't have my gun with me. But I would have brought him in for questioning the following day, taken him to Detroit, and turned him over to my superiors."

"So he could be hanged."

Jacob shot her a dark look. "Cosy, war is war."

Maybe so, but it didn't seem right to her to kill a man over a failed attempt to set prisoners free. She needed time to sort through her feelings and to come to terms with this side of Jacob.

"Have I made you hate me?" he asked.

Cosy chose her reply carefully. "You mentioned snakes," she said. "You're wrong about them. Snakes aren't slimy."

"What the hell kind of answer is that?"

"I only meant if you can be wrong about snakes, isn't there a chance you can be wrong about other things?"

He gazed at her in puzzlement. "But you told me yourself that Dan was Major Eaton."

"That has nothing to do with it. But if you insist on a direct answer, I could never hate you, Jacob."

They walked in silence after that, and the way home had never seemed so long to Cosy. When they at last drew near, she said, "Are you coming in or taking up your post in the pine grove again?"

"I'd like to come in if you'll let me."

"Why wouldn't I? We'll use the back door so I can slip upstairs and change. Father doesn't like to see me in these clothes, and I don't wish to upset him."

Mina was not in the kitchen when they entered the house. Hilda came out of the pantry and stared at Jacob. Looking at Cosy, she asked, "Will *he* be staying for lunch, too?"

Jacob's head went up like a lynx scenting prey. Belatedly Cosy took in the meaning of Hilda's question—someone else had also arrived unexpectedly—but Jacob was already striding through the kitchen. Heart in her throat, Cosy hurried after him, only to stop abruptly as she came into the front entry.

Jacob had halted, too, and they both stared at the couple embracing in the archway to the parlor. Rosalind was wrapped in Dan's arms, and they both were oblivious to anything else.

Almost immediately Dan looked up. He broke away from Rosalind so that he and Jacob stood face to face.

"I thought you'd return, Rackham," Jacob said. "Or should I say Major?"

Dan flicked a look at Cosy, turned to smile at the bewildered Rosalind, and said calmly, "I've no military title. Why would you call me Major?"

"Major Eaton, perhaps?"

"Sorry, my name's Rackham. Always has been."

"Jacob," Rosalind cried, "whatever's the matter with you?"

"Keep out of this, Rosalind," Jacob warned. "Cosy, take her to your father."

"I won't leave Dan!" Rosalind cried.

"Jephthah's in town with his bride-to-be," Dan said, fending off Rosalind as she tried to clutch his arm. "Go to your sister," he ordered, pushing her toward Cosy.

Cosy caught Rosalind's hand, drawing her farther away from the two men.

"What's your business with me, Thompson?" Dan demanded.

"You're under arrest for your part in the piracy of the *Phoenix* in May of this year. You may also be questioned about a similar piracy this month of the *Philo T. Parsons.*"

"Under whose authority?"

"The United States Army." As he spoke, Jacob drew his pistol.

Rosalind gasped and clung to Cosy.

"I defy you to prove I had anything to do with the incident of the *Phoenix*," Dan said. "As for the *Parsons*, I was nowhere near Lake Erie when she was taken and I have witnesses who'll vouch for me. Reliable witnesses, Thompson. Or should that be Major Thompson? *You* must have a rank even if I don't."

"What you say about the *Parsons* may or may not be true," Jacob said, "but in the case of the *Phoenix*, there are witnesses who'll testify against you."

"Jacob, you can't be serious," Rosalind said, letting go of Cosy. She held her head high, apparently having regained her poise. "Do put that silly gun away. Of course Dan had nothing to do with any pirating? In May, you said?" She put a hand to her face. "I blush to confess this but Dan and I were together for the entire month of May."

"Why, you told me——" Jacob began.

"I told you lies," Rosalind said. "You couldn't expect me to admit what I'd done. It would have ruined my reputation. The truth of the matter is I met Dan on the train from Boston and he—well, suffice to say we were immediately attracted and I'm afraid I encouraged him to take advantage of me. In the hotel in Sandusky we——"

"For God's sake, Rosalind," Jacob growled.

She made a moue. "I'm sorry. I made up the other story, the one I told aboard the *Pewabic*. It sounded romantic to claim I'd been on a pirated boat. I never set foot on the *Phoenix* and, naturally, Dan didn't either because we were having our own little idyll. I realize it was very naughty of me—both what I did do and also what I told fibs about."

Cosy stared at her sister, fascinated. She thought Rosalind had told her the truth about the *Phoenix,* but listening to this new story made her slightly unsure. Because it could be true.

Jacob, who'd been flushed with what Cosy assumed was outrage while he heard Rosalind out, was now pale, his face taut, the gun held steady in his hand.

"Furthermore," Rosalind went on, "if you don't drop this ridiculous accusation against my husband, I'll see to it that everyone knows exactly what you tried to do to me aboard the *Pewabic*. Yes, and since. Here in my father's house, too, even after I became a married woman. I won't try to protect you any longer, Jacob Thompson!"

Cosy gaped at her, now positive she was lying.

Dan laughed, an easy, relaxed sound. "Better give over,

Thompson," he said. "My Rosalind's just begun. She'll have your hide stripped off you and hung on the shed for drying before you know what's happened."

"We were going upstairs to pack," Rosalind put in, glaring at Jacob. "Dan didn't go far after he left Houghton. He's been staying with Mr. Appleton at the Nonpariel Mine while he decided what to do next. Now we're on our way to California. San Francisco." She walked toward Jacob, moving between him and Dan. "I shan't ever forgive you," she told him. "What a devious man you are."

Jacob lowered the gun, returned it to its holster, and turned to Cosy with a wry smile. "You sister calls *me* devious when I can't hold a candle to her."

"No one can," Dan announced, putting an arm around his wife. Together they walked past Jacob and Cosy and started up the stairs.

"I doubt San Francisco is where they're actually going," Jacob said to Cosy once the two were out of sight. "He's too clever to leave a straight trail. I sincerely hope I never set eyes on the pair of them again. I thought he could be trouble; but Rose Red, your sweet little sister Rosalind is the dangerous one. If she'd had the gun, I'd be stone dead by now."

"I wouldn't have let her kill you," Cosy said, "any more than you would have let Lame Wolf kill me."

Jacob put an arm around her waist, drawing her to his side. "If we stand here, we'll be forced to watch them leave once they're ready to travel. I prefer not to. Shall we go into the music room?"

She sat on the window seat with Jacob beside her. Clouds had covered the sun, she saw, threatening rain. It reminded her of her sister's wedding day.

"Rosalind loves Dan," Cosy said. "He's what she wants, and she's determined no one will take him from her."

"Someone or something will someday," Jacob predicted, "even though I failed to bring him in. He's a man attracted to danger, and such men aren't long-lived."

"I can't help being glad you weren't the cause of Dan being hanged."

Jacob nodded. "Since he's your sister's husband, I realize it would always be between us; and I don't want anything, ever, to come between us. You must promise me, after you finish your training as a physician, that I'll still be the most important thing in your life—as you'll always be in mine."

Cosy stared up at him. "Physician? What training?" she asked.

"After we marry, we'll live in my home town, at least for a while. And Philadelphia just happens to boast one of the finest medical schools in the country. Some twenty years ago, they refused admission to Elizabeth Blackwell; but times change. She proved a woman could become an excellent doctor and, should they try to balk, I'll force your admission. By God, I'm a lawyer, after all."

"But I'm not sure I—"

"You're a remarkable woman, Cosy. You can do anything you set your mind to. And I'll always be with you, should you need help. I see no reason you can't begin your studies while I'm involved in this blasted war. We're on the verge of winning, so it won't last forever, but I'm obliged to go where they send me until it does end."

Cosy had been so astonished at Jacob's plans for her that she hadn't quite taken in all he'd said. Had he actually said "after we're married"?

"Did you ask me to marry you?" she demanded.

"I was afraid you might refuse, so what I did was sneak

in the idea." He lifted her chin with his forefinger, gazing into her eyes. "Will you marry me, my Snow White, my Cosy? I'm so in love with you no other woman will ever do. Only you."

Philadelphia? she thought. She understood that the city was in Pennsylvania, but she knew nothing else about it. Except Jacob had said it had a famous medical school. One he expected her to attend. It was exciting but frightening at the same time. Still, whatever must be done to become a healer, she would do. And she'd be willing to be his wife under any circumstances.

"Jacob," she murmured, "Nothing could make me happier than to marry you."

He kissed her with passionate exuberance. Before she lost herself completely in the pleasure of his embrace, she pulled back slightly.

"In the story of 'Snow White And Rose Red,' " she reminded him, "the prince chooses Snow White while Rose Red has to make do with his brother. That didn't suit Rosalind, so she insisted the story had to be wrong. But it isn't. Snow White *does* marry the prince." She put her fingers to his lips. "You."

"I'm no prince," he protested.

She smiled, her eyes alight with love and mischief. "Not even the Prince of Snakes?"

He laughed and lifted her off her feet, whirling her round and round in a circle. "Prince or not," he said as he set her on her feet again, "I chose a woman more remarkable in every way than any fairy-tale princess. You."

When he held her close this time, she gave herself completely up to the wonder of his kiss and all that it promised . . .